HARVEST
HOME

HARVEST HOME

THOMAS TRYON

ALFRED A. KNOPF
New York

This book is for

ALLEN LEFFINGWELL VINCENT

In Harvest-time, harvest folk

servants and all,

Should make all together

good cheer in the hall,

And fill the black bowl

Of blyth to their song,

And let them be merry,

all harvest-time long.

THOMAS TUSSER

Elizabethan farmer-poet

PART ONE

AGNES
FAIR

1

I awakened that morning to birdsong. It was only the little yellow bird who lives in the locust tree outside our bedroom window, and I could have wrung his neck, for it was not yet six and I had a hangover. That was in late summer, before Harvest Home, before the bird left its nest for the winter. Now it is spring again, alas, and as predicted the yellow bird has returned. The Eternal Return, as they call it here. Thinking back from this day to that one nine months ago, I now imagine the bird to have been sounding a warning. But that is nonsense, of course, for who could have thought it was a bird of ill omen, that little creature?

During the first long summer, its cheerful notes seemed to stand both as a mark of fulfillment and as a promise of profound happiness, signifying the achievement of our hearts' desire. Happiness, fulfillment—if promised, they came only in the strangest measure.

The house, though new to us when we purchased it in the spring, was almost three hundred years old, an uninhabited wreck we had chanced upon, bought, and spent the summer restoring. In late August, with the greater part of the work behind us, I was enjoying the satisfaction of realizing one's fondest wish. A house in the country. The great back-to-the-land movement. City mouse into country mouse. Mr. and Mrs. Theodore Constantine and

daughter, landed gentry, late of New York City, presently resid-
ing at 11 Penrose Lane, in the ancient New England village of
Cornwall Coombe. We had lived there less than four months.
I had thrown up my job as advertising executive with a large
New York firm and was now working as a serious artist, painting
in the studio I had made from the chicken house behind the
garage. My time was my own; I kept no scheduled hours, but
worked as I chose. Yet, habitually an early riser, I liked to take
advantage of the pristine morning solitude, often abroad in the
still unfamiliar village environs to discover a housefront to sketch,
a river view, a tree, whatever might catch my fancy. Today, however, I felt slothful. Hung over, lumpish, unwilling to rise, I told
myself it must be Saturday, and hoped it was true. I was dimly
aware that the day held some particular significance, though what
it was I could not recall.

My stomach made a hollow noise, and Beth's head turned toward me. She reached and touched my hand, the corners of her
mouth lifting with the fleeting traces of a smile; even in her
sleep she knew I was suffering for my last night's overindulgence.
I tried to give her back her hand, placing it where it had rested,
at her breast, but her fingers remained entwined in mine. She
offered companionable little pressures between them as she lay
reclined at an easy angle, tendrils of hair partly covering her
closed eyes.

I listened to her easy, rhythmic breathing, watched the rise
and fall of her breast, my eye lingering on the rounded fullness
of the pale flesh, the darker, almost carmine-colored tips under
the pleated, translucent cotton. Though pillow-creased and
sleepy, a trifle wan and strained, her face to me, sixteen years her
husband, was infinitely pleasing. I was not only her spouse, her
lover, but her admirer as well, and I speculated as to how many
married couples were as good friends as we were.

As I gazed at her, not wanting to wake her, I realized that her
face was thinner. Since our coming to the village, with the work
and worry of the house, and the continuing crises with our young
teenage daughter Kate, fatigue had shown itself, and I wondered

if having traded being city mice for being country mice was not a mistake.

She was not asleep. The smile widened lazily, her lids fluttered, she drew a luxurious breath, and opened her eyes.

"Good morning, darling."

I smiled back and said good morning.

"Hung over?"

"Mm."

"Poor sweet."

A blue vein throbbed in her neck and I bent and pressed my mouth to it. Her arm came around my head, holding it there, her fingers playing in my hair. My wife, my love. She moved closer, her hand sliding down my cheek, feeling my night's growth of whiskers. "Bluebeard," she murmured, and I turned my head to find her lips. I kissed the sleep from her mouth and from her eyes; gentle kisses, but as her body pressed against mine I felt a stirring, a compelling surge. She must have felt it, too, for contented sounds came from behind her lips, and I pulled her nearer still. It was not our custom to make love in the morning— we had not, in fact, made love for some time—but quite suddenly, of all ideas it seemed the best and the most natural.

I waited while she disengaged herself, slid from under the sheet on her side of the bed, and stood. Splaying her fingers, she combed them through her hair and shook it out. It fell across her face again, obscuring her profile as she looked down to undo her nightgown. Sun rays filtering through the window framed her from behind, the flesh opaquely dark against the sheer white fabric, and the melting light produced a sort of corona around the sweep of her hair. She raised the shift over her head, bending to lay it aside with a grace and innocence that reminded me of one of those lovely pastel bathers of Degas.

When she put herself into my arms, she was warm and smelled of sleep and softness. I could feel the fragile cage of her ribs under the flesh of her back as she arched against me; yes, she was thinner. We made love affectionately, communicatively, tenderly, but without passion; we had become too used to each other, and to the act, for it to hold any new mysteries. Beth's nature was not one of passion, but rather of compliancy. She was accessible, submissive, yielding in a mild, utterly feminine way. Myself, I did not dream of great passions; she was my wife, I loved her, we had a child, and though we could not have another, still we were a family. I had never been unfaithful, either in body or in spirit, and if passion was lacking, there were other things, more important things, that made up for the lack.

Later, we lay still joined, uttering satisfied resonances into each other's necks and cheeks. I remember thinking how lucky I was, feeling safe and secure in the world we were creating for ourselves, this new world in the village of Cornwall Coombe. And this, our bedroom, seemed the very heart, the alive and throbbing, most particular and exact center of that world. Lying at peace, I let my eye rove around its already familiar, lived-in spaces, enjoying the pale buttery yellow of the simple plaster walls that took the sunlight and amplified it, the thick, creamy enameled woodwork, the matching Chippendale chests serving as bureaus, the Hudson River landscape over the fireplace, the airy curtains Beth had made, the bowl of flowers she had arranged on the mantel, her dressing table with its array of crystal bottles—perfume she seldom wore. Our room, I told myself; our house, our world.

And still the bird sang in the locust tree.

"*Listen* to it," Beth sat up, pulling the sheet to her chin and leaning forward on her knees.

"I could have killed it. What's today?"

"Saturday."

"Thought so." I snuggled some more, pleased that I had been right. "Then we can stay right here—"

"Don't you know what *day* it is?" She laughed a gay, light laugh that was all her own. "It's fair day, remember? The Agnes Fair?"

Of course—I had forgotten. The last Saturday in August was the day of the village fair, an annual tradition. I had been hearing of little else for weeks. "Did I drink a lot last night?"

"No. But drinking's never been your long suit."

I tried to lure her back into my arms. She resisted, saying she must get up and do the picnic lunch. Slipping away, she held her shift against her as she ran to the shower. I pulled the pillow onto my stomach and cradled it, stretching and feeling great crackings along my night-knotted frame, and wondering what the Agnes Fair would be like, this village festival everyone set such store by. Agnes—who was she? I confess I was intrigued by the prospect no less than Beth appeared to be. Where but in Cornwall Coombe did people have folk festivals any more?

I still found it difficult to believe places like this existed in the world today. Only it wasn't in the world; it was another world, a world of its own. On that morning, I lay there thinking how perfectly it suited me. We had been part of that discontented host longing to escape the city; like so many others, we had sought to rediscover more stable values, to satisfy a yearning to set our feet upon the land again. We had become frightened in New York, of the lurkers in the doorways. So we had fled to the country, hoping the country would provide what the city could not: peace, tranquility, and safety. All to be found in Cornwall Coombe, and while Beth showered, I drowsed on the pillow, contemplating the joys of being possessed of an eighteenth-century house.

2

Sometimes we said we *must* have been possessed even to buy the house. It was a matter of the merest coincidence that we had found it at all, so out of the way was it. After years of Sunday brunch discussions with friends about the joys of country life, we'd begun hunting. Started close to the city, looked in Westchester, in Rye, in Croton-on-Hudson, Bedford Hills; then sneaked across into Connecticut, in Greenwich, Cos Cob, Darien, Westport. Took Polaroids of anything that seemed likely, then scotched them one after the other: too large, too small, too expensive, poor schools, not enough character. The truth was we were afraid to make a decision.

Finally, the decision was made for us, or so it seemed. In February, Beth's father, Lawson Colby, had died. We had gone up for the funeral, and in mid-March we packed Kate in the back seat and drove up again to settle the last of his affairs and arrange for the storage of his belongings. When we drove back the weather was bad. There was no snow, but a fine sleety drizzle made the prospect of the long drive a dreary one. Beth was silent and withdrawn, haunted by whatever guilts she may have been harboring about her father; Kate, who had the sniffles, was in one of her moods.

Then, an hour or more along the way, the rain stopped and the sun struggled from behind the overcast. On Beth's whim, we left the four-lane parkway and got on an old turnpike to take in some of the small towns along the way; then we left the turnpike and drove along a back-country road; then we got lost. We came to a place called Saxony, and that was on the map, and beyond that was something called Tobacco City, also on the map, and across the river Cornwall Coombe, hardly on the map at all.

Suddenly, as we came over a hill, we saw in the upper left-hand corner of a vacant prospect an old, swaybacked covered bridge spanning a narrow reach of the river. Though our side was still ghost-gray, the farther side was bathed in a pale yellow light, as though that land were in some way more special, more deserving of the benediction of sun, and as the clouds moved above the lowering expanse, I saw something that made me smile and wait for Kate's cry. It came on cue.

"Look, Daddy—Mummy! A rainbow!"

Faint, yet it was there, a wide bridge of colors above the one of wood, and it was only inevitable that we find the route to the bridge and cross over. A sign read, "Lost Whistle Bridge."

Had the sky been filled with fire and brimstone, a rain of St. Elmo's fire, or some other ancient portent, a man might well have continued along his planned route. But a rainbow? Who could mistake that for anything but a sign of the most auspicious kind? Every schoolboy knows a rainbow is lucky; at the end there lies a pot of gold.

I turned the car, and what we discovered thereafter became a source of wonderment to all of us, for we had not gone far before I realized we truly were in Heart's Desire. No more than a hamlet, Cornwall Coombe lay nestled among some low hills, girdled by groves of just-budding maples and locust trees. Everywhere the forsythia and pussywillow were in bloom, as well as the shadblow bushes along the riverbank, and the air became suddenly flush with spring.

A remote section, its roads seemed hardly traveled, but for an occasional truck or farm wagon. First it had been only empty countryside, farms and farmland, sagging silos, fences of wire or stone, the fallow earth ready for planting, and not a soul to be seen. Then, rounding a bend, we saw in a large plowed field a farmer with a hoe. He was not, like the man in the poem, "bowed by the weight of centuries," but a tall, upright fellow, a giant of a man, blond-headed and almost proud-looking. Alone among the furrows, he stood easily, the hoe over his shoulder, and he looked off at the tilled land in a waiting attitude as, over the shallow brow of the hill beyond, a horde of figures appeared, waving aloft a forest of hoes, ragged against the skyline. The man raised his hoe in a kind of welcoming gesture, and the figures spread out across the field, women and children poking holes in the soil with their hoe handles, the men bending to drop seed from bags slung over their shoulders. Now the holes were closed up, and, the planters moving in structured patterns across the dark umber of the field, the pallid yellow sun breaking through the slate-gray clouds, I thought of a Flemish landscape with its primitive simplicity, right and natural and perfect.

I remember experiencing at that moment an emotion I could not then—nor can I now—describe, a vague stirring inside me, some fugitive longing, a desire to stop the car, get out and feel my feet upon that earth, to be among those farm people planting seeds that would grow. Watching, Beth reached and pressed my hand. This was what we had been trying to express to each other, she and I. This was the reality of the dream.

The country road became a street: Main Street, naturally enough. Proceeding past a crossing with a sign reading "Penrose Lane," we continued toward the center of the town, where Colonial houses bore plaques on their aged fronts proclaiming the date they had been built and who had built them: Penrose, 1811; Harper Penrose, 1709; Gwydeon Penrose, 1668. A good, Penroseate, New England town. Beth said it reminded her of a Currier & Ives print, and Kate squealed in delight at the flock of sheep cropping the turf of the broad Common in front of the white steepled church.

We wondered why the streets seemed so empty, for it was midday; then the answer became obvious: they were all out in the field, the entire village. We circled the Common, looking at the houses, the church, and other buildings, then drove back the way we had come. Beth squeezed my hand again, struck by the beauty of the place, and on that fine spring afternoon I had to admit it was unlike anything I had imagined would exist in this day and age. Its charm was instantly apparent, with an indefinable but unmistakable something that made it so attractive. Perhaps it was the spare, immaculate houses with their lawns just coming green, the plots of winter-tended gardens, the bright, beckoning window-gleam, the spruce paint on the clapboards and shutters, the lofty trees whose bare branches arched over the road.

When we came to Penrose Lane again, on the merest impulse I turned in. It proved an interesting turning: a wide, tree-lined street with handsome old dwellings behind elegant fences of wood or iron pickets, here a stone mounting step at the curb, there a stylish gilded weather vane atop a cupola.

Then, largish, dilapidated, forlorn, the house appeared on our left. We had passed the smaller house next door, on whose porch sat a man wearing dark glasses, while a woman worked in a flower bed close to the hedge separating them from the adjoining property. Perhaps I might have driven on by, but my eye was attracted to the brickwork on the chimneys, carefully executed work that said something to my artist's eye. But it wasn't the chimneys, really; it was the house. I was drawn to it as though it were fate itself, Kismet in clapboards. Without thinking, I swerved across the road and pulled into the drive alongside the hedge. Kate bounded out and ran up on the porch, while Beth and I sat craning our necks behind the windshield.

Clearly, the place was empty. The patchy lawn had gone to crab grass, there were weeds in the flower beds, the windows were bare with some of the panes broken.

"Oh, darling, look," Beth breathed, opening the car door, and together we went across the lawn to the side of the house, looking up at the massive clumps of shrubbery under the windows. I recognized them as lilac bushes, and knew why she turned to me with her smile; I had brought her lilacs in Paris one spring. At the corner of the house there was a large locust tree, and up in the branches we could see a last-year's nest. Abandoned nest, abandoned house. We spent some time peeking behind cupped hands through grimy windows along the front; then Kate, who had gone adventuring on her own, came reporting a discovery: a tumble-down chicken house behind the garage. While she ran around it making hen squawks I let its ample proportions begin giving me ideas about a studio. On the pitched roof was an empty dovecote, and beyond what must once have been a stable.

Halfway down the lawn was a large beech tree with the remnants of a birdhouse dangling from a lower limb. A hundred or more branches sprang from a triple fork which in turn grew from an enormous trunk, with thick, gnarled roots spreading out at the base. A beautiful tree, lofty and immense, gray, wrinkled, scruffy; it looked like a grand old elephant.

I put my arm around Beth's shoulders and walked with her back across the lawn. Out in front, we went up on the sagging porch and peeked some more while Kate tried the door, which was locked. The living and dining rooms revealed some interesting paneled wainscoting and wide pegged floors, and the former a large fireplace.

We found our prowlings had not gone unobserved. The woman from next door stood at the bottom of the steps, looking up at us. She listened affably enough as I explained we were interested in old houses—not strictly a lie—and she smiled when I inquired if anyone had a key. She told us the place had been shut up for years; it belonged to someone named, appropriately, Penrose, the village postmistress, but the upkeep had been too much and she had moved to other quarters.

Was the house by any chance for sale? I inquired.

By no chance, the woman replied. Not unfriendly, just firm. I wondered if perhaps she didn't want neighbors.

Would it be possible to speak with Mrs. Penrose? I persisted.

Miss Penrose, she corrected, Miss Tamar Penrose would be at the post office, unless she'd closed and gone to the field with the others. But, the woman added, Miss Penrose would definitely not be interested in selling.

I descended the rickety steps with Beth. "Quite a gang out in the field."

The woman laughed. "You've come on Planting Day."

I said we would try the post office, and thanked her. I took the Polaroid camera from the glove compartment and snapped a picture. Beth and Kate were waiting in the car, and as I got in, the woman stood on the walk, watching. On the other side of the hedge I heard the sound of a voice reading aloud, and caught snatches of a paragraph I thought I recognized from Mark Twain's *Life on the Mississippi*.

The post office was closed. I looked at Beth and shrugged; clearly it wasn't in the cards, and I wasn't about to track the lady down in some cornfield. Beth's wistful smile said what it had at other times: Never mind, there's a house for us somewhere. Leaving Kate to acquaint herself with the sheep, we walked together across the Common to the church, where a quaint black buggy with a dapper mare awaited an absent owner. In the churchyard a figure was laying flowers on a grave, an old woman in voluminous black, with something white on her head. Having no wish to intrude on her privacy, we kept our distance, and instead of reading the tombstone inscriptions as Beth had suggested, we admired the clock tower and belfry in the steeple. When we left I saw the old woman observing us.

As we returned to the car, we heard Kate calling to come and take her picture with the sheep. The shot came out darkish and I tried another; it was better. Pocketing the first, I handed the second to Kate, who laughed and showed it to Beth. It was a good one, a last memento of Cornwall Coombe: Kate's smile telling her delight to be amid such exotic creatures as sheep, behind her the Common, the old New England church. Then, looking again, I saw in the photograph, standing on the church steps, the same figure we had seen in the graveyard. I glanced up quickly and saw her watching us from the spot where the camera had caught her.

Again on impulse, I left Beth and Kate and went back across the Common to inquire of the old woman if she knew anything about the empty house in Penrose Lane. She pointed to the post office, and I said yes, I knew about Miss Penrose, but did she think the property might be shown? She paused to consider, then replied she had no way of telling; you never knew how folks might behave around here. I reached in my pocket for a pencil, took out the first snapshot, and scribbled our New York telephone number on the back. If, I said, she talked to the post-office lady, and if the property might be shown, would she call me collect? She accepted the photo, looked at the number, then turned it over and peered at the picture. Nice girl, she said; handsome family. Then she made another remark as she started down the steps.

"Beg pardon?" I asked, not quite catching it.

"I said, 'Handsome is as handsome does.'"

The picture disappeared among the ample folds of her skirts as she marched to the buggy at the curb. Getting in, she glanced at me again, and I thought I saw a twinkle in the ancient eyes. "Well, must get on for the plantin'."

"What do they plant?" I asked.

"Corn," she replied as the buggy rattled away.

There was little talk for the rest of our journey home. I was disappointed, and though Beth and I didn't exchange thoughts we each knew what the other was thinking. We had not driven very far when Kate started sneezing; then she began a mild attack of asthma. We always kept a Medihaler in the glove compartment, an oral device which helped reduce the chest congestion, and when she had found relief I stepped on the gas.

If it had been spring in the country, winter still hung on in the city, dirty, slushy, blowy. Our West Side apartment seemed drab and dark and, as if for the first time, I saw how badly it needed repainting. Beth, naturally enough, was depressed following the death of her father, though she tried not to show it. Kate's asthma attack had worsened, and she had to be kept out of school again.

I was edgy and nervous, and had another row at the office with old Osborne regarding the Staples Coffee account. The argument concluded, I burst out, ready to quit, and though cooler heads momentarily prevailed, I knew my days were numbered. The following noon, I resigned my position by mutual agreement. By four the same afternoon, Sandler-Haigh heard I was available and called to make me an offer; I said I'd think it over.

I had fitted out a small room in the back of the apartment as a kind of studio where I had been painting in my spare time, and there I retired, nursing my ruffled ego and telling myself now was the time. Get out of the rat race, don't go back, do what you've always wanted to do. Beth agreed. We had saved a fair bit; there was a lot more to come from her father's estate, and it seemed a good time, she pointed out, to take stock. I had begun as an artist, why not continue? I said I'd think that over, too— though I'd been thinking it over for two years or more.

What neither of us could stop thinking of, or talking about, was the house. Marvelous lines, I said; fabulous possibilities, she said; front porch would have to come off, I said; needed lots of chintz, she said; but we couldn't have it, we both said.

Sometimes I would take the photograph of the church on the Common and sit staring at it. It seemed to beckon me, saying,

"Come." But if this was a form of destiny, it was a thwarted one; clearly we were not meant to come.

Kate improved. I went around the corner to buy her some chili at Pepe's Chili Palor—as we called it, because as long as we had lived in the neighborhood the first "r" in the neon sign had never worked. Pepe Gonzalez, the proprietor, was out; his daughter 'Cita waited on me. Poor 'Cita: a dozen or more years later, she was still apologizing for the case of mumps I had caught from her when she was a child.

Kate got better, returned to school. Beth decided to paint the living room. I worked in the back studio. It seemed as if spring would never arrive.

Then, several weeks later, the telephone call came. I was working in tempera on a gesso panel when Beth came in and said it was long distance; something in her face told me it was no ordinary call. The warm voice identified itself as Mrs. Dodd; perhaps I remembered her, in Penrose Lane up in Cornwall Coombe? It was about the house next door, and if we were still interested, the house might be shown. Would we care to come up?

Would we! Leaving Kate with Mrs. Pepe, we set out early Sunday morning and got there shortly before noon. The weather was gorgeous. Spring had advanced in the countryside since our last visit; the dogwood was in bloom and the laurel, and rows of yellow daffodils blared trumpet-like in the greening gardens. When we arrived in Cornwall Coombe, I parked in front of the drugstore as had been arranged, and we waited on the Common for Mrs. Dodd until church was over.

We could hear the organ in the church, and the bright sound of voices singing the lofty chorus of "A Mighty Fortress Is Our God," the hymn swelling in the clear morning air. I looked at Beth and winked. The sheep were still grazing on the grass. Soon we heard the congregation giving the last responses, then the minister's benediction, and people began spilling from the church vestibule. I saw Mrs. Dodd appear, helping the man in the dark glasses down the steps. Leaving him chatting with a figure I recognized as the old woman I had given our telephone number to, Mrs. Dodd hurried to meet us. She said her car was parked on the other side of the Common, and if we drove around we could follow her. Yes, she had the key.

When we pulled up behind her Buick, the old woman gave us a backward glance as she drove away in her buggy. We were introduced to Mrs. Dodd's husband, who was blind. I ventured a commonplace about the church music, and Mr. Dodd said with some pride that it was his wife who played the organ. Today, Mrs. Dodd interpolated, was Whitsunday. I looked at Beth: did people still observe Whitsunday?

We drove to Penrose Lane, where Mrs. Dodd led her husband to the porch and settled him in a chair, made him a drink, then joined us on the lawn next door. The lilacs were in bloom along the drive, and a bird was rebuilding the nest in the locust tree, a little yellow bird.

The house, Mrs. Dodd explained before unlocking the front door, was one of the oldest in the village. It had been built by the son of one of the founders, Gwydeon Penrose, whose house was on the Common. This one needed a plaque: 1709.

A bit in need of repair, too, I'm afraid, she said as we entered the musty hallway; well, yes and no. The kitchen was impossible, but for money could be made possible. Likewise the baths. The rest was all we had hoped for, and more. Its charm was infinite. The wide hall divided the house; on one side was the living room, spacious, with pegged floors and the marvelous fireplace, and across the hall a large dining room with the paneled wainscoting under what looked like thirty coats of paint. Connecting the dining room and kitchen was a smaller room with another fireplace. I suspected it was what used to be referred to as the "second parlor," but Mrs. Dodd called it something that sounded like "bacchante room." It was only later I realized she must have said "back anteroom."

Upstairs there were four bedrooms; the largest, with agreeable proportions, revealed another fireplace and overlooked the locust tree at the front corner, with the Dodd hedge below.

We came down, and, leaving the two women talking in the

kitchen, I went out back to look at the chicken house again; I was right; it would make a perfect studio. Walking past the stable to the foot of the property, I gazed back at the wide sweep of rutted, weed-choked lawn and made silent decrees. There I wanted a terrace, there a wall, there border gardens. I wanted pigeons in the dovecote, and another birdhouse in the beech tree. I wanted the house painted white, with dark green shutters, and except for removing the front porch, not another line would I touch. The baths would have to be modernized, the kitchen as well. I would put in a picture window. I would clean out the chicken house and put in a skylight and whitewash the interior. I would paint the stable barn-red; I would find Kate a horse. I would have it all just as I had always dreamed of it. In short, I would buy the place.

When I learned how much it would cost.

I walked back to the house to find Beth standing alone in the drive under the lilacs. She had pulled a bloom down to smell it; then, thinking herself unobserved, she put her face in a bunch of them, as though wanting to drown in their scent. Hearing my footstep, she turned, and I still carry the memory of how lovely she looked at that moment, her face buried in the purple clusters.

"Oh, Ned," she sighed; there was no need to say any more. While overhead, in the branches of the tree, the yellow bird feathered its nest, we, below, laid plans to feather ours. I held Beth's face in my hands and looked into her eyes. Because of the old trouble, I wanted, this one last time, to be sure she was certain in her heart it was the right move. Her face gave me the answer. I cautioned her to play it deadpan and not seem too anxious; then we went to find Mrs. Dodd again. She met us at her door and ushered us into the sun porch, which also served as the blind man's study, a small, many-windowed room with half-drawn shades. The walls were lined with shelves holding a helter-skelter collection of books, papers, folders, memorabilia. Over drinks, we learned that Mr. Dodd was, in fact, Professor Dodd, and had taught in a college in the northern part of New

England before retiring. Choosing my moment, I inquired when we might speak with Miss Penrose about the house. Professor Dodd said there was no need; he had been authorized to make the sale in the event we found the property satisfactory. He would name a price and that would be it; there would be no dickering. I asked what that price might be, scarcely suppressing a look of astonishment when he mentioned a figure well under what we were prepared to pay.

We asked about available schools and doctors. Mrs. Dodd shook her head. The village could not afford its own doctor; the nearest one was in Saxony, on the far side of the river; he came in emergencies. Aside from him, the Widow Fortune, a sort of midwife, homeopath, and veterinarian combined, was all Cornwall Coombe had. Legal matters were usually handled by a lawyer in Ledyardtown. Though there was a school of sorts, most of the farm children didn't go beyond the eighth grade. For those who wanted to attend, there was a high school over in Saxony, but hardly anyone from Cornwall Coombe, except the paperboy, went there. Learning was scant in the village. I looked at Beth; this was something we hadn't foreseen. No doctor, no school; both were necessary.

There was, however, Mrs. Dodd suggested, a good place over in Ledyardtown, the Greenfarms School, which had a fine reputation. Many parents in the neighboring towns who desired better education for their children sent them there. No bus, though; Beth would have to drive. Car pool? No, none of the village children attended Greenfarms. If we cared to, Mrs. Dodd would take us over after lunch. I asked Mr. Dodd if we would encounter difficulty finding workmen to do the renovation; he mentioned a Bill Johnson, who lived out on the turnpike, and said this man could probably give us a more than satisfactory job. Mrs. Dodd offered a bite of lunch with them, but we declined tactfully. She suggested the Yankee Clipper, also out on the turnpike, or if something light would do, there was the Rocking Horse Tavern in the village. We chose the latter, finished our drinks, and when

Mrs. Dodd brought her husband's lunch on a tray, with the food carefully cut up for him, we left, asking if we might have a few hours to discuss the situation. Mr. Dodd said to take all the time we needed, the house would still be there.

Crossing the lawn, I heard again the voice reading from a book: *"Miss Havisham often asked me in a whisper, or when we were alone, 'Does she grow prettier and prettier, Pip?'"* I recognized *Great Expectations*, and thought of our own.

We parked beside the Common, then paused to admire the wooden rocking horse over the doorway of the tavern, a polychromed figure with gilded mane and tail. Inside, the air was thick with pipe smoke and talk of corn among the farmers gathered around the bar; several eyed us with curiosity as we found a table in the back and ordered beers and steak sandwiches, and began exchanging ideas about the house. Beth laughed when I told her about having misunderstood Mrs. Dodd's comment about the bacchante room, and said it cried for mulberry walls, and could we have a hunter-green sofa? She remembered there was a Victorian sideboard in storage we could hide the TV in.

Some others came in, an older man and five younger ones, and they also were stared at as they heaved past the bar with heavy-booted tread and took a table in the corner. While the men at the bar talked corn, these talked tobacco, a burly, almost ruffian-looking gang, obviously a family. The older one, an angry, bristly man, we decided must be the father.

After lunch, as we waited for Mrs. Dodd, we stood outside the tavern and had a look around the Common. This large central area of the village was more than an eighth of a mile long, oval in shape, encircled by a road which began at the north end where Main Street left off. On the west side were a Grange hall, a firehouse, and a grocery; then the post office, an ancient squat, oddly shaped building of wood and stone, with a large, lopsided chimney. Next door was the Gwydeon Penrose House, then the drugstore, a barbershop, and more houses. Our side began with the tavern; next to it a building apparently combining the facilities of town hall and library; another ancient clapboarded dwelling, now converted into a bank, with Ye Beauty Shoppe upstairs; more houses; and the church, directly opposite the post office.

People were taking their Sunday ease along the walks, looking in the shopwindows or forming little knots of conversation, while their offspring played on the Common where the sheep bleated as dogs without leashes ran among them.

What cars were parked along the curbing seemed of Eisenhower vintage, their wheels and fenders still muddy from the winter. A wagon creaked by, a stolid farmer holding the reins. He pulled up, got down, and went into the tavern we had just quit, sliding a look at us as he passed. I thought how wonderful to hear horses' hoofs, the sort of sound one expected in such a place.

Taking Beth's arm, I walked with her in the direction of the church. An old man sat on the top step near the vestibule doorway, his chair tilted back, his lap filled with knitting as his gnarled hands plied large wooden needles. He, too, was observing us. I felt Beth's hand squeeze mine, two nervous little tugs. I squeezed it back, and we strolled into the cemetery to wander among the tombstones again, reading the antique inscriptions. Like the living village, this dead one seemed well populated by Penroses.

We climbed a grassy knoll whose far side was also planted with graves, sloping away into a marshy meadowland, with the river gently curving inward beyond. A low iron fence marked the boundary of the cemetery, and on the other side, half hidden under a tangle of briars, was a solitary marker. Curious, I went to investigate. All around the plot the grass was long and untended, the ground wet and soggy. I pushed the briars aside and read the inscription:

GRACE EVERDEEN

Deceased

1958

Wondering who the unfortunate lady was who had been thus consigned to unconsecrated ground, I returned to Beth on the slope above, and we left the cemetery and passed the church where the old man pursued his woolwork—a muffler, if I was correct—his eye not missing a trick as we continued along the walk to the point where Main Street began. Then we gazed back at the panorama. The sun was bright, the sky blue and cloudless, and spring was everywhere. A man was dressing up a picket fence with a fresh coat of paint; another carried a bucket out behind a house and used an old-fashioned hand pump to fill it. A third sprinkled ashes on a cultivated plot beside his doorway, while beribboned girls dawdled over boys with Sunday-slicked haircuts. Another wagon lumbered past; a dog ran under the horses' traces, barking at their hoofs.

I loved the feel of the place: the tranquil, bucolic look, the sense of peace that spoke from every doorway, from each plot of well-tended grass, from every newly blooming garden. I loved the solidity and agelessness of it, of the passersby themselves, simple country people with simple country faces. There was a sense of veneration for that which had gone before, a rigid, disciplined effort to preserve things as they were—even, perhaps, a reluctance to acknowledge things as they are.

Mrs. Dodd came for us. We spent a pleasant hour driving over to Ledyardtown, about fifteen miles away, and talking with the head of the Greenfarms School, where we were informed they would be happy to interview Kate for admittance next fall. The school, adequate beyond our expectations in such a remote locale, appeared to meet any educational requirements; there was even a riding academy where a course in "equitation" was taught. Kate would be ahorse yet.

On the way back, I mentioned to Mrs. Dodd that I hadn't realized tobacco was grown in these parts. Oh, yes, she said, on the other side of the river it was all tobacco, used for cigar wrappers. Beth mentioned the bristly-looking man in the tavern. That must have been Old Man Soakes and his brood from over in Tobacco City, Mrs. Dodd replied. A reprehensible lot, they sometimes came over to buy corn to make whiskey with. Moonshining in New England? Indeed, she replied; the Soakes clan had been making bootleg whiskey for years. It was rumored they kept a still in the woods outside town, though no one had ever bothered to try to locate it. People, she told us, mostly minded their own business. Besides, Soakes's whiskey was regarded favorably by the village farmers; and it was cheap.

We returned to the Common to pick up our car, again following the Buick out to Penrose Lane where, coming up the walk, I overheard another passage from Dickens.

We found the blind man in the sun porch listening to a record player, a device he called his talking-book machine, on which he played books that had been read onto a disk. Shutting the phonograph off, Mrs. Dodd offered us another drink, and we informed her husband we would take the house. A handshake was all he asked to seal the transaction, with papers to be drawn up subsequently, and we lingered in the sunny room for three-quarters of an hour, becoming acquainted with our neighbors-to-be. The Professor seemed to know a good deal about the history of the village and was happy to answer any questions Beth or I put to him. I tried to explain to him my feelings about the place, the excitement I felt at discovering Cornwall Coombe. He listened, nodding at each sentence, and when I had done he said it was understandable enough, but people often ignored the fact that life a hundred years ago was not easy. Time put a patina of affection on yesteryear, and we tended to forget how appalling existence could be in those times, how long and how hard a man had to labor for his food, how difficult childbearing was, how few medicines and conveniences there were; how stern the realities of life.

Tradition, he continued, was the important thing here: tradition and custom, customs that had been preserved through the villagers' lineage since olden times. They were a tightly knit, insular group, these corn farmers, apparently determined to cut themselves off from the rest of society in an effort to preserve their own folkways, much as had the Amish in Pennsylvania, the Mennonites in Ohio. What had been good for a man's father and grandfather was good enough for him; what they had worn, he wore; the tools they used, he used—a scythe to mow the hay, a sickle to cut the corn.

The Professor sat comfortably in his chair, savoring his drink from time to time, his head directed straight before him, his eyes completely hidden behind his dark glasses, whose side pieces admitted no light. The people of Cornwall Coombe were good people, he continued, from good stock, but their ways were different from most people's, and they took a deal of getting used to. Some might find it difficult adapting to the village ways, he pointed out, with, I thought, a hint of something in his tone, as though he thought perhaps we might not be able to—or, to put it more strongly, not be willing to.

The village was not rich, which was all right; small, which was fine; quaint, which was nice. The farmers were sociable according to their custom; worshiped according to their custom; ate, drank, fasted, worried and wept, married, gave birth, and were laid to rest according to their custom; were not particularly interested in what went on in the world and, according to their custom, never went there to see. Were we, he wondered, prepared to adapt?

Rising with Beth, I said we were. We were prepared for anything. The Professor sipped from his glass and tapped his nail against the rim. He hoped, he said, we would prosper.

3

While Beth squeezed fresh orange juice, I sat at the farm table in our new kitchen scanning the morning news. It all seemed familiar. There had been another skyjacking, an Eastern flight. It was the second that week; the first had ended in shooting, two bandits dead in the cabin, terrified passengers, a disgusted crew. A man in California had gone amok, had killed his wife and four children. It made me sick to look at the paper. The trouble in Ireland—religious persecution in this year of our Lord, 1972; heavy artillery banging away on the Golan Heights; Americans dropping bombs on insignificant Vietnamese huts.

I turned the page to look for *Peanuts*.

"Don't forget your vitamins," Beth reminded me. She pointed to the array of capsules and pills she always set out beside my plate: ascorbic acid, Super-Potent B-Complex Alerts, Multi-Vita-Mineral tablets, brewer's yeast, niacin, and riboflavin.

I washed them down in sets with the orange juice. Beth poured coffee from the electric percolator, then continued making breakfast while I sipped from my cup. On the radio, Milton Cross was advertising the "Barcarolle" from *The Tales of Hoffmann*, plus a million other sensational semiclassical glories, all for the low price of $3.95.

Beth paused to gaze out the picture window at the terrace beyond, with its unfinished wall. "It's like a beginning, isn't it?"

"What is?"

"Oh—today. Somehow it feels like a beginning." I supposed the fair, locally signifying the end of summer, had something to do with her thought.

"A new beginning for us?"

"Something like that."

"Maybe we ought to start by going to church tomorrow."

"I didn't necessarily mean *that* new a beginning." Daughter of a minister, Beth had shunned churches ever since we'd been married.

"A token appearance might not be a bad idea, just to grease the skids a bit."

She turned, brightening. "Have you noticed? They seem to be changing. Don't you think they are? Toward us?"

We had arrived outsiders, city people, not wanted on the voyage. "They" had been aloof—not unfriendly, but as remote from us as their village was from the roads and highways. After our arrival, in my infrequent forays about town, I had met with singular indifference. Then, happily, and for no apparent reason, I began getting friendly nods, a word here and there.

Fred Minerva would come around to offer some canny advice about insulating the house or to dump a load of fresh manure for the new lawn; Edna Jones would stop by with a begonia cutting, some kale or Swiss chard from her kitchen garden. Suddenly I felt we had neighbors, friends, that we were at last becoming a part of the life around us and were not merely interlopers.

"It must be the Widow, don't you think?"

I was forced to agree. At least I could see no other answer. The Widow Fortune had become our benefactress. Robert Dodd, our next-door neighbor, had said she was the oldest inhabitant in Cornwall Coombe, a sort of matriarch whom all the villagers respected to the point of reverence, a local antique. She was the woman I had spoken with on the church steps on Planting Day, and she was the first to arrive, in her buggy, at our kitchen door. I suspected Beth was right: after her had come the others. The Widow Fortune—I had told myself her name was lucky.

I beckoned to Beth, and she came and sat on my lap. I could smell the sweet, natural fragrance of her hair, the lingering aroma of the Pears' soap she always used. "Is it O.K., sweetheart? You're not sorry we came?"

"It's O.K. And I'm not sorry we came. It's just—it's difficult getting used to their ways."

"If we want them to get used to our ways, we're going to have to get used to theirs. It'll be all right, you'll see."

She got up and spun a little happy turn. "I love my new kitchen."

"Beats Chock Full o' Nuts."

"*Ned*—you *never* had to eat breakfast at Chock Full o' Nuts!"

"Only kidding, sweetheart." Listening for Kate's footsteps overhead, I watched Beth as she scrambled eggs, browned sausage, took rolls from the oven, dropped bread into the new toaster. Her movements were deft and economical, and she moved about the various work areas in a planned pattern, with no wasted motions. I found her extraordinary—but then I always had.

"Are you going to sketch after breakfast?" she asked.

"I'd like to finish those tombstones; then I thought I'd walk out to the Lost Whistle Bridge."

"All that way?"

"It's not far." With my right forefinger, I felt the small lump that had recently formed on my left third finger, a wart which seemed the result of continual pressure from my various drawing instruments. "It'd be good for Kate to be seen in church, don't you think? Wouldn't hurt us, either, getting in good with the—"

"Natives? Maybe. But I don't think Kate wants to spend Sunday morning listening to Mr. Buxley preach. It's difficult enough—"

Still no sound from upstairs. Kate must be sleeping late—not unusual; she didn't rest well at night. A violent asthmatic since the age of nine, our daughter had been subject to even more vicious attacks since coming to Cornwall Coombe. At that very moment, we didn't know what condition she would appear in, whether, in fact, she would be able to go to the fair at all. Or want to. Kate *was* difficult. Still, we offered ourselves the pretense that all was well, and hoped we were right.

While breakfast cooked, Beth brought things from the refrigerator and began making the picnic lunch, stuffing plump chicken breasts with a tempting mixture from a blue-ringed mixing bowl.

I squinted at her, reducing her figure to a silhouette, taking in the series of curves and angles, the splash of dark hair falling over one eye. Bethany Constantine, née Colby; thirty-seven years old; Scotch-Irish-English ancestry; Miss Kemp's School, Boston; Bennington, Liberal Arts major. Measurements: 35″, 28″, 32″; trim, neat body; a full mouth, perhaps a little too wide for the triangular face; a pussycat sort of face, quick to smile, not so fast to frown.

But thinner. And dark smudges under the eyes; a brittleness to her posture betraying the fatigue that caused her extra effort in standing straight.

"Aren't you eating?"

"Certainly." She was snitching bits from the pans on the stove while she continued working. She found a paring knife in a drawer, pulled out the chopping board, and began chopping chives. She made an exasperated sound as she stopped and drew her thumb over the edge of the knife blade.

"Honestly, I paid Jack Stump thirty-five cents for this knife, and I don't think it would cut warm butter." She laid it aside and finished the job with another. "I swear he could sell ice to an Eskimo." Jack Stump was an itinerant door-to-door peddler who regularly came bouncing his cart up to the kitchen door, trying to soft-soap Beth into buying the latest cooking gadget or housewife's convenience.

"Haven't seen Jack in a while," I remarked.

"I *know*. Hasn't been around in days. Thank God for small favors. I never heard a man talk so much."

Movement upstairs: Kate was awake. Beth heard the sounds, too. She looked at the ceiling, glanced at me, then returned her attention to the chives.

"More coffee, darling?"

"Um-hmm." A woman in Ohio had drowned her baby in a bathtub. Someone had done the same thing the day before. I looked at the date on the newspaper. "This is *yesterday's!*"

"Paper didn't come yet this morning."

"Didn't?"

"No. And Worthy's usually Johnny-on-the-spot. You don't suppose he's sick?"

"I saw him in the drugstore yesterday."

Beth brought a cloth and napkins from a drawer, the checked ones she had found when we were in Paris. I took a cinnamon bun, my cup and saucer, yesterday's paper, and went through the open doorway into the bacchante room. From the kitchen I could hear pleasant domestic sounds: the slam of the refrigerator door, running water, the garbage disposal, Beth humming along with the radio. I got a pencil and began the crossword puzzle. Presently she came in and leaned over the back of the sofa to raise the window behind me. "What a lovely day." She straightened the things on the piecrust table, and pulled a few leaves from the flower arrangement on the sideboard. "It's such a nice room, isn't it? Such a nice house. Aren't we lucky Tamar Penrose decided to sell!" She kissed the top of my head. Remembering what the place had looked like when we moved in, I inwardly winced and thought back over the endless weeks of renovation: the torn-up rooms, the paint smells, the insidious silt of plaster dust on everything, our tired bodies dropping into bed at night. Now the work was almost done. New kitchen, new bathrooms, new hardware, new screens and awnings. The insulation men were finished, the floor men, the electricians, the heating men. The house was painted inside and out, the dining room papered; Lawson Colby's furniture, a collection of good antiques, had been brought from storage and arranged in the rooms. Among the remaining jobs were the terrace wall and the skylight in the studio. But our mainstay, Bill Johnson, was leaving next week to spend the autumn and winter in Las Vegas, and we would have to look elsewhere for a handyman.

"I think she's got designs on you."

"Huh? Who?"

"Tamar Penrose. I see her making goo-goo eyes at you when we go in the post office." Tamar Penrose had designs on me? I recalled the way she would manage to stretch across the post-office counter, or sling her hips while lounging at the postal scales. Still, designs? We'd hardly exchanged two words.

"Half the village is named Penrose, from what I can see," I said.

"It's awful the way they've inbred. They're all direct descendants of the original family. 'Once or twice removed,' cousins marrying cousins—that sort of thing. Some of them are a little— you know." She tapped her temple. "Like Amys."

"Amos who?"

"Not 'A-m-o-s'," she spelled " 'A-m-y-s.' He's that marvelous old curmudgeon who sweeps the streets and rings the church bell. The one Kate calls 'vinegar puss.' And the Widow's husband was a Penrose on his mother's side."

"Was he—?" I tapped my temple.

"Oh, I don't think so. How old do you think she is?"

"Who?" I was trying to think of a four-letter word for "decree."

"The Widow."

"Dunno." I wrote in "fiat."

"I suppose she could be anywhere from sixty to ninety. Maggie Dodd says it's the best kept secret in the village." She carried my empty cup into the kitchen.

"How long a widow?" I said through the doorway.

"Ages. Maggie says it was quite a love match. It's the honey that does it, I guess."

"Makes love matches?"

"No, dopey. It's the Widow's honey that keeps all those old farmers young. Mr. Deming must be eighty, and he looks—"

"Seventy." Ewan Deming was chief among the village elders.

"The same with Amys. Half the farmers in the village are over sixty and they still work a whole day."

"How do you account for it?"

"The Widow calls the body the human house. She says to stay healthy, watch the cows. Cows have common sense and know what to eat. Like lots of people don't," Beth continued from the kitchen.

I heard the sound of Kate's feet on the stairs, then glimpsed her as she passed through the front hall beyond the dining room; in a moment she was with her mother.

"Hi."

"Morning, darling. Sleep well?"

"Nope."

"Don't forget your vitamins, dear. All set for the fair?"

"Guess so. Bet it'll be corny."

It was going to be one of her smarty days. "C'mon," I called, "it'll be fun."

Carrying her orange juice, Kate came in and kissed me. "Hi."

"Hi, sweetheart." Her hand trembled as she drank from her glass, and I could tell she'd had another bad night.

"It's not every day you get to go to a real country fair."

"Cut the commercial, Daddy." She stared out the window, popping the vitamins between gulps. Her sleepy face looked doleful and lethargic. Kate with her unmanageable hair, her urchin's face, her sandpapery voice—poor knobby, angry Kate. Her eyes were red and puffy, her face pale.

"They sure got a lot of yokels around here."

"Yokels?"

"And some of 'em are crazy."

"Who's crazy? I haven't seen anyone crazy."

"Missy Penrose is crazy."

"Darling, don't say that," Beth said from the kitchen. "Missy's not crazy; she's a little unusual, that's all."

"And she's a bastard."

Worse than smarty; mean. When these moods came upon her, a result of lost sleep, it was difficult to know how to handle her.

"Lots of children are illegitimate, but it doesn't mean they're any less or any worse than we are. People can't help the circumstances of their birth."

"She's still crazy. She hardly ever talks, she mumbles, and when she does talk she says nutty things. And she goes into the woods to trade looks with the boys. And her mother's a sex fiend."

Through the doorway, I caught Beth's eye as it flashed a humorous look at me behind Kate's back: *Has designs on you.*

"Come and have your Granola, dear."

"Not hungry."

"Kate, you've got to eat something. I've got scrambled eggs and sausage. Honestly, with people—"

"—starving in India; I know." Kate ambled into the kitchen and I heard a chair scrape the floor as she sat at the table. "What are we having for lunch?"

"Darling, try to think about your breakfast first, huh? We're having vichyssoise with chopped chives, chicken breasts stuffed with crab—"

"What's for dessert?"

"Mousse au chocolat."

"Are there any extras?"

"No. And you're having fruit cup, anyway. You know what the Widow said about sweets. There are four mousses—two for your father and me, two for the Dodds."

"Rats." There was a pause while Kate munched a piece of toast, then: "Daddy, you know what an oracle is?"

"I have an idea—"

"Like they have at Delphi, right? And it tells you things, right? Well, Missy Penrose is supposed to be an oracle."

"Is she filled with revelation, then?" I managed to suppress my smile by turning it into a yawn.

"Don't laugh. They really believe it. You know about the Minervas' barn?"

"Kate," Beth put in, "that's just a story; nobody believes it—"

"Sure they do. They really do. Yokels."

Fred Minerva had been having a run of bad luck, all of which had stemmed, or so the villagers maintained, from his stumbling in the dance at Spring Festival. Soon after, he stepped on a rake and got blood poisoning; then his barn had caught fire in a July electric storm.

"But before it burned," Kate went on, "he asked Missy Penrose if he should build a cupola and have a weather vane, and she told him, 'Save wood, save iron.' She was telling him a cupola and a weather vane would be a waste because the barn was going to burn, and it did."

"Haven't they ever heard about lightning rods?" Beth said.

"They don't have them," I said. "It's not permitted. Nor insurance."

"But it only stands to reason—"

"They're not interested in reason, sweetheart. It's the custom."

"See? Yokels." Kate put down her fork and went to the refrigerator. Beth said, "Darn, I've forgotten the picnic hamper. Now, where did I see it last?" She went out through the hall. Kate was rummaging in the refrigerator freezing compartment.

"Kate, are you happy here?" I said.

"Sure. I guess so."

"Are you looking forward to school?"

"Um." She closed the refrigerator and got a spoon from the drawer.

"We can always move back to Seventy-eighth Street."

"Aw c'mon, Daddy." She ate for a moment. Then: "You said I could have a horse." Angry, resentful.

"Sorry, sweetheart, you know what—"

"The doctor said. I know."

I felt guilty about the horse. Unthinkingly I had promised it before we left New York, not realizing then the serious allergic effects of animals on Kate's asthma. The doctor in Saxony, who had been treating her, had told us to keep her from direct contact with any four-footed creatures, but the trouble was far more serious than a mere allergy.

Since the age of nine, Kate had suffered from a congenital condition known as status asthmaticus, which continually imperiled her life. After years of treatment, to little effect, we had learned from a new doctor that the symptoms were self-induced, a form of psychosomatic asthma, whose origins had been eventually traced to the trouble Beth and I had had between us six years ago. It was, the doctor said, Kate's unconscious way of getting even with us. Once, she had almost died, and only the respirator from the fire department had saved her. It became important that she not get overly excited or emotionally upset, either of which conditions was likely to induce another attack. Her last, a week ago, had come as a result of her disappointment about the horse. There was a tantrum, followed by a seizure, and the doctor had to be called over from Saxony.

"It was in the attic." Beth came in with the picnic hamper. "Kate, open the window over the sink, can you? It's such a beautiful day out, a real New *England* day." She set the hamper on the counter and turned. "Kate! Rocky Road ice cream? For breakfast?"

"It's just eggs and milk, Mom, just breakfast food."

"And condensed-milk sandwiches for lunch. You'll be breaking out in pimples again, and none of the boys will—"

"—look at me. Who cares."

After making an issue of the ice cream, Beth now chose to ignore it. Anything to avoid a scene; but while the rod was spared, the child was spoiled. I had long since given up protesting.

"What are you going to wear today, dear?" Beth asked brightly.

"This."

"Blue jeans and a T-shirt? Wouldn't you like to wear a dress? Something pretty? For the fair?"

"What's so special about the fair, anyway? Honest, it's all anyone talks about. Yokels."

"Kate . . ." Beth remonstrated gently.

"Do you know they go crazy?"

"Who?"

"The villagers. Moon madness. When the moon's full, they go dancing in the fields and do crazy things."

I looked up from my puzzle. "Do they turn into werewolves and vampires?"

"Well, it's *true.*" Kate banged her spoon for emphasis. "And there's a ghost, too."

"I haven't heard anything about ghosts," Beth said.

"There's a ghost out in the woods—"

"Who told you?"

"Missy Penrose. It comes out at night and eats babies and goes riding down the road on a headless horse—"

I decided Kate's sense of drama had confused local superstition with Washington Irving. From conversations with Robert Dodd, I had learned that Cornwall Coombe tended to be slightly mythic in its lore, but I had not heard anything about a ghost.

Beth tried to calm Kate, who was prancing around the table making wild moaning sounds and generally imitating a spirit. "Darling, don't go getting excited now. Go up and put on a dress, please? You'll look so pretty."

When she had gone, Beth gave me a brief look and I knew what she was thinking. *What are we going to do about her?* It was the one thing troubling our existence, and the thing we both felt guilty about.

I could hear the creak of the wicker as she filled the Hammacher Schlemmer picnic hamper. Across the hedge, Professor Dodd's sun-porch window slid open. In a moment a voice called, "Anyone up over there?"

Beth crossed to the sink and leaned to our window. "Morning, Robert. Lovely day for the fair."

"Yes, it is."

"Good morning," Maggie Dodd called. "Marvelous day. Just listen to that bird." Maggie was enthusiastic about everything, as if she took it as a personal responsibility that we should like everything about Cornwall Coombe. Yet it seemed to me that though her touch was light, in her own bantering way she was always putting the village down. "How's the picnic coming?" she asked.

"Just finishing."

"I think you're crazy, doing the whole thing yourself. I could have done the dessert, at least."

"I wanted to. It's chocolate mousse. How are the martinis doing?"

"I'm just going to fix them. Ned doesn't want martinis?"

"Doesn't like them."

"I'll put in some Scotch, then. See you later. I'm going to get Robert's breakfast."

Beth turned off the tap, dried her hands, and began wrapping the chicken breasts in foil. Beyond the hedge I could hear Maggie speaking to Robert, then silence, then another voice:

"*D'Artagnan trembled.*

"*'Certes,' said Aramis, 'I do injustice to the beauties of this thesis; but, at the same time, I perceive it would be overwhelming for me. I had chosen this text—tell me, dear D'Artagnan . . .'*"

I recognized what we had come to call the Invisible Voice, the man who had recorded Robert's talking-books. It was a daily sound that we had become accustomed to, and through the summer I had caught portions of the remainder of *Great Expectations*, followed by *Madame Bovary*, and this week *The Three Musketeers*. Robert was reading his way through the classics.

"Darling, did you say you were going out to sketch?"

"Mm."

"You'd better hurry; it's getting late."

I finished the puzzle, tossed the paper aside, and went from the bacchante room into the kitchen, then started out the back door.

"Wait, Ned." Beth went to the cork bulletin board, referred to a penciled slip of paper, and did a few rapid calculations. "Have you got some cash? Stop at the Widow's and pay her five dollars. We owe for eggs and honey. And here—" handing me a paper sack—"take her the rest of the cinnamon buns." She gave me an uncertain look.

I took the bag, at the same time drawing her into my arms.

"Ned?"

"Mm?"

"Kate—?"

"I know."

"You *don't* know . . ." Her frustration put an edge to her voice that I seldom heard. "You're not a mother. You *don't* know."

I held her for a moment, then released her and said, "Don't worry. It's going to be O.K." But I said it with an assurance I scarcely felt.

4

When the great back-to-the-land movement began, Beth had suggested we make a clean break with the past. By mutual agreement we decided that no New York friends would clutter up our guest room, at least until Christmas. Consequently we were both isolated geographically and cut off from our old acquaintanceships as well. Which was not a problem: our parents all were dead, and what friends we might elect to have come and visit could well wait.

Still, though I had never confessed my doubts to Beth, at times I worried. Where were we to fit into this yesteryear place? Apart from the Dodds, whom would we have for friends? How was Kate going to fare at Greenfarms School? Were we crazy, burying ourselves in a one-horse town, where it was necessary to drive way out to the turnpike to find a shopping center or to see a movie, where people still believed that what was good enough for their fathers was good enough for them? How could they talk to me of painting, or I to them of corn?

Therein seemed to lie the answer. When in Rome . . . Though I had never been intimate with nature, next year I would plant corn. I would plow up the field at the foot of the property and put in corn and beans and tomatoes and early peas. I would get gardening books; I would learn about the soil and how it might produce, even for a city dweller. Formerly a lover of the pavements, now I would be a lover of the earth. There, at the corner of Penrose Lane, on this bright morning of the Agnes Fair, I laid claim to the land, swearing fidelity to it. I felt it was as Beth had said: today was a new beginning.

I turned left onto Main Street and continued in the direction of the Common. The Widow Fortune's house, several blocks along Main, was almost obscured behind a corn crop so high it hid a man's hat. I had heard Robert Dodd say the old lady talked to the corn to make it grow, a concept I found fanciful, supposing plants must grow as they chose, or as they received sustenance; but growing because someone talked to them . . .

I went down the lane at the side of the small, gabled house and into the dooryard, where I set the sack of buns on the back-porch steps, next to a pair of worn shoes. Beside these was a bunch of flowers in a leaky pail. A large black iron pot sat over a smoking fire in the dooryard, the contents simmering and making thick plopping sounds. Savoring the aroma, I discovered other smells, the pungent musk of damp earth, the dusty tang of broken flowerpots and manured trowels, a tinge of fertilizer. Good country smells. Everywhere I looked, I sensed an earthy richness, an appreciation of growing things, plant life and animal life, all of life. There were patches of garden under the window sills and, along the fence, a bed of cabbages, their pale green heads set in perfect alignment, the rows meticulously tended. No weed, I felt sure, would dare show its face under the Widow Fortune's careful scrutiny.

My eyes traveled along the rows, to discover the old lady herself, kneeling among the cabbages. Oblivious to my arrival, she held herself upright, with bowed head, her hands clasped over her breast, and I guessed she might be praying, though why in a cabbage patch I had no idea. The soft morning light lay about her in a wash of water-color tints, all mist and mother-of-pearl, violet and gray and rose; and observing the motionless form, I thought, Here is someone who appreciates the joys of a solitary contemplation of the day. Presently she lifted her head, and, still not noticing me, she rose, digging her fisted hands in the small of her back to ease it, and scanning the sky overhead, lost in some cloudy reverie. Then, lifting her skirts that she had pinned up for purposes of convenience, she peered at the ground around her and spoke.

"Come, now, slow one, have a bite." She bent and broke off some cabbage leaves and dropped them beside a large brown stone at her feet. As though by some feat of sorcery, the stone moved. I blinked, then realized it was a large tortoise whose shell resembled a stone. While it proceeded to eat the cabbage leaves, she bent down and spoke to it like a witch to her familiar, then straightened, her black form real and corporeal amid the dissolving mists.

"Good morning," I called at last. She turned, peering at me through round, silver-rimmed spectacles, waiting for me to approach. "Watch your hoofs," she said in a forthright tone, "don't tread on my cabbages." A sizable woman, she presented a handsome figure, Junoesque in its stateliness: large head, straight neck, full shoulders. Though time had tugged her here and there, causing the neck to sag under the firm chin, her skin was pulled tight and shone with a robust glow over the rosy flesh. How old *was* she? I wondered again. Age had not seemed to wither

her; there was nothing crone-like in her appearance; her constitution appeared firm, her heart stout, and if her teeth were not her own she did not yet walk with a cane.

If someone had driven up at that moment and asked me my first, surest impression of the Widow Fortune, I would have said comfortable and motherly.

"You're an early riser," she said briskly.

" 'Carpe diem,' " I quoted, watching where I walked.

"Can't speak French," she replied; the merry twinkle in her eye told me she knew it wasn't French.

" 'Seize the day,' " I translated.

"It's the early mornin' that's got the gold in its mouth, as they say. I like to be up before all the trammel starts."

When she spoke, it was with a firm authority, a distinct voice that knew what things were about. Listening, she had a gentle, luminous expression, humorous but not mocking.

"Beth sent you some cinnamon buns for breakfast." I nodded toward the back-porch steps.

"Well, now, that's neighborly. I've got the kettle on; let me put the cow to pasture, and you'll come and have a cup of tea with me." It sounded less an invitation than a command performance, and I found myself nodding in accord. Her step was spry as I followed her along a footworn path to the barn, where she disappeared for a moment, then reappeared, herding a large brown-and-white cow into a small pasture, carefully setting in the fence bar to keep the animal out of the corn.

"Brown Swiss." She spoke with a touch of pride, explaining that the cow, whose name was Caesar's Wife, was descended from the first herd of Brown Swiss brought from Switzerland to New England almost three centuries before. Caesar's Wife was the Widow's treasure.

She led me back the way we had come, stopping to stir the boiling pot with a large wooden paddle. "Hog," she said briefly, and I watched the pieces of meat and fat rise to the surface. "One of Irene Tatum's. Slaughtered it myself last week. Most mysterious thing! Hog had two stomachs, if you can believe it."

She gave me a look. "Guess what I found in one of 'em? A collar button." Her look sharpened, as though testing me. "Wouldn't you call that an augury?"

"I guess I might," I said, laughing.

"Sure you would. Anybody would. But what sort?" she asked in a dismayed voice, looking at the sky again. The pig, she went on, had been put down for salt pork, and she had made sausage with her own casings. The leavings went for blood puddings, and now all that remained was the head which was boiling in the pot; that would be for scrapple.

She pulled out the paddle, shook it, and laid it aside. Now she took a splint basket from a peg on the wall and marched to a corner of the garden where she began examining her plants.

"Only a minute," she called, snipping several sprigs with the large silver shears suspended from her waist by a length of black ribbon. Someone was sure to have iced tea at the fair, she said as I came up behind her, and a sprig of mint always went nice. She held it out for me to inhale its cool fragrance, then cut some more and offered me another sniff. "Pennyroyal. Good for colic." When she had done, she led me to the back door, took off her boots, and coaxed her feet into the worn shoes. Enjoining me to wipe my feet, she showed me into the kitchen. She laid the basket on the table and indicated a chair where I might be seated. While I put aside my sketchbook and drawing case, she tucked the cinnamon buns in the warming oven, put out a second cup and saucer beside the one already in evidence, poured tea, brought butter from the refrigerator, and a pot of honey.

The kitchen was low-ceilinged, small, and comfortable, and furnished with the clutter of a lifetime. One counter, on which sat a score of green bottles, with a scattering of corks and labels, was a small bottling works. Another held several shallow crocks whose contents looked as if they had only recently come from the oven: the blood puddings she had spoken of. A large tin kettle bubbled merrily on the stove. She spooned some of its contents up, blew on it, then tasted. It was not to her apparent liking, for she made a face, then bustled about, adding a little

of this, a pinch of that, until the brew was more to her satisfaction.

"How's your family?" she asked, pursuing these small homely
details.

"Fine." I noticed her hands, large working hands, yet marked
by their own simple grace, shapely, tapering fingers and smooth
oval nails. "Except for Kate—she's been having asthma attacks."

"I know. Asthma." She spoke the word sharply, marking such
a condition with her personal disdain. "That child oughtn't to
have asthma." She took out the buns and set them on a plate
before me. "Help yourself." Her nimble fingers separated the
small harvest of herbs in the basket, tying them in bunches and
hanging them from nails set into the edge of a shelf over the
sink. Everywhere were jars and other containers, filled with various herbs, stalks, blossoms, seeds—what appeared to be an entire
pharmacopoeia of country cures. "What's that used for?" I inquired, sniffing at the kettle on the stove which gave off an aro-
matic, almost exotic essence.

"For what ails you."

I wondered if she was bottling the concoction to sell at the
fair, medicine-show style. As though reading my mind, she explained that she did a satisfactory back-door business; hardly a
soul in the village didn't stop by one time or another for one
of her herbal infusions.

Her eye fell on my sketchbook. "How's the paintin' comin'?"
I assured her I was working hard at it, and had a New York
gallery swindled into handling my work.

"You any good?"

"Probably not."

"You're a liar." She beamed behind her glasses. "Let me see."
She leafed through the book, murmuring approval; then uttered
a little gasp as her hand flew to her breast. I saw she had come
upon the page of tombstones I had drawn yesterday. "My, my,
'course you're good. Dear me. Clemmon's stone." Gazing at the
rendering of the grave marker, she seemed a trifle overwrought.
"Aye, there's where dear Clem sleeps." Closing the sketchbook,

she set it aside, and took the chair opposite me, stirring her tea with a small silver spoon. "Clem bought me these cups the year we was married. The whole set, and not a one broken, not even a chip." She lifted the cup, staring thoughtfully at it for a moment, then sipped. "How long you folks been married?"

"Seventeen years next June."

"That's a good time. Must be prett' near settled in each other's ways by now. Marryin's good, keeps a body on his toes. Me, once I lost Clem, I never cared to wed again."

I watched her peering through the window at the great cook-pot in the dooryard, following with her eye the trail of white smoke as it rose in the air. "Straight up," I heard her mutter, "we'll have a nice fair."

She turned back. "Your place seems to be comin' along, don't it? You got a good man there in Bill Johnson."

"Did have." I explained about Bill's imminent departure.

"Why, he didn't say nothin' to me 'bout goin' to Las Vegas." She sounded surprised and a little miffed that Bill had not taken her into his confidence. "You'll be needin' another, won't you?"

"It's not easy getting help around here, with everyone thinking about the corn crop."

"Things'll slack off a bit now before harvest." Her heavy tread caused the floorboards to give as she got up and tied one of the puddings in waxed paper and slipped it into the sack I had brought the buns in. "Got to drop this off to Justin Hooke's. He's partial to blood puddin's."

Justin Hooke, I had learned, was the tall plowman we had seen in the field the day we first arrived in Cornwall Coombe. Owner of the most prosperous farm in the community, he was generally regarded with a mixture of awe, respect, and benevolence. His wife's name was Sophie, and their union had been one the entire village looked upon fondly. Justin must have been a decided favorite of the Widow's, for now she placed another pudding in the basket.

"How'd you like that tea?" she demanded, producing a box from the shelf. "Weber's English. It's a One-B Weber, not a

Two-B. I mail to London after it. Ever hear of Fortnum & Mason?" I said I had. "That's where. Fancy store. They don't seem t'carry One-B Weber's tea in America."

I carried my cup to the sink, washed and rinsed it, and started for the door.

"Off so soon?" She laid a large quilt beside the basket.

I thanked her, and said I planned on hiking out to the Lost Whistle Bridge to make some drawings. Remembering what I had come for, I gave her the five dollars for eggs and honey. She pocketed it and said she was going out Lost Whistle way herself, if I cared to ride along. "Worthy ought to be here any moment to hitch up the buggy. Unless you prefer shanks' mare."

Again I had the feeling of command, rather than suggestion. But, yes, I replied, I'd be happy for the ride. She excused herself, saying she must ready herself for the fair, then left me, and I heard her going up the stairs and passing overhead.

I wandered back out into the dooryard. Chickens and geese pecked at random among the rows of pole beans. In the distance the church bell sounded eight sonorous peals. Hearing a noise behind me, I looked to see someone pedaling a bicycle down the drive. I recognized Worthy Pettinger, who delivered the morning paper.

"Morning," he called.

I returned the greeting and walked to meet him. "Morning, Worthy."

"Sorry I'm late this morning, Mr. Constantine. Ma's frazzled today over the fair." He gave an energetic nod and his smile was bright as he took a paper from the handlebar basket and folded it. He was of high-school age, thin and lanky, with handsome, well-boned features, and a bright, eager smile; a thoroughly ingratiating young man. An industrious one as well; one could always see Worthy mowing someone's lawn or chopping in a woodpile or planting a garden.

"Worth-ee?" A second-story window had flown up and the Widow's head popped out. "Hitch up the mare and don't dawdle." She popped back in. "Oh, dear," came her disembodied voice, "now where in the nation's my brooch?"

Worthy kicked down the metal stand and leaned his bike on it, then deposited the newspaper on the steps. I ambled along behind while he went into the stable and led the little mare out. "Hey, old girl, hey, old girl," he said cheerily as he slipped the bit in her mouth and adroitly maneuvered her into the traces. He brought the harness, hooked it up, and hitched the leads into the shafts, all in a matter of seconds.

"You seem to keep pretty busy," I observed, admiring his dexterity.

"Yes, sir. Plenty of work hereabouts, if a fellow cares to do it. I'm trying to make enough money to go to agricultural college next fall. There's still a lot that farmers don't know about growin' corn, even if they'd have you think otherwise. Organic, that's the thing." He spoke in a buoyant, forthright manner. "I figure by different planting methods you could maybe double the yield of corn. Good land around here, but people don't take advantage of it. There's machines that'll do the work of ten men, with time to spare, for plowing and sowing, harvesting—everything." He spoke to me confidentially: "I got a tractor." I gathered from his tone this was a treasure on a par with the Widow's cow. "It's a beauty. I can take the whole motor apart and put it back together again, and she works just fine." He spoke in such a secretive, guarded tone that I decided having a tractor in Cornwall must be a daring enterprise indeed.

"Why don't the other farmers have them?"

"Not allowed. Machinery'll put the small farmer out of business, and we're sort of all in it together. But tractors could be the salvation of the whole town, them and harrows—"

"Shame on you, Worthy! Are you preachin' sedition, then?" The Widow had appeared in the doorway, waiting while the boy led the horse and buggy to her. "Here's a bun. Eat. You look thin."

She had changed her work clothes for an elegant, full-skirted black dress, with a long black alpaca apron over it. Her white hair was carefully brushed and pinned up in a knot, and neatly covered by a snowy cap with a ruffled edge, the strings hanging down either side of her chin. The missing brooch adorned her ample bosom.

"Thanks, Widow." Worthy picked up the paper and exchanged it for the bun.

"Don't thank me, thank the mister's missus—she made 'em. Drat that newspaper, I don't know why I spend the money. Nothin' but rape and murder and higher taxes." She flung the paper aside and went into the kitchen, reappearing in a moment with her basket and quilt, and a small valise made of worn black leather. She kept a watchful eye until Worthy stowed all this safely under the seat.

"Drat, forgot my shears." Again she disappeared, returning with her waist girdled by the black ribbon from which hung the silver shears, looking as though they were the companions of her life. She took the flowers from the bucket, wrapped their dripping ends in part of the discarded newspaper, and added these to the other things that had already been loaded. Thus fitted and accoutered, she gave the boy her hand while he aided her ascent into the buggy seat. "Did I remember to turn off the stove? Worthy, run and look." She turned to me. "See how a good-lookin' man like yourself flusters an old lady." She indicated the place beside her, I took it, she picked up the reins and gee'd the mare, turning the buggy in a wide arc so the wheels slid into one of the herb beds. "Hell's bells, there's my fennel ruined. Worth-ee?" She dropped the reins and waited for rescue. Worthy flew down the steps and led the mare from the dooryard onto the drive, smiling good-naturedly. "Think you'd never driven a buggy, Widow," he said, returning the reins to her. "Maybe you'd better break down and buy yourself a car."

"What should I do with one of them infernal contraptions? All smoke and noise and gas-eatin'. Better a horse that eats hay. Clem gave me this buggy for a weddin' present, and I'll be buried before it is." She flipped the reins, the mare started forward, but she immediately pulled up. "I was forgettin'. Worthy, Mr. Constantine here's goin' to need some help around his place. Bill Johnson's takin' himself out to Las Vegas for the gamblin'. Think you might find some time to lend a hand?" She fixed him with a look behind her spectacles.

"What kind of work, Mr. Constantine?" I explained about the skylight in the studio, and the terrace wall. He agreed to come at the first opportunity and see what might be done, then sped off on his paper route.

"He seems like a good kid," I offered conversationally, grateful for the Widow's concern in my difficulties.

"Aye, Worthy's a likely lad. Good as they come and better'n most. He's cheerful and obligin' and he's handy. He'll make a good farmer one of these days." I said I thought it ambitious of him to want to go to agriculture school. She did not reply immediately, but sat considering the matter. When she spoke, it was with a thoughtful tone. "He's only makin' trouble for himself. Folks won't take to newfangled ways around here. He's got his heart set on goin' away to school, but his father en't about to let him. Him nor his mother both."

I expressed surprise that parents would stand in the way of a child's wanting to better himself. The Widow shook her head. "I s'pose it sounds small to you. But you have to understand folks around here. They're set in their ways and it'd take one of them atomic bombs to move 'em. Worthy, now, he's different. Always has been. I midwifed him and I've seen him growin' up spirited. Needs a bit of cautionin' now and then, but he'll do fine. They're the hope of the world, the young. Your girl, now, Kate. Is she takin' to our country ways? Does she seem happy?"

I said yes to both questions, and she continued to query me, a catechism that I decided stemmed from her sympathetic interest in Kate's asthmatic condition. What did she eat? How many hours of sleep did she get a night? Had she ever been allergic before? What kind of exercise, and how much? Was she subject to fits of temperament or melancholy?

"She's an only child, now, en't she? Sometimes an only child'll take on sicknesses a child with brothers and sisters never gets."

I explained that while we had both hoped desperately for more children, Beth had suffered obstetrical complications and Kate's delivery had been enormously difficult. I did not tell her, however, that secretly I harbored the fear that my adult case of mumps had left me sterile, and that it might be my fault, not Beth's, that we'd had no other children.

The Widow's questions next focused on Beth, an only child herself. And me, she wanted to know, had I brothers and sisters? No, I said, though Greeks often had large families.

"Fertile, yes." She tilted her head at a quizzical angle, as though sizing me up. Her eyes twinkled as she said, "Beware of Greeks, don't they say?"

"Only if they come bearing gifts."

"Which you have—cinnamon buns. Wily folk, the Greeks. Look how they come in the night with a hollow horse to tumble the walls of Ilium."

"I'm not out to tumble the walls of Cornwall Coombe."

"Never knew the joys of children myself," she went on. "Still, every last boy and girl in the village is mine, in a way. I like to watch 'em from my parlor window, see 'em rompin' down the street. I rap my thimble on the pane and wave; they wave back but they keep goin'." I felt her gruff, crusty air hid the loneliness she must have experienced during the long years of her widowhood. In another moment, she startled me by reaching out and patting my hand. "You folks be happy, hear? That's all you've got, each other, and bein' happy together." I was about to murmur acknowledgment when the Widow called briskly, "Mornin', Tamar. Mornin', Missy."

Skirts hiked up, her bare legs showing, the postmistress was sitting on a porch glider, braiding her little girl's hair. The child eluded her and, carrying a ragged-looking doll, came down the walk to the picket gate and watched us pass. Framed by the red braids, her elf's face was milky pale, pinched, and drawn-looking, and her large, washed-out eyes contemplated us with the dull-witted, curiously vague expression that can come of closely bred bloodlines.

"Horsy, Missy." Slowing the buggy, the Widow jounced on the seat, making a to-do of the mare, causing it to bob its head and jingle its harness. The child made no reply, but only continued gazing at us. "Goin' to pick a good sheep today, Missy? There's a girl." The old woman's voice was friendly and hearty, and she gave a little nod of satisfaction. I had the sensation the child was staring not at her or at the horse but at me, and I felt unaccountably ill at ease as I looked back at the pale milky face, with its spate of reddish freckles over the bridge of the nose.

Her mother called from the porch, "Missy, come make poopoo." Before obeying, the child turned, still clutching the ragged doll; again I felt the same odd sensation that the look was in some significant way directed toward me. As we passed on, I casually inquired of the Widow if it was true that Missy Penrose could tell the future. The old lady gave another nod; Missy had strange powers, of that there was no doubt. It was the freckles, she said, two dozen of them, rather in the shapes of the constellation Orion, with its two great stars, Betelgeuse and Rigel. These markings were the stars of her face, a kind of cosmos printed there, and as men might read the mysteries of those stars, so it had been given to the child to read other mysteries.

I continued thinking of the star-speckled face and the deep nature of Missy Penrose, and we rode in silence to the end of Main Street, where the Common lay before us, dotted with tall, spreading trees, the church steeple gleaming in the bright morning light. There was the bell in the tower, the great face of the clock below, and beside the open vestibule doors, old Amys Penrose, the bell ringer, dozing in a chair. On the Common, the green of the grass and leaves was intensified by the clarity of the clean blue sky and the white canvas of the booths and tents that had been set up for the Agnes Fair, with gay pennants fluttering from their peaks. All seemed in readiness for the day's events: livestock enclosures had been put up, chairs and long tables had been set out for people to eat at, and three tall shafts had been dug into the ground for the shinnying contest.

The idly grazing sheep baaed as we stopped at the churchyard, where the Widow made her way to her husband's grave and arranged her fresh flowers, then stood silently with head bowed.

I walked to the top of the knoll and looked down the backward slope to where the churchyard ended, bounded by the iron railing. Beyond it was the untended plot, with its marker almost obliterated by weeds and growth. Again I wondered about Grace Everdeen, whose remains lay under the forlorn tombstone, and why she had been forbidden the company of the other village dead.

I turned back.

Head still bent, the Widow was speaking: "Well, Clem, things are lookin' fine for fair day. Now all we can hope for is the right choosin'." She angled her head as though awaiting reply. I moved away, affording her a larger measure of privacy for this genial dialogue between the quick and the dead, which for some reason seemed to me a perfectly natural thing.

At length she broke off, raised her head, and, catching my eye, smiled. She came toward me, stopping at one point to look down at another headstone.

"Well, Loren, well," she murmured, stooping to pinch off a flower whose stem was broken. "Loren's gone, too, and that's in the manner of things. The Lord giveth, the Lord taketh."

I looked down at the stone. The inscription read:

LOREN MCCUTCHEON

Who Hoped but Failed

Age 28

"How did he die?" I asked.
"Of drink."
"At twenty-eight?"

"'Twa'n't the drink so much—but the fall he took while drinkin'. Slipped off the barn in the night."

I was about to ask what misfortunes had caused the unknown Grace Everdeen's exile, but the Widow, giving short shrift to the dear departed, lifted her skirts and marched from the cemetery, shears swinging on their ribbon.

The street was quiet and deserted, except for the postmistress, who came along the sidewalk on the far side, leading her daughter, Missy, by the hand. When she got to the post office, she turned the child toward the grazing sheep, gave her a pat on the bottom, and sent her off, then unlocked the post-office door and went inside. The child ambled across the roadway and onto the Common, where she slowly made her way among the flock.

Meanwhile the Widow, hands planted on hips, was surveying the old bell ringer, still dozing in the sunshine.

"He's a codger, Amys." She chuckled and accepted my hand as I assisted her into her seat. "Forty years our sexton and still he don't hold with Agnes Fair. Nor much of anything, if it comes to that." She clucked up the mare and the buggy rolled onto the roadway. "Good Missy," she called to the child, who did not look up but only stared at the sheep as they moved around her, their bells making a pleasant tinkling sound. The Widow snapped the reins on the mare's flanks, a swarm of flies arose, and the horse stepped out at a smart pace, back the way we had come, heading out the country end of Main Street.

5

"How'd you come by that wart there?"

She had handed me the reins and now she brought my hand closer to her spectacles to examine the growth on my finger. I explained about the pressure from my brushes, and said I'd been meaning to see a doctor about it.

"Ha! You do that. Old Doc Bonfils over to Saxony. Maybe he'll rid you of it—maybe he won't. What you need is a little red bag—that'll take care of your wart, and then some."

"Little red bag?"

She laid her finger alongside her nose and closed one eyelid. "What we call the Cornwall cure. We'll see to it," she added mysteriously, giving me back my hand.

We were proceeding along the winding road, called the Old Sallow Road, which leads to Soakes's Lonesome and the Lost Whistle Bridge. In the east the sun rose higher in a sky already pure cerulean. The corn grew tall on either side of the road, and when I commented that the year promised a good crop, the Widow agreed.

"I knew t'would be. I been listenin' all summer to the corn a-growin'. Oh yes sir, you can hear it all right. You come out with me one night next year—don't smile, I'm not talkin' about country matters—and you'll hear it too. The softest rustle of leaf, soft as fairies' wings, and you know them stalks is stretchin' up to the sky, the tassels is length'nin', the ears is bit by bit gettin' fatter, till you can hear their husks pop. That's somethin', on a hot dark night, standin' by a cornpatch in the light o' the Mulberry Moon, and hearin' the corn grow. Then you can say the earth has returned the seed ten thousandfold."

She pointed upward. "See that blue sky now, that's God's sky. And up there in that vasty blue is God. But see how far away He is. See how far the sky. And look here, at the earth, see how close, how abiding and faithful it is. See this little valley of ours, see the bountiful harvest we're to have. God's fine, but it's old Mother Earth that's the friend to man."

And corn was king. Foolish folk, she continued, on a cold night might insist on burning their cobs in the fire. Burn corn? Never. Return the corn to the earth, bury it, then, when the plowman turned the furrow in the spring, the tilth would come up rich and dark against the shear, a fertile soil willing to bear generously for whatever hand was put to the harrow. Love the earth and it must love you back.

"Yes," she concluded thoughtfully, "we'll have a bountiful Harvest Home."

"Just what is Harvest Home?" I asked.

"Harvest Home?" She peered at me through her spectacles. "Why, I don't think I ever heard a pusson ask that before. Everybody knows what Harvest Home is."

"I don't."

"That's what comes of bein' a newcomer. Harvest Home's when the last of the corn comes in, when the harvestin's done and folks can relax and count their blessin's. A time o' joy and celebration. Eat, drink, and be merry. You can't have folks carousin' while there's corn to be gathered, so it must wait till the work's done. It means success and thanks and all good things. And this year's the seventh year."

"The seventh year?"

"Ayuh. For six years there's just feastin' and carryin' on, but the seventh's a special one. After the huskin' bee there's a play, and—well, the seventh year's particular for us. Harvest Home goes back to the olden times."

"When does it come?"

She looked at me again as if I were indeed a strange species. "Never heard a pusson ask that either. Harvest Home comes when it comes—all depends."

"On what?" I persisted doggedly.

"The moon." While I digested this piece of information, she pursed up her lips thoughtfully, watching as some birds flashed by. "Three," she counted, observing their smooth passage through the sky. "And larks. Larks is a good omen if ever there was."

"You believe in omens."

"Certain. You'll say that's ignorant superstition, bein' a city fellow." Most of the villagers, she continued, were descended from farmers who had come from old Cornwall, in England, more than three hundred years earlier, and the Cornishman didn't live who wouldn't trust to charms or omens: stepping on a frog would bring rain, wind down a chimney signified trouble in store, a crow's caw might foretell death or disaster, and, she concluded, did I find all this odd?

"No," I replied, "not particularly." Being Greek, I knew about superstitions; my grandmother had been a walking almanac of "do"s and "don't"s, including broken mirrors and hats on beds.

"Superstition's just a condition of matter over mind, so t'speak. I'm a foolish old woman and I don't see things so clear. Missy, now, she can see plain as well water."

Again I saw the child's dull but watchful eyes.

The Widow continued, "Take that collar button in the hog's stomach. Missy'll know for sure how to read it."

"You mean it could be a bad omen?"

"Certain! It just depends. Still and all—" Her voice again took on a worried tone as she looked away over the brimming fields. "But what could go wrong now? Surely the crop's grown? Surely we'll have a bountiful Harvest Home? Surely God won't take away what He's promised the whole summer long. Look at the corn there, as fat and ripe as a man could hope for. Surely everything's been done that a body could do? Surely seven years was penance enough?" Her rapid questions being, I assumed, strictly rhetorical, I could do no more than nod my head at each while I studied the mare moving in front of us. Yet her voice told me how much she, and the entire community, counted on the harvest. Finally I asked her what was meant by the seven years' penance.

"The last Waste," she explained obscurely, and went on to relate how in Cornwall in the olden times, as she put it, there had been the Great Waste, when the land lay under a plague of Biblical proportions, the crops blighted, when nothing would grow. It had been the fault of Agnes, that same Agnes in whose name this very fair today was being held. For undisclosed reasons, this Agnes of old Cornwall had risen up before the entire village and cursed the crop. In fury, the villagers had dispatched her on the spot, but as a result of her maledictions they had suffered years of pestilence and drought. Then, one night, the spirit of the dead Agnes appeared to one of the elders—a repentant Agnes

—saying that if a fair would be given each year in her honor, the land would again flourish and the crops would be plentiful. Thus the establishment of the annual Agnes Fair, a provenance I found interesting if fanciful.

Yet the next part of this strange history as the Widow related it struck my ear as real enough. Thirteen years ago, right here in Cornwall Coombe, there had been another Waste; the river had not risen in the spring, the ground was dry when the seed was planted, the rains did not come, the corn withered in the husk, and hard times came upon the village. Small wonder, I thought, that the farmers were superstitious.

Behind us I heard the noisy clangor of kettleware, the familiar furious din announcing the various comings of Jack Stump, the peddler. Looking back over the seat, I saw him working his cart in a frantic effort to catch up with us. Never turning, but with a serene smile, the Widow made no effort to restrain the mare's progress, and only let her have her head.

Jack Stump, newly arrived like us, had during that first summer become a familiar sight along the byways and thoroughfares of the village. His improbable-looking rig was little more than a pieced-together relic of a cart constructed atop the several parts of an ancient bicycle. Astride a shiny, cracked leather seat and flying a small tattered American flag on one of the handlebars, he would drive the cart, ringing a cowbell or squeezing the rubber bulb of a brass horn to witness his comings and goings; these and the continual clang and rattle of the tin pans, kettles, and skillets strung above on lines made a mobile pandemonium that alerted the countryside to his continual progresses. And where he came and went, Jack Stump talked.

"Jabberwocky," the Widow said, "that's what that one spouts." She jerked her head to the rear where the peddler strained under his load. "Poor benighted soul." When he at last pulled alongside, she nudged me with her elbow and offered him the best of the day and weather.

"Whatcha say, Widow. Whatcha say, sir?"

The Widow slowed the mare to a walk. "Well, Jack, glad to

see we're not harboring a slugabed. What gets you up so bright and early?"

He huffed, seeking his breath, until the huff turned to a wheeze. "I'm an early bird, Widow, catching my worms. Yes, ma'am, there's plenty to do and I'm the fellow to do the doin'— oh, yes. The way I see it, the world's an oyster, and you got to be quick to catch the pearl—"

"Before—" the Widow tried to put in.

"Before the other fellow steals it first. How are you today, sir?" Before I could reply, he had his answer ready. "Fine, sir, fine as rain, I can see that. And your lovely wife? Fine, too, is she? Good enough. You folks come from down New York way, ain't that so? Seen a bit of the big town myself in my time, damned if I haven't—sorry, Widow—"

He was a scruffy old fellow, a mite of a man, all head and torso, with hardly any underpinnings to speak of. His merry monkey face was flat and wide. He wanted shaving, his teeth seemed nonexistent, and his hair stuck out under his ruined fedora like scarecrow's straw, half covering large jug ears. He was scrupulously dirty, as if he worked at maintaining the traditional image of the disreputable hobo. In spite of the temperature, he wore layers of tattered clothing, and where a button had failed a pin would do as well.

"How's your shears, Widow?" he asked, pedaling alongside the buggy. "Sharp as a tack, I'll bet, darned if they ain't. I sharpened 'em up myself, didn't I?"

"That you did, Jack."

"And not a cent of charge." He gave me a droll look. "Not for no Florence Nightingale such as this dear lady is."

"How's your backside, Jack?" she inquired.

"I'm sittin', ain't I?"

"Jack's been sufferin' from a sight o'boils," she explained, solving the mystery of what had kept him from his daily rounds.

"And that's no handy place, I'll admit, for a fellow who sits as much as I do," Jack continued. "But this sweet creature, she bends me over a barrel and puts on some of that there salve of hers— Say, Widow, what all's in that salve?"

"That'd be tellin'. How's the toothache?"

"Gone, just like you said."

"Still wearin' your little bag?"

He dug down in his shirt and displayed a small bag of red felt hung on a drawstring around his neck.

"No—don't you feel inside there," she cautioned as he poked with a grimy finger. "You'll let out the charm for sure. Where you off to now?"

"To the woods."

"Soakes's Lonesome?" Her eyes on the road ahead, she spoke deliberately. "What takes you there?"

"Got to check my traps. I got 'em staked out all through them woods—"

"Oughtn't to go in there, Jack."

"Haw—them Soakeses don't scare me none."

"You catch me a rabbit, I'll make you a rabbit pie, Jack. Wait now, dearie, just a minute," she said to the mare. "We've got a stop here." She reined up the mare at the roadside and I helped her down. We stood before the Hooke farm, the largest and handsomest in Cornwall Coombe. The house was a gem of Early American architecture, with lawns and gardens in front, broad cornfields on either side, fruit orchards beyond, and cows grazing in the meadows that stretched away to the river.

"Shan't be a moment." The Widow took her basket and marched down the drive to greet the mistress of the house, Sophie Hooke, who was feeding a flock of chickens in the yard beside the kitchen door. She kissed the Widow's cheek and they spoke while the fowl pecked at their feet. Suddenly a rooster appeared among them, sending them into a panic of squawks and feathers.

"That's the biggest rooster I've ever seen," I declared.

"That's the gen'ral talk. Everyone says Justin Hooke's got the biggest rooster in town, if you catch my drift." Jack Stump snapped his hat brim and slipped me a lewd wink. According to village repute and ladies' gossip, nature had generously endowed Farmer Hooke sexually; hence, "Justin's rooster."

"You mean the women talk about that at their kitchen door?" I tried not to sound shocked, but I was surprised that such locker-room subjects were discussed among the housewives of this community.

"You live on a farm, you see everything," Jack replied philosophically. "They're a bawdy bunch, farmers. Women, too. I tell 'em the one about the fellow with twelve inches but he don't use it as a rule, and don't they squeal some! They know what Justin's got, all right. I guess it's what keeps Sophie smilin'! There's the old cock himself." He nodded to the barn where Justin Hooke appeared in the hayloft door. He swung out on the baling rope and made a dramatic sweep to the ground. When he, also, had kissed the Widow's cheek, she lifted the napkin from her basket and offered him the two puddings.

Straddling his seat on the cart, the peddler shook his head admiringly. "Ain't she a fine woman, the Widow Fortune? A good strong soul, damned if she ain't, good for a man's work as well as a woman's, no worse in the barnyard than in the kitchen. There's never a time I stop by her door when there ain't a slice of pie or a hunk of sausage waitin' for me. You'd look a far piece before you'd find a more kindly, generous soul, and I tell it at every door I pass."

"Goodnight nurse, Jack, how you carry on." The Widow had returned from her errand to overhear the last of his praises.

Doffing his hat, Jack bowed in a deferential manner. "The world don't seem so bad a place when a man can find dear ladies like yourself in it."

"Hush; enough." She let me help her into her seat, took up the reins, and we continued along toward Soakes's Lonesome. Here and there in the cornfields, I saw scarecrows stuck between the rows, rising above the tops of the stalks. Not the ordinary, garden-variety of scarecrow, these were fanciful fellows, decked out in extravagant bits of motley costuming and rags. There was one in particular, the head and body stuffed with straw and corn-

husks, a battered hat tilted rakishly over one button eye, a long
feather stuck in the band like a cavalier's plume.

Just then two crows swooped up out of the field, their wings
black and shiny against the sky. "Two crows," I heard the Widow
murmur. "Now, that's bad for sure." She shook her head, and
clucked up the mare.

"Jack, I'm in the market," she hinted to the peddler.

"In what way, Widow?"

"Old clothes. I'll be needin' them to make my scarecrows for
next year."

"How many do you make?"

"Nearly all you've seen. Hardly a farmer in the village doesn't
come plaguing me around Spring Festival time to do him up
a scarecrow. Can you fetch me some good outfits? Somethin'
swanky?"

"Sure I can."

"Cheap, now. I don't pay good money for rags."

We had come to the top of a rise, where Jack tipped his
scroungy hat again and took his leave, coasting off toward the
bottom in a cloud of dust, the echo of his tinware trailing behind.

The Widow laughed, watching him go. "His heart's in the
right place, but his tongue's an affliction."

As we moved down the hill, the cornfields spread wide and
far. Past the fields and grazing meadows, the treetops rose in lush,
billowy foliage, their leaves still a long way off from turning.
A curl of smoke rose from the Tatum farm opposite the edge
of the woods. Beyond the woods—Soakes's Lonesome, as it was
called—lay the river. On the other side I could make out the
brown patches of Tobacco City land, where the crop had already
been harvested, and the rolls of white netting which had not
yet been taken down. A dirt road wound between two fields,
ending at a jetty by the riverbank. A cloud of dust rose as a
pink car, an Oldsmobile, pulled up close to the bank. Several
men got out and clambered into a motor skiff tied at the jetty.
Soon it was cutting a path through the water—the hum of the
engine lost to us at that distance—and heading for a point of

land on our side where the woods grew down to the river's edge. I watched the craft's progress, and as it approached, the voices of the men became faintly audible. When they stepped ashore I caught the dull gleam of sunlight on rifle barrels. Then they entered the woods and disappeared.

"Soakeses," the Widow commented in a sour tone, as though identifying the men by name were sufficient to sum up their entire and particular natures. Forthwith she revealed to me the salient facts concerning Soakes's Lonesome, whose history was an interesting one, full of the blood and havoc for which the Cornish people had long been known.

Originally, the sizable tract had been designated by the village founders as communal land, within whose preserves anyone was entitled to hunt or fish. Then, somewhere in the early 1700s, it had become the property of the Soakes family, who accordingly reserved the hunting and fishing rights to themselves. Though the village fields had proved rich for crops, the Soakeses and some others of the old settlers moved across the river, where, eschewing corn, they engaged in raising tobacco. The move, said the village fathers, constituted forfeiture of all rights to land on this side of the river, and henceforward Soakes's Lonesome would no longer belong to them. The Soakes clan, then extensive, refused to relinquish its title, which was now held in dispute between the family and the people of Cornwall Coombe. The present generation—an old man, his wife, and five sons—were generally regarded as a fierce and savage tribe of "tobacco scut," who for their part still continued to look upon the land as theirs; and woe to the trespasser.

Which, the Widow pointed out, accounted for the tales of the Ghost of Soakes's Lonesome. A people who readily believe in ghosts needs must have one. Rumor had it the Soakeses maintained a well-hidden still deep in the woods. Some years before, a revenue agent had come to investigate; it was said he went into the woods and never came out. And around his mysterious disappearance there had sprung up a tale about the Ghost of

Soakes's Lonesome, whose shade was said to haunt the Old Sallow Road close to the Lost Whistle Bridge.

We got to the Tatum farm and the Widow reined up again. "Here's where I must leave you now," she announced. Across the way, a dirt track ran up to the Tatums' back door, where the lady of the house was stirring something in a large iron kettle. Nope, not pigs, the Widow explained; Irene did homemade soap. Laying down her paddle, then pulling the smoking fire apart, the red-haired Irene bawled to her children not to track ashes in the house as they came from loading food baskets and hampers into the back of a pickup truck.

I took my drawing case and hopped from the buggy to help the Widow alight. I thought she would pay a call on Irene, but no, "I must be about my herbin'," she said, "and you've got your bridge to sketch." She hung her shears straight, took her basket, arranged to meet me again in an hour, and, so saying, picked up her skirts and made her way toward the woods through the tall meadow grass.

I continued along the road on foot, cornfields on my left, then an orchard, and on my right the curving edge of a palisade of lofty trunks, and, beyond, the dark recesses of Soakes's Lonesome. A little farther along, I passed the peddler's rig, half hidden behind some thick laurel shrubs where he had sought to conceal it—a precaution, I decided, against the Soakeses' chancing upon it.

Arriving at the bridge, I sat under a tree and made several rough drawings, then began a detailed one of the portal. In exactly fifty minutes, I closed my pad, zipped up my case, made a quick tour of the bridge approach to locate the best angle for the painting I planned doing, and then started back down the road.

Again I passed the sequestered peddler's cart, and, rounding the next bend, I glimpsed the Widow's white bonnet bobbing among the trees at the edge of the meadow. I waited until she reached the road, then helped her into the buggy. Suddenly we heard the sharp report of guns within the woods. A voice shouted, and another; then for a time all was silence. In another moment the peddler's gnome-like figure broke from the woods. He pulled the rig from its hiding place, ran it down the gully and onto the road, hopped onto the seat, and pedaled toward us as fast as his feet could turn the wheels.

"Ho, Jack," the Widow called, "what's about?"

He made no reply, but an expression of terror contorted his grizzled features. Passing, he gave us a dazed look, as though he had never seen us before, and hurried off toward the village.

Behind us, a formidable figure appeared between the tree trunks, a shotgun at the ready. He watched the peddler's hasty retreat; then, shaking his fist, he entered the woods again.

"The old man himself," the Widow said. I replied that I supposed he had caught nosy Jack investigating his still and had scared him off.

"It's likely. Jack's nose is afflicted, too," she said as she took up the reins.

Well, thought I, if the sleepy, yesteryear village of Cornwall Coombe provided such intriguing mysteries in this ready-to-hand way, I would prove easily diverted, and without telling my companion, I resolved to find Jack at the fair and discuss exactly what had happened to him in the woods at the hands of Old Man Soakes.

6

With terrific rumblings and backfirings of failing motors, shiftings and grindings of ancient gears, the creak and grate of decrepit wooden wheels in the dusty roadway, amid shouts and calls and laughter, we arrived at the Common shortly before noon, along with scores of others, old people and middle-aged and young and younger, and crying babes in arms, to say nothing of barnyard beasts of varied description: cattle lowing, horses neighing, sheep and goats bleating and baaing, hens cackling, dogs barking—all these and more. Which was to be expected, for, like Christmas, the Agnes Fair came to Cornwall Coombe but once a year and, like Christmas, people were bound to make the most of it.

I parked the car close to Irene Tatum's wreck of a pickup truck, and opened the door for Beth. When Kate got out of the back seat, we cautioned her to keep well away from the furred animals, then stood watching the holiday crowd, jocular and gay as they thronged about the booths, exchanging greetings and hugs and kisses as though they hadn't seen their neighbors for a month.

They were mostly farm types: sober-sided, raw-cut, stringy men, but well-seasoned like old lumber, with bad barbering and a dusting of talcum, wearing workaday outfits, shirts open at the neck, patched and faded overalls; the women in plain, unfashionable dresses that might have belonged to their mothers, with light straw hats or bonnets looking as though they had been worn forever; the smaller girls in dresses obviously stitched up at home, their older sisters with buxom meaty bodies pushing at the seams of their colorful best frocks, their hair plaited with ribbons or hanging free and halfway down their backs as they grinned at the hooting overalled boys, replicas of their fathers.

A great scurrying ensued: the men hastening to tie up the animals inside the livestock enclosures; the women, with their baskets and bags and boxes, to set out for display homemade canned goods and bakery items, to spread out their handicraft work and sewing in the booths provided, and betweentimes to gather unto themselves for purposes of gossip and news exchange; the children to lug chunks of already melting ice to cool the milk and butter and cream and eggs in the shade before dashing off to see the fair.

"Look out for King!"

Grunting and swaying, a giant hog footed its way along two planks from the back of the pickup truck, on whose dented panel was the legend "King the Pig."

"Here he comes!" Irene Tatum proudly bawled as the animal reached the ground.

"Never seen such a clean pig, Irene," a farmer said. "Could put that pig in your own bed and sleep with it." "Yes, you could, Will Jones, could you get your wife to move over," Irene said, laughing. "Sister, fetch your ma her umbrella, this sun's thick as honey." Children were spilling out of the truck like clowns in a circus act. Using the tip of her umbrella, Irene prodded King to a standing position, and while a crowd collected, she showed the hog off as if he were one of her own progeny.

"How do, Mrs. Zalmon, Mrs. Green," she shouted. "Junior, you get King over to the enclosure. Sister, bring along the hamper. Treat that pig like family, Rusty. Put him on the cool side so's he'll get the good of the breeze. Debbie, pull your skirts down!"

While they trooped off, along came the Minerva clan. "Your Jim's growed some this summer," Mrs. Green allowed to Mrs. Minerva. "Ain't he a husky fellow. Could be he might be the lucky one t'day—"

"My Jim?" Asia Minerva looked both shocked and pleased. "Naw," she said, "naw . . ."

"See where the Hookes come, yonder." Mrs. Green pointed at Justin, who had arrived, his wife on his arm. As a feathery murmur swept the crowd, several girls hurried to cluster around him, Sophie standing a little to one side watching with an air of amused detachment, while her husband was offered smiles and admiring glances.

The object of these attentions, Justin Hooke, was a perfect child of nature. In spite of his country clothes and simple straightforward manner, he had an élan, a verve that along with his heroic size set him apart from his fellows. An altogether remarkable specimen of a man, tall, husky, broad-shouldered, bluff and hearty, a golden look to him, with his bronze skin, his sunyellowed hair, the flash of strong teeth showing behind his easy smile.

Just now he seemed embarrassed by the flutter his presence

was creating as the girls pressed closer about him, and I wondered why all the fuss?

"I've got gooseberry tarts in my basket, Justin," said one of the girls coyly, and another hinted about her raisin pie; a third, making sheep's eyes, asked if he were partial to stuffed eggs. "Who will it be today, Justin?" the first asked, putting her hand on his arm. "Yes, who will it be?" said the second; then they were all demanding to know of Justin who he thought "it" would be.

There were more voices and laughter as other girls joined the circle, and calls and shouting, and constant comings and goings, and more newcomers. Worthy Pettinger arrived on his tractor, and from the expressions of some close by, it appeared the noisy gusto of his old John Deere was an affront to their ears.

"Ain't Missy the prettiest thing in her dress," cried Irene Tatum in her gravelly voice, while others agreed, parting and forming an aisle through which Tamar Penrose led the child onto the Common. "Did you pick your sheep, Missy?" someone asked respectfully, and "Good Missy," another said, reaching to touch her ribbons.

Pallid, thin, with bony joints and brittle-looking limbs, and oblivious to the interest her arrival was causing, the child was regarding me gravely. Even braided and in ribbons, her red hair looked lank and limp, and I noted again the spattering of freckles across her nose.

Next to appear was Jack Stump. He wheeled his peddler's rig onto the grass with a cacophony of tinware, sprang from his seat, and hopped about dropping the canvas tatters that passed for awnings on his cart and lowering the panels to display his wares. Now he produced a scratched and battered fiddle from one of the compartments, and then a soda-pop box, which he stood on as he began sawing away on the instrument.

The music was suddenly and thoroughly drowned out as, with horn blatting, a car careened in a wide circle at the edge of the Common; I recognized the pink Oldsmobile belonging to the To-bacco City group. Doors banged open and the five big and beery-looking Soakes boys got out; then, from behind the wheel, came bristling Old Man Soakes himself. Their arrival caused evident consternation to the musician, for the fiddling ceased abruptly, the instrument was whisked from sight, Jack Stump scrambled onto his seat, and, with kettleware crashing, he disappeared into the crowd.

Old Man Soakes's look was grim as he waited while his offspring freed a galvanized tub of ice and beer from the trunk of the car and lugged it into the shade of a tree, where they flopped on the grass and began popping tops and passing the cans among themselves. Then the father busied himself at the trunk, bending to set out for sale an assortment of home-sewn stuffed canvas decoys.

Making my way through the crowd that now separated us, I found Beth and Kate talking to Worthy Pettinger.

"Worthy's offered to show us around the fair," Beth said, and as we moved off together I saw that Kate's lively interest in the boy was masked by an elaborate show of indifference as he pointed out various sights. We watched the livestock competition, which had already begun; then the pie contest, where Robert Dodd was chief among the judges; then the trained bear; and the Punch-and-Judy show, a small, cheapjack affair that reminded me of one Beth and I had seen years before in Paris. While Judy assaulted Punch from one side of the stage, a white wraith-like figure beat him with a stick on the other, and the sorry victim fended off both spouse and ghost with equal vigor. When we left the tent, I made further reference to the battling phantom, and asked if Worthy had heard tales of ghosts around Cornwall Coombe.

"You mean the Ghost of Soakes's Lonesome?" He shrugged. "Folks around here are dumb enough to believe all kinds of things. I guess ghosts are the least of 'em."

As we went along, Beth's attention was continually diverted by the various home arts and handicrafts displayed at the booths: quilted bedspreads, crocheted counterpanes, hand-woven materials, figures cleverly carved and whittled from pine, little dolls, basketwork. "They could make a fortune selling these down in New York," she said.

Some distance away, I glimpsed the Widow Fortune sitting behind a booth, talking energetically with Sophie Hooke, and at the same time doing a sharp business in the honey trade. Other booths had pickles and preserves for sale, fresh garden produce and dairy things. Strolling among the tents and booths, I was interested in the workmanship embellishing the canvas sides: primitive, country-type designs, crudely but gracefully executed with the naïveté of cave paintings. There were suns and moons and stars, various animals, a horse here, a cow there, a barn, a stick-figure man. And, everywhere, corn: sheaves of corn and shocks of corn and ears of corn, people growing, harvesting, cooking, eating, storing corn. Corn not only in its facsimile, but in reality, some of the tent entrances being framed by bound shocks and festooned with garlands of dried husks and leaves, and bunches of unshelled ears, their kernels yellow, red, brown, some variegated with all three.

Our guide identified it as Indian corn, breaking an ear off and tendering it to Kate with a smile. He seemed to sense her feeling of awkwardness and kept up an easy line of conversation which, while directed at Beth and me, was designed to make our daughter less self-conscious.

King the Pig, he assured us, was bound to win the hog competition. Farmers thereabouts had a way of letting their pigs stay penned up, leaving them to root among their own filth. He had persuaded Irene Tatum to try a new method, that of building King a movable trailer home. When the ground beneath became soiled, Worthy would drive over with his tractor, hook up, and move the pen to a fresh location.

"Pigs don't *like* to be dirty," he explained earnestly, "any more than people do. Feed them grain like a horse, give them plenty of water for washing, and keep them off the dirty ground."

He went on speaking of the things that were nearest his heart, talking with neither constraint nor pretension, but in a frank, affable manner. He had none of the cruder aspects one might expect in the rural character, revealing a sensitivity to both people and surroundings. Though his frame seemed slight for heavy farm work, his complexion was ruddy and healthy, and he had a lithe, agile way of carrying himself that hinted at untapped reserves of strength.

Next, he pointed out the teams of horses being readied for the horse-drawing contest, and the place where the wrestling matches would be held. One of the largest of the Soakes boys, Roy, had come 'cross-river to take on Justin Hooke, and though Roy had more weight, Justin was stronger, and sure to win. From the way Worthy spoke, I could see Justin was something of a hero to him, too. Still, he planned to take the pole-shinny competition himself.

" 'Course, it's better for things if the Harvest Lord wins, but he can't win *every*thing."

"The Harvest Lord?" Beth asked, and Worthy explained. This singular honor had been bestowed on Justin Hooke at Agnes Fair seven years before. He had been crowned at Spring Festival, and it was this traditional role he would continue to assume through the weeks of harvest; a pageant was to be held in the Grange hall some weeks hence—the Corn Play, as it was called—where his queen would be crowned. She was called the Corn Maiden, and Sophie Hooke had been chosen for this part.

"Who chose them?" I asked.

"Justin was elected by vote, and he chose Sophie himself," Worthy said.

"Oh, look!" Beth had stopped to admire a collection of ivory jewelry on display at a booth. She picked up a pair of earrings and held them to her ears. "Soup bones," Worthy laughed. The pieces—brooches, rings, and the like—were made locally, carved and engraved from odd pieces of bone. They were worked in the elaborate scrimshaw fashion of the old whaling sailors, and the ivory-like patina came from patient sanding and waxing.

By now we had made a complete circuit of the fair and found ourselves back where we had started. Beth leaned on the jewelry booth counter to pick a stone from her shoe. "Listen," she said,

"I'm about done in. Why don't I get the picnic hamper and find the Dodds? We can meet under that big tree and see the matches from there."

"Maybe Kate would like to watch from the platform with the other girls," Worthy said, pointing out a wooden structure at the side of the field where the Corn Maiden and her court would be seated for the events. Kate accepted, though she remained silent as Beth invited Worthy to picnic with us. When I had got the hamper from the car trunk and Beth had reminded me not to forget Kate's Medihaler in the glove compartment, she went to find the Dodds.

"Mr. Constantine," Worthy said. "I'd like to take Kate to see King the Pig, if it's all right with you. He's sure to get a blue ribbon." He pushed back the wedge of blue-black hair that kept falling across his eyes, and waited politely for my answer.

I said I supposed that even a Kate could look at a King, so long as she wasn't late for lunch. I watched them go off, then went back to the jewelry booth and purchased the bone earrings Beth had admired.

Nearby, the trunk of the Oldsmobile was still open, and Old Man Soakes appeared to be doing a brisk if sub-rosa trade in the decoy business. One farmer after another stole up to slip him some money and carry off not only a canvas duck but a pint of home-brew as well.

Not far from Soakes sat a group of old men making designs from strips of cornhusks, braiding them into simple but elegant figures, some like pinwheels, others like fans or stars or helixes, still others whose shapes were the product of fancy. I took my sketchbook from my case and my pen from my pocket, and began drawing. One of the men looked up; I asked what they were making.

"Decorations for Harvest Home," he replied; "for good luck."

"Aye, good luck," said a dry voice. It was the bell ringer, Amys Penrose, chewing on a straw, sourly watching the men weaving. "They say the devil makes work for idle hands, so if you fellers can't find the devil one way you'll find him another. Me, I'd spend the rest of my days loafin', if I could."

"Ain't got too many left, have you, Amys?" asked one of the gentlemen, winking at his cronies.

Amys tickled his ear with the tip of the straw and thought a moment. "Well," he said finally, "and if I don't, I wouldn't give up what's left of 'em to be about such damn foolishness. Look there, will you."

Some farmers went by leading a sheep on a rope. Missy Penrose suddenly appeared from the crowd, put her doll aside, dropped to her knees, and threw her arms around the animal's neck. The little bronze bell tinkled as she buried her head in its woolly pelt, while passing mothers smiled and turned to their offspring. The bell ringer made a shredded sort of sound in his throat, then spat.

"Don't be so irksome all the time, Amys," one of the old men chided, his fingers working nimbly with the straw in his lap. "Content yourself with the space the Reverend Buxley's reserved for you in his churchyard."

"Aaarch." Amys spat again. "Don't tell me them cheap boxes the church totes us off in ain't goin' straight to worms before year's end. Lookit young McCutcheon—don't you just know them worms is already et up half that coffin and all of Loren."

"Bury the dead," said one of the men, nodding philosophically. The group worked in silence for a time, and Amys stood hunched against the tree trunk, toying with his straw. I continued with my pen, sketching one face after another, and several pairs of hands.

"Who's it to be today, do you reckon?" one of the gentlemen asked after a time.

"Talk among the ladies allows it's bound t'be Jim Minerva," another responded.

"Still, it's hard to say," a third put in.

"Fine fellow, young Minerva," said the first. "Father's a good farmer, got a new barn, Jim's got growin' brothers to help out. Couldn't go wrong there."

"Some of Fred's bad luck might have rubbed off on the boy," the second replied.

"Luck's luck," Amys observed dourly, "which is what folks around here need the most of."

While this mystifying conversation proceeded, I had turned my attention to Missy's doll, making several quick sketches of its incredible appearance. Her mother pulled her aside as Jack Stump reappeared on his rig, banging a kitchen spoon against the row of kettles and offering jovial nods right and left as he doffed his hat. In his wake came an excited group of women, Irene Tatum among them, proudly showing off a blue satin ribbon with a rosette attached. "Whatcha say, ladies," Jack greeted them. "Whatcha say, Irene Tatum? Congratulations are in order, yes? That's a swell sow you got there. Chinee Polack, ain't she?"

Mrs. Tatum gave a rowdy laugh. "It's a Poland China, Jack Stump, and it's a he, not a she. Can't you tell the difference?"

"He's don't have tits."

"You're right there, Jack. Tits on a boar hog is 'bout as useful as you are. You know where Poland is, Jack Stump?"

The peddler scratched thoughtfully, hair, beard, armpits. "Poland's north of It'ly, ain't it? And China's due east, I reckon. That what Marco Polo discovered."

A red face appeared among the onlookers. "Marco Polo's the one sailed around the world, ain't he?" asked one of the Soakes brothers.

"You better get yourself back in school, boy," Jack called. "This here Marco Polo's the one fought the heathen and went into China and discovered spaghetti."

"China?" said Edna Jones. "I always thought spaghetti's Eyetalian."

"'Course it's Italian, you bewitching creature." Like a magician, Jack produced a flowered scarf from a drawer and flourished it in her face. "Marco Polo found it growin' in China over the sea and he brought back some seeds and planted them in Rome and that's why spaghetti's Eyetalian. Listen, Doris Duke's got spaghetti plantations all over Honolulu."

"Peddler, you're an ignorant fool!" Old Man Soakes had loomed from beside the Oldsmobile, looking dangerous. "You never been to school, you can't even write your name. Why don't you shut your mouth before someone shuts it for you? Spaghetti's nothin' but flour-and-water paste!"

For a moment I thought Jack would be forced to retreat from this spate of fury, but, taking heart from the crowd, he held his ground, setting up his pop-bottle box and stepping onto it. Snatching open a drawer on his rig, he flashed a bright chrome gadget.

"Whatcha say, ladies, lookee here what I got for you, the finest little kitchen helper in the world, garnteed to do twelve—count 'em, twelve—*diff'rent* household jobs, and all for the price of sixty-nine cents, a fair price which goes with the day."

Tamar Penrose stood listening to the spiel, holding the child Missy in front of her. During Jack's come-on, I had been made aware of the postmistress, and I took the opportunity to assess her evident charms.

Scarcely what would be termed a beauty, Tamar Penrose had good skin and a head of rioting dark hair. She was taller than most of the women about her, with a full, firm body, wide hips, but a narrow waist. She held herself in a lazy, though erect posture, so her breasts strained under the bright print of her dress, showing her nipples to provocative effect. Her lips were very red against the pale skin, and when her hands moved on the child's shoulders at her waist, I saw that the fingernails were lacquered a matching color. And though I never caught her looking directly at me, still I had the feeling she was observing me. As for the child, her pale eyes were now focused on a farmer standing close by, sharpening a sickle on a handstone.

Jack's audience having thinned appreciably, I stepped over to the corner of his cart just as Old Man Soakes came striding up. He grasped Jack by his coat lapels, whisked him around to the back of the cart, and spoke in a rough, angry voice.

"I wasn't doin' nothin'," I heard Jack protest feebly. "Never mind what you wasn't doin'," Soakes replied, "stay out of them woods. You've had your warnin'." He strode back to his place at the rear of the Oldsmobile while Jack reappeared, his fingers shaking as he adjusted his jacket.

"Damned grizzly is what he is," he muttered, shooting a look from the corner of his eye. "Them woods ain't private property, y' know." He rubbed the stubble on his chin with the back of his hand.

"What happened in there this morning, Jack?" I asked. He stopped his hand and looked at me closely, as though deciding whether or not to take me into his confidence.

"As strange a thing as I ever hope to see," he said after a moment, his eye on the bent back at the Oldsmobile trunk. "And I seen it with these here two eyes, which is as good as they come. Twenty-twenty vision, I got—"

"But what happened?" I persisted. "What did you see?"

"I seen a ghost," he whispered.

I stepped closer to catch his every word. "What sort of ghost?"

"A ghost that once was dead, but now's come alive. A living ghost, as sure as I stand here. And it was screamin'." He ducked another look at Old Man Soakes who accepted some money from a passer-by in exchange for a bottle and then slammed the trunk lid with a loud crash. Straightening, the man cast another baleful glance in our direction.

"Later," Jack whispered; he left me standing by the cart and quickly hopped over to the farmer who was sharpening his sickle with the handstone.

"Whatcha say, Will Jones, whatcha say," he began, flicking a glance to where Old Man Soakes stood at the edge of the crowd, still watching. Assuming an air of nonchalance, Jack reached for the sickle and tested its edge with his thumb. "Lemme tellya, Will," he said to the farmer, "you can sharpen up that there sickle a lot faster on a wheel."

"Haven't got one," the farmer replied.

"Come along, I got one on my rig." Jack brought the farmer back to the rig, moving me aside to reveal under a flap a grindstone clamped to a piece of the cart frame. Instructing the farmer to turn the handle, he laid the blade to the wheel and proceeded to grind the edge. Sparks flew up like meteors, and the peddler cocked his head this way and that, ostensibly checking the angle, but I could see he had an eye on the departing back of Old Man Soakes. The child Missy left her mother's side and slowly approached, watching the shower of sparks shooting into the air.

"Missy," Tamar Penrose called insistently, but the child paid no attention as Jack put his thumb to the blade to test it. "Hot damn, now that's sharp, Will." The blade glistened like a silver crescent.

"Pretty good," the farmer agreed.

"Good, hell! It's perfect! There y'are, Will, sharp as a dime and no charge." He handed over the implement, leaped onto the saddle of his rig, and started off.

"Jack," I called, hoping for the rest of his story, but he only shook his head and, without a backward look, pedaled away into the crowd.

When Tamar came to take Missy's hand, the child hung back for an instant, her bleak eye lingering on the gleaming sickle blade in Will Jones's hand. Turning, her look fell on me; she gazed for a long silent moment, and I suddenly felt the hairs on the back of my neck tingle as she continued to stare, her body a trifle stiff, her mouth slack. Then she permitted herself to be led away.

I stood alone for a moment, trying to examine the sensation I had felt, a fugitive feeling I could scarcely define. I moved into the crowd, my eye on the tree where Beth was already laying out the picnic things. Though I saw Beth plainly, it was the child's face that hovered before me; and it was perhaps for this reason alone that I forgot to take Kate's Medihaler from the glove compartment of the car.

7

"An elegant repast, my dear," Professor Dodd said to Beth, wiping his lips with one of the checkered napkins. "You have found the way to my heart. Now if you're truly good, Margaret will give you her recipe for old New England succotash. Most people use salt pork, but she makes it the old Indian way."

"How did they do it?"

"They baked a dog with it."

"Oh, Robert, really, the Constantines aren't going to believe a thing you tell them if you keep that up." Maggie Dodd took a cigar from Robert's breast pocket, rolled it between her palms, clipped the end, and held the match while he lighted it.

"I assure you the Indians considered it a great delicacy," Robert continued. Having finished our picnic lunch, we were sitting under the tree—Robert Dodd in a lawn chair, Worthy Pettinger close to Kate—eating Maggie's chocolate mousse. Beth, who was wearing my gift of the bone earrings, stretched and lay back on the grass, looking up at the sky.

"It's hard to believe places like this exist any more. It seems like a—" She groped for the word.

"Throwback," Maggie supplied.

"No such thing," said Robert.

"I mean someone found it and forgot to throw it back."

"Margaret's always making jokes at the village's expense," Robert said.

I was quick to recognize the flash of intimate response between the couple as Maggie leaned and took Robert's napkin, shaking off the crumbs and folding it. Watching them, I felt we truly had found friends. To me, Maggie personified that thing I had been trying to express to myself about the villagers, an air of simple, placid grace, with her unmade-up features, her still-clear skin and eyes, her neatly coiffed hair whose style I was sure had not changed since she was a young woman. Her voice was low and serene, with a kind of easy, humorous lilt to it: an imperturbable woman.

"What Robert means," she went on, "is just what you're trying to say: there's a sort of timelessness about Cornwall Coombe that often strikes outsiders—or even newcomers—as unusual."

Beth lighted a cigarette and blew smoke through her nose. "What does it mean—Coombe?"

"It's an English word—Celtic, actually," Robert explained. "Means a valley or a sort of hollow. I suppose it implies a certain remoteness, which we are given to hereabouts. Margaret's partially correct: there are a number of 'throwbacks' around here, like certain of the names which have an ancient and venerable history. Take the Lost Whistle Bridge, for instance, which is a corruption of 'Lostwithiel,' one of the towns in old Cornwall." He pointed his cigar to the house next to the post office. "And when Gwydeon Penrose built that house over there, he named it Penzance House, but it's come down to us as 'Penance' House."

The horse-drawing contests had begun, and presently the Widow Fortune appeared with some friends, seating herself at a table under a nearby tree. The old lady set down her piecebag, her splint basket, and her black leather valise, then arranged her skirts and shears while others drew around her and opened various baskets and hampers from which they produced an array of provender. Another lady came with a tall glass of tea, holding it while the Widow reached in her basket and broke off a sprig of mint, crushed it, and put it in the tea.

"Say hello to the Widow, dear," Maggie prompted Robert.

"How do, Widow," Robert called, and she called back, putting her tea aside as one of the ladies offered her an ear of corn in a napkin.

Maggie laughed. "Look how she takes that corn off the cob. My teeth wouldn't stand for it. Isn't it amazing how she keeps her faculties? And her energies. You'll see—after her lunch she'll sit there and quilt the whole afternoon, she and Mrs. Brucie and Mrs. Zalmon."

"A quilting bee?" Beth asked.

"Quilting's become fashionable everywhere these days, but it's never stopped in the Coombe. Our ladies can turn out a dozen quilts a month."

"Patchwork quilts bring a lot of money down in New York," Beth said speculatively.

Out on the field, Fred Minerva had hitched his team to a skid with wooden runners like a sled. Worthy explained that this was called a stoneboat, onto which sacks of sand had been loaded. Deftly manipulating the reins, Fred encouraged his horses to pull the stoneboat along the turf, and at a certain point he unhitched his team and another took his place. The various pairs of horses were decked out in bell-laden harness, and I saw that Justin's team had little corn rosettes stuck up behind the blinders.

I turned back to Robert. "The thing I don't understand is how, in a day of modern technology and machinery, farmers still continue to use a horse and plow in place of tractors."

"They don't *believe* in tractors," Maggie said.

Worthy sat up, attentive to the conversation, as Robert said, "The farmers hereabouts discovered long ago what farmers elsewhere are just coming to realize. There's a good deal of work on a farm that can be done more cheaply by animal power than by gasoline. And your seed will go in early, before you can use a tractor on the wet ground."

"Maybe you lose a little time at early planting, Professor," Worthy put in, "but in the long run you make it up. And I'll bet if I hitched my tractor onto that skid I could move it farther and faster than all those horses put together."

"Hot, hot, hot. Never saw a fair day so hot." It was the redoubtable Mrs. Buxley, the parson's wife, accompanied by her husband. Wearing a flyaway hat and billowing chiffon, like a four-masted schooner in a high gale she descended upon us. She blew out her cheeks and lowered her bottom into one of the chairs Mr. Buxley had brought along. "Can't remember a fair day hot as this, not since—James, can't you bring your chair closer and join us?—the year of the last great flood. That was the year you and Robert came to us, wasn't it, Maggie? Remember, Robert?"

"I remember." Robert laughed shortly.

"Gracious, that was fourteen years now, hardly seems possible." She lavished a smile on Beth. "And for you, this will be your first. We don't see you in church—do we, James?"

Mr. Buxley's reply was inaudible. Mrs. Buxley wrinkled her brow, her smile becoming one of infinite patience. "And we miss seeing your little girl for Sunday School—isn't that so, James? You know that I take the Sunday School myself, James has so much work composing his sermons. You like our church, Ned? I may call your Ned? Allow me to see some of your work, may I?"

Her insistent hand slipped my sketchbook from my lap and began leafing through it. "Why, there's Amys Penrose to the life. And old Mr. Huie! And those *hands*—you *are* talented, Ned. Your husband's *very* talented, Mrs. Constantine." She displayed the page for all to see.

"What are those things?" Beth pointed to several drawings of the corn designs the men were weaving.

Mr. Buxley spoke up for the first time. "They're harvest symbols. Supposed to bring good luck. You'll see them on almost every door and chimney in town for the next month."

"And look how he's captured that doll," Mrs. Buxley chimed in. "Ned, wherever did you find it?"

I explained it belonged to Missy, the postmistress's child.

"Of course. What do they call it, Robert—a 'gaga'?"

"A corn doll? Yes, a gaga."

"Gaga? What does that mean?" Beth asked.

"Vaguely, it's Indian for 'fun' or 'funny.' Just a child's plaything."

"I should think it'd keep a child awake at night."

Mrs. Buxley laughed. "One of our little traditions. You're

bound to think us positively heathenish hereabouts—isn't that so, James?"

"We've had our fill of progress," Beth said.

"Coming from the city and all, yes—they seem to progress right into damnation down there, don't they? I see you're wearing some of our earrings—pretty, aren't they? Imagine, from soup bones. Clever, what our carvers can do. Roger was the best carver, wasn't he, James? James! Roger *Pen*rose? The best carver? That brooch the Widow wears on Sundays—Roger carved that, as I recall. Look at those strong *horses*—"

Out on the field, the horse-drawing contests continued. When each team had pulled the skid as far as it could, it was unhooked and another was put in place, and so on. After each round, more sacks of sand were added to the load, which became increasingly difficult to pull.

It came Justin Hooke's turn again; his horses strained under the burden, their flanks streaming, their forelegs buckling. Unlike the others, Justin did not use a whip, but coaxed the animals ahead by manipulating the reins and calling to them. The stoneboat moved a good distance, and a cheer went up among the spectators. Mr. Deming, the chief elder, after measuring out the last distance, pronounced Justin the winner.

As the teams were withdrawn from the field, the sound of Worthy's tractor was heard. Looking around, I saw that he had vanished, and now his head appeared over the crowd as he drove the John Deere onto the field. He had hitched chains behind, which he quickly attached to the stoneboat, then resumed his seat and began throwing levers. The front end of the tractor nosed up in the air and the tracks dug into the ground, then, obtaining purchase, began to slide the load. Shifting quickly, the boy skillfully sent the tractor forward, and when he had got up speed the stoneboat went jouncing over the grass, the crowd parting and closing behind until stoneboat, tractor, and driver were lost from view.

"Oh, dear," Mrs. Buxley muttered, "Mr. Deming's not going to like that at all. See how the grass is all chewed up. Worthy ought to know better. I hope there won't be trouble again. James—?" She gave her husband a piercing look. Mr. Buxley opened his mouth to speak, then closed it, and suddenly remembered his socks needed pulling up. Mrs. Buxley rose. "There's the Widow, James. We must go and say hello. See you in church." She waggled her fingers and—the Reverend Mr. Buxley trailing after with the chairs—she went to greet the Widow Fortune.

When they had gone, Robert chuckled and shook his head. "Leave it to Worthy to rile things up around here. You won't get him set in his ways, not while he's got that tractor."

Worthy came back to take Kate to the platform for the wrestling matches, and since we had a good view from our picnic spot, the Dodds, Beth, and I remained under the tree. The Widow Fortune, carrying her own chair, came and set it down close by, adjusting her things around her.

"Why does a tractor stir up such consternation?" I asked Robert.

"You get plenty of resistance around here to new ways. I suppose Cornwall Coombe's always been a world unto itself." He paused briefly while Maggie held a match for him to relight his cigar.

"Look," she said when she was done, "here comes Justin onto the field." Shading her eyes, she described to Robert the action that preceded the wrestling matches. Roy Soakes shuffled out onto the turf, where he took off his shirt and stood around looking surly and sweaty, rubbing the palms of his hands on his jeans. There was a pause, then a tumultuous shout went up. Justin Hooke appeared, stripped to the waist, looking more gigantic than ever as he surveyed his opponent. Raising his arms in salute to the crowd, he advanced with long, rapid strides to the platform, where he bowed to Sophie and all the girls, then returned to the field and shook hands with his opponent. The referee spoke to them, stepped back, and the bout began.

It was wrestling of an order I had never seen before, the good old-fashioned country kind, with no holds barred. Whenever

Soakes got the upper hand, he received no encouragement from the crowd, though his father and brothers suggested mightily, "Kill the guy!" "Break his arm, brain him, Roy!" And for all that Roy had weight on his side, Justin's strength carried the first round, then the second, then the third. When at last Tobacco City's finest went limping from the field, Old Man Soakes angrily shoved another of his offspring out in his place, and, after taking off his shirt, he faced Justin. Without waiting, the newest opponent shot out his foot, tripped Justin up, and dropped on top of him. There were boos and catcalls at such dirty tactics, and Jack Stump darted out on the field to protest to the referee, but Old Man Soakes came roaring after him, seized him by the collar, and tossed him back into the crowd.

Even with the unfair advantage, it was no contest. Heaving himself up, Justin threw Soakes to the side, fell on him, and put a half-Nelson around Soakes's neck until his eyes rolled up. Then he released him and stepped away. As Soakes got to his feet, Justin whirled and gracefully planted a well-placed kick on his backside, which sent him sprawling. Amid cheers and laughter Justin left the fray.

Justin took a towel from Worthy and wiped himself down, then went to the platform where he talked with Sophie and the girls, waiting for the next event to begin. At one point, he stooped and cordially spoke a few words to Kate, who was seated on the steps. When the whistle blew, announcing the next contest, he handed her his towel, then ran lightly onto the field again, accompanied by Worthy and half a dozen other young men. It was time for the pole-shinny.

The referee held up his hand and the first contestant readied himself at the base of the pole, testing its surface with his palms until the whistle blew and up he went. He touched the top, then slid down, and Jimmy Minerva took his position while the referee called out the time from his stopwatch. He signaled again, and Jim went up and came down. Third to go was Justin, moving with dexterity for a man of his height and weight, quickly arriving at the top, where he paused briefly, then slid down. Applause

followed the announcement that his time had beaten the first
two. On the platform, Sophie and her girls had risen, also Kate,
who was standing on the steps, caught in the excitement of the
moment as Worthy addressed himself to the pole. He spat on
his palms, rubbed them together, and grasped the wooden shaft,
waiting, his knees bent so they almost touched the ground. Hearing the whistle, he came up out of his crouch in a slick leap
and, hand over hand, feet gripping, he went up like an agile
monkey to tap the top of the post.

He waited, grinning down at the crowd, until the referee
called out the time, well under Justin's. Holding on with one
hand, he waved, and I saw Kate waving back at him excitedly.
He did not come down immediately but, grasping the tip of the
pole with both hands, he began to sway with it back and forth.
Mr. Deming hurried out on the field gesticulating, while the
crowd murmured excitedly, watching Worthy's body describe an
ever-widening arc against the sky. Kate rose from the steps, staring wide-eyed, fearing for his safety.

Using the pole as a fulcrum, the boy extended his body outward in a horizontal position. Suddenly there came a single, loud
report, almost like a pistol shot. Dropping to the vertical again,
Worthy began sliding down, but when he had got less than halfway another cracking sound was heard as the pole continued
to split. Without looking below, he flung himself outward in
a graceful movement, and plunged to the turf. I was certain he
must be hurt, but in another moment Justin had him on his
feet, dazed but laughing and shaking his head. He was hoisted
aloft and borne around the field, until Mr. Deming stepped up
and ordered them all off. Glancing over at Kate to catch her
reaction, I saw only the back of Sophie's dress as she bent above
a crumpled form on the steps. I started at a half-run, then stopped
as the Widow Fortune seized my hand.

"No," she said, pointing to the valise beside her chair. "The
black bag—bring it!" She hurried toward the platform while, un-
noticed by the others under the tree, I snatched up the black
bag and dashed after her.

Kate lay collapsed against the steps, and when I arrived Sophie was cradling her in her arms while the Widow leaned over her, listening to her heart. Kate's face had gone livid; the blue veins in her forehead bulged and throbbed. The eyes were wide and glassy in the way I had seen so many times that summer, and her skin was flooded with perspiration. Great gasping noises issued from her throat as she fought for air; her fingers clutched at her neck as though to tear away the invisible hands that were strangling her.

"A doctor—" I looked wildly around. The Widow shook her head, fumbled open the valise, located a bottle, and pulled the cork. Holding the glass neck to Kate's mouth, she put several drops of liquid between the parted lips, then stroked the neck muscles until the drops had been swallowed. She repeated the operation, and in a moment the terrible gasping sounds subsided, to be replaced by a dry rattle. Then the chest became almost motionless, and Kate's breathing slowed. I seized her wrist and tried to find her pulse; there was none.

As the crowd came toward the platform, the Widow motioned for me to carry Kate into a nearby tent, where I laid her on a table and again tried to find her pulse, cursing myself for having forgotten the Medihaler. I dropped her limp wrist, raced from the tent, and thrust my way through the figures thronging the platform where the elders were making a presentation to Justin's winning team of horses. Catching sight of Beth, I shouted "Kate!" and jerked my head toward the tent, then pushed on through the crowd. I found the Medihaler in the car, and hurried back. Expecting the worst, I tore aside the tent flap to discover Beth, Sophie, and the Widow grouped around the table where I had left Kate in a paroxysm of agony. I stopped in my tracks at the sight that now greeted me. Kate was sitting up, her hands in her lap, listening as the Widow spoke to her. Beth gave me a wild look; we knew from experience that the attacks usually lasted from an hour to two or three days, but here was our daughter breathing easily if feebly.

I started forward, the Medihaler in my outstretched hand.

Beth drew me beside her and I put an arm around her, holding her close, not daring to speak. The Widow stood behind Kate, leaning slightly forward, her head even with the girl's, her lips close to her ear. The tips of the ancient fingers were working at the cords of Kate's neck, then at her temples, and as she worked she spoke in low, soothing tones. I felt Beth's hand fumbling for mine; I took it and held it hard, observing the old woman's careful but firm ministrations, the movements of her large womanly hands, her intent, grave expression, and I was flooded by a sense of relief and release, relief for Kate's recovery, release from my own guilt.

Sophie came over to us and, assuring us that all would be well, took us outside the tent. Maggie Dodd was there with Justin Hooke, and together we waited. Then, silent, stricken-looking, Worthy Pettinger joined us. From inside we heard the Widow's gentle, yet insistent alto voice.

Justin's head turned and our eyes met. Then he nodded, once, twice. He did not speak, but I could tell he meant us to know what Sophie had already voiced: all would be well.

Shortly we heard Kate's husky laugh. "All right now?" the Widow asked; there was a sound of assent, and in a moment the flap was raised and Kate appeared, looking pale and shaken. Beth rushed to embrace her; then she and Sophie led her away. With another look, Justin followed with Worthy. The Widow, who had been watching, bit her lip in contemplation, clasping and unclasping her fingers across her apron front, then went back into the tent and reappeared with her black valise.

I remembered how Kate's attacks would seemingly abate for a time, only to return with increased vigor, and I wondered if this was not merely one of those stages. The old woman seemed to read my mind, for she rested her hand on my arm and exerted a firm pressure, as though to buoy up my spirits.

"She'll be all right now. Don't worry yourself, and tell your wife not to worry. And whatever you do, don't fuss the child. Act as though nothing happened." Brushing aside my expressions of thanks, she employed the shears hanging at her waist to snip an errant thread from the cuff of her sleeve; then, beaming behind her spectacles, she patted my cheek. When she had accepted Maggie's arm and permitted herself to be led away, I remained staring at the useless Medihaler in my hand, then absently slipped it into my pocket and followed after the others, wondering how the old woman had effected a cure at once so swift and so miraculous. And though I did not realize it then, it was not the last time the Widow Fortune was to rescue Kate, to rescue Beth, and to alter all our lives.

8

An hour later, it was as if nothing untoward had occurred. Kate went off with Worthy again, while Beth, calm now, talked with the Dodds. The Widow had removed her chair to its former spot under the other tree, and I could see by her impatient gestures how she dismissed among the circle of ladies grouped around her all talk of the earlier incident. With the heat, the women had drawn well into the shade of the overhead branches, digesting their lunch, as well as such tidbits of gossip as still remained unconsumed from the morning's repast.

Though I could not explain it, I felt that a great weight had been lifted from me, and that the threatening fact of Kate's illness had suddenly dissolved; the occasional looks the Widow Fortune directed to me as she conversed only served to substantiate this feeling.

Leaving Maggie and Robert engaged with Beth, and taking my sketchbook, I made myself inconspicuous while I ambled closer to the Widow's group, where I uncapped my pen and began to sketch the group of ladies putting their heads together and talking. The Widow took out her glasses and inspected the lenses for lint, then put them on. "Mrs. Zee, I believe we might bring out our quilts now." She smoothed down her apron while the other ladies drew their chairs closer and took quilts from their baskets. The complacent bleat of a sheep rose in the torpid air as it stood patiently in a wooden tub while some men washed it. Overhead, the sun flickered through the green canopy of leaves, glinting on the rims of the Widow's spectacles, the thimble on her finger, and her shears as she scissored out a piece of bright cloth and pinned it to her quilt.

"Wa'n't Justin the marvel today?" Mrs. Brucie said. Mrs. Zalmon put her hand to her breast. "I've never seen such a handsome Harvest Lord."

"Worthy Pettinger'd be obliged if he didn't try to make such mischief," Mrs. Green said.

"Such jackanapes tricks," Mrs. Zalmon said.

"Don't it put you in mind of somethin'?" Mrs. Brucie said.

"It surely *does!*" Irene Tatum pulled up a chair and flopped. She had a piece of newspaper, which she pleated, and began fanning herself. "If I didn't know better, I'd say Worthy's gone off his rocker just like the bad one." A chain of looks went around the circle like small, silent explosions.

"Hush, now," the Widow Fortune ventured gently.

"I've said it before so I'll say it again: she was a bad one." Irene Tatum's tongue was sharp, as if she kept it whetted on a stone, ready to carve on all occasions.

"A bad apple spoils the barrel," said Mrs. Green.

"Went bad long before Agnes Fair," said Mrs. Brucie.

"We gave her honors and she flaunted them in our faces," said Irene Tatum.

"Hush, now, Irene." The Widow's needle flashed. " 'The evil men do lives after them, the good is oft interred. . . .' Some things are best not spoken of. Leave her in peace."

"Never find no peace, Grace Everdeen," declared Irene hotly.

"Goodnight nurse!" the Widow exclaimed, then deftly changed the subject. "I never saw such a leap as Worthy made. A daredevil is what he is."

Mrs. Brucie shook her head. "Devil, yes. The boy holds contrary notions. Let one get ideas, and they'll all get them, and then where are you? On the verge, on the pure and simple verge. Widow, oughtn't you to talk to the boy?"

"Worthy?" The Widow looked surprised. "Why, Worthy's nice as pie. And a good boy, I'll be bound." She drew out a length of cotton and rethreaded her needle.

"Well," Mrs. Green said firmly, "if anyone's to be chose, it's sure to be Jim Minerva, mark my word. I'll put my corn and stock to wager."

Though I found the conversation puzzling, wondering who was to be chosen and for what purpose, and by what means, I was forced to smile at the agreeable circle.

"Dear sakes," the Widow said, "if that sheep's not positively snowy." The men had rinsed the animal's coat, and one of them lifted it from the tub and set it on its feet to dry in the sun; another retied the bell around its neck. While the women continued together, sewing and gossiping in their group, the unoccupied men likewise drew off together, meditatively picking their teeth, an easy lackadaisical drone to their voices, their attention occasionally directed to the sheep's bell, whose soft tinkle hung in the air as the washers brushed the white woolly coat, none of them speaking, all of them seeming to be waiting.

A little distance away, Missy Penrose stood stock-still, idly staring up at the sky where a silvery jet traced a white contrail across the blue. The Widow called out to a passerby, "Miss Clapp, take her out o' the sun. Out o' the *sun*, I say. It's too hot. She'll never last till they're ready." Miss Clapp brought the child under the tree, where the Widow took her on her lap. She rummaged in her piece-bag, produced a length of twine which she tied in a loop, and began showing Missy how to do cat's cradle. The old lady seemed at pains to amuse the child, and when they had played for a time, she set Missy on the grass and resumed her stitching.

Mrs. Green looked up at the church clock. "Soon it'll be time."

"Soon," said Mrs. Brucie.

I felt a touch on my shoulder, and turned to find Beth beside me, watching me sketch. She smiled, then walked across the grass and circled the tree until she stood behind the Widow, where she looked down at her work.

"It's a beautiful quilt."

The Widow smiled up at her. "Bit o' fancywork. A way to pass the time."

"Why, it's Noah and the Ark."

"Aye, dear, it's only lackin' two giraffes and the dove."

"How long does it take to make one like that?" Beth asked.

"Depends. Four or five of us can finish this off before the moon goes a full quarter. What you ought to do, dear, is try a bit of fancywork yourself. Everyone in these parts sews. Set a spell, dear. You start savin' your hand-me-downs and worn-outs, you'll have enough to begin quilting right off. Never throw nothin' away, that's what my granny used to say."

I smiled to myself; the idea appealed to Beth, I could tell.

"Here, dear, let me thread up a needle," Mrs. Zalmon said. "Mrs. Brucie, pick out a patch there, can you? See—you just pin it on, then it's ready to be stitched."

Beth glanced over at me with a smile, her expression clearly saying, *My God, look at me—I'm in a sewing circle.*

Later it cooled slightly, the shadows began to lengthen as the sun dropped, and the Common settled into somnolence. The air was still and heavy and smelled faintly sour, the odor of weeds or grass cuttings. The pennants hung limp and tired on the booths. No traffic passed, no voices called, no dogs barked. All was silence.

I went across the roadway in the direction of Penance House, where I had seen some of the men disappearing. Wondering what had taken them there, I walked past the post office, and when I heard low voices from behind the barn next door, I went to investigate. Abruptly the voices stopped. In the stillness, I could feel the same prickling at the base of my neck I had felt that morning, and a lifting of the hairs along my forearms. An uncanny feeling, telling me something was about to happen. I took several steps toward the barn, then halted, riveted by a sound

I instantly recognized, climbing to a terrible pitch, a wild cry, rising upward and outward as though from the heart of a bell, to float, then to die in the air, trailing away to nothingness. A pair of swallows, alarmed, took abrupt flight from the eaves of the barn, arcing out against the sky, dipping and swooping past my vision. I rounded the corner of the barn and was confronted by a baffling semicircle of backs. No one turned. Why so still, these men and boys, why so grave, so silent?

Then I saw the child, and thought at first she must be hemorrhaging, so red were her arms. I saw Will Jones's simple farmer's face looking at me. In hat and overalls, he stood meekly in the center of the circle, the handle of his sickle clasped loosely in one hand, the sharp silver crescent gone red. At his feet lay the felled sheep; below the red wool its thin legs still jerked. The child knelt in the dust, busily engaged as she gazed dreamily down at the red mass of viscera she held in her palms, her arms red to the elbows.

She raised her blank face and, as though waking from a dream, peered around the circle of men stolidly looking upon her and upon the red maw of the sheep's cleaved belly and upon the still-palpitating entrails she tenderly cupped in her hands. Dripping red, the glossy tubular glands and bulgy membranes slid about and slowly slipped through her splayed fingers and fell back into the parted red cavity beneath them. Never removing her eyes from her hands, she raised them palms upward before her, toward the sky, their redness trembling against the blue. There was no sound, only the dry rattle of the watchers' breath trapped in their throats; one man coughed, another blew his nose into a bandanna. Still the red hands remained outstretched; as if in a trance, the child rose and began a slow circuit, her eyes glazed, uttering not a word as she moved around the circle of younger men. Stiffly she walked past young Lyman Jones, past the Tatum boys, past Merle Penrose, past several others, until she stood before Jim Minerva. A faint sign of recognition appeared in her face, a perceptible widening of the eyes, a murmur in the throat. Her hands moved slightly as if to touch him; then she passed on in her dream and in her dream stopped again, reaching out her hands and laying their redness against the cheeks of Worthy Pettinger.

A sigh, a murmur; stillness. The whir of insect wings.

When she took the hands away, a replica of each palm lay upon Worthy's flesh, and as she slowly turned, she dropped her hands almost to her sides; not quite, for in her dream something told her to hold them away from her dress. Some of the men gathered closer to Worthy—pale now around his bloody marks—and thumped him on the shoulders, congratulating him, while others dragged the sheep aside, leaving a smeared trail of red upon the brindled ground. Several men lit up their pipes, scratching blue-tip matches on the seats of their overalls, exchanging nods and low remarks. Out on the street a car backfired, jolting me into shocked reality. I looked again, saw dust and straw and blood, heard the dull buzz of flies, the dry hiss as someone took breath in through his teeth, smelled the stench of the animal. The women came running from the Common in pairs and groups, looking at the ring of men, all amazed.

"Did she choose?" they wanted to know. Who? Who was it? Was it Jim? Jim Minerva? "No," said the men, shaking their heads, moving aside, and "Praise be!" the women cried, seeing the marked boy. They kissed him, hugged him, bore him away, the men following, until there was no one behind the barn except me.

And the gutted sheep.

And Missy Penrose.

Breathing through her mouth, she was making strange, incomprehensible sounds as she stared at the open cavity. "Mnn —mean—um—nmm—" Where all had been red before, now a black liverish-looking bile was running from the rent tissue. She stopped, put her fingers into it, brought them out bloodier, darker, held them against the sky, her body going rigid and beginning a tremulous shaking.

"Mean—um—nmm—mean—"

Her eyes rolled upward in their sockets; a slight spittle appeared at the corners of her mouth, became a froth. She twitched, jerked, then a stiff arm rose, a red finger pointed at me. A rising breeze caught her hair, lifted it across her eyes; she brushed it away; red appeared on her forehead like a stigma.

I stared back, feeling the same chill again, the same cold sweat. Wind was whipping the grass at her feet. I said nothing. She said nothing. Her eyes were glassy, blank; I knew she could not see me. Yet she saw—something. Then, still pointing, red, she began screaming. I stood frozen in terror. From the Common came the tumult of celebration. No one had seen, no one saw. She was screaming louder than I thought it possible for a child to scream, and, screaming, she pointed.

She stopped. Her arm fell and hung limp, her eyes came into a kind of focus; she stared briefly at the dead sheep, then turned and walked away.

The air began to freshen, the wind to change, and the sky by slight but perceptible degrees to darken, and out on the Common I could see the men standing back as the women rushed to engulf the child, touching and petting her, a murmur sweeping through them, becoming chatter, then acclaim; then, as the child fainted, their voices were suddenly stilled, like birds before a storm.

I went behind the barn and vomited into the grass.

PART TWO

THE DAYS
OF THE
SEASONING

9

The Days of the Seasoning began, that lax period before harvest when the sun did its final drying of the corn, and the farmers readied themselves for the winter. And as the Days of the Seasoning went by, little by little I cleared my mind, and stopped thinking about the red pointing finger. At least I tried to tell myself I had. I convinced myself it had been nothing, a child having a joke on an outsider. During those early September weeks, I went about the village, sketching, doing water-color studies, and telling myself the incident had had no meaning. Sometimes I would see her—behind her gate, on the Common, along the road—but it was as if nothing had happened. So I told myself nothing had.

Though my perceptions might have sharpened since then, it is perhaps because I have learned the art of substituting one thing for another: it is the law of compensation put into sober practice. Later I was required by force of circumstance to negotiate a painful series of readjustments, but in that early autumn my only concern was the business of painting that small but particular corner of New England called Cornwall Coombe. It was all bright then, illuminated by the light I saw it with, and the brightness gladdened my painter's eye. The light in cities is flatter, grayer, less defined. In the country it was quite different, an evocation of all the glowing light I had ever wanted to record, like some rare golden elixir that had been poured over the hills and fields. There were few grays in my palette, but an abundance of yellows and ochers and deep umbers with which I slopped and spattered the gessoed panels I painted on, working in a fury of haste to capture what I was seeing.

I felt I was becoming a fixture in the village, accepted not because I was the same as they, but because I was different, because I could "draw" things. I was respected because of my work, and because they sensed I wanted nothing more than to be able to put onto a board with brush and color the life I saw around me. And on my part I offered them ungrudging admiration. If I have presented them as picturesque and quaint, I have erred. Countryfolk they were, but a bunch of tough nuts. Dawn-to-dusk, fourteen-hour-a-day workers, unshirking and unstinting, stylish in their own New England right, whose plainest, homeliest task became a kind of ritualistic act: the quartering of an apple, the whittling of a stick, the laying of a brick. I appreciated them for their country wisdom, their humility, their hardiness. The sturdy sons of sturdy fathers. I found them people of simple but profound convictions, and I admired them for their love of the soil, their esteem for their village, their reverence for the past, and their determination to hold on to it at all costs. I liked their forthrightness, their modest know-how, their reticence; if they were worried and wearied by debt, or fearful of natural disaster, they alone knew it, for they never confided such things, except perhaps among themselves. It was the freemasonry of those who live close to the earth, with its harsh, often bitter realities.

And we were being offered a share in it. We were finding ourselves accepted as in the natural order of things, and were treated accordingly. Several Sundays after the Agnes Fair, we went to church. Mr. Deming and the elders were by tradition awarded the choice seats—up front, with cushions. Also included in this preferential treatment were, I discovered, the Hookes, Justin and Sophie. The remainder of the worshipers were ranged, also traditionally, in accordance with their social position and wealth, wives and husbands together—their offspring suffering time-honored banishment to the galleries, boys on one side, girls on the other—while the choir was seated in the loft behind, with Mrs. Buxley to conduct and Maggie Dodd at the organ.

When the last bell peal had died away, we all rose, and while the minister entered from the vestibule in his black gown, Amys drew the doors shut, their closing timed to coincide precisely with Mr. Buxley's arrival in the pulpit. Soon thereafter the bell ringer stationed himself at the rear of the boys' gallery, where he maintained a long wooden rod, ready to tap to consciousness any dozing young fry.

Our family sat toward the rear, in the straight-backed, un-padded, and decidedly uncomfortable pew one of the elders had assigned us, and we joined with the others while Mr. Buxley led the opening prayer. We sang the Doxology to Maggie's ac-companiment. After that came the pastor's church notes and items of general interest; next was a hymn, followed by another prayer, and then, at the indicated moment, amid clearing of throats, rustling of programs, creaking of pews, and dropping of hymnals into racks, the congregation settled itself for the ritual Sunday sermon.

Harken, the village of Cornwall Coombe. Meek and humble lamb though he might be Monday through Saturday, the Rev-erend Mr. Buxley on the Sabbath was a lion. This was his church, this his pulpit, this his flock. For his text he had selected Second Kings, Chapter 18, Verse 32: "Until I come and take you away to a land like your own land, a land of corn and wine, a land of bread and vineyards, a land of oil olive and of honey, that ye may live and not die . . ." Having read from the scripture, Mr. Buxley closed the Book, removed his glasses, placed his hands on either side of the pulpit as though for moral support, and launched into a lengthy peroration. His broad ministerial gestures described the bounty of the promised harvest and the warranted thankfulness for a full grain elevator, fuller pocket-books, still fuller stomachs. But then, alas—arms falling in despair —with such bounty, what else was there in this land of plenty?

Sin.

Here it comes, I thought, hellfire and brimstone; shades of Henry Ward Beecher.

". . . sinning in this land of corn and wine," deplored Mr. Buxley, and though he spoke of Israel, who was there gathered before him who knew not he alluded to Cornwall Coombe? Sin lay in the hearts of those who, like Jezebel, were greedy beyond their just portion. But—finger directed heavenward—the great Lord Jehovah, nothing loath, had prophesied that Jezebel, unfortunate creature, should have her worldly flesh eaten of by dogs at the wall of Jezreel.

I reached for Beth's hand, lying on the hymnal in her lap. She smiled at me under her lashes and I gave her a silent *I love you.* On this glorious Sunday in Cornwall Coombe, where was there to be found a luckier man than I? She nudged me, directing my attention to the boys' gallery where Amys Penrose, leaning over the back pew, administered a smart rap on a head with the tip of his rod. Blinking, Worthy Pettinger sat up abruptly, awakening in time to learn of Jezebel getting her just deserts: having painted her face and done up her hair, the hussy was leaning out a window, whereupon three eunuchs were induced to throw her down. "'Go see now this cursed woman,'" the minister quoted, "'and bury her: for she is a king's daughter. . . .'"

My eyes lingered on Worthy's saturnine features as he lent appropriate attention to Mr. Buxley. In the several weeks since the Agnes Fair, the boy had been in our employ, helping complete the terrace wall, setting in the skylight, plus seeing to the myriad other chores Beth found in unending succession. Day by day, we were becoming more dependent on his help and, in consequence, day by day fonder of him. He had proved to be bright, able, quick to learn, and willing to please. Still, observing him as he worked, I could see he was somehow troubled, but when I tried to draw him out, I discovered nothing to solve the mystery of the boy's melancholy. In the back of my mind always was the memory of the fair:

The red hands of Missy Penrose printed on his cheeks; from sheep's entrails, like an ancient seeress the half-wit child had chosen the boy. Her pale face staring in triumph at Worthy's paler one: plainly he had not wished it. Children and sheep's blood and oracular vision: the startling ways of Cornwall Coombe.

Still, though I had said nothing, I felt glad that no one had witnessed the scene behind the barn at Penance House, the black guts of the sheep, the red pointing finger.

I turned my head, looking up at the gallery where the village girls sat. Missy Penrose's expression darkened as she saw my apprehensive glance, and her brow lifted in slight acknowledgment, as though between us we shared some unspoken and forbidden secret.

What bond could possibly connect us—me, Ned Constantine, and her, the village idiot? Why had I been singled out for her notice? And, having attracted it, why had I experienced that strange mixture of awe and dread? Why, in dreams, did I now see that accusing finger?

Was there some unplumbed depth in her make-up? Not a chance, I told myself. Missy Penrose wasn't deep—she didn't have the brains God gave a chicken. She made up crazy things from her own addled sense of specialness, and the superstitious villagers, eager to believe her, treated her accordingly.

On the far side of the church, in the pews for the unmarried women, I accidentally caught the postmistress's eye. Tamar Penrose's lazy stare caused me to look immediately away. Had she winked? In church? With Beth beside me? I glanced back: prim and proper, the postmistress was dutifully attending her pastor.

When at length the sermon was concluded, the minister cleared his throat and announced the closing hymn. We sang again, the benediction was offered, the service ended.

As I walked into the vestibule, Amys Penrose was again tolling the bell rope, announcing that church was over. "Nice music," I complimented Maggie Dodd as she descended the stairs from the loft.

"Why, thank you," sang Mrs. Buxley, following her. "Success,

James," she called to her husband, greeting his parishioners at
the door. "Our truants have entered the fold at last. Lovely day,
isn't it? Where are Mrs. Constantine and your little one?" Like
a large, damp mollusk, Mrs. Buxley attached herself to my side
and we passed through the vestibule doors to stand on the top
step. "Ring loud," she called gaily to the bell ringer. "Good morning, Robert. Didn't Maggie play beautifully? That Bach! Worthy,
dear, did you get all the hymnals put away? Close the cupboard
door? That's a good boy."

I stopped to remind Worthy about a patch of broken slates
that needed replacement on the studio roof. He said he would
investigate, then ducked through the crowd gathered at the foot
of the steps for after-church greetings. While Robert took one
of Maggie's elbows, I offered him mine on the other side to guide
him to the sidewalk.

"Fallish day, Robert." Wearing her best Sunday black, with
carved bone brooch at her breast, the Widow turned away from
Beth and Kate, with whom she had been speaking, to acknowledge the Dodds and myself. " 'Pears autumn's goin' to take us
by stealth 'stead of by storm this year. Mornin', Asia. Where's
Fred today?"

Mrs. Minerva stopped to pay her respects. "Fred's feelin' sort
of achy—and just before Harvest Home, too. Hate to think of
what it'll be with a change of weather."

"Fred's had the worst luck. You just come along to me, Asia,
and let me give you something for him."

"Some sermon today," Mrs. Zalmon said, greeting the Reverend, who was once again meek, as though this very day he might
inherit the earth. Divested of his robes but maintaining his circular white collar, Mr. Buxley accepted congratulations on his
preaching while his wife basked in reflected glory.

"You can't tell me he didn't mean Gracie Everdeen," someone
said.

"Oh, dear, now, really, we mustn't—I mean, it's such a lovely
day, we oughtn't—now, Sally Pounder—" It was Mrs. Buxley's
habit not only to mince words but to make hash of them as well.

"We mustn't sully a Sunday with such talk—I'm sure James didn't mean—did you, James?" Tucking her husband's arm under hers, she took him off as though he were a parcel.

While the Widow continued talking quilts with Beth, Jack Stump's cart was heard approaching, the clatter of his pans and kettles fracturing the churchtide quiet.

"Whatcha say, ladies, bounteeful day, ain't it? Whatcha say, Widow?"

"Come 'round later, Jack," she said, and he tipped his hat to her. Pedaling up to Sally Pounder and Betsey Cox, the bank teller, he yanked open a drawer and flourished a piece of beadwork.

"Yessir, we got us a bounteeful day, girls, so let's make hay while the sun shines. How's your pig, Irene?" He tipped his hat to Mrs. Tatum. "Girls, lookee here what I got. One of a kind, a pure original, you'll never see another one like it."

"Don't you know this is the Sabbath, Jack Stump?" Irene Tatum bawled. "Since when do we allow Sunday buyin' or sellin'? You got some dispensation? No? Then haul your contraption off and don't go merchandisin' at the very church door when people's just finished speakin' with the Lord." Her anger was as righteous as if she were Christ driving the moneychangers from the temple.

I nodded to the Hookes, who now descended the steps; Justin was immediately surrounded by a ring of admirers, while Sophie stood aside with resigned good humor. I moved back as Tamar Penrose, fishing a key from her bag, passed close by. She gave me a sullen glance, then, turning quickly, she crossed the roadway onto the Common.

Mrs. Green was speaking to Mrs. Zalmon. "Look at them tatty beads," she said as the peddler palmed the necklace off on Betsey Cox. "A body can't set much store by what he trades in."

"Ayuh," Mrs. Zalmon agreed, making her words significant. "He's not a likely person, is he?"

Mrs. Green's mouth drew down. "Not likely at all."

The Widow laughed. "Oh, I like Jack Stump. He's independent. Folks have to be independent—gives 'em character. I like a

fellow who thinks for himself. People are so busy today tryin'
to be just like all the others. I like people who has peculiarities."

Justin offered to drive her home in his El Camino, and she
asked him to wait while she went into the churchyard and spent
some time with Clem. As was evidently her habit, she had been
inviting certain of the gathering to come to her house and be
sociable before Sunday dinner. Justin accepted the invitation,
then disengaged himself from the ladies and took Sophie off
down the sidewalk.

"You come along for those scraps in a while," the Widow told
Beth, and, lifting her skirts, she went into the cemetery, shears
dangling at her waist.

Maggie said, "Ned, take Robert down to the Rocking Horse
for a drink; then we'll go to the Widow's." While she and Beth
turned to talk quilting with Mrs. Green and Mrs. Brucie, I gave
Robert my arm and led him along the sidewalk toward the tavern.

"Another local custom?" I asked.

"One with the deepest significance. Ladies not welcome."

Passing the churchyard, I saw the solitary figure beside Clem
Fortune's grave. It made a striking picture, I thought, the old
woman in her widow's weeds and white cap, standing among
the ancient tombstones, head bowed, her lips moving.

It was indeed a grand day. The broad New England sky was
sunny and bright, the air nimble with the slightest hint of autumn
in the brisk breeze that tumbled leaves along the roadside. Groups
of people were strung out along the sidewalks, enjoying the fine
weather and discussing Mr. Buxley's sermon. The belled sheep
grazed on the Common, cropping the turf, their coats woolly and
thick for winter shearing.

"What are those ridges in the grass?" I asked Robert. He angled
his head as though to look.

"Bonfire circles. When the grass burns away and they reseed
it the next spring, it always seems to come up a different color."

"Bonfires?"

"On Kindling Night, just before Harvest Home. A farm custom. Up in Maine and New Hampshire, they still have big fires

on Election Day, which is somehow mixed up with the British Guy Fawkes Day, though I don't suppose they remember quite how. Here they have a fire to mark the end of the growing year, and they dance around it."

"What kind of dance?"

"What's known as a chain dance. It goes back to the ancient Greeks—you can still see vases in museums with chain dancers painted on them, some of them dating back to the Bronze Age or further."

I saw Missy making her way through the sheep, the incredible-looking doll in her hand. Her mother stood in the doorway of the post office, and I had the feeling that as we walked along, both pairs of eyes were fixed on us. At the tavern, the village males— Sunday suits, collars opened, ties yanked—moved aside to permit the blind man to reach a place at the end of the bar nearest the door. In the corner at our right sat Amys Penrose, drinkless, but looking hopeful. Amys, I had discovered, was regarded as the village eccentric. Caretaker of Penance House across the way, he also looked after the sheep on the Common, swept the street, and was church sexton, bell ringer, and grave digger. A typical Yankee, he kept himself beholden to none, never kowtowed to the village elite, came and went as he pleased, and, being a Penrose, was maybe a little "tetched."

As we sat down he hiked his stool over to accommodate us. "Mornin', Professor."

"That you, Amys? Your bells sounded fine this morning."

"Ringin's ringin', and drinkin's drinkin'."

Though blind, Robert knew when he was being cadged. "Have a beer on me, Amys," he offered. We ordered drinks from Bert, the bartender, and while they were being brought I heard one of the farmers in the vicinity speaking to a group around him.

"I guess Gracie's ears were burnin' today."

"If the hellfires haven't burned her first."

Again I wondered what Grace Everdeen had done to merit such general censure.

Robert was speaking to Amys: "I was telling our friend here about the chain dances on Kindling Night."

"Kindling Night." Amys used the spittoon. "Crazy notion. They been doin' them fool dances ever since I can recollect." Like the Ancient Mariner, he seemed to compel me with his glittering eye. "You stop around here long enough, you'll see lots of things."

I sipped my drink, my head bent slightly so I could see off across the Common. Tamar Penrose was still in the post office doorway. "Why does the post office have such a large chimney?"

Amys took his face out of his beer mug. "Hell, that ain't been the P.O. for no time a'tall. Used to be the old forge barn to the Gwydeon Penrose place, over there where I live." He pushed his hat back, leaned his elbows on the bar, and ground some peanuts between his bony jaws. "Cagey feller, old Gwydeon. Once, during an Indian attack, he barricaded himself and his family inside that forge. Them Indians tried to burn him out, but he'd built the place of stone, so fire wouldn't touch nothin' but the door. When the Indians finally got in, all ready for scalpin', they wa'n't there. Foxy old Gwydeon'd dug a tunnel months before, and he got out and his whole family, too. 'Course, the forge ain't been a forge for years. After the Revolution, the barn was sold and it became a general store; then we got the P.O."

"Tell me another thing, Amys," I said. "Is it true what they say about Missy Penrose?"

The bell ringer's brows darkened and his mouth curled sourly. "Depends on what they say, son."

"I was talking about her freckles. Do they form a constellation?"

"There's fools aplenty 'round here who'll believe anything you tell 'em. If they care to think that whatnot child's got the evil eye —why, then, I guess she's got the evil eye. 'Cept I'd put my money on the mother, not the daughter."

"Easy, now, Amys," Robert said soothingly.

Amys drew himself up and pounded on the bar. "Listen, if it comes to that, you tell me why the Reverend takes after a dear soul like Gracie, and never points a finger at the likes of *her*." He jabbed his thumb in the direction of the post office. "Never a gooder girl than Grace Everdeen, and for her sins she comes to grief, while that one, no better than she ought to be, is your fancy miss post office lady. And blast Roger Penrose, who couldn't tell the gilt from the gingerbread." His voice had risen to an angry quaver, and heads in the vicinity swiveled to stare at the old man. "Never mind, around here you can't teach your grandmother to suck eggs."

"Easy, now," Robert repeated. To change the subject, I inquired if there were any boats on the river available for rowing. The old man confided that he kept one in a particular spot, and said I might borrow it anytime, a snug craft that needed no bailin'. He thanked Robert for the beer and left, and when we had paid the tab we stepped outside to find the peddler's rig drawn up at the roadside, where Jack Stump was exhibiting for a gathering the identical one-of-a-kind piece of cheap beadwork he had purveyed to Betsey Cox in front of the church. "Sunday special, ladies," he began, "a chunk of gen-u-wine Victorian, that's whatcha got here. Victorian, ladies, which means it's practically a antique, if you figure by years, because anything that's Victorian means it goes back to before Columbus discovered America."

The crowd laughed and someone called out, "Tell us, Jack Stump, what came before Victorian?"

"Before Victorian you had your Dark Ages, which was when them fearsome Tartars come across the steppes of Russia and tried to rule the world. But they used the back steps so they wouldn't get caught." Jack wheezed at his joke.

"And what came before that, Jack?" Robert called good-naturedly.

"Hell, Professor, you orta know. You had your religious age, when Martin Luther spiked his thesis to his front door."

"Who was Martin Luther?" a voice demanded.

"Why, Martin Luther was a Lutheran. That's what it means, a Lutheran is someone named Luther."

"My name's Luther, and I ain't no Lutheran," said one of the

Soakes boys, lolling in the tavern doorway, a can of beer in his hand.

Jack chose to ignore him. "And Martin Luther told folks the Pope was nothin' but a greedy cuss and any Christian worth his salt ought to show them roguey priests the door. Said Cath'lickism was nothing but organized crime, and folk shouldn't have no more to do with 'em."

"Ain't no Cath'lics this side of the river," called someone in the crowd.

"I heard that, Grandmaw," Luther said. "Ain't no call to talk that way."

"Ain't no call for some folks to be off their own side of the river," replied another.

Roy Soakes, the defeated wrestler, stepped out. "We come and go as we please. We don't want no trouble."

Jack Stump tossed the beads aside and out flew another drawer. "Soap, soap, ladies? Pretty little balls, shaped just like a pineapple, mighty pretty for the bathroom—no? Whatcha say, Sophie? Justin? How's married life treatin' you? Honey, if you're lookin' for a new dress for the huskin' bee, I got some mighty lofty goods." He snatched a bolt of fabric from a shelf. "You'd have to go some to find a dress pretty as this here'd make." He unrolled the bolt partway and offered it to Sophie, draping the end of it over her shoulder. "And here's needle and thread, pins galore, if you've a mind to do your own sewin'."

"Use 'em yourself, old man," Roy said. "Use 'em to zip your lip."

Jack put on a knowing expression as he returned the stare. "Well," he retorted slyly, "maybe I orta zip, 'cause if I didn't I bet I could tell of some might' funny doin's in them woods."

"Peddler, mind your business," Old Man Soakes said, shoving Luther out of the way and taking up a hulking stance in the doorframe. His voice had a hollow boom that silenced general comment as he pointed his finger at Jack. "Them woods is private property. That land is been Soakes land since before the first

Continental Congress and it's Soakes land to this day. We don't like trespassers."

"Ain't your land," someone said. "It's ours. We're corn, you're tobacco."

" 'Tain't called Soakes's Lonesome for nothin'," the old man maintained stolidly. He turned to Jack again. "You've had your warnin'."

"You don't scare me," the peddler retorted.

Roy's look was murderous as he shook up his beer can and tossed it at the cart, sending wet foam in all directions. Jack danced around in a circle, holding out the bolt of cloth. "Lookee —you splattered all over! What d'you want to do a thing like that for? Maybe you fellows need for me to call the police?"

"You do that, peddler," Old Man Soakes said darkly.

Roy laughed. "Don't recall they got police over here. Cornwall Coombe must be gettin' all the latest conveniences."

Luther sauntered behind the peddler and bent down on all fours, and Roy gave Jack a shove that sent him tumbling in the dust. He scrambled away with a crab-like movement, then shouted as Roy skidded under the rig and lifted his back against the undercarriage to tip it over.

In a flash, Justin Hooke was on him, arms around his waist and yanking him from beneath the cart. Roy rose, then swung, knocking the farmer on the side of his head as three of his brothers lunged out the tavern door and joined in the attack. Jack Stump took several brutal blows in succession, which dropped him to the roadway. When he cried out, I sprang forward, grabbed Luther, and sent him reeling. Roy came at me and I threw two quick jabs, following them up with a heavy blow to the gut. Justin, meantime, had recovered himself and now ran to put his back against mine, waiting for the others to rise.

Even at double the odds, it was no contest. No sooner would one get up and step in for a swing than he would be knocked down again.

I grinned over my shoulder. "I didn't know country boys knew how to use their fists." Justin swung again; Luther took his third tumble. "This country boy does!" Justin was enjoying the fight.

Not so Jack Stump, who had taken a merciless beating. He lay in the dust struggling to get up, and as Old Man Soakes raised a foot to roll him over, a figure like a dark avenging angel confronted him.

"Give over, Mr. Soakes!" commanded the Widow Fortune, standing before him, her face hot and angry. Almost as tall as he, and as broad, she stared him down while the sons dropped their fists, waiting for the father's signal.

"Whether they be your woods or not, we do not require the peace of our Sunday to be disturbed." Her voice rang out loudly in the silence.

"I come to buy corn," said Old Man Soakes, who had removed his hat and was inching the brim through his fingers.

"Then buy your corn and go home. Fight on your own doorstep, and leave peaceable folk to theirs." She waited until the group had moved back to the tavern entrance and the crowd closed in; then she bent to look at Jack Stump, who lay at her feet.

"Well, Jack, are you mortally wounded?" She turned to me. "Help him up and give him a dusting; then bring him along to my house and we'll see what we can do to repair him."

10

"Brawlin' in the streets," the old lady exclaimed, sitting Jack Stump down in one of her kitchen chairs and bending over his battered face. Pale and shaken, the peddler felt his jaw and winced as he tried to move it. It appeared badly dislocated, and though he offered no complaint I could see it was causing him intense pain. Beth, Kate, and I stood watching as he entrusted himself to the Widow's capable care.

"Here, now, Jack," she said in a kindly tone, "lay your head against the back of the chair—that's good, just so." She peered down at him through her spectacles; then, standing behind him, she laid a hand on either side of the jaw, her sensitive fingertips probing their way along the mandible bone until they had located the desired spot. Her back muscles tightened, she gave a quick yank, and there was an audible sound as the jaw snapped back into place and Jack's face went white under the stubble of beard.

"Lord, Jack," she told him, "can't a man shave for Sunday? There, now, how's that suit you?"

He felt his jaw again, wiggling it back and forth, then nodding.

"And now you'll be tellin' me they started the fight, them Soakeses."

Jack nodded vigorously while I related the details, including the episode of the flying beer can which had precipitated the attack. The Widow darted me a look.

"You're as bad as him—and Justin, too. The three of you. What'll Mr. Deming say?" She clucked behind her teeth and asked Beth to hand her the black valise from the counter; she set it on the table and opened it. Taking a piece of cotton, she selected one of the labeled bottles, poured some of the liquid on the cotton, and cleaned Jack's swollen eye.

"You'll be a fine sight tomorrow, you will. And a fat lip to boot." She touched the swollen tissue lightly. "Now, then, I won't hurt you. You've had enough hurtin' for one day. That eye's goin' to need a poultice. Kate, put the kettle on."

Kate filled the copper kettle and set it on the burner, while the Widow employed some fragrant-smelling ointment, carefully dabbing it on the injured lip. Then she slid a small tin of it into Jack's pocket, with instructions for use.

She took a mixing bowl from the cupboard, and a cloth bag from a shelf, measured out a handful of what looked to me like plain corn meal, and added to the contents a pinch from one jar of herbs and a pinch from another, until the kitchen became one delicious amalgam of aromas. When the kettle began singing, she poured some boiling water into the bowl and mixed up a mash which she put into a piece of cheesecloth and rolled into a poultice. Letting it cool slightly, she gently tilted Jack's head back again, and laid the poultice on the half-closed eye, tying it there with a strip from a rag. "Jack, you look piratical. Right debonair, y'are." She gave him a pat and dispatched him to bring in the used clothes he had for her, then showed us into the parlor while she dug out scraps for Beth's quilt.

If the homely character of her kitchen told much about the Widow, her parlor told more. A room I suspected to be a repository for all her "best" pieces, it was cozy and comfortable-looking, and well used. Without ever looking shabby, the furniture showed long wear, and the rugs, hand-hooked or braided, were thin in spots, testament both to the feet that had trod them and to the years of treading. I asked if she had made them.

"Beth, you'll most likely find that rocker comfortable. Kate, try the sofa. Yes, I done 'em, every last one. Keeps me busy through the winters when I'm not makin' scarecrows."

I went to the bay window, which was filled with potted plants, and looked at the neatly carpentered bench that bore beautifully carved Roman numerals from one to twelve.

"Clemmon built that bench. My clock bench, he called it." The bench was a sundial, and where the sun streamed through the window, hitting the frame, it cast a shadow. "I been tellin' time from that bench the better part of my life."

"How do you set it ahead for daylight-saving time, Widow?" asked the peddler, coming in with an armload of clothes.

"You're a fool, Jack Stump. I been here long before daylight savin's and I guess I can set my head for any such government notion." As Jack began laying out his hoard on the piano bench, I glanced at the mantel, where an old-fashioned shaving mug sat, and beside it an ivory-handled razor. Mementos of the dead Clem Fortune, I decided. His widow, meanwhile, was examining each of Jack's secondhand garments carefully, and with a smile in her eyes, but in a gruff voice, she demanded, "You don't think I'm goin' to buy any of these old rags, now, do you?"

The peddler held up a tattered coat. "Feel that material, the finest worsted. And the lining's good as new."

"*New? Horsefeathers!*"

"Practically. Needs a bit of sewing, mebbe, but you're just the one to do it."

"I wouldn't ante up a quarter for that rag, Jack Stump. What else have you?"

He displayed another jacket, then some pants, then one or two dresses. "Here, now, what's this?" she asked, ignoring them and snatching up another garment, her eyes flashing as she inspected it at arm's length.

"I knew you'd hanker for that one, Widow." Jack hopped to her side and held out the sleeves to better effect. It was an army tunic, green with age, the epaulettes on the shoulders tarnished to gray, the threads unraveled. "Got this from a woman over to Ledyardtown. Belonged to her great-uncle. Spanish-American War uniform."

"Sort o' dashing, en't it?" She turned it backward and sniffed the material. "Smells o' mothballs. And the Lord knows what else." She darted a wary look at him. "How much?"

"Well, I figure I ought to ask ten dollars—"

"Jack Stump, you're out of your mind if you think you can come into an old lady's parlor and sell her a motley coat for ten dollars."

Beth and I exchanged glances, smiling as the pair began haggling over the price, and we benefited by a lesson in good old New England trading. Well, the peddler said, she really had him; he was off on one of his territory circuits which would take him all through the northern part of the state and even over into New York; he couldn't go dragging them clothes along with him—would she give him eight for the coat? The Widow held out for five dollars for the coat, plus some dresses he had laid out, and two pairs of pants, though what she might do with those she was sure she didn't know.

The bargain was struck, and, scorning the remainder, she paid for her purchases and took them into the next room, where she dumped them in a corner. Through the doorway, I could see her hanging the tunic on a dress dummy and regarding it speculatively. "All of you, come and see," she said. "This'll make a fine scarecrow."

"Pay no attention to the higgledy-piggledy mess," she told us as we came in. "Here's where I make my scarecrows, and this is what I make 'em from," indicating a chaotic array of odd garments. "And that's what I make 'em on, my old Fairy Belle." She pointed to an ancient sewing machine, the kind with a foot treadle. "The only new thing I ever hoped for was a fancy sewing machine with an automatic bobbin, but I expect I'll sleep beside Clem before I ever stitch on one of them." She sighed over the Fairy Belle, then looked around her. "All hodgepodge. It's the same thing, year in and year out. Seems like I just get to know my scarecrows through the summer and I have to say goodbye to them."

"Goodbye?" Beth asked.

"Scarecrows don't last but the growin' year. Come Kindlin' Night they'll all be burned. That's a treat you folks have in store." When the crops were harvested, she explained, the scarecrows were collected from the fields and brought to the Common to be put on the bonfire; then the ashes were sprinkled in the fields as a token to the following year's crop.

She dug around in a large box until, with an exclamation of delight, she produced a cracked and battered cocked hat which she sat on top of the dummy where the Spanish-American tunic hung. She dragged out a pair of tall leather boots, and then a belt which she buckled around the middle of the coat. "Reg'lar warrior, en't he, Kate? Needs a sword, I expect. This here'll be someone's next-year's scarecrow, and won't that be a sight for the crows?"

She yanked another box from a corner and spread the cardboard flaps. "Why, here's what I wanted, right where I forgot I'd put it. Beth, come and look at all these scraps, what you'll want to begin your quilt." While she tugged out remnants of fabrics and examined them, I helped Jack gather up the pieces

of clothing the Widow had not taken, and we carried them out
to his cart, where he put them away.

"Now, there's a woman," he repeated, shaking his head and
wheezing. "Ain't she a woman, though?" He peered at me with
his good eye, looking, as the Widow had said, somewhat piratical.

"How's your jaw?" I asked.

"Good as new." He waggled it again and grinned; then his
brow creased as he frowned. "Skunks, that's what they are, them
Soakeses. A pack of drunken skunks. See what they drew." He
dug in his pocket and produced a message scrawled on a scrap
of soiled paper. "What's that writin' say?" I took it from him and
read aloud:

"I ain't afraid of no Soakeses, and they ain't goin' to keep me
out of no woods, neither," Jack said.

When I asked again what had happened there on the morning
of the Agnes Fair, he launched into a heated jeremiad about the
cost of his traps, the difficulty of setting them, and how it had become a job of warfare finding places to put the traps where the
Soakeses were not likely to discover them. Between his rapid
style of talking and the wheeze punctuating nearly every sentence, I had difficulty following his drift at times, but the essen-
tial facts I gathered were these:

On the morning the Widow and I had seen him go into the
woods, he had checked his traps and discovered two of them
missing. In a third was the scrawled warning to keep out of
Soakes's Lonesome. In another, he found a rabbit, which he put
in his bag; then he continued on, finding most of the traps removed from their places. In time he had wandered into a part
of the woods where he had not been before. It was there he had

discovered the Ghost of Soakes's Lonesome. Folks might think it a ghost, for it howled like one, but he hastened to assure me it was not the ghost that had frightened him.

"No ghost is goin' to get the best of Jack Stump, no sirree. I had my look and I seen my fill, and I left, and I'm walking along through those woods when them fellows pop out from behind a tree and snatch me. The old man grabs me around the throat, and another's got this shotgun and it's pointing right at my nose. Well, the boys find that hare in my pocket, and they stole it from me, and they pushed me around, and finally they let me go, but the old man grabs up that gun and sets off a blast. By that time, I'd gotten behind this ol' tree and he don't see so good, anyhow. That's when I come bustin' out of them woods, and him chasin' right after me."

And since then he'd gone back to the woods, a fact not unknown to the Soakeses—hence the Sunday altercation. Had he, I asked, come upon the "ghost" again?

"Sure I have," he boasted. "I seen it, and plenty." He pointed off, as if the woods were close at hand. "And it's a very dark and secret place—out of the way, as you might say." He waved an axe, saying he had marked the trail from where he had seen the ghost by making blaze cuts on the trees along the way. They began on a tall pine on a rocky knoll.

Just then, the Widow's face appeared at her kitchen window, and in a moment she brought Kate out into the dooryard.

"Sell me that axe, Jack," she called. "I need one." She led Kate into the hen house, and I could hear her through the doorway, explaining the facts and economics of poultry life. Jack handed me the axe, which I laid on the step. "And does the ghost still holler?"

"Sometimes it do, sometimes it don't. Sometimes it wails like a banshee, sometimes it don't make utterance." Asia Minerva was coming up the drive, and Jack, still talking, tipped his hat to her; in a moment the Widow appeared from the hen house and took her into the kitchen.

I fingered the sinister warning, trying not to smile. For all the peddler's scruffiness and talky ways, I liked him—even if he couldn't write his name.

"I'll tell you what about them Soakeses," he continued confidentially.

"What?"

"You know they's supposed to be a still in them woods?"

"Yes."

"And you know about the revenuer that come around?"

"Yes."

"The ghost is the revenuer."

"How do you figure?"

"I don't figure—I know. I seen him. They done him in, them Soakeses. They killed him. That's the ghost people talk about. But I touched it." He held up his thumb.

"There's a body?"

"Bones. The fellow's bones."

"How does he howl, then?"

Jack silenced his reply as Asia Minerva's face appeared briefly at the kitchen window. Then, "You believe me, don't you?" he asked, blinking, his watery eyes appraising me.

"Jack Stump, stop palaverin' about bones out there with my guest." The Widow's face popped up at the window and she shook a wooden spoon. She disappeared immediately, and Jack's hand tugged at my sleeve. "You believe me, sir, you believe me," he maintained stoutly, as though a lie were never to pass his stubbled lips. "Lookee, I'm off around my territory for a few weeks, but before I go I'm gonna have to have another look."

I returned the scrap of paper, which he made into a small roll, and slipped it into the red felt bag in his shirt. "The Widow's magic's good for toothache; mebbe it's good for Soakes-ache." He dropped the bag back inside his shirt, then set his feet on the bike pedals and careened the rig up the drive, narrowly missing the Hookes's El Camino as it pulled in.

Kate came out of the hen house saying she'd like to raise chickens, and we went into the kitchen together, where the Widow was decanting some concoction into a bottle for Asia Minerva.

She corked it, then snatched a piece of paper off a spindle and scribbled some directions. Asia appeared upset as she took the medicine.

"No bother, Asia," the Widow told her. "Fred'll be well in a jiffy. Come in and have some coffee." She ushered us into the front parlor which had filled considerably, the Demings having arrived, and Constable Zalmon and his wife, as well as Robert and Maggie and Beth. The conversation broke off suddenly, and I knew they had been discussing the melee with the Soakes gang. I thought I detected a look of approval from the staid Mrs. Deming, and I wondered if perhaps the fight had done something to solidify my position in the community. Even Mr. Deming smiled, and as Justin Hooke came through the front door he hurried to shake my hand like an old friend.

"Here's the Harvest Lord himself." The Widow Fortune kissed his cheek, then turned to Sophie. "And his Maiden." She offered him her own chair, while Sophie sat beside Beth, who was speaking with Robert, and I went and sat on the sofa arm. "You're right," Robert was saying, "you'd have to travel far and wide before you found a place like Cornwall Coombe." He felt in his breast pocket for a cigar, which Beth took and lighted for him the way she had seen Maggie do.

"Thank you, m'dear. You see, part of the reason is geographical, as I said. We're a small valley—an enclave, really—ringed on three sides by hills, and we sit in a larger valley. On the fourth side is the river. The old turnpike road ran close by for two centuries, but it was thirty miles east of us, and I don't think anyone who traveled it knew Cornwall Coombe was here. Thirty years ago, the parkway was put through but still no one came near the village. Railroads, sure they built one—six miles due east on the Saxony side. The nearest airport is some sixty miles away, and there still isn't more than the one road in and the one road out of Cornwall Coombe. That you, Ewan?" Robert turned his head as Mr. Deming joined our group. "I can smell that apple tobacco of yours. I was attempting to tell our new friends how we all came to get fitted into the Coombe. Perhaps you could explain better, having been here longer."

Mr. Deming puffed his pipe thoughtfully and scratched his head. "Well, I dunno. Possibly I'm correct in assuming one of the things that attracted you to our little hamlet was its quaintness, is that so?"

"Of course," Beth said. "That's its charm. It's so unspoiled."

"Unspoiled, yes. And the reason is that the march of time, so to speak, has passed us by. People think we're fighting a lost cause, but don't tell that to Fred Minerva or Will Jones. They plant when the locust leaf is the size of a small child's littlest finger, and not before. They clean out their corncribs when the moon is in the second quarter, no other. When Fred courted Asia, or Will was making sheep's eyes at Edna, it wasn't in the summer, nor did they marry in June, because that went against custom. They had to wait until winter, when the crops were in. All these things are governed by patterns that go back so far they're obscure and indefinite even to them. But they do it not knowing why they do it. And outsiders are bound to think it strange. The social unit here is not the family, it's the community. And the community is founded on corn. As the corn flourishes, so does the village."

When Mr. Deming had finished, I went into the dining room and put down my coffee cup. Leaning against the doorjamb, I fished out my sketchbook and began a surreptitious drawing of Sophie. Clearly, she had been and still was the village beauty. Her hair was long, dark blond underneath and, where the sun had touched it, soft and yellow like corn silk. Her eyes were the bright blue of a china plate, expressing a bewitching innocence, and her voice had a lilt to it that I found captivating. She seemed easy and relaxed, with an air of calm assurance about her. There was a kind of strength in her face, and the quiet simplicity of the New England goodwife of old. She had no fuss about her, no feathers, and her eyes revealed an honesty and determined cheerfulness that, as I sketched them, only occasionally seemed to betray a slight yearning. I was sure she was a good wife to Justin, a capable homemaker, and probably one day would be a good mother.

Close by, Mrs. Deming, Mrs. Zalmon, and Mrs. Minerva listened from their circle of chairs as the Widow reminisced about her dead husband.

"You still miss him, don't you, Widow," Mrs. Zalmon said.

"Ayuh. It don't do to look backward, I know, but all the same I don't suppose a day goes by but what I don't think about him. He was a good man."

Aye, Clemmon Fortune was a man worth hoeing corn for, they agreed, listening while the Widow talked about that long-ago time when she had been young and was Clem's wife.

"Oh, he had a singing voice," she said. "He could sing the day through, dear Clem could." She remembered how they used to hitch up the buggy and take the Lost Whistle Bridge 'cross river, and how he loved hearing the clop of the horse's hoofs on the planks, and how the resounding chamber of the bridge itself made his voice sound even more powerful. He'd pull up right in the middle of the bridge and serenade her, singing "Lady Light o' Love" or "Sweet Nonnie in the Willow Shade," and put his arm around her waist, romancing in her ear. Well, she said, though Clem was gone now, the covered bridge remained.

"Seems a shame to lose so many of them bridges, somehow," Mrs. Deming observed. "They give a touch to the countryside, don't they?"

"They give a touch to Soakes's Lonesome, anyways," the Widow said.

"Ah," said Mrs. Zalmon tellingly. "Did you go a-gatherin' herbs this week, Widow?"

" 'Deed I did." She flicked an eye about the room to see that her guests were enjoying themselves. "Summer gatherin' for winter ills. Good bit o' elecampane out in them woods. Except"—making an awful face—"them hog-footed Soakes boys trample a plant to pieces."

"Why don't them Soakeses keep to their own side of the river?" Mrs. Zalmon demanded.

"That Old Man Soakes is a tyrant if ever there was." Mrs. Deming tugged Mr. Deming's coat. "Ewan, the elders ought to do something about them Soakeses." She turned back to the ladies. "The way he raises them wild sons. They got no more brains than one of Irene's pigs, and stomachs to match."

"Aye, they're troublesome," the Widow said thoughtfully.

"Why, how's that, Widow?"

"To tell the time, read the clockface. You'd have laughed to see how Jack Stump come shootin' out of them trees on fair day, as though the devil himself was on his heels."

"Jack Stump was in Soakes's Lonesome?"

"Ayuh."

"Scared him, did they?"

"You never seen that cart go so fast as it did down the Old Sallow Road." Peering through her spectacles, the Widow smiled up at me. "What happened was," she pursued, "Jack went nosin' about the woods, and the Soakeses caught him snoopin' and scared him off."

"He goes trappin' in there, don't he?" Mrs. Deming asked.

"Aye. Rabbits and such."

"Well," said the Constable's wife significantly, "if I had an interest in them woods, I'd surely keep a close watch—if I was a Soakes or not."

"Pooh, them Soakeses." The Widow slipped me a wink, then changed the subject quickly to arrange an impromptu quilting party that would take place that night at Irene Tatum's. While she spoke, I observed Justin Hooke. With his yellow crop of curls and blue eyes, he could have been Sophie's brother, not her husband. Folding his ham-like hands across his front, he talked graciously with Mr. Deming, who had moved next to him, but under the farmer's easy humor I detected greater depths, a sense of a man knowing what he was about, that he had been brought up to a purpose in life, one that he found satisfying in all its respects: a destiny achieved.

Mrs. Zalmon meanwhile had drawn Kate to her and was explaining the calendar of yearly festivals celebrated in the village.

First came Planting Day, some of which Kate had briefly witnessed. Next was Spring Festival, then Midsummer's Eve, the Agnes Fair, the Days of the Seasoning, and finally the four days of Harvest Home, including the Corn Play and Kindling Night.

"What's the Corn Play?" Kate asked.

"Sakes, child, it's just a play. It comes at the huskin' bee." Mrs. Zalmon looked over to Justin. "Yonder is the Harvest Lord, Mr. Justin Hooke, and the Corn Maiden, Mistress Sophie Hooke."

"It's very old, Kate, our Corn Play," Justin said. "I guess there's been the play before there was a Cornwall Coombe, even. It was brought from the old country, and it goes back to the olden times, isn't that so, Widow?"

"What's it about?"

Justin looked to the Widow, who said, "Why, the Play tells the story of the growin' of the corn. You've never heard that story, have you, Kate? Sophie, run and bring the quilt from the chest at the foot of my bed."

As Sophie went on the errand, Maggie passed me with a tray of empty coffee cups, and I followed her into the kitchen.

"Ned—hi!" she said gaily, brushing my cheek with her lips. "I haven't had a chance to talk with you. You're drawing—let's see."

I showed her the sketch of Sophie. "Oh, Ned, it's lovely." It was not, I felt, an offhand compliment. She carefully studied the head, which in a rough, sketchy way captured something of Sophie's glowing character. Maggie rinsed the glasses and one by one set them on the drainboard. I pocketed my sketchbook and took a dishtowel.

"Ned, I don't think I've said how nice it is to have you here. It's nice for the village, of course, but I mean for us—Robert and myself." She spoke with an easy warmth, and I could not doubt her sincerity. "I hope you didn't think I was unfriendly that first day. We're not used to visitors here. But I told Robert that evening the best thing that could happen would be for you to buy that house. So you see, it's really from selfish motives

I'm saying this. We need you here, we really do." She turned off the tap and dried her hands on the other end of the dishtowel.

"Hey, isn't that bad luck?"

She laughed. *"I'm* not superstitious. There're enough others around here for that."

"Maggie, how did her husband die?" I inclined my head toward the other room.

"Clem Fortune? Oh, dear. It was a tragic thing. Of course, it happened long before we came back here—" She broke off, tidied her hair, stared out the window. "He killed himself, accidentally. With an axe. He'd gone out to Soakes's Lonesome to cut a tree, and the axe slipped. Gashed him terribly in the thigh, and he must have gotten lost in there somehow—it's easy to do— and before he found his way out again, he'd bled to death."

A figure stood in the doorway. I turned, saw the Widow. She nodded, hands clasped over her black apron. "Aye. He was like a tree, Clemmon was, and like a tree he cut himself down. Ironwood tree. Never did find out what he wanted with ironwood. Come along, if you want to see the quilt."

I glanced at Maggie, then laid down the dishtowel and followed the two women into the living room. A giant quilt was spread out on the sofa back, while the guests stood around admiring it. The Widow invited us to draw nearer, settled her spectacles on the bridge of her nose, and began describing the various personages and events that had been stitched in bright-colored pieces. "Now, Kate, here's himself, the Harvest Lord. Here's his crown, all made of cornhusks, and his red cloak." She traced the outline of the figure, immense, stalwart, strong, wearing a diadem of husks and a long bright mantle, with a colorful, short-skirted costume beneath. There was power in the figure; enormous vitality seemed to radiate from it.

By his side was a female figure, surrounded by others in the act of lifting a veil from her face. Another stood by with her crown. This was the Corn Maiden and her court. It was the Corn Maiden who, mated to the Harvest Lord, caused the corn to grow.

Standing beside Justin, Sophie listened with both gravity and dignity. She caught me watching her, and her serious expression changed into a bright smile, as if to say, *Isn't it all silly?* The Widow was pointing out other symbols: the rain which nourished the earth, the moon which told when the planting must be accomplished, the sun urging the stalks up through the soil.

She described the rest of the participants as well: the Harvest Fool, in his funny corn clothes, looking rather like a medieval jester, and the Young Lord—he who, by Missy Penrose's choice, would be played by Worthy Pettinger.

Beth asked whose hands had stitched the quilt originally, and the Widow replied that it had been made by the wife of old Gwydeon Penrose, who had founded the original settlement. Not by herself, of course: almost all the village dames had worked on it. No need to mention that this was more than three hundred years ago, and that this quilt was a copy of another, even older, which had remained in old Cornwall. Of course, in that quilt there wasn't any corn; corn hadn't been known in England till after Columbus's New World discovery. Before that it was just wheat and rye and such; but still they'd had a word, "korn," signifying the various kinds of grain.

When we had admired the workmanship again, Sophie carefully folded the quilt and bore it off to its storage place. Beth sent me for the box of scraps and soon thereafter the Widow's sociable began breaking up.

When we had made our goodbyes and thanked our hostess for her hospitality, we went along. Going down the walk, I saw a doll lying on the lawn; then, in the corn patch, a furtive movement between the rows. As we got in the car, the child Missy Penrose stepped out and snatched up the doll. Then, scraping a stick along the fence pickets, she made a noisy clatter as she went away up the street.

11

The studio had turned out fine. The skylight provided good illumination, there were shelves aplenty for my art books, storage space for my paints and brushes, racks for my canvases and larger drawing pads. Plaster casts hung on the white walls: a foot, a nose, a giant eye; above these a mask of Danton, guillotined, which I had bought in Paris years ago.

I painted for an hour, immersed in my work, until I heard Beth announcing the roast was done. I rinsed my brushes and shook them off at the sink, then washed my hands. Kate shouted up to the roof overhead, where Worthy was hammering, inviting him to eat with us. "Hey," I called to him, "there's a leak down here." I kicked a bucket under the pipe to catch the persistent drips, and as I dried my hands I noticed how the wart on my finger was shrinking. I slipped out the little red felt bag the Widow had hung around my neck a week ago, wondering what secret Cornish charm she had put into it that caused warts to disappear.

I called to Worthy to come down from the roof and went into the kitchen with Kate.

"What's the matter with Worthy, Daddy? He's been so glum lately."

"Don't know, dear. Maybe he's got problems."

"Don'tcha think he's good-looking?"

"Very."

I fingered the back of Kate's neck. "You getting a crush?"

"*Come on*, Daddy. Mommy, when can I have a date?"

"Ask your father, dear."

"Daddy?"

"I think you'd better take that up with your mother, sweetheart."

"I could go to the movies with a boy, couldn't I?"

I thought the interest in the opposite sex a healthy sign, and decided Kate was beginning to come out of her shell. "When you get asked, I'm sure your mother'll let you go to the movies."

We sat down to dinner, Beth and I at the ends of the table, Kate between us on one side, Worthy on the other. Since coming to Cornwall, we had more or less adopted the habit of the village, which was to have the main Sunday meal in the afternoon. Standing over the large platter of roast beef, I sliced off the end cut that Beth preferred, laid it on a plate, and passed it along to Kate for vegetables. "Worthy, how do you like your meat? Rare?"

"I like it well done, too."

The other end usually went to Kate; I looked at her and she said quickly, "Oh, that's good, because we like ours rare—right, Daddy?"

I served Kate, then myself, and pulled up my chair. When we had begun, I quizzed Worthy as to the condition of the studio roof. He had ripped out the section of broken slates, but said that the understructure showed no signs of dry rot; all that was needed was to replace the slates. Where, I asked, did one buy them? He thought a minute, then remembered a woman over in Saxony whose breezeway had collapsed in a snowstorm last winter. The woman had not rebuilt, and he thought possibly she might still have the used slates, which would be better than buying new ones. Her name was Mrs. O'Byrne.

The talk got around to gardening, and I informed the table of my intention to plow up the meadow next spring and plant vegetables. Worthy instantly became excited, and said he would bring his tractor around. We got into a discussion of organic gardening, and he described the kind of operation some friends of his had over in the neighboring town of Danforth. Like ourselves, they, too, had come from the city, and had pooled all their money and resources to form a commune. They had bought a defunct place which they rechristened Nonesuch Farm, and though the townsfolk called them hippies and weren't being helpful, they hoped in two years' time to put it on a paying basis.

"I'm going over there this afternoon, if you'd like to see it."

Another time, I suggested; I had plans for Beth and myself. But perhaps Kate might enjoy the ride. I signaled Beth, who had opened her mouth to protest; she quickly picked up the cue and consented.

"Back to school soon?" I asked him.

"Yes, sir."

"Are you looking forward to that?" Beth said.

"Yes, ma'am." He was in his last year of high school, and, as he had told me, hoped, against his father's wishes, to enter agricultural school next fall. He had been working hard to earn the money, and had been studying nights, "when Pa doesn't catch me." As the conversation continued, I watched him closely. His moodiness, habitual of late, seemed to have washed off at the kitchen sink, and he laughed and joked with Kate, who, seated across from him, kept plying him with various dishes. Perhaps the Widow was right, perhaps he just needed more feeding.

I asked him what the latest village news was. Not much, he replied; never any news in Cornwall Coombe. Mrs. Mayberry was ailing, wouldn't last till Harvest Home; Mrs. Thomas was going to have a baby, probably before next Tithing Day; Elsie Penrose, the librarian's daughter, was going to be courted by Corny Penrose, her second cousin on her father's side. Corny had given Elsie a cob.

"Mrs. Thomas is going to have a baby? How wonderful!" Beth exclaimed. "Why is Elsie getting a cob from Corny Penrose?"

Worthy said it was an old village custom; when a boy was interested in a girl he sent her a corn ear, and if she accepted his attentions she husked the ear and returned it; if she wasn't interested she sent it back unshucked. Sometimes a girl, if she was bold enough, would send an ear to a boy. But whatever ears might be sent, the results had to wait until the crops were in.

"Has anybody sent you a cob?" Kate asked.

"Not yet."

She looked relieved and began relating what she had learned

from the Widow's quilt concerning the Corn Play. Worthy's face darkened. "That's silly stuff."

By diligent questioning, Kate found out a little more about the choosing of the Harvest Lord and the Corn Maiden. Since the original Agnes Fair, the Harvest Lord had always been picked on that day. He would be crowned with honors the following year at Spring Festival, when the villagers would bring him presents. Then, during the next seven years, he would be given all sorts of privileges, including free communal labor to work his fields and farm. And at some point during that time, he would select a Corn Maiden to reign with him.

"Is it always a husband, who chooses his wife?" Beth asked.

No. The village had been surprised when Justin had married Sophie, then picked her for his Corn Maiden. Usually it was a single girl. When the Corn Play was given, in the Grange hall, the new Corn Maiden would be crowned.

Beth and Kate cleared the table and brought in dessert and coffee. When they were seated again, Kate asked, "Worthy, you're going to be the new Harvest Lord in the play, aren't you? Who'll you pick for Corn Maiden?"

I exchanged a look with Beth: bold as brass, our daughter. Worthy frowned and didn't answer; he wasn't interested in all that.

"Do they have square-dancing at the husking bee?"

"Sure."

"Can you square-dance?"

"Sure." But he didn't like doing it. Square-dancing was old-fashioned, for old fogeys who lived in the past. He didn't want to live in the past; he wanted to live in the here and now. His brows were drawn down in a gloomy line as he toyed with his napkin. "Mr. Deming carrying on like that at the fair. All I was doing was having some fun, but you're not supposed to bring a tractor on the Common. You're not supposed to play on the shinny pole. Old geezers like him don't think anything's funny. The minute you do different or act different, people talk. It makes you stand out, and people around here don't want to stand out."

"Do you?"

"Well, I don't want to be like everyone else. There's no point in doing things just because other people do them, is there? I think it's crazy doing them their way just because it's their way. Look at Gracie Everdeen."

"What about Gracie Everdeen?" I put down my fork and prepared to listen.

"I don't know, really. It all happened when I was small. But there's been lots of talk."

"What kind of talk?"

"They say she went crazy."

Gracie Everdeen, a product of the overly mixed bloodlines of the village? "Was she a Penrose?"

"I don't know, sir. She may have been. Almost everybody is, one way or another. She was supposed to marry a Penrose."

"She was?"

"They were engaged, then she ran off."

"But she came back, didn't she? She's buried in the cemetery—or out of it, rather. Why is that?"

"I don't know, sir."

"Who was she engaged to?"

"Roger Penrose."

Ah, Roger Penrose the bone-carver. "Did he marry someone else?"

"He died."

"How?"

"He got killed jumping his horse. A broken neck, I think. Like I say, it all happened a long time ago. Before—"

"Yes?"

He shrugged. "Before I was old enough to remember." He glanced at the clock on the wall. "Gee—it's getting late—"

"Don't you want dessert?" Beth said.

"Maybe we'd better get started," he suggested quickly and I had an idea he was trying to extricate himself from a conversation he was sorry he'd begun in the first place.

When we had seen them off for Danforth, with instructions to
be back before nine, Beth and I put the dinner dishes in the
dishwasher, then walked down the lane and through the meadow
to the river, where we found the boat Amys had mentioned.
We had brought along a blanket and a transistor radio, and Beth
tuned in some music, sitting in the stern, while I turned the
boat and began rowing upriver.

It was one of those days a happy man records for his mental
posterity. Sunday afternoon, New England, summer's end. A
dreaming landscape; faultless sky; dazzling clouds; bursting sunlight; river calm, placid, seductive in its peaceful turnings; the
splash of water, creak of oarlocks. Birds singing along the shore;
the play of light and shadow among the trees; a little music;
your wife, whom you love. What might be called the ingredients
for a perfect day.

I could tell Beth was in one of her reflective moods and I
did not try to make conversation, but only gave myself up to
the beauty of the afternoon. Along the shore, the oncoming autumn was showing itself, not outright, but secretly, in the smallest corners. There was a tang of smoke in the air, making a kind
of uneven haze that seemed to lay a golden sheen over everything
—water, trees, foliage—with the soft luminosity of a Turner painting. It was a special kind of ease and contentment that envel-
oped me as we followed the meandering course of the river for
perhaps a mile, until we came within sight of Soakes's Lonesome.
When we had got around several more bends, I saw on the opposite bank the Soakeses' jetty. Half a dozen ducks floated idly
in the water, while on the landing the old man and the boys
were hunched over some kind of activity. They looked up, eying
us briefly as we passed. I got a feeling of menace from this furtive
appraisal, and as I glanced back the old man opened his knife
and stropped the blade on his boot. Putting more force into my
strokes until we were well past them, I looked back again to
see one of them getting into the skiff.

I could hear the dull reverberation of the motor as we rounded
the next bend, and I wondered if we were to be followed or

in some way interfered with, but when the skiff appeared again it was heading for the Cornwall shore. Shortly we had the river to ourselves once more. I wiped my arm across my forehead, rested on my oars, and let the boat drift close to the bank, enjoying our solitary state.

The sun felt warm on my back and shoulders, and I stripped off my shirt, which Beth took and held in her lap. She still continued rapt in some kind of reverie, and I made no effort to disturb it. Once she looked at me with a trace of a smile; then she looked down again, watching her hand in the water. She was wearing a gold snake I had bought for her in Venice, and I saw a fish dart close to it, attracted by the bright gleam of the metal. Then Amys Penrose's flat-bottomed tub became a gondola and the river was the Grand Canal, the sky not American but Italian, and we were back in Venice, that summer seventeen years before, in 1955.

It had begun the previous winter, a bone-chilling one in Paris, where I was studying at the Sorbonne on the G.I. Bill. I picked Beth up on the grand staircase of the Louvre, under the "Winged Victory." She'd come over from London with a college chum she'd been sharing a flat with in Chelsea. I heard her reading from her catalogue: "The 'Winged Victory of Smothrace.'" *Smothrace,* for God's sake; the opportunity was too good to let pass; I stopped and pointed out her error. Yes, she knew it was *Samo*thrace, but it always came out *Smo*thrace with her. The three of us spent the afternoon together, and then, out of my mind and over my budget, I invited them to dinner.

The other girl, Mary Abbott, went back to London alone and Beth stayed with me in my loft in the Rue du Bac. *Sous les toits de Paris,* and all very romantic and my bed was a lot warmer than it had been in some time. We saw the spring in, and spent a fortune keeping the rooms filled with lilacs, which she loved, and in June I bought a secondhand car, packed up my paints, and we worked our way down to the South of France, then into Italy. We lingered for days in the Uffizi in Florence, then went on to Venice, and finally to Greece.

We spent that winter in North Africa, where a steady stream
of letters arrived for Beth, addressed in a firm, authoritative
hand. Reverend Colby, Beth's father, was demanding that she
return home. Hers was an unusual situation, and though she
was not inclined to talk about it I gradually learned enough to
put the puzzling pieces of her life into some sort of order.

She had been christened Bethany, after the town in Connecticut her mother had come from. Mrs. Colby had been rich, and
her money enabled the Reverend to enjoy a style of living not
permitted to most men of the cloth. Their house, in a suburb
of a large New England city, was expensively furnished, but
although Lawson Colby liked his creature comforts, he mentally
donned a hair shirt, forcing his wife into a strict and regimented
observance of Protestant virtues. Mrs. Colby had died of diph-
theria when Beth was only two, and from then on Beth lived
under the bitter and tyrannical eye of her father, who forced
church at her on all occasions. What he raised was not a God-
fearing child, but a God-despairing one.

After college, Beth had persuaded him to let her come to Europe with Mary Abbott, to "visit cathedrals," but now the year
was up and he demanded that she return home. I had decided
I was going to marry her, and had notions of what sort of recep-
tion this would meet with at the Reverend's Methodist hands.
Bethany Colby marrying the son of an immigrant Greek from
Jersey City—Catholic Greeks, at that. Raised in a happy home,
I could appreciate Beth's basic needs. Being motherless, she felt
rootless. She was not religious, she did not love her father. She
had never experienced any warm stream of affection as a child,
and after her mother's death the father had become a stricter
parent—harsh, even—making sure that the minister's daughter
didn't go wild. In the Puritan ethic of his Cotton Matherish
forebears, to be happy was, by extension, to be sinful, and until
we met I do not think Beth had ever been very happy. But there
was this about her: she had the characteristics of the chameleon,
which takes hue and color from its surroundings; stubborn
though she might be at times, Beth was open to influence. I

was a happy person, and by some subtle transference she, too, became happy. With me the minister's daughter went wild on the Left Bank and all the Reverend's decrees about Thrift, Work, Virtue, and the True God were tossed out the windows of our Paris loft.

It was impossible to toss the father as well, so we went home and faced the music, which at best proved discordant. The Reverend had heard tales of bohemian artists living in garrets; he did not deem me a suitable choice for a son-in-law. But by spring Beth's defiance of the old man was sufficient to elicit his agreement to our marriage if I would "settle down to some honest work."

We were married in June and moved into an apartment in Greenwich Village. I put the paintbrushes away, and found a job with Osborne & Associates. The brushes stayed put away for fifteen years.

Shortly after Kate was born, we took a larger apartment on the West Side, around the corner from Pepe's Chili Palor. Since Mrs. Pepe often baby-sat for us, we would return the favor, and it was while sitting for their daughter that I contracted the painful case of mumps that 'Cita was still apologizing for.

I swelled up, Beth nursed me, I deflated; and went back to Osborne & Associates, hating every day of it. But during those years Beth and I were happy together. I knew that partly she had married me in order to be free of Reverend Colby, and in many ways she had replaced him with me. Now, if she had no mother, she at least had two fathers. As Kate grew, Beth lavished on the child all the attention she herself had lacked. I could see what was happening from the beginning, that Kate was being smothered with a maternal blanket of the heaviest weave. When she was nine, she had her first asthmatic attack.

These began in the winter of our ninth year of marriage, when something happened to Beth, a breakdown whose origins were both deep-seated and obscure. She withdrew into another world. I thought at first she must be having an affair with some other man, but I was wrong. She came home one evening and announced that she wanted a divorce. She was going to leave and take Kate with her. No amount of reasoning on my part could sway her from this stubborn course, but a friend of ours at Columbia persuaded her to see a psychiatrist. The cause of her morbidity became quickly apparent, and I met with the doctor to learn what he had discovered. Beth had lacked a mother, which had led to a hatred of the father. I had replaced the father, and now her subconscious was transferring the hatred to me.

We got through it. She became whole again, became the Beth I had known, and we even joked about her having the nine-year itch. But there was still the problem of Kate's attacks, which no amount of medical treatment was able to help, which nothing had helped until we had come to Cornwall Coombe and the Widow Fortune.

I felt the keel of the boat strike something, and I opened my eyes. Beth was smiling at me. "We've run aground, darling."

The boat had nosed onto a sandy shoal, and I lifted an oar from the lock to push off. "No. Let's stay here a little," she suggested. I took off my shoes and socks, rolled up my trouser cuffs, and got out to pull the boat onto the shoal. I helped her ashore and we clambered onto the bank, where we spread the blanket and lay down.

The river formed a small cove, a secluded inlet screened by shadblow bushes and overhung with willow branches. It was the perfect spot, a country idyll all its own. We had left the radio in the boat and the music came as though from far away. I felt a pastoral serenity and peace that communicated itself to me through the lazy drone of the bees working the patches of meadow flowers close by, the sunlight trembling on the pool below and flickering in the leaves overhead.

In the distance, I heard the sound of gunshots, and I realized we were very likely trespassing in Old Man Soakes's preserves. One of the boys was probably after squirrels in the woods. There were several more shots; then the air became still once more. We took off our clothes and slid down the clay bank into the water and swam, then lay on the shoal to dry ourselves off. Back

on the bank, I moved the blanket even farther under cover, and
we made love in God's great outdoors.

"What do you talk about when you and the ladies get together?"

"Oh, you know—girl talk."

"Mrs. Brucie and Mrs. Green are hardly girls." We had put
our clothes on again, and were lying together on the blanket,
I with my head back against a fallen log. Beth said, "Mostly
we're talking about selling their quilts."

"Selling them?"

"Mm-hm. Remember Mary Abbott from Bennington? She's
got that shop on Lexington, and I know if she put a couple
in her window they'd sell in no time. I'm going to talk to her
about it. And there's all that carved bone jewelry, and the dolls.
There's a good market for that kind of handicraft work today.
Look at the way they sell things from down in Appalachia."

I agreed it sounded like a good idea. "What else do you talk
about?"

"Men."

"Come on."

"Don't you find the Widow fascinating?"

"Mm-hm."

"The things she knows. I don't mean just cooking and sewing,
but all that herbal business and her cures." She was playing with
the little red bag hung around my neck. "It's really working,
huh? Let me see." She inspected my wart, then kissed my finger.

I leaned to brush a leaf that had fallen on her shoulder. As
I pulled away again, she stopped me with her hand.

"Ned?"

"Mm?"

A look came over her face, one I did not immediately understand. "Would you like to have another child?"

"Us? We can't—"

She nodded eagerly. "The Widow says we might be able to.

She's got a remedy. Wouldn't you like it—a baby brother for Kate?"

"Hey—wait a minute. Not so fast. What kind of remedy?"

"I don't know. One of these elixirs she makes. She says that often it works. Mrs. Thomas has wanted a baby for the longest time, and she couldn't have one, until the Widow had her and Mr. Thomas taking something. Now she's pregnant."

"Aren't we sort of old to start the nursery business all over again—even if the Widow's elixir worked?"

"We're not exactly ready for Sun City. I'm not about to go through the change of life. Kate will be married in no time—darling, she *will.* And—"

"What?"

"I'd like to be a mother again. Once more, while there's still time. Oh Ned, I *want* it. Your child. A son."

I wasn't sure how I felt about it. I had put the idea out of my mind for so long that it felt like a completely new one. And what if the Widow failed? What if Beth's hopes were raised and we couldn't produce? And whose fault would it be? Beth with her obstetrical problems or me with my mumps? I suggested tests; let a medical man determine the case before—

No, she said. Stubborn Beth. No doctor—the Widow.

"Well," I said. "Well." I grinned, then kissed her, a tacit submission to her wishes. I guessed the spare room could become a nursery, if between us we could provide an occupant. I kissed her again, and decided we had had the perfect afternoon. When we spoke of it later, it became That Day, one I've relived many times since; and I sometimes wonder if she has too.

I decided to go that evening to Saxony and talk to Mrs. O'Byrne about the slates for the studio roof. A sirocco-like breeze had come up when I left Beth and drove out along the Old Sallow Road, and the sun was dropping behind the cornfields on my left as I headed toward the Lost Whistle Bridge. Coming over the rise, I looked down on the panorama of the Tatum farm, its barn and sheds already becoming dark shapes on the hill. Across the road lay the edge of Soakes's Lonesome, with the river winding along its farther side.

Passing the Tatum house, I noticed that the fire under Irene's soap kettle was cold. Figures were moving in the front parlor where the lighted windows cast their shadows on the porch. In the drive were several vehicles, and the Widow's little mare stood between the buggy shafts. Silently wishing the ladies a pleasant evening of quilting, I continued along past the woods. When I passed the next bend, I saw the peddler, Jack Stump, on his rig. I tooted the horn as I went by, and he waved. Glancing in the mirror, I saw him trundle the cart over the gully and pull it up among the trees.

I could feel the wind buffeting my car as I drove onto the covered bridge. There were still figures hunched over some work on the Soakeses' jetty, where the skiff was again tied up. Curious to see what they were doing, I stopped halfway across, took the binoculars from the glove compartment, and got out to look through the latticework that trussed the bridge.

Leaning on the railing between the cross-trussings, I adjusted my lenses and brought the group into close view. I recognized Old Man Soakes himself, and the boys I had fought with that morning. There were ducks in the water, and I realized they were not live ducks at all, but decoys, attached to strings. It was the manufacture of these fake birds that the Soakeses were engaged in, the father cutting canvas sections from a pattern, one of the boys sewing them together, another stuffing them with some sort of material. The one sewing was using a sailmaker's curved needle to stitch up the seam along the back.

Twenty minutes later I was in Saxony, and I stopped at a drugstore and looked up the name O'Byrne. The drug clerk gave me directions and I located the house a short distance away.

Mrs. O'Byrne was amiable and friendly, and readily disposed to sell me the slates, which were piled out behind the garage. With the wind whipping her skirts, she took me out to view the slates, and she showed me where the breezeway had collapsed between the house and the "summer kitchen," as she called the large shed that had once been connected to the main structure.

"I figured when that rooftree came down, there wasn't any point in rebuildin'." Besides, she said, she was alone, and couldn't afford any household repairs. I decided the price of slates had just gone up. But they were the proper size and color, each drilled with holes for nailing, so I bought forty of them. When I had loaded them in the car trunk, I wrote out a check for the figure she asked.

Was I, she wondered, interested in old clocks? She had a particularly fine one which she would like to sell, a genuine signed Tiffany. I said I might be interested, and she took me into the house to show it to me.

The clock was a beauty, black onyx and ormolu, with works that made a pleasant ticking sound, and a delicate chime. I offered her a hundred and twenty-five dollars and she took it.

While I wrote out a second check, Mrs. O'Byrne quizzed me about life in Cornwall Coombe: how long had we lived there; did we raise corn; was our daughter in school there; did I know an old lady over there somewheres who birthed babies—she must be passed away by now. No, I said, the Widow Fortune was very much alive. Well, Mrs. O'Byrne said, she was competition for Dr. Bonfils, who lived here in Saxony. Yes, the doctor had treated our Kate several times.

Then: "Have you come across someone named Gracie Everdeen?"

Yes; in a way, I said. Did Mrs. O'Byrne know her?

"Indeed I did. She stayed with me most of one whole summer back some years ago." She spoke with interest of the girl, whom she immediately dubbed "that poor unfortunate creature."

"She was the most melancholy thing I ever saw. She just appeared one day, right there at the door. I was canning cherries, so it must have been late June. Usually I'm able to can all season as the various things come along, but just about that time I'd boiled up a mess of corned beef. I was carrying the kettle out to dump the water between the bricks when I slipped and scalded my foot. That would have put an end to my canning that year, except here came Grace Everdeen looking for work. I told her I couldn't pay much, but she could have board, and sleep in the little attic room. That was fine with her, she said.

"So she moved her few things up to the attic and looked after the house pretty well till I could get back on my feet again. She canned the quinces when they came in, and the tomatoes, and all. She was a good worker and a neat one but, as I say, melancholy."

Mrs. O'Byrne shook her head. The wind had caught a shutter and was rapping it against the clapboards; she asked me to oblige her by securing it. When I had done so, she continued her story.

"She'd been in some trouble, and she'd run off. I took it she'd done a deal of travelin' and was gone most of two years. But now she'd come back. She had a sweetheart over in the Coombe and she wanted him, though how she expected she might have him, looking as she did, I'll never know. In any case, there was another woman."

Who, I asked, might that have been? Mrs. O'Byrne did not know. "But she cursed the pair of them, and I could hear her up in the attic crying to break your heart. Then she wrote him a letter, which she asked me to check for spelling, demanding he come and meet her. I stamped and mailed the letter for her, and by well into July—we were canning peaches, I remember— there still wa'n't any answer. Then one day it come. That evenin' she went to meet him. What happened then I got from Mrs. Lake."

"Mrs. Lake?"

"Old Mrs. Lake that lived by the bridge. She's dead nine years at Easter, and the house was pulled down. In any case. She lived close by the Lost Whistle, as they call it 'cross river. Mrs. Lake heard and saw, and when she came to visit me, if I didn't see, I heard."

Mrs. O'Byrne having heard from Mrs. Lake, now I was to hear from Mrs. O'Byrne. Roger Penrose had ridden out on his horse to the bridge, where Grace was waiting for him on the other side, but neither of them, for unknown reasons, would cross to meet the other. Roger begged Grace to return over the river, while she demanded he come to her. But the meeting was a stalemate; Roger rode away without Gracie.

They continued to rendezvous through the summer, always in the evening and always with the same result. Thwarted, Roger became angrier and angrier with Grace, while she, standing at the bridge portal, shouted wild and passionate pleas through cupped hands. It was to no avail; still the lovers did not see each other.

"Mrs. Lake said their voices echoed somethin' fierce through the bridge, and the pain of them two was somethin' terrible to hear, like wounded animals. In any case, raspberries came and went, and then we was into blueberries and damson plums, and by this time I was off my crutches, so I did up the gooseberries and currants from the fields, and that must have been September, for that's when gooseberries is ripe. One evening I decided to walk down to the bridge and have a look for myself. I left before Grace had redded up the dishes, and Mrs. Lake and I hid on her porch, with the light off, and here comes Gracie, with a scarf wrapped around her head, standing this side, while there he came ahorseback—I could hear the hoofs as he rode along the road, then cloppin' up on the approach. Then he stops and calls: 'Grace, come home!'

"Finally, he must have gotten mad beyond reason, for now over he came at a gallop. Grace tried to run, but he pulled alongside o' her and scooped her up right out o' the roadway, and carried her back across the bridge."

"Back to Cornwall?"

She sniffed. "Not likely. They went off onto the side of the road, but they was just there on the other side, for we could hear the horse whinnying in the orchard. 'Well,' I said to Mrs. Lake, 'if it come to country matters, I must give Grace her notice in the morning.'

"Then, what do you know, here comes Gracie afoot, back across the bridge, and he's riding off down the road. Her head was still wrapped in her scarf, and she was so unhappy I didn't have the heart to send her away. I brought her home and put her to bed. Next day the old lady comes."

"The Widow Fortune?"

"If that's how she's called. Rides up in a buggy, and Grace says can she use the parlor. Which I let her, even to permitting her to offer tea and such. I stayed upstairs, but I could tell the old lady was most sympathetic to Grace's situation—a kind soul, if you don't mind. Then she left."

Grace was now driven to the extremest measures. First she told Mrs. O'Byrne she would leave, then she swore she could not, then she didn't know what to do. In the end, however, she went away, never to return.

"'Twas the night of full moon, I remember that," Mrs. O'Byrne continued. "Grace went out again in the evenin', and that was the last I saw of her. She just left everything here and went. Never came back for her things, neither. Her sweetheart died, didn't he?"

I said yes, wondering how she had come by this particular piece of news. I related what I had learned from Worthy about the horse accident, and Mrs. O'Byrne's look was woeful as she opened the front door for me. "But you didn't say—is Grace there still? Does she fare well?"

"She's dead, too."

"Oh, no—you don't say! Poor thing. Still, I suppose she's better off. I wouldn't want to go through life suffering like poor Grace did."

I stowed the Tiffany clock in the trunk, along with the slates, while the wind, which had increased perceptibly, drove everything before it.

"Hurricane weather," Mrs. O'Byrne called. "Stop by again." She battled the door shut against the gale.

Driving back toward the bridge, I looked at the sky. The moon, round and white, shed a strange light over the landscape, while across its face drifted an intermittent cheesy curd, lending the white light a greenish-yellow cast. Lightning flickered bluely on the horizon, and a steady wind whipped the grass along the roadside.

The car tires beat a tattoo on the bridge planking as I crossed. Emerging from the farther end onto the Old Sallow Road, I could feel the wind take the car again. The air sizzled intermittently, as if wired with a network of faulty electrical connections. I made the turns slowly, keeping the car toward the center of the winding road as I passed the Tatum orchard. I felt melancholy, thinking back over the story of Grace Everdeen. I found it strange and sad, and a little mystifying.

The lights were still burning at Irene's house, and as I rounded the next bend, the embankment I had passed earlier was now on my left, and above me I glimpsed an edge of treetops waving wildly in the wind. On the other side of the road, the cornfields were whipped to a frenzy; the wind drove leaves and debris along the rutted track leading up to the house, scuttling them around the wheels of the parked cars and the buggy, past the soap kettle, spiraling ashes and carrying all up the steps onto the porch itself, where the parlor windows were glowing.

I slowed as the wind buffeted the car again, and a large branch broke from a tree and flew onto the road. I swerved, then stopped. Leaving the motor running, I got out and pulled the branch to the side of the road. Straightening, I heard what sounded like a cry above the sound of the wind.

As I kicked the branch into the gully, lightning flashed again, a sharp electric current of blue that turned the sky a sickly green color. Then suddenly, above me, at the top of the embankment, materializing out of the darkness, there appeared what I immediately thought must be the Ghost of Soakes's Lonesome. Ghastly, eerie, the figure was a gray ashen hue, the white garments flapping like cerements, a specter returned from the grave. I have never seen a ghost, nor do I believe that ghosts exist, but at that moment I was absolutely certain I was looking at one. It seemed to glow against the lurid sky, hovering some twelve feet above me, the body cut off by the edge of the embankment, head upraised, arms outstretched. I tried to tell myself I was imagining all this, but there it stood, a haggard, silvery shape, like some ghoul risen from the dead.

It turned on me the most terrible countenance I had ever seen. An appalling face, the flesh was as white as the clothes, except for the dark recesses of the eyes and the red, grinning mouth. It was this grin that made it seem more horrible, scarcely a smile at all, but the parody of one. A poor, painted smile, witless, demented, grim, the inane smile of a rag doll. Dark gouts of liquid erupted from the corners of the mouth while one hand—feeble, supplicating—lifted in a pitiful gesture and tore at the grin, as though to strip it away.

Then the haggard thing performed a grotesque reel, a dance of agony, twirling slowly, slowly, head once more thrown back to the night sky.

In another moment it had disappeared, vanished as though, in the tradition of ghosts, it had dematerialized. I ran and shut off the car motor, then laboriously made my way up the embankment, using rocks and projecting roots to clamber up the steep incline and onto the grassy plateau at the top.

There was nothing, only the swath of wind-whipped grass, the edge of the woods beyond, and, beyond that, darkness. I called out. No answer came, and no sign at all of the white apparition.

The clouds scraped across the face of the moon. Suddenly bright and shiny as it moved slowly toward the west, it again poured a dazzling white over the dark landscape. I thought how big and bright and shining it was, and how far away, noting its visible geography, its clearly delineated craters, mountains, deserts, seas. Again I lowered my gaze, taking one last look for that other, impossible shape I had seen. And standing there, listening to the wind, I felt sure this was no ghost, no supernatural creature, but something as real as the moon itself, real enough to have been human and alive.

12

Real enough; but had it been alive? Or was I falling under the influence of Cornish witch tales and charms? I thought of telling Beth of the strange apparition, then, remembering the old trouble, and how easily influenced she was, I decided against it. Better to let the village weave its more salutary spells, whose good effects were so clearly already at work upon her. I was persuaded that it was better to leave my tale of the Ghost of Soakes's Lonesome for another, more appropriate time.

The next day, Monday, I worked in the studio sanding the gesso panel I would use for my painting of the covered bridge. When Worthy came, I interrupted my work to help him tackle the roofing job. He was moody again today, with little to say regarding the excursion to Nonesuch Farm, other than that Kate had enjoyed it. I made no allusion to the strange event of last night, and between us we limited ourselves to the scantest of small talk until Beth called us to come in. We ate lunch from folding tables in the bacchante room so we could watch the replays of the Olympic events. Mark Spitz had captured another gold medal, and they were saying he would take an even seven and make Olympic history; I wished him the joy of all that gold.

When we had eaten, I left Worthy to complete the roofing job alone and, taking my water-color equipment, I set out for the Lost Whistle Bridge. On a sudden thought, I pulled in at the Pettinger farm to have a word with Worthy's mother and father. The place wasn't much by anybody's standards, not "all-electric" like the Hookes's, and without indoor plumbing. Like the rest of Cornwall Coombe, the Pettingers had planted corn wherever the ground might bear it. There was a well and a springhouse, a chicken run, and a barn. If Fred Minerva was jokingly referred to as the biggest hard-luck farmer in the community, Wayne Pettinger surely was the poorest. He had two other sons to help him with the work, but it quickly became evident that he begrudged the time "the boy" was giving to others, myself included.

Both of them, the mother and the father, had the tired, careworn look of the workaday farmer fighting a losing battle against the soil, and neither seemed inclined to discuss Worthy's trouble when I bearded them in the kitchen, but only sat bleakly and with unswerving gaze as they heard me out. I told them I felt that Worthy should be given a chance, that a great disservice would be done in stopping his schooling.

Mr. Pettinger was angry and adamant. The boy was full of fool notions. Theirs was a poor farm, but with seven years of Worthy's being Harvest Lord it could become a rich one. Men would come and work it for him and not charge for labor; it could be the place they'd always dreamed it might be. Honor had been conferred; but no, the boy didn't want honors, he wanted to be off with them hippies over to Danforth. Mr. Pettinger damned left and right: damned machinery, damned modern methods, damned folks who wasn't satisfied with what they had but was so greedy they had to have more. Kids today didn't know how well-off they was.

He turned to Mrs. Pettinger. "It's your fault, givin' him learnin'. There's where the trouble starts—never should've let him go to school." He clumped out to the barn, leaving me facing his wife, whose eyes were now streaming.

Clutching her red hands on the oilcloth-topped table, she confided to me that she had heard Worthy planning to run off. I replied that I thought young people should be allowed to do with their lives as they saw fit. She listened with a woebegone expression, dabbing at her eyes with her apron.

"He don't laugh no more," she said. "He was the most agreeable of all of 'em, you never seen a boy so pleasing, and so easy to please." Her smile was frail as she stared at her hands. "And he's bright, too. Not like—them." She jerked her head toward the dooryard where Worthy's brothers were shoveling manure. "Seems like he's always had his nose into everything."

But then she'd heard him, out behind the mulch heap, telling Junior Tatum how he planned to run off to Danforth if he couldn't go to college. Her heart had been sorely tried. Planning to leave the village, leave Cornwall Coombe. Had she failed? Hadn't he been raised right?

Finding the mother's grief hard to witness, I tried to speak some words of comfort, but she continued as though I weren't there.

"I tell myself, hope and custom will be my stren'th. But he's a mind of his own; he's different. And in Cornwall Coombe it don't pay to be different. You got to go by what folks say, and what they think." She rose. "And what they do," she added. I sensed that these words were for my benefit as well, as though through some instinctive kindness she did not want me to make a similar mistake.

She followed me to the door, then seized my hand impulsively and said with a passionate look, "Help him, mister, can't you?"

I spent the afternoon by the bridge, before my easel, my thoughts on the boy. Last night's hot wind still continued, and it made outdoor painting difficult, but I persevered until I had accomplished two passable water-color studies. Shortly after four o'clock, I packed up my gear, stowed it in the car, and drove back up the Old Sallow Road.

I turned the bend where I had seen the "ghost" the night before, and pulled onto the shoulder. I climbed the embankment and made a careful investigation of the terrain, noting that the grass had been trampled, which bolstered my theory that what I had seen was no supernatural being, but human.

With a backward glance at the Tatum house across the way, I crossed the patch of trodden ground and approached the edge of Soakes's Lonesome. From within its shadowy recesses came the plaintive barking of a fox. Birds overhead chirped and sang as they flitted from branch to branch. Beyond the trees I could just make out the flat blue plane of water that was the river, and heard the dull chug of the Soakeses' skiff from the farther shore. The heat of the day was gradually cooling, condensing into mists along the bank, only to be unraveled by the wind.

I moved farther into the wood, resolved to find last night's phantom or, if I could not, at least to discover the more substantial form Jack Stump had described to me. Parrot-green ferns fanned a toothy pattern in the wavering light. Beyond, the darker green was laurel and alder, with sprawling thickets of gooseberry bramble whose vicious barbs caused me to wend my way with care. Passing from glade to glade, I felt the ground give softly and noiselessly beneath my feet, a carpet of pine needles, strewn with wind-tumbled cones.

I heard a faint rush of water: a creek. I continued on till I discovered it winding among the trees, then began following the water's upstream course, stepping from hummock to hummock across pools on whose dimly reflective surfaces water creatures skittered. My feet flattened a patch of skunk cabbage, the squashed leaves emitting a faintly sour stench.

I heard the snap of a twig behind me. I whirled. Something moved in a thicket. I waited, then decided it was the fox, wary and watchful; I continued on.

Now I was deep within the woods, girdled round by leafy shade, stilled by a silence that was almost uncanny. It grew dimmer. The tree trunks were black, their malachite moss bled of color. Somewhere a woodpecker rapped; crickets sounded; occasionally I heard the goitered throb of a bullfrog.

The terrain became hilly and rocky as I proceeded into a remote arm of the woods, and I discovered a worn foot trail which I now proceeded to follow. I kept a keen eye out as I went along the trail, and it was lucky that I did so, for otherwise I might have died—as Clemmon Fortune had—lost within those woods. Certainly I would not have discovered the trap that lay waiting for me.

The trail forked, and I had slowed, wondering which of the two paths to take, when I saw it, carefully concealed, a small, unnatural-looking mound where pine needles and other debris had been sprinkled for camouflage. I halted within feet of it, my eye tracing the tail of chain links winding through the leaves, and the unsprung jaws awaiting the foot of the unwary.

Choosing the left-hand fork, I stepped carefully around the trap, and continued along. The trail made a slight turning, and some low-growing branches partially obscured my way. I half crouched, pushing aside the branches, and when I had passed them I straightened—and walked almost into the bristly face of Old Man Soakes. In one hand was a shotgun; with the other he reached out and grabbed me around the throat and spun me up against the trunk of a tree. His arm pressed against my windpipe, intent, it appeared, on choking the life out of me. Through bulging eyes, I stared back at his angry face, the lips compressed with fierce determination, bits of white spittle along the lower one, his breath coming in spurts as he exerted a deadly pressure.

Releasing his hold enough to produce his knife—the large, sharp-edged one I had seen him using on the landing—he stuck its point against the side of my neck. I turned my head, trying to avoid not so much the knife as the rotten smell of his breath. His eyes looked crazed as he demanded to know what I was doing in the woods. I tried to pull away; the knife point held me as though driven through my neck into the trunk behind. There were footsteps; he looked away for a fraction of a second. I yanked my knee up and caught him in the crotch; he let go of me, his face going bloodless as he doubled over. I placed both hands against his shoulders and shoved, then lurched away. Roy Soakes was coming at a jog along the path ahead; I spun, racing back the way I had come. As Roy charged after me, I heard the old man curse him to get out of the way so he could get a clear shot. The shot came; and another. One spanged off a trunk near my head, the second went wild. A quick look behind told me Roy was hot on my heels, and I dashed pell-mell back down the trail. When I neared the fork, I made a quick leap over the trap, then ducked down the right-hand trail, not slowing until a cry reached my ears, followed by a loud metallic sound as Roy's foot sprung the trap. I paused briefly until I heard the

old man coming behind him, spouting foul oaths at Roy's stu-
pidity, and more as he tried to release the iron jaws.

I almost felt like whistling. Having moved the trap to catch
the innocent and unsuspecting, Old Man Soakes had only snared
one of his own brood. I hurried along the trail, occasionally looking back over my shoulder as I plunged still deeper into the inner-
most reaches of Soakes's Lonesome. I looked up at the sky, trying
to find my bearings. A bird slid downward in a wide-winged
dive, and I turned first one way, then another, not knowing
where I was heading, trying to avoid the malignant tangles of
growth blocking my every path. Coils of creepers wound about
my feet, dark bramble thickets rose before me. Heedless of the
thorns tearing at my legs, I lifted my arms to protect my face
and forced my way through.

I came to another stream and crossed it, stepping from one
grassy hummock to another. My foot slipped, there was a sucking
noise as it slid into cold, thick muck. I pulled; the foot held
fast. A moldy stench arose from the mud as I bent and tried
to release myself. At last the foot came free and I raced on.

I found another trail, a narrow corridor allowing me passage;
I followed it blindly. The country was utterly unfamiliar. I could
tell only that I was on an upward climb. Ahead lay an outcropping of shale, a humped ridge of rock that sprang half buried
from the earth. I lay down, panting from my exertions, batting at
the insects swarming in a thick damp cloud around my head,
settling on my neck and throat. I tried to cover them, felt the
sticky wetness. My hand came away with blood where the old
man's knife had jabbed me.

I rested until my breath returned. Then my eye strayed to
the tree which grew, it seemed, almost from the very rock I rested
on. It was a tall pine, with an abundant growth of branches
towering some fifty feet into the air. On the trunk, as high as
a short man might reach, was a naked spot where the bark had
been cut away. I got up and went to it, putting my fingers to
the open wood, still viscous with sap.

One of Jack Stump's blazes: the tall tree on the rocky knoll.

What I had sought with purpose I had found by accident. I circled the knoll, looking for a second blaze. I discovered it below me, on the left side of the outcropping. Now I could make out the trail which wound around the knoll and back into the woods. I pushed on ahead, looking for the next blaze.

The terrain was sloping downward now; lichen-spotted boulders lay strewn along my path like fallen meteors. I could hear the gentle purl of the stream on my right. Overhead the treetops again closed above me in a vast net of wind-tossed, soughing branches; the sky grew dim.

Minutes later I was still following the hatchet marks, pushing my way through a waste of tall pines where, on either side of me, more outcroppings of rock rose in sedimentary convulutions where the earth had heaved them up in wall-like formations. Proceeding toward them, I saw a deep V between the two sections, through which the stream flowed, more placid now as it widened its course and sluiced past.

I paused again, watching the dark flow of water, listening. A bird called, another replied. Then, silence; the rush of the wind. I had the eerie sensation I was being followed, and not by my friend with the shotgun. My imagination began to work. Shadowy shapes, hostile and sinister, loomed. Again I conjured up the figure of last evening, the whitened face, the red grinning mouth, the pale, supplicating hand.

I passed through the gap, footing my way over some rocks in the stream bed, until I could reach the bank again. It was there, standing on a rock in midstream, that I heard the scream.

If it was a scream. Though I thought of it as such, it was utterly unlike any sound I had ever heard. Scream? Cry? Lament? I turned my head one way and the other, cupping my ears, trying to determine its origin. It seemed to come from several directions at once, and I decided this was caused by the shale walls rising at precipitous angles on either side of the stream to form a sort of echo chamber. Was it a moan? It seemed to float along the current of the stream, rising, then dipping, then falling away to nothing, only to return again, a terrible, inhuman sound.

I leaped from the stone onto the bank, advancing through dense growth, while the voice, if it was a voice, always increased in volume. Another few steps brought me to the edge of a wide clearing, where I froze in astonishment.

The trees bordering the clearing were not pines, but white birches, the silvery bark curled in papery spirals, revealing the tan underside. This grove of pale trunks formed a ring around the grassy open space, and in the purplish light I saw at the center of this space another stream issuing forth from a wide pool. It was not the pool that made me stare, but the tree that grew beside it, for it was from this tree, I was certain, that the cries came. It grew above the clearing like some gaunt, storm-twisted Titan, a once-lofty tree, now lifting no more than three or four dead and leafless branches toward the sky.

Again I heard the cry, and I approached, circling the tree until I was looking at it from the opposite side. From gnarled roots to blasted top, the large trunk was split open, a dark wound where a bolt of lightning had rent it apart and fire had burned its center out, leaving it hollow. A mesh of thick vines grew upward from the base, crawling along the withered trunk, sutures trying to close the gaping wound where the sides lay back like flaps of charred flesh. The wind streamed through the gap, tugging the cuffs of my wet pants, brushing at the grass, tearing at the leaves of the new growth around the tree. Then I heard the cry again, and once more I froze, for I discovered the thing that voiced it, almost hidden behind the moving greenery.

I was looking at a human skull, and it was from behind the parted jaws that the screams came.

There is always something about the slow workings of nature upon death's victim as it eats away the mortal flesh and reveals the armature beneath that is shocking to the living man, knowing that he, too, must at some time fall similar prey. But to come across a skull staring from the heart of a hollow tree screaming maledictions gives rise to a greater fear; and I was afraid. Still,

I found it impossible to run, and I remained where I stood, listening to the monstrous thing as it harried me, now screaming, now sighing demoniacally.

My eye was caught for a second by a black form floating down from the sky, a crow which silently glided to a branch of one of the birches across the clearing, watching me as the cries rose in the clearing. Then, the wind suddenly dropping, the cries dropped with it, and I realized what was happening. It was the wind itself that caused the sounds. Pouring through the gap behind, streaming across the clearing, the draft was sucked in through the open base of the tree and funneled upward through this flue to where the skull lay caught in the vise-like grip of the new growth; the sound came from the head itself, a freakish woodwind pipe whose stops were the decayed knotholes and whose horn was the gaping jaws.

I came nearer and pulled the vines aside. The skull lay slightly to one side, the rear of the brainpan wedged deeply into the open cleft and locked in place by the growing tendrils. A skull that was large and thick, with a slightly Neanderthal slope to the brow: the cheekbones were prominent, the jaw was large, and what teeth remained were unevenly spaced. A spider had spun a web across one eye socket, while slugs had trailed shiny tracks across the temple. Looking closer, I saw a long cranial fracture, running from the temple to the bridge where the nose had once been. I judged the skull to have been split by some heavy object. I tried to dislodge it, but it seemed to have been forcefully jammed into the hollow interior, which held it fast.

Below the skull, the rest of the skeleton remained intact, reclining backward as though in repose, shaping itself to the angle of the trunk itself, the encroaching vines still giving it human shape. The hands were long and large, the bones heavy and coarse-looking; the man had been slightly under average height. Kneeling, I now examined the lower extremities, which, comparably large, were held pinioned in the tangle of growth.

Again the wind; again the thing gave utterance, finding its tongue as the current swept in around my face and was pulled upward. I stepped back, one foot almost slipping into the pool of water. Making a small circle around the base of the tree, I tried to probe the secret of this grotesque discovery. In that fiercely defiant expression there was both mystery and revelation. Proof of a life snuffed out, obliterated in a moment of denial or protest. Dimly in the distance I heard the fox barking. Once, then twice more. Sly fox, wary enough to know the deceitful heart of man, to know that in these woods lurked both the hunted and the hunters.

The crow made a lonely, plaintive sound, bleak as death. I felt very alone in the clearing. I looked back at the tree again. If this was Jack's "ghost," what then was the apparition I had been confronted by last night? Yet if that being was phantom, this was not, this nameless carcass in the tree whose death had been managed in the grimmest fashion. Who beside myself had chanced on it? Were these the bones of the missing revenuer? How long had they lain here?

How many winters had sifted snow through those dead sockets, how many springs thawed the ice that rimed the jaws, summers cured the narrow ribcage, lying snug and sepulchred in its charred catacomb? Free at last of worms and scavengers, mere instrument of the capricious wind that even now rose and caught at the imprisoning vines. Again the skull sounded its doleful lament, while on its perch above, the black crow brooded over the spectacle, that victim of so sorry a plight, warning against trespass in Soakes's Lonesome.

13

During the next several days, I had little chance to dwell on my shocking discovery in Soakes's Lonesome. Nor did I discuss it with Beth, not wanting to worry her with further distressing tales of grisly woodland apparitions. Though we still rose together and breakfasted together, we usually parted company early in the morning, I to my particular pursuits, she to hers. She would drive Kate over to Greenfarms School, return to do the housework; then, when things were in order, she busied herself organizing a sort of village crafts guild whose products she had arranged to sell in Mary Abbott's New York shop. These affairs sometimes took her to the kitchen of one lady or another, and often I found our house curiously deserted. I realized that I was still accustomed to the bustle of the city, and though I pretended I was becoming used to the country, the emptiness and silence at times were disconcerting. Still, there was much to be done, and I limited myself to afternoons at my painting, first taking care of the countless chores that needed seeing to.

The windstorm having uprooted a maple in the back yard, earth had to be dug from the meadow to fill the hole, the tree sawed up. Storm windows were ordered. I talked to an insurance man down in the county seat about an appraisal on our new furnishings. I sent away for some pamphlets and literature on organic gardening. I looked at station wagons for Beth over on the turnpike. I got myself a bicycle. And I bought Kate a horse.

It was not the doctor but the Widow Fortune who sanctioned this, her discussions with Kate being as effective as her various medicines. Magically, the asthma disappeared. Though I never discovered what the old woman did to effect the cure, a miraculous one it was. And as Beth and I came to trust her, we came more to trust in our own safety and happiness.

As we trusted in the fact of the baby, and that the baby would come as promised. Our daily vitamin doses had been supplemented by a bottle of some pleasant-tasting mixture that the Widow had brought—with directions—to our house. And though we joked about taking it I could see how profoundly Beth wished for the fulfillment of her dream of a son, and how profoundly she believed in the Widow's power to make it possible. It was not misplaced belief.

Thinking back, I suppose those first weeks of early autumn in Cornwall Coombe were the happiest we had ever known together. We seemed to have undergone some subtle transformation that had drawn something to ourselves, both separately and as a family, from the land and the people, who daily were more inclined to accept us as part of their lives. And daily I would see the changes wrought in Beth. She slept better, the smudges under her eyes disappeared, and the lines in her forehead. The brisk air did something to her appetite; she ate sitting down, for a change, and started putting on weight. Her skin took on a fresher look, and I began calling her Peaches because her cheeks reminded me of one, with that same rosy glow.

Kate, too, seemed to be enjoying the beneficial effects of country life. It was a pleasure to see her able to enjoy animals, having been denied them so long. Fred Minerva had steered me to a man in a nearby town who was selling his farm and moving to the city, and had several horses for sale. The mare I ended up buying was large for Kate, but I decided she would soon grow to the proper size. The farmer had warned me that the horse was inclined to be headstrong, and when I presented her to Kate I cautioned her not to get carried away.

It was inevitable that the mare, whom Kate named Trementagne—a French word for north wind she had found somewhere that she shortened to "Tremmy"—would assume an important place in her life, but she seemed interested in sharing her love for the horse with us, and eager to show off the skills she was rapidly acquiring in Greenfarms' "equitation" classes.

Not since the Agnes Fair had she evidenced any symptoms of her tormenting illness. She was healthier and happier and never appeared in the morning with the out-of-sorts expression I used to dread. Watching her, I thought I could discern small but obvious changes in her. She was becoming a young woman. She was losing that gangling, knobby look, and, perhaps because of her association with Worthy, she seemed less shy and diffident.

A frequent visitor to our house, the Widow Fortune might stop by, usually late in the afternoon, to watch Kate ride her horse in the field below the stables, or I would hear her and Kate talking in the kitchen, and I knew she was helping Kate

allay the fears that brought on the asthma attacks. After a cup
of tea, she would take her splint basket and hurry away to nurse
old Mrs. Mayberry; then Kate would come out to the studio and
watch me paint until Beth returned home.

In the evening, the weather remaining fine, we would barbecue steaks on the terrace, often joined by Worthy Pettinger, for
whom Beth and I decided Kate was developing a strong attachment.

Viewed in the light of what occurred later, it was a fool's paradise, but I could not have known that then. Fool's paradise in
those weeks was still Heart's Desire, and it seemed nothing could
possibly happen to spoil the idyll of our new existence. Above
all, and very real, was a profound sense of belonging not only
to my family but to the villagers, to the countryside, and, though
I did not till it, to the land.

Yet while I worked about the house and at my easel, the grisly
souvenir in the hollow tree remained in my thoughts, that and
the "gray ghost," as I had come to regard that other, even more
puzzling apparition. If I failed to fathom the unfathomable, it
was perhaps not so much due to my lack of mental agility as
that I did not feel I could confide my thoughts to anyone. I
did not want to tell anyone I had been seeing ghosts, nor did
I want people saying I was a fool. Whatever I said, and to whom,
it was bound to be repeated, and I hated the thought of these
farmer people thinking I was as moon mad as they, and as superstitious.

There were, however, two with whom I was anxious to talk:
Robert Dodd and Jack Stump. Robert, with Maggie, was out
of town—visiting his university, with which he kept up considerable contact. And the peddler had not as yet finished his territory circuit, for nowhere in the village was his tin-pan clatter
to be heard, and I listened in vain.

The only other shadow darkening my existence at that period
was the boy, Worthy Pettinger. In its quiet but firm way, the
village was adamant on the subject of his "accepting the honor,"
as the phrase was couched. Worthy must and would be the

Young Lord in the Corn Play. Though he came regularly to our house after school to do chores, he was now invariably late, invariably offhand, and, when I asked him what was troubling him, invariably reticent.

It was hard to know what to do; how could we help when we didn't really know what the problem was? My own assessment was that the boy's dark distress stemmed from a reluctance to commit himself to Cornwall Coombe for a seven-year tenure as Harvest Lord—no matter what honors or wealth accrued from this—when it was his desire to be quit of village encumbrances and old-fashioned ways. Who could blame him for being "newfangled"? But if the father continued to hold to his parochial attitude, forcing him to "accept the honor," there seemed little to be done.

One noontime, having left Worthy using a chain saw on the uprooted tree, I decided to pay a visit to the Hookes. I found the sketch I had done of Sophie at the Widow's Sunday sociable, put it in a little frame I dug out of a box, and drove out to the Hooke farm.

When I got there, I left the car on the road and walked down the drive circling the house, having learned that the back door was where Cornwall Coombe folk paid weekday calls. Approaching the open Dutch door at the kitchen steps, I was greeted by a flying object, a great squawking feathered projectile, which came flying through the opening. I watched the chicken land, then, wings flapping, run off into a patch of nasturtiums. In another moment, Justin's smiling face appeared.

"Come in, come in," he said heartily, reaching to shake my hand and opening the lower half of the door for me.

"Anybody home beside the chickens?" I asked, mounting the steps.

"Tossing a hen through the door brings good luck. Sophie, look who's here." Sophie rose from the table where she had been working on some ledgers and offered me a cup of coffee. When she had moved the ledgers aside and set the cup on the table,

I presented her with my gift. She took the package and looked from me to it and back again.

"Go ahead, Sophie," Justin urged, "open it."

A little gasp escaped her lips as she undid the paper and saw the sketch under the glass. She looked at me gratefully. "Nobody ever drew me before," she said simply.

Justin came around the table to see. "Why, it's Sophie to the life." He pulled out a chair for me to sit. I put sugar in my coffee, and cream from the pitcher Sophie had brought from the refrigerator. Justin asked where she would like the sketch hung.

"In the living room, I think."

He went to find a hammer, and Sophie led me into the front room, where she picked out a spot for the drawing. "Sophie," Justin said when he had tapped in a hook and hung the sketch, "take him and show him the upstairs. When you've done, Ned, come have a look around the place. I've got to get back to the men or they'll be sitting on their hands." He clumped down the hall in his heavy boots and Sophie preceded me up the stairs.

I glimpsed a crisp white bedroom with a large four-poster bed similar to the one Beth and I slept in. Sophie took me in and showed me the crocheted counterpane her grandmother had made, pointing out the fine workmanship. "It's called popcorn stitch." The room had a serene but solid look to it, with printed curtains at the window, and at the foot of the bed a blanket chest painted with flowers to match the curtains. When I admired it, she blushed, saying she had done it herself.

"You're very talented, Sophie."

"But not like you." A thought suddenly crossed her mind, and she stepped to the window, looking down at the barnyard. A hole had been dug along a strip of lawn between the house and the cornfield, and beside it stood a young tree, ready for planting. Justin came with a shovel, bent to set in the tree. Sophie turned back and said, "Could I ask you something?"

"Sure."

"I have my egg money put aside, and I was wondering— How much would you charge to do a painting?"

"I'd love to paint you, Sophie."

"Not me. Justin. I'd like a picture to hang over the mantel while he's still Harvest Lord."

I said I thought that was a fine idea, and that I would be happy to execute the commission. "It's the first I've had." But I added that since I did not enjoy doing studio portraits, I would want to find a natural spot, revealing of his character, to pose Justin in. She grew more excited at the idea and asked when I might begin.

"Well—I've got some commitments I've got to finish up for my gallery in New York first."

Her face clouded. "How soon could you start?"

Since it seemed important to her that I paint it while the Harvest Lord was still in office—so to speak—I said I would begin some preliminary sketches as soon as possible.

She brought me back downstairs and into the kitchen again where the ledgers lay stacked on the table.

"Do you keep the books, Sophie?"

"Oh, yes. That's my part. Or *part* of my part. Someone has to keep track of where the money goes." She showed me one of the books, the neat columns of figures in her fine hand, the accounts payable, and the accounts receivable, which were apparently nil until the corn was cut.

"They'll fill up by Harvest Home," I said.

She closed the ledger and rubbed the tips of her fingers lightly over the gold stampwork on the front. "Yes," she said softly. Impulsively she reached for my hand. "We're so glad you've come to live in Cornwall. You're the first outsiders we've had, and it's going to be nice knowing you, and Beth, and your little girl." She thanked me again for the drawing and said she hoped I would stop by anytime.

"I'm often out this way," I told her. "I'm doing a painting of the bridge."

"The Lost Whistle? That should be lovely." But I saw her face cloud at the mention of the bridge, as though the place had unpleasant associations for her.

"Something wrong with the bridge?" I asked.

"N-no." She spun, looked at the table. "Gosh, I've left the cream out to spoil." She took the pitcher and held it up. It was of porcelain, shaped like a cow. The tail curled up for a handle and the cream poured out through the mouth.

"It was a wedding present. It comes from Tiffany's. In New York? It's a very fine store."

Her ingenuousness regarding Gotham jewelers made me want to smile. Still, I noticed how she had changed the subject from the Lost Whistle Bridge. I admired the pitcher, saying it reminded me of La Vache Qui Rit, the Laughing Cow cheese Beth used to buy at the deli in New York. She put the pitcher in the refrigerator and sat at the table. When I left, she had begun going over her books again.

"Don't forget," she called after me, "about the painting, I mean."

I found Justin still planting. Like me, he had lost a tree to the storm, and this one was to replace it. Laying his shovel aside, he took a box filled with ashes and sprinkled them around the balled-up roots, explaining that they made good fertilizer. He picked up his spade again and shoveled in the rest of the earth, tamping the dirt with his foot and, from time to time sighting along the narrow trunk to make sure it was straight. When the work was done, he stepped back, looking up at the bare branches.

"There's a tree for next spring. Ought to bloom just about Spring Festival time." When I asked what kind of tree it was, he said a flowering pear tree. Then, taking me by the arm, he led me on a tour of his domain, an obvious source of pride.

First he showed me the "blessing stone," a large block of quarried granite set into the foundation of the barn, with the date 1689 marking the year of its construction. The fine old boards had never been painted but through the years had aged to a beautiful patina. Painting a barn, he said, was a kind of sacrilege.

He took me to the toolshed where all the implements were also dated, giving one the sense that their makers had intended them to be passed on, so that in the distant future by these simple artifacts the past might be better understood.

We saw the pigpens, the hayloft, the stables, all with plenty of light and ventilation, and everything neat as a pin, spruce and straight and clean, with none of the slump and sag of other farms in the community. Looking over the place, I thought—jealously, perhaps—how much greater was the legacy of Cornwall Coombe than was ours, we who had lived half our lives in the city. Here, all around us, was the richness of Justin's heritage. It was plain to see that there was no master here but himself, and that he knew it; knew, too, what his forebears had bestowed.

He pushed his hat back on his head and looked at me, anxious that I should appreciate his fields for both their beauty and their worth. As I had seen him do before, he stood with feet wide planted in the soil as if, like Antaeus, he renewed his strength by contact with the earth.

Often sober-looking and grave, he showed flashes of a youthful humor that I found ingratiating. There was a delight in him, as if he could not really believe his good fortune. He was easy to like, and I was secretly pleased that Sophie wanted me to paint him. When he returned to being a plain farmer, and Worthy had taken over as Harvest Lord, he and Sophie could look at the portrait on winter nights and tell their children how it had been back then.

"It looks like a good soil for crops," I observed.

"Best around." Cornwall Coombe would see a bountiful harvest this year, he said, speaking with a reverence I had seldom beheld in a man. Corn was easy to grow; all that was needed was rich earth, plenteous rains while the kernels formed in the husks, and the long slow heat of the August nights. He asked if I'd heard the Widow tell about hearing the corn grow.

I laughed and said yes. "One of her fancies, I guess."

Justin shook his head. "It's true. You can hear it. And it's one of the best sounds in the world. Thirteen years ago, we had a Waste, and a man would have given his eyeteeth to hear the corn growing then."

"A bad time—the Widow told me about it."

"When you've seen one of those, you never forget it. A drought that leaves every stalk and leaf withered and the earth dry as dust. And if corn won't grow, nothing will. It's a terrible thing to see, bad enough when it happens to you, but worse when it happens to your neighbors, who maybe don't have as much put by as you do. They get to depend on a fellow, Fred and Will and the others." His brow contracted. "And she that brought the drought made them suffer."

"She?"

"Grace Everdeen. As big a fool as God ever put in Cornwall. She's the one who brought the last Great Waste."

"How did Grace die?"

"She killed herself. As she ought to have."

"How?"

"She threw herself off the Lost Whistle Bridge. Drowned."

Sophie's face clouding over the cream pitcher; no wonder the bridge had unhappy associations.

Changing the subject, Justin took pains to lay out for me the economics that welded the village into such a tightly knit community. The individual land titles dated as far back as the 1650s, the tracts having been portioned out by Gwydeon Penrose and the elders in accordance with the size of the family and the number of males available to farm the land. The acreage thus balanced, everyone worked it in communal fashion. Today, as then, when the corn was finally dried on the stalk, it would be harvested by hand, the ears loaded into wagons and taken over to the granary at Ledyardtown, where the wagons would be weighed with their contents, emptied, and weighed again; the farmers were paid for the difference in weight, their profits depending on the amount of land they tilled.

If the corn went to the granary, I asked, was it all husked first at the husking bee? Justin shook his head. "My fields will be the first to be harvested, and the corn from my south field will be the last to be husked. That's what goes to the Grange for the husking bee."

When I asked why this was so, he shrugged and said, "It's always been that way." He bent and pulled a weed and stuck it in the pocket of his overalls. "It's part of the rights of the Lord."

"And when Worthy becomes the Harvest Lord, then do the rights go to him?" Yes, he said. I replied that from my observations the idea seemed to have little appeal for Worthy Pettinger. Justin's brow contracted again. "He's got no choice in the matter. He's been chosen."

"By Missy."

"Chosen," he repeated stolidly. "Worthy's just got too darn many modern ideas. He doesn't know how lucky he is."

"You've been lucky."

"Sure have. I got my farm and I got Sophie and I've been Harvest Lord. Maybe that's not so much to you, but it's a lot for me."

I pictured again the first time I had seen him, the unknown giant with the hoe in the tilled field. Now, as then, he seemed the human manifestation of the growing process, the descendant of the ancient yeoman who works his land and lays by his crops, who hopes for the best and will take the worst, whose lot in life, good or bad, comes from the land.

He smiled warmly and clapped me on the shoulder. "I've got to be getting back to work. Sophie's mightily appreciative of that drawing. We both thank you."

I said I was glad it had pleased her, and told him of her plan regarding the portrait. Justin smiled. "Well, now, I don't know as I'd make much of a subject. You want me to put on a coat and tie and come sit in your studio?" I explained my method of work, that I would begin some sketches when he had the time, and that I would like to pose him somewhere here on the farm. I would paint at my portable easel, and when he wasn't available I could work at home.

Almost in spite of himself, a light had sprung into his eye. I could see he was both touched by Sophie's gesture and flattered that I would paint the portrait. He shook my hand warmly, and as I looked at his honest face it seemed I saw his honest heart.

He moved down the drive to the pear tree he had set in the ground. He took the shovel leaning against it, and for a moment his hand grasped the slender trunk. I decided then and there that this was how I would paint the farmer Justin Hooke: beside the newly planted pear tree.

I turned and started along the drive to my car, watching the long rows of drying corn as they passed my line of vision. Then something caught my eye and I stopped. At the head of one of the rows, leaning against the broken face of a rock, I saw a little figure. At first I thought it must be Missy's doll, or one like it; then I realized it was something else. I picked it up and looked at it. It was about eight inches tall and, though of the doll family, it was entirely different. For while Missy's gaga was merely a child's plaything, this clearly was something far more extraordinary. It looked like a kind of totem, a fetish of some sort, a little corn god.

In a cornfield? The idea seemed ridiculous, and I wondered if some superstitious farmer, jealous of Justin, was trying to put a country hex on him. I looked back to the barnyard where the men were still working. No one had seen me stop. Tucking the doll inside my jacket, I hurried on my way.

It had been my intention to go to the covered bridge to see whether my true impressions of it had been reflected in paint, or whether I was doing nothing better than a calendar-type reproduction. Driving out along the Old Sallow Road, however, and passing the nearer edges of Soakes's Lonesome, I came across the Widow Fortune's buggy parked on the shoulder of the road. A short distance beyond, I saw her black-clad figure making its way through the grass bordering the woods. I tooted my horn and would have passed, but she waved for me to pull over.

"Hello," I called, getting out.

"Hello yourself. Faired off nice, didn't it? How's your bridge picture?"

"Well, it's a picture of a bridge. Can't say as it's much more."

"You're gettin' awful New England in your twang."

I crossed the gully to meet her, looking into the splint basket on her arm. "What are you after today?"

"Mushrooms is up."

"Are they?"

"All over. Rain brings 'em. Come along, if you like. I'm on a reg'lar expedition."

I ran back to the car, took my keys from the ignition, and slid the little corn doll into the glove compartment and locked it. I locked the doors, then joined the Widow at the edge of the woods. Her face looked warm and moist, and I detected a note of excitement in her air as, with her usual spry step, she started off among the trees, letting me catch up as I might, she with her head down, so that her keen eye should miss no needed herb or plant.

"Elecampane's abundant this year." She bent and broke a sprig from a plant, and held it for me to sniff. "Lovely smell. But we're not lookin' for elecampane today."

"How about toadstools? Can you tell the difference?"

"No difference. Toadstool's a moniker, nothing more. Find an ugly mushroom, folks think it's something a toad might sit on. But they're all mushrooms. Trick is in knowing which from which." She proceeded along, from time to time using her spectacles like a lorgnette, for a closer study of the terrain.

"What do you do with elecampane?" I asked.

"That's what Fred Minerva's takin'."

"What other ingredients?"

She laughed and gave my shoulder a knock. "That'd be tellin', wouldn't it? It's not sal volatile—you can bet your boots."

I hadn't imagined she would give a recipe for medicine any more than she would for hoecake, unless she left one of the ingredients out. She saw a tree around whose base had grown a series of shelf-like formations, pale brown in color, and she hurried to it, knelt, and examined the growths with her hands, nodding, and muttering anxiously to herself. She rummaged in her basket, and when I asked what she was looking for, she "Drat"ted and said she'd forgotten to bring along a knife. I lent her my pen-knife, and watched as she scraped around the outer edge of several of the growths, catching the parings in her hand. These she slipped into a scrap of tinfoil paper, made a twist, and dropped it in her basket. We proceeded on again, and she stopped here and there, once to scrape some sulfur-colored lichens from the bole of a tree, another time—producing Jack Stump's hatchet from her basket—to hack up some pale roots she had unearthed under the layer of decayed leaves and humus around a strange-looking shrub. A novice in the mysteries of herb-gathering, I was fascinated by the variety of material that struck her eye. Once, when she was on her hands and knees feeling about under the pine needles, she pulled me down with her and brought my ear close. Hear, she said; listen to them, they're at work. There were sounds of minute scurryings under the needles, and she pulled them apart to show me the little beetles and worms crawling about, pale, wet, segmented, decomposing nature as fast as they could—pulverizing leaves, grass, roots, bark, branches, cones, everything—forming the new matter that would fertilize the next generation of growth in the woods.

We went on, farther into Soakes's Lonesome. When I mentioned the Soakeses, and wondered if we might be considered trespassers, the old lady cried "Faugh!"—an expletive plainly denoting her contempt for the savage 'cross-river tribe.

We walked along a path where the leaves had drifted in thick windrows, our feet making shushing sounds among them, while up in the tree branches birds sang. I was unfamiliar with this section of the woods, and I wondered in what direction lay the tall pine, with the blazed path of the grove of white birches. Once I almost started to confide in her the secret of the skeleton in the hollow tree, and of the gray ghost I had seen, but again I feared being laughed at, and most of all by her.

Suddenly, distant shotgun fire reverberated through the trees, a series of muffled detonations. "Devils," the Widow muttered.

"There's your Soakeses, over t'the river. Killin'. You a hunter? No? Good. Too many hunters."

Now she uttered a little excited cry and dashed ahead of me. When I caught up with her, she was standing beside a large tree and looking down where, close to the base, grew a ring of mushrooms that had sprung up through the ground covering. She quickly knelt and began breaking the stems at the base and handing them to me. I examined one: though it was handsome, it certainly looked like the most poisonous thing nature could provide. The cap was about four inches across, a brilliant red, with small, warty bumps on it. The surface felt sticky, and bits of pine needles had adhered. The stem was white and pulpy-feeling, and the gills on the underside were a delicate formation of pale white. I had never seen the old woman so excited; her face was flushed from her exertions as she demolished the ring little by little. Then she carefully wrapped each mushroom in a piece of tinfoil. When she had finished, she gave me her hand and I helped her to her feet.

"There," she exclaimed with pleasure, dusting her dress and handing me the basket to carry. "I knew we'd find some fly today, if we persevered."

"Fly?"

"Those," pointing to the mushrooms, "are fly agaric." They were called "fly," she explained, because they were once used to kill flies and other insects. If it would kill flies, how about humans? I asked. She laughed.

"I expect it could, you eat enough of them. Or at least they'd make a body mighty sick."

"What do you use them for?"

"A woman always thinks it takes two to keep a secret, but I'm here to say I think it takes one." She touched my arm and we proceeded back along the way we had come. At one point, we passed a spot where some more mushrooms grew; she pointed them out but scorned touching them. "Now there's some little mites that only a fool'd touch." Small and white, with dome-shaped caps, these were known as the Destroying Angel, and were deserving of their name. As for the red-topped beauties in the basket—those, she hastened to say, properly used could cure chilblains or, as in the case of Ferris Ott's father, to halt his attacks of St. Vitus' dance; Farmer Ott had had to miss church four Sundays in a row. "You and Beth are gettin' to be quite the churchgoers," she observed as we walked along. I said we were finding it pleasant, that I hadn't been to church since I was a boy, and as for Beth—

She laughed. "She told me she's a nonbeliever. Still, nonbelievers *can* become believers."

"Old dogs and new tricks?"

"Why not?"

"I think Beth believes only in what she knows for sure to be true."

The Widow had been searching about her as we went along, now stopping to peer intently around a clump of ferns, now upon the ground. "What is truth?" she demanded finally.

"That which exists."

"Many things exist. Things beyond—"

"The ken of man?"

"And others even within his ken. Depends on how broad a ken a pusson's got." She gave the word "ken" an emphasis that caused me to pay closer attention. "Here in this village, in this little place where folks seldom go beyond its boundaries, they tell themselves they understand the world and life. Coming from the city, you perhaps understand more."

"Possibly."

"But not all." Her next question startled me. "You believe in the psychics?"

"Like Missy Penrose?"

"Missy, and other—"

"Phenomena? It's possible."

"Phenomena can be realized, too. By those who—seek." Again the little snick of emphasis. "Take yourself, now. You're a man of perception. Seein's not necessarily believin'. There's many kinds of reality, y'know. Many kinds o' things." She seemed to be leading the conversation, as if making some subtle probe of my nature. "It's a matter of understandin' things that maybe seem impossible to understand."

"How?"

"By a pusson openin' himself up to the possibility." Again she shot me a look to see how I was absorbing this.

"How would a person do that?"

"There are ways."

"Would you show a person?"

The familiar twinkle behind the glasses. "What makes you think I could?"

It was my turn to shoot her a look. "I think you could."

She laughed and gave me a thump on the back. "Flattery's a poisoned gift, they say." She brushed some strands of cobweb from her skirts where her scissors usually hung. I pricked up my ears at her next words. "Still," she said in a barely audible tone, "an 'experience' might be arranged."

"How's that?"

"I said an 'experience.'"

"When?" My response was too eager, too forthright. I suddenly realized we were dealing in subtleties. Again she used her glasses lorgnette-style to peruse the ground carefully.

"Who knows?" she said at last. "A pusson mustn't go too fast. The sphinx in Egypt's been there a long time but no one's solved its riddle yet. Not even the great Napoleon. 'Course, some folks is *smarter* than others. If they was presented with a sphinx, *they* might be able to solve the riddle."

"They?"

"*They.*"

"Me?"

"Maybe." She replaced her glasses and her glance was mischievous as she picked up her skirts and went by me. "A man must learn to discover what is possible."

"Would that be the 'experience'?"

"You got too many questions." I could hear the humor in her voice. "Come along."

14

The next few days brought more intermittent rain followed by a cold snap. We turned the heat on for the first time since our occupancy, and steam clanked through the labyrinthine pipes, rattling the radiators in furious bursts of energy, but producing little heat. The thermostat, of ancient vintage, was found to be defective, and I called a heating crew from over on the turnpike, asking them to replace it with a new one. Meanwhile we used the fireplaces. These proved to be defective as well, for in each room—the living room, the bacchante room, and our bedroom—more smoke seemed to come down the flue than went up.

Clearly what was needed was Jack Stump, whom I remembered hearing brag that he was handy in the matter of chimneys. He was long overdue to have returned, and I biked down the River Road to the bait shack where he lived.

Jack Stump had never claimed the virtues of homemaker, and his poor dwelling appeared to be in the same sorry state as when he had first taken tenancy back in March, after the spring floods. I could see a watermark girdling the battened sides about halfway up, and I wondered why the shack hadn't been carried away altogether. The lawn was weeds, with cans and other debris scattered everywhere. At one side was a windowless shed where he probably stowed his rig, but the door was padlocked when I investigated. I knocked at the shack door, and got no reply. I knocked again, then called; still no reply.

I would have to tackle the chimneys myself. I turned my bike around and pedaled back up the road, pulling over to the side as a red Volkswagen came toward me from the other direction. I recognized Jim Minerva, who waved as he passed. What was he doing down on the River Road when he should be working at the grocery store? Playing hooky, maybe, and getting in a bit of fishing.

Driving back along Main Street, I saw Tamar Penrose in the doorway of the post office. She was holding a cat in her arms, and she watched me sullenly as she cradled the animal against her shoulders, her red nails running through the fur like so many red beetles.

In its unpredictable, New England way, the weather turned fine again. The following Saturday I engaged Worthy's assistance and together we went about dealing with the chimneys. We laid old sheets at the bottoms of the fireplaces, covered the mantels, then got up on the roof. Using safety ropes, we fished a heavy chain down the chimney and flailed it about, loosening the soot and unclogging the flues.

The Dodds had returned the night before, and I called down to Maggie, who was planting bulbs on her side of the hedge; after a while she brought Robert out to enjoy the sun in a lawn chair and they talked while she gardened. When Worthy and I came off the roof before lunch, we carried away the sheets and emptied them in the trash, then cleaned up at the kitchen sink. While we handed the bar of Lava soap back and forth, I reminded him of the leaking sink in the studio, which he had neglected to take care of.

We had calf's liver for lunch, and when we had eaten, Beth drove over to Mrs. Green's to pick up a quilt. I paid Worthy and sent him along, then walked down the drive to the studio. I closed the door behind me and sat, bemused, on my stool. The thing I was thinking about was in the room, but for the space of a quarter of an hour I did not look at it. Finally I went to one of the racks and took out the sketchbook I had used at the fair. I flipped through the pages until I found what I was looking for: the drawing of Missy Penrose's doll. I stared at it for some time, then, placing the pad on the drawing board, I drew a shoebox down from the top shelf, where I had hidden it. I removed the cover and placed the doll from Justin's cornfield beside the sketch and compared the two images.

Both had corncob bodies, both had huge eyes secured in the straw head, straw legs bunched together with raffia ties, and tattered bits of rag that passed for garments. The doll was just a child's doll, but the other thing—I stared down at the strange, eldritch face, again trying to comprehend its being. It was clearly meant to represent the female figure, for attached to the cob body were large protuberances passing for breasts, and its sex was clearly defined by a deep cleft between the legs.

What was it? Whose hand had fashioned it? Recalling a section in one of my reference books, I found the volume and turned to "Primitive Art," my eyes scanning the pages: a grotesque figure of a painted clay effigy vessel, possibly representing the goddess Demeter; another, a contemporary doll of the Angolese, representative of the fertility rites practiced by primitive agrarian societies; a giant basalt head found in Mexico, believed to represent Coatlicue, the great Mother Goddess, destroyer of men; an ivory doll carved by an Eskimo, the figure of a shaman or tribal priest; a Pueblo Indian kachina doll with wooden body, dressed in cloth and feathers; a Mayan stone face found in Honduras; a god of the ancient peoples of Oceania; a carved relief of a female, dug up in France, and believed to be the object of worship of the ancient Celts. All, as the accompanying text explained, manifestations in the different cultures of a similar deity, that Earth Mother who was older than Rome or Greece, older than Crete, than Babylon or Egypt; as old as the dawn of time.

I turned back to the drawing board, comparing the images again. It was the eyes, mainly. In the sketch they had a blank, almost innocent gaze, but in the figure they seemed mysterious, even malevolent. All-seeing eyes, all-knowing. Omnipotent. Whose did they remind me of? There was a cruelty in their ominous stare, implacable, remorseless. Suddenly I felt a chill. Had I tampered with something I had no right touching, some witch doll or voodoo object one of the superstitious villagers had stuck in Justin's field to cast a spell?

I whirled at the sound of footsteps. Worthy Pettinger stood hunched in the doorway, a wrench in his hand. "I forgot to fix the pipe—" He broke off and his face paled as he stared at the thing on the drawing board. "Where did you get it?"

"I found it." He stepped back as though struck. "Can you tell me what it is?"

"Where did you find it?"

"In a field."

"Where?"

"At Justin Hooke's." The wrench clattered to the floor; I picked it up. "Have you ever seen one before?"

"No. I never." A whisper as he backed away to the door. "You got to get rid of it."

"What *is* it?"

"I—don't know. Does anyone know you took it?"

"No. I don't think so." I lifted it, shook it, heard a swift intake of breath from Worthy. I put it in the box and set the lid on. "I'll burn it."

"No! You can't burn the corn—it's got to go back into the ground. Bury it." Snatching up the box, he ran from the studio. When I stepped out, I saw him taking a spade and hurrying behind the garage, the box under his arm.

He dug the hole under a clump of bushes close to the hedge separating our property from the Dodds'; he shoveled the box deep into the soft ground, covered it, and jumped on the earth with his feet. Then he scattered leaves and twigs over the spot. When he finished, he leaned on the spade handle, sweating and wiping his mouth, his eyes riveted to the newly covered hole.

I waited another moment, then spoke. "Worthy, tell me what it is."

He took a breath and seemed to recover himself. "I don't know," he said with an offhand shrug. "Just some crazy thing." He sounded sheepish. "I guess I got carried away. Well, long as it's there I suppose we can leave it. Nobody wants a crazy-looking thing like that anyways." Still he could not disguise the urgency in his voice.

I looked at him coolly. "Missy Penrose might."

"Huh?" He looked up sharply.

"She has one like it. A corn doll. You've seen it, surely."

He shrugged again. "Oh, sure, that. Lots of the kids do. 'Gagas,' they're called. Just poppets."

"You don't care for Missy much."

"Sure, she's O.K."

"Can she prophesy?"

A dark look had come over the boy's face, the blood rose to his cheeks. He fell silent, absently chopping with the tip of his spade along the edge of the flower bed closest to the hedge. His shoulders hunched, his mouth assumed a grim line.

"Worthy, I'm asking you something." Still no reply. "You don't *want* to be in the play, do you?" He waited; silence. *"Do you?"* I stepped to the boy and spun him around. "Answer me, damn it."

"No, I don't!" He spat the words hotly. "It doesn't matter any-way—I won't be here!"

"Why not?"

He yanked his shoulder from under my hand and his dark eyes flashed angrily. "Because I'm leaving. I hate this town, and I hate the people in it. They're fools, all of them."

"Why?"

"Because they think that what they think is the only way to think. They think if you plow a field you should use a mule, not a tractor. Mules are the old way, and wooden rakes are the old way, and hoes are the old way, and that's all you hear around here—the old ways. I don't want to be a corn farmer."

"Corn seems inevitable in this place."

"Not for me. Nothing to do but plant corn, nothing to talk about but harvesting corn. And their Spring Festival and their Midsummer's Eve and their husking bee." His voice rose in pitch, then broke, and when he spoke again it was with a softer tone.

"Honest, Mr. Constantine, I got to get out of here. I've got to get away."

"One-horse town?"

A trace of a smile. "Sort of. You know. A fellow gets feeling cooped up in a place like this. I never been anywhere farther than Danforth."

"Will you go there—to your friends?"

"That'd be the first place they'd look."

"Who?"

"All of them. I'm thinking of joining the navy."

"And see the world? Maybe that's a good idea."

"I been savin' my money. I got some put by, enough to tide me over. There's a fellow I know runs a pool parlor and beer bar in Hartford. I can go stay with him until I decide what to do."

"How old are you, son?"

"Sixteen."

"The navy won't take you without your parents' consent, you know. Not till you're seventeen."

"I know. They'll never give it, anyway, but I'll be seventeen soon." He lifted the shovel and stepped from the hedge, moving past me.

I stopped him. "You're right. You ought to go if it's what you want to do. It's your life, no one else's, and you can't let other people tell you what you should do. We'll miss you." I took out my wallet, extracted some bills, and held them out. Worthy shook his head.

"Go on, son, take it."

"You already paid me."

"This is just to help you along till you get things figured out." I pressed the money into his hand.

"O.K., but only till I can repay you." He folded the bills until they were a small square and tucked them in his watch pocket. "Thanks, Mr. Constantine. I'm sorry to be leaving you. You've been kind to me. Will you tell Kate goodbye?" He looked back at the buried box. "And look—"

"What?"

"Nothing."

I was sure he was going to say more, but had thought better of it. "Will you write me and let me know what you decide?"

"Sure. Would you want my tractor?"

"That's right—we were going to plow with it next spring. How much are you asking?"

"No—you can have it. It's a present."

I said I couldn't accept it, but if he thought I could manage to keep it running, I'd like to buy it; where could I send a check?

He thought a moment, then said, "Here's what I'll do. I'll write to you, and put 'John Smith' on the envelope. That way you'll know it's from me." Again he looked back at the covered hole. "Don't tell anybody," he whispered. I took the shovel and we shook hands.

"Tell your wife goodbye, too," he said, and went up the drive. One thing was clear: he was lying. Something had frightened him.

I looked down at the spot where he had buried the box; then, taking the shovel in my hands, I began digging.

When I had hung the shovel in the garage and come out, the shoebox under my arm, I heard Robert's hallo from the other side of the hedge.

"That you, Ned? Come and sit."

Turning the corner of the hedge, I found the blind man in his lawn chair, with his usual stoical attitude, as though he had learned long ago never to expect anything but what life chose to bring him. "Well, m'boy, Margaret tells me you've been up on the roof all morning. Be careful—those old shingles can be treacherous."

I pulled up another chair, explaining that all necessary precautions had been taken, and that Worthy Pettinger had done most of the dangerous work anyway.

"Handy fellow, Worthy," Robert said ruminatively. "Good-looking boy, too, they tell me. Got the old Cornish blood in him."

"I thought the Cornish were fair. He looks more like an Indian."

"In England it's generally held that the so-called 'black Irish' were sired by those Spaniards who made it to shore when the Armada was sunk, but anyone who knows their apples will tell you it's not the Spanish who blackened the Cornish hair, but men from a civilization far older than that. I'm speaking of the sailors from Knossos, in Crete, long before Caesar's legions were even settling in England."

"And Missy," I asked pointedly. "Is she of the Cornish strain, too?"

"Her mother is, that we know. As to the father—that would be anybody's guess."

"Is it true she can prophesy?"

Before Robert could reply, Maggie appeared with a carriage robe which she tucked around his knees, laughing at his protests at being coddled. "Just pretend you're on shipboard, darling."

"What time do we get to Le Havre?" He smoothed the cover over his knees while Maggie knelt close by with her gardening things. "What have you fellows been talking about?" she asked, digging in some large new bulbs.

"Ned was asking about Missy's predictions."

Maggie laughed again. "Ned, you've got to get used to the country notions around here."

"I don't think you can toss them off as notions," Robert argued. "Certainly there are people who appear to be endowed with special powers. Cassandra foretold the downfall of Troy. Montezuma's priests were able to predict ahead of time the coming of the white man to the New World. Modern psychical research recognizes precognition as possible. People get portents of disaster all the time, and they're often confirmed."

"Maybe Missy just makes lucky guesses," I put in.

"Maybe. But because of her freckles the villagers believe she had communication with the god. Not our Christian God, mind you, but the god that was worshiped in the olden times, as the Widow calls them. In those days, they believed men had the power of divination which stemmed from their knowledge of the stars."

"And Missy's stars are written on her face."

Maggie placed a bulb in the hole and covered it over. "You see, Ned—country notions."

"What you have to remember," Robert continued, "is that human nature doesn't change much. You can't negate the ingrained imagination of a whole culture. When they came from Cornwall to the New World, the original settlers were a deeply religious sect. What did they find when they got here? Cold, illness, the constant fear of attack; they were foodless and homeless. They were forced to adapt to circumstances, to learn new ways in order to survive. But in learning the new they refused to give up the old, a faith based on the moon and the stars and the tides, and on ancient deities they could turn to for succor in this time of stress. During the first year the village was settled, there was a good harvest, which the Indians had shown them how to grow, and they had food."

But then, he went on, had come what was still remembered as the Great Waste, the famine where the corn shriveled up and died, and the Cornish settlers felt the cold hand of fear at their throats, and they raised themselves up and prayed for help, not in church but in the fields, inviting the blessings of the old gods, those who had come with the dark-haired Cretan sailors. And the gods answered them, for the land was blessed with crops in the fields and fruit in the orchards.

"But it's all vestigial," Maggie hastened to point out. "Like the Spring Festival and the bonfire."

"Country notions, yes," Robert replied. "You'll find evidence, though, that when the Christian priests tore down the pagan temples, the people made them leave the trees that grew around the temples. And, more importantly, the priests couldn't destroy the thinking that impelled the building of the temples in the first place."

"What would Mr. Buxley do if he found something like this in Justin Hooke's corn patch?" I took the lid from the shoebox and brought out the doll.

Maggie, about to set in another bulb, laid it down with her trowel. "What on earth—?" She reached and took the doll from me. "What a strange-looking thing." She turned it over in her hands, examining it. Then she placed it in Robert's hands and let him feel it, describing its form to him in all its details. When Robert had done, she stood it up on the ground among her iris cuttings and bulbs and pronounced it a most unhandsome thing.

"It's really quite awful-looking, Robert."

"Is it?"

"What do you suppose it means?" I ventured. "Do they believe in hex around here?"

"Hex is Pennsylvania Dutch, isn't it?" Maggie said. "I never heard of any hex in Cornwall, did you, Robert?"

"No. I don't believe so."

"Where did you find it, Ned?"

"In Justin's cornfield."

I watched Robert closely, seeking some visible expression behind his dark glasses. It was impossible to see beyond them. He drummed his fingers thoughtfully on the arms of his chair. From the corner of my eye I saw Maggie collecting her gardening things, dropping the iris cuttings and bulbs into her basket. She rose, dusting her knees. "I'm going to leave you men to sort it all out. It's too much for me."

"What *would* Mr. Buxley do?" I asked Robert again when she had taken her basket and gone.

He shrugged. "I suppose he'd look the other way, just as the Catholic Church does. The church and the law have learned it's a lost cause trying to censure such beliefs. How can you hope to fight them, when it's proved that the old Cornishmen arrived here with the same gods the Indians already had?"

"But—vestigial, you say?"

"Margaret's word, but I suppose it suffices. All these things are the traces of the older culture. Who knows why Fred Minerva will let his barn burn before he'll put up lightning rods? Or why the Widow can cure things the doctor can't? Or how Missy can tell the future?

"Justin traces his lineage back in an unbroken line to the earliest families in Cornwall. Now, those forebears of his were—

as Cornishmen are—deeply religious. They believed in one way for countless years, and then the priests came and renamed all the streams and wells and glens, and tore down the temples and built churches and gave them Christ on a cross. They accepted all this for more than a thousand years. But all the time, they were feeling some nameless longing inside. What do they do? They hark back to the olden times, where they find a source of comfort that even they can't comprehend, a fever that cools the fever, a mask that hides the mask.

"Superstitious? Oh, yes, Justin's superstitious. It's in his blood, his bones, his very nature. In his father's, and in his grandfather's. Because he believes that come hell or high water, bad crops or plague, what's going to save him is that inner voice that he listens to. His or Missy Penrose's, no matter which. That's why they still have fires and dancing on the Common." He put his hands on the arm of his chair to lift himself. "No, no, I can do it. Come in and have a drink? No? Come over again, it's always good to have company."

He went across the lawn as if he had eyes to tell him the way, and when he got to the back door Maggie came and opened it, holding it for him while he entered. "Thank you, Margaret," he said, going in. I waved, but she appeared not to have seen me, and I turned to go home.

15

When I reached the corner of the hedge, I heard the sound of hoofbeats along the road, and saw Kate coming down the lane astride Tremmy. She sat the horse well for the length of time she had been riding, though it briefly occurred to me that she was coming at too fast a pace. When she reined up beside me, her face was flushed and excited with the elation of being on horseback.

Remembering the former owner's warning, I told her to be careful not to give the animal so much head. She leaned from the saddle and smoothed the mane over the ridge of the chestnut neck muscles. "She's just high-spirited, Daddy. Watch!"

She flicked the reins, spun the mare, and rode her in circles around me as I stood in the middle of the road.

"Fine, sweetheart. But I think Tremmy's had enough for one day, and so have you. Cool her off now, and give her her dinner. Don't forget to rub her down," I called as I went in the back door.

In the bacchante room, I discovered ladies come to call.

"Behold your seraglio," said the Widow Fortune, looking up from her sewing. Her horse, she said, had a stony hock today, so she had come shanks' mare with Mrs. Zalmon and Mrs. Green to bring us a gift, a little wooden keg of honey mead. She pointed to the dusty vessel on the piecrust table, saying she had not wiped it off, since she wanted me to see how old it was. I made myself a Scotch-and-soda and sat in my club chair. Kate came in with a can of polish and began using it on her boots.

"Kate," the Widow said, "you sit that horse like a reg'lar hussar."

"I want a new saddle for her, only I'll have to wait until next year."

"How's that?"

"Haven't the money. I have to save out of my allowance."

"Chickens," the Widow announced. "You ought to go into business and raise chickens." She gave me a look. "You put up some wire and stakes and build the child a chicken run. When the chickens get tired of laying, you can always eat 'em. Beth, you promised me that recipe for chicken and crabmeat."

"I'll copy it out before you go."

"What's for dinner?" Kate asked.

"Steaks and salad."

Kate made a face. "I'd rather have chili."

"*Chili?*" the Widow said.

Beth laughed. "Kate's favorite thing in the world is Pepe Gonzalez's chili."

"You come to me for dinner one night, Kate, and let me fix you a nice clam chowder, and you're bound to change your mind."

"Clams is all spoiled over to Boston," Mrs. Green said.

"No." The Widow was shocked.

Mrs. Zalmon said, "There's poison in the water makes 'em go bad. People are dyin' of it."

The Widow shook her head. "Not content to ruin the land, now they must poison the sea. Think of that. No clams."

"And oysters," Mrs. Green put in. "Imagine. Today folks eat oysters whether the month's got an 'R' or not. Things certainly have changed since I was a girl!"

"Cozy room, Ned," the Widow observed, looking around. "Be nice for winter evenin's."

Mrs. Green made a mock shiver. "Ooh—winter, and so soon."

"Aye, soon. People claim a New England winter's hard, and I s'pose it is for them what's soft. But I like to feel all tucked in by a blanket of snow come Thanksgivin'. And they say when winter comes, spring can't be far behind. The shadblow will pop before you know it, and it'll be Plantin' Day again. There'll be Spring Festival, and dancin' on the green."

"The maypoles," Mrs. Green said.

"Maybe Worthy'll be takin' Kate to the maypoles." The Widow gave her a bright look.

"Kate, darling," Beth suggested, "why don't you clean your boots in the kitchen?" Kate took her boots and polish away, mourning Pepe Gonzalez's chili.

Suddenly a gust of wind blew down the chimney, scattering the ashes from the fire I had made to test the cleaned-out flue.

"Oh, dear . . ." Mrs. Green looked doubtfully at Mrs. Zalmon. The Widow glanced up behind her spectacles, then borrowed Beth's shears to snip a thread.

"An omen, for sure," Mrs. Zalmon said in a hushed tone.

Beth used the fireplace brush to tidy up the hearth. "Well, we can't say the chimney isn't drawing."

I said I hoped so; Worthy and I had worked like dogs.

"I told you he was a good worker," the Widow said with some satisfaction.

"What do you suppose can be the matter with Worthy?" Beth said. "I never saw such a change in a boy."

Mrs. Zalmon replied, "Some young people want too much from life. More than they're meant to have. Worthy don't know how lucky a boy he is. To have been chosen the Young Lord is an honor most boys wouldn't sneeze at. Look at Justin. See the fine farm he's made, the finest in the Coombe. Worthy could do a lot for his family by settin' his mind in the village ways and not wantin' to be a revolutionary. Ought to thank the Lord he's been chosen, Worthy ought."

"How was the Harvest Lord chosen before Missy's time?" I asked.

Mrs. Zalmon explained. "It was done by vote of the ladies. Everyone met in the church the afternoon of Agnes Fair and dropped a ballot in the collection box." Then, Mrs. Green continued, the most votes won. But when Missy came along and it was discovered she had the power, it was decided this year to give up the voting and let her make the choice.

"Still and all," Mrs. Zalmon put in, "that's not to say Missy done the best, choosin' Worthy."

"What will happen if he isn't in the play?" I asked.

"Not in the play?" The Widow gave a sharp look. "He'll be in the play, will he, nill he. People expect it of him."

"People don't always do what people expect of them," I ventured. "Maybe he's got other plans."

Mrs. Green sniffed. "He can't have other plans. Boys must do their duty, same as men. That's the way it's always been. Isn't that so?"

"Maybe." The Widow was thoughtful. "Clem always thought so. But then he was a most unusual man."

"Clemmon's gone to glory," Mrs. Zalmon said. The Widow nodded, and bit the end of her thread off.

"Aye, gone to glory," she repeated softly. "Where, God willin', I'll follow afore long."

"Afore long? Never think it, Widow!" exclaimed Mrs. Green.

"One day soon I'll be gone." She sighed. "Then who'll there be to pass it all on? Who'll there be to tell the young? Young folks is so diff'rent today than when we was girls. Still, there's Tamar—"

"Pshaw, Tamar." Mrs. Zalmon was indignant. "Tamar take *your* place?"

"Tamar's hoydenish, no doubt," the old lady said mildly, "but she's got character and strength. She's of the earth, Tamar is. Maybe she's not so spiritual as we might hope for, but she's apt. If a pusson could talk to her—bring her 'round, so to speak—"

"She'd be a sight better than the bad one," Mrs. Green agreed.

"Who was Grace Everdeen?" I suddenly asked.

The Widow looked up blankly. "Who was Grace Everdeen?" she repeated, looking not at me but at some invisible point between us. She thought for several moments. "Why, Grace Everdeen was old Bess Everdeen's girl. Gracie Everdeen." She repeated the name slowly, as though she had neither spoken nor heard it in a long time. Mrs. Zalmon frowned behind her glasses. I knew I hadn't chosen a pleasant topic, but still I pursued it.

"But who was she? Why did she run away?"

"She was a wicked girl," Mrs. Zalmon said firmly.

"The local Jezebel?" I remembered the comments after Mr. Buxley's Sunday sermon about the jade of Samaria.

"In the Biblical sense." Mrs. Zalmon's needle paused in the air. "Grace was worse than any Jezebel. You could see the evil workin' in her. Look how she changed. Took all those foolish notions, carried on as she did, shinnyin' up the flagpole."

"And if that wa'n't bad enough," Mrs. Green put in.

"Ayuh. Rasslin' Roger to the ground at Agnes Fair."

"In front of the whole village, mind you," Mrs. Green said indignantly. "Shamin' the Harvest Lord. Oh, she'd changed all right."

"I could see it in her face. I could see the badness eatin' at her.

I knew she was lost long before the rest did. I saw her face all pinchin' up, saw her eyes changin'. Look what come about the night of Harvest Home."

"What happened then?" I asked.

"Mrs. Zee . . ." the Widow cautioned.

"She was a disruptive influence. At her worst she come, and—"

"Goodnight nurse, Mrs. Zee . . . !"

"Was a disruptive influence!"

From the village we heard the sound of bells. All talk and activity among the women stopped suddenly. Mrs. Green looked at the Tiffany clock on the shelf. "That's not the six o'clock ringin'—"

The Widow laid aside her quilting. "It's Mrs. Mayberry, passed over."

Mrs. Zalmon glanced nervously at the fireplace. "Wind in the chimney. I knew it was an omen."

The Widow removed her spectacles and pinched the bridge of her nose to ease it. "Aye. She's passed, bless her heart. I done all I could, and Jim Buxley come to be there at the last. We must say a prayer tonight for her repose."

Shaking their heads over the departed Mrs. Mayberry, the two other ladies said they'd better be going along. The Widow Fortune lingered for another cup of tea, and while Beth went to do something in the kitchen I took a sketch pad from my case and settled back in the club chair. On the small piecrust table beside it I kept a number of my bamboo pens, one of which I took out and sharpened with my penknife. Uncapping a bottle of ink, I began sketching the old lady as she bent over her quilting. From the unconscious pursings of her mouth and the slight lift of her brows, I could tell she knew what I was doing.

"What sort o' pen is that?" she asked after I had been working for some moments. I held it up for her, showing her the hollow bamboo tube. "The Japanese use them," I explained.

"Wily folk, the Japanese." She glanced at my drawing hand. "How's your wart?"

"About gone." I produced the little red bag from inside my shirt and dangled it. "Wily folk, the New Englanders."

"Here, put that away. Don't go showin' it to the neighbors."

I dropped the bag back inside my shirt and we continued working, she on her sofa, I in my chair. When I had finished the sketch, the Widow asked to see it, and I held it up for her.

"Sakes," she said, taking it and looking at it thoughtfully. "It's to the life. The old lady and her sewin'."

I tore off the page, rolled it up, and presented it to her. She accepted it with a nod and tucked it in her piece-bag. She took the bamboo pen from me and held it to the light, sighting through the hollow tube, then pressing the tip against her palm, as though in wonderment that a drawing could come from such an instrument. She patted my hand. "It's the hand, of course, not the pen. It's a tough row to hoe, art—en't that so?"

"Art's hard, they say."

She lightly touched her fingers to my chest. "Art's power, and it comes from there. In the heart."

"Can I see you home?"

"No need. No tramp's going to snatch an old lady. Not *this* old lady, anyways." She called goodbye to Beth, then shouted up the stairs to Kate, who came to the top step and waved. While the Widow gathered up the rest of her things, I stifled a yawn. "Too much art. I've got to get to bed early."

She had gone back in the bacchante room for her piece-bag, and as she returned, she paused, her hand resting briefly on the little wooden cask. Her expression was enigmatic as she crossed the hall, and I opened the front door for her. "But not *too* early to bed," she said. She went down the steps and turned again, her glasses twinkling. She bobbed her head once, then went down the walk and turned up the lane.

I made a fire in the barbecue while Kate helped Beth carry out the dinner things. We were to dine on the terrace, on the wrought-iron glass-topped table that Beth was particularly fond of. We sat on the iron chairs with the white duck cushions, and there was the smell of autumn leaves in the air. While the steaks broiled we had the salad, and as Kate prattled on about her ambition to raise chickens I looked at Beth over the ironstone tureen. She wore her hair, as usual, in one long sweep, and she'd put on a touch of lipstick. I don't know if it was merely the long late light, but she looked particularly beautiful. She had on blue jeans and a simple oxford button-down shirt, a marvelous shade of saffron, the color that monks wear in Tibet. I suddenly realized I had begun seeing her in a new light, that in some way she was undergoing subtle changes. She was still the chameleon, taking on the hues and attitudes of those around her, but a different quality had crept into her character, one of purpose and strong-mindedness. She seemed a more distinct personality, as if she were discovering things about herself. She seemed less my wife and more a woman in her own right, more self-reliant and independent. I felt I was looking at her in the round, so to speak, as one views a statue, from all sides, not merely a bas-relief with the figure partially imprisoned in the stone.

"Worthy left the lawnmower out again," she said. I mentioned nothing of the earlier scene with the boy, and kept my counsel regarding his proposed departure from Cornwall Coombe.

"Oh, nuts," she said, "I forgot to give the Widow that recipe." While Kate carried away the tureen and brought out the baked potatoes and succotash, I took the steaks from the fire and forked them onto the platter. "Wouldn't you know we'd be having steaks," Beth said. "I've only got three; otherwise I could have invited her to stay for dinner."

"The Widow?"

"Mm."

As we ate, the sun slowly receded, and the golden light turned purple, then blue, then gradually black. Stars appeared like tiny lights being flicked on. A 747 went over noiselessly, its wings catching the last of the sun, glittering metallically. I lighted the candle in the hurricane lamp. A ragged moon had come up from the east, lopsided and bulbous, spreading a luminous silvery film over the tops of the waving cornfields beyond the meadow.

Kate had draped her linen napkin over her head, and suddenly she leaped up, pushing her chair back and doing a madly antic dance out onto the lawn and back.

"Moon madness! I'm a victim of moon madness!" she cried, popping behind the trunk of the beech tree, then out again. "Boo! I'm the Ghost of Soakes's Lonesome." Beth got her to quiet down, and she came back and sat again, still playing with her napkin.

"I saw him," I said after a moment's consideration.

"Who?"

"The ghost."

"Aw, Daddy, come on."

"It's true, sweetheart."

"Ned."

"Well, I did. Believe it or not."

"You saw the Ghost of Soakes's Lonesome?"

I nodded, sliding my plate away and leaning back in my chair. The time seemed so right for it, the ill-shapen moon, the quietude—a good night for a ghost story. I recited the details of my encounter with the gray figure on the embankment, building it up in pitch and fervor, making it all misterioso—the strangely twirling figure, the flapping garments, the red, grinning mouth. I made no mention of the bones in the hollow tree, thinking that that part was too real and grisly for even a ghost-story session. Kate was enthralled; her father, who spoke only Truth, had actually seen a ghost.

After I finished my strange recital, she and Beth cleared the things from the table, leaving the hurricane lamp, and I moved into one of the larger, more comfortable terrace chairs. I could hear their voices inside, talking as they rinsed the plates and put them in the dishwasher. The refrigerator door opened and closed several times; then Beth asked Kate to copy out the chicken-and-crab recipe and take it over to the Widow's. Maggie called through the sun-porch window beyond the hedge and she and Beth exchanged a few words. Presently I heard the Invisible Voice relating more Dickensian adventures. The dishwasher went on, and the garbage disposal, distinct but muted. When Beth came out with the coffee things on a tray, I went in and brought out the little cask from the table and two glasses from the cupboard. The cask was a beautifully made thing, carefully coopered, and bound with iron hoops at either end; a small wooden peg served as a stopper. I broached it tentatively, then drew it out. Tipping the opening to a glass, I poured out some of the liquid, moving the glass so the sides became coated. It was extremely viscid, with a soft yellow color. I sniffed; it had a pleasant aroma, rather like oranges or some other citrus fruit. The taste was sweetish, but with the tang of a cordial. I filled the other glass half full, handed it to Beth, then finished filling my own. She tried some with the tip of her tongue and pronounced it good, and we alternated sips of it with the coffee.

"What's Robert reading these days?" she asked.

"I think it's *A Tale of Two Cities*. I keep hearing 'Carton,' and 'guillotine.'"

We finished our coffee, then continued sipping the Widow's mead and enjoying the evening. The yellow bird in the locust tree at the front of the house made muted chirruping sounds, and I thought with what constancy it clung to its nest. Inside the kitchen, the dishwasher clicked, signaling the end of its various phases of mechanical ablutions. From all directions came night sounds, those serene and tranquil noises that have a lulling and most satisfactory effect on the senses. As we sat drinking and talking quietly, a breeze sprang up, carrying the gray barbecue smoke off across the lawn, rustling the leaves of the beech tree. The leaves had continued to fall in profusion, and even as I watched, here and there a current of air dislodged them from the branches and wafted them away.

"Have to rake tomorrow."

"Mm. Worthy can do it, can't he?"

I didn't say anything. Beth pointed up at the sky. "Look—a shooting star." I caught the faint silver parabola as it swished a small arc through the sky. It seemed vaguely unreal, impossible for something to travel so far, so quickly.

"Make a wish," Beth said.

"I did." I watched her light a cigarette. "Did you?"

"Yes."

"What?"

"If I tell, it won't come true." She blew out a stream of smoke. "It couldn't anyway. It's impossible."

"Nothing is."

"I wished Mother were here."

"Your mother?"

"I wished she could have seen us. Seen Kate. Seen our house. All of it." She was sitting only a short distance away; I put out my hand for hers, and she took it and bridged the gap. I felt the reassuring pressure of her fingers on the back of my hand.

"What did you wish?" she said.

"I wished for a straight nose."

"I love your nose."

Next door, the arm was lifted from the record, and the Invisible Voice fell silent. I waited for the sound of the window being closed, but it must have remained open, for I did not hear it. The sky was ablaze with stars, and as I gazed up at them they seemed unnaturally bright, as though on this night they had somehow come closer to the earth. I picked out the constellations I recognized, the Big and Little Dippers, and the North Star, and, low over the cornfield, Mars glowing red and warlike. I wondered where Orion might be, with Betelgeuse and Rigel; then I thought of the prophetic child, the freckles across the bridge of her nose, the red pointing finger.

I lifted the cask again and poured from it into the glasses, first Beth's, then mine. I was experiencing a marvelous feeling of relaxation and contentment, and I was fully conscious of the night, of our being together, of this corner of our small domain. I did not speak, but continued enjoying what I sensed was some fleeting moment of comprehension. I felt supersentient—and supersensual. I felt I had never loved Beth more than I did at this moment, had never felt so close, so near to her, not merely touching her hand, but completely and utterly joined to her. How extraordinary she was, my wife. How extraordinary her being. I had a supremely clear sense of who I was, who she was, who we were together. We continued sitting in silence, and I was noticing how the bark of the beech tree seemed to stand out with remarkable clarity when I heard the sound of music. I thought immediately that Robert had put another record on, and was about to make some remark about his selection of what sounded to me like a flute solo, when I realized the sound was coming in the other direction, from the cornfield below the meadow. It rose on the breeze above the sounds of the crickets and peepers, a light roulade of notes, silvery and melodious, faint at first, then taking on a definite form and melody. There was magic in the sound, a kind of mysterious, siren strain gratifying to the ear, alluring and enticing with the plaintive quality of the shepherds' pipes we had heard in the hills of Greece.

I glanced at Beth; she sat with her eyes closed, enjoying but not questioning it. There was something absolutely and completely pagan about the proliferation of notes, not wild, but primitive. It was sinuous and serpentine, winding itself through the air and breeze, seductively mixing with the sough of the leaves and the grass, the rustle of corn leaves. It was strange. It was magical. It was, I suddenly realized, an experience—the kind of experience, perhaps, that the Widow had hinted at.

Sounds were added. I could detect a second flute, coming from another part of the field. There was the faint tympanic flutter of a tambourine with its fluted disks, and a delicate bell-like chime that made me think of the finger bells of Balinese dancers. A delightful, musical tinkle, whose charm rose in support of the winding flute. We were hearing the pipes of Pan, and at any moment across our lawn would troop horned and goat-legged creatures in the moonlight, satyrs at a wine festival. I tried to comprehend what was happening. This was no impromptu village concert, but a testament of some kind. Then I thought of the honey drink, the cask of mead. It was drugged. Sitting on my terrace, my wife beside me, I felt as if I were being transported, and if this was so, I was utterly willing for it to happen. If it was an experience, I willingly gave myself up to it, tried to open myself to it, as the old lady had suggested; tried to become part of it.

Then, as mysteriously, as magically as it had begun, it ended. The tremolo of the flutes intoned a last strain, then died; there was a brief tintinnabular clink of the tambourine, and a final sound, one I did not recognize, as if some sort of instrument of bones were being used, a tiny subsequence of clicking noises; then all became still again. I breathed deeply, and very softly, not to upset the delicate equilibrium that had balanced within me. I stole a look at Beth. At some time during the playing, our hands had parted, and hers had gone to her breast where it lay, pale and immobile, the fingers curled at the base of her throat. I waited for some movement, some kind of recognition, but she remained immobile, eyes closed, the trace of a smile on her lips, child-like. Was she asleep? Had she heard? Or had I imagined it? I looked up at her as she rose.

"Did—"

Leaning, she laid her fingertips across my lips. I glimpsed her eyes bright in the moonlight before the sweep of her hair fell across them; I knew the answer. I had not imagined it. I stood, moving close and putting my arms around her. She was still holding her glass, and she lifted it and drained off the contents. I watched the slender column of pale throat as the liquid went down, and I could taste the liquor on her lips as I kissed them. Never had she felt more desirable, never had I wanted her more. Yet, and I realized this fully, it was not merely desire, the loin lust we often joked about, but a profound, deep-seated craving to continue the experience on another, on a physical level.

"Let's go to bed," I whispered hoarsely. She made a little acquiescent sound in my ear, then stepped away from me, pressing me back in the chair.

"No?" I asked.

"Yes. In a little while. Come to me. I want to see to Kate, and then—"

"Mn?"

"I want to—be ready." I saw the line of dark lashes as she

dropped them. Getting ready was one of the little bits of modesty about her. She went away softly, as though not to break the spell. I picked up my glass again, and drank. I knew now why the cask had been brought, and why the Widow had cautioned not too early for bed. I knew tonight was meant to have a special significance, to evoke a particular awareness in Beth and myself, both separately and jointly.

And it was not over; I was certain there was to be more to the 'experience.'

The night seemed to expand around me, to encompass and envelop me. The deeper colors of the chrysanthemums grew richer, more vibrant in the moonlight, like the colors in old tapestries. The coppery sheen of the beech leaves became brighter, hammered from precious metals. The sky pulsed and throbbed, evoking a low, touchable canopy, bejeweled, lighted by a globe I could at will reach up and extinguish. I was feeling a rush of intensity I did not understand, but did not care to; to have it was enough. I was aware; I was at one with my surroundings, with sky and earth and light and sound, with trees, flowers, corn, with all of nature.

Then it began, the rest of it.

I saw a figure. I did not move even a fraction as it appeared. I was right; the music had not been the end of it. It was a male figure, and I supposed it had come out of the cornfield, for it waited just at the edge, in a dark strip of soil between the meadow and the beginning of the corn. It stood enormously erect, wearing some kind of garments, though I could not perceive what they might be. I say the figure was enormous, for so it seemed, larger than any human I had ever seen. It took first one step, then another, and came into the full light of the moon.

It might have been a spirit of vegetation—I remember that the idiot trademark of the Jolly Green Giant immediately crossed my mind. Yet there was nothing humorous about it. It was deadly serious, earnest, real. In all its vividness and aliveness, it stood there, the embodiment of vigor and of growing; not demoniacal, but a benign spirit. Now I saw that the arms and legs were sheathed in tied-on bunches of straw, while the torso and lower quarters were girdled in corn leaves. A tight-fitting helmet-shaped cap of leaves covered the head, and the face itself was hidden behind a large straw mask. The expression formed by the angled eye slits, and that of the mouth, was again one of benevolence, the slightly vacant yet obtrusively concentrated expression of ancient Greek sculpture, a look at once bland yet enigmatic: the unknowable. The figure took the classic stance of *contrapposto*, the forward leg engaged, shoulders and hips in opposition. Thus it stood, nothing more—for the moment.

It was the figure from the corn quilt, of course. The Harvest Lord; but not a representation or facsimile. He brought his arms up very slowly, a gesture I found both equivocal and absolute: a wide, encompassing movement, as though within the curve of his arms lay revelation. With arms outstretched, he bowed, acknowledging me—a somewhat theatrical bow, I thought. I told myself it must be Justin Hooke, yet I was not sure. I looked for a glimpse of golden hair at the back of the neck, but could see none. He straightened again, and lowered one arm. With the other hand he made dumb gestures, pantomiming a flow of words from behind the mask. Then he turned slightly and another gesture indicated the raising of a curtain or drapery, behind which lay the cornfield, which he now indicated in a single wide sweeping arc. Then the arm came down, and he turned to his right.

My attention was drawn to where he looked, and I now saw another figure some distance away along the edge of the field. I had not seen this one appear, either; it was simply there. A female figure, hidden from top to toe under some sort of luminous veil. She remained immobile under the silvery shroud, facing me, then turned toward the male figure. I waited, wondering if they would approach each other simultaneously or if one would go to the other. Then I saw it was the woman who waited, the man who went, advancing to her slowly, ceremoniously, and simply. When he had got to within three or four feet of her, he lay down, couching himself in the short grass, one knee up, resting on one locked arm. For a moment neither moved; then the woman's pale draperies parted and an arm appeared. In a slow gesture it revealed itself, the hand supple, graceful, the fingers relaxed, slightly bent, the forefinger extended. She leaned her shoulders slightly forward, and now the man raised his free arm and, with his pointing finger, awaited her touch. The space between the two fingers grew smaller, and as they closed I saw a quick flash, a single white sputter of light that leaped between them. It was the Sistine Chapel, Michelangelo's awakening of Adam, the divine spark given from Jehovah. But that was a fresco, this was real. The kinetic gift of the vital life force. The man got to his feet, bowed to the woman, to me, then returned to where he had originally appeared. I turned my eyes back to the figure under the veil. Her hand and arm had been withdrawn beneath the draperies again, the disguise assumed again.

Who was she? Who was she *meant* to be?

I had thought at first it must be the Corn Maiden. But, observing her, I realized she had come in a form different from what I expected, something other than what I had seen in the quilt. I sensed it was not she but someone else, someone whose identity I was supposed to guess. The sphinx. In her very being lay the conundrum. Tell me who I am, she seemed to say. She remained motionless for a period, as if giving me time to make my guess; then she lifted her hands outward from her sides, and they met slowly over her head, raising the veil as the covered fingers touched above. I was both shocked and excited as I realized that under the veil she was completely naked, and I could see the gleam of her thighs, pale and marmoreal in the moonlight, with the dark, mysterious cleft between.

I thought she must remove the veil. I thought she must invite me, make some gesture, some signal that I was to come to her, to take the place of the other figure, but when the hem of the drapery had lifted almost to the waist, it immediately dropped again. I rose and took a step forward, revealing myself. I looked to the place where the man had been standing, but he had disappeared. Then the woman figure inclined her head beneath the veil, posed for an instant, turned, and stepped from the grass onto the strip of dark earth, into the shadows of the cornstalks, then into the corn itself.

She was gone.

I ran partway down the lawn, then stopped. I was not meant to follow. Something had been revealed to me, not only the woman's charms, but also some deeper, metaphysical equation I could not solve. Watching the field, I heard the dry bone sound I had heard earlier, followed by a short flute passage, brief but effective, like the final coda in the Strauss *Till Eulenspiegel.* A beguiling strain, yet somehow mocking, as though the whole thing had been a game, some little divertissement for an autumn evening.

All was silence. I turned and went back up the lawn to the terrace. I found the peg for the cask, fitted it in, picked up the glasses, and carried them and the keg into the house. I rinsed out the glasses and set them in the rack. I let the cold water run on my hand; the flow had an incredible feeling to it. I turned off the tap and put the cask on the topmost shelf of one of the cupboards. I locked the kitchen door, switched off the lights, went through the hall, checked that the front door was locked, and went upstairs. I stopped and listened at Kate's door, then opened it softly. She was asleep. I closed it again, and crossed the hall to our bedroom. The door was ajar. I went in to find Beth in the rocking chair by the window. Her hand was raised in what appeared to be a gesture, and at first I thought she was motioning to someone; then I saw she was only reaching for the tassel of the shade. She drew it down, and her hand dropped into her lap. She spoke softly, calling me darling, and rose to extinguish the only light, the small one on the bureau. She disrobed and got onto the bed, which she had turned down. She was waiting for me.

The moonlight streamed through the front windows, enough to undress by. I was careful with my clothes, folding them and placing them on the chair, my shoes beneath, and when I turned again Beth drew a little breath as I went to her, and I thought of a bride on her wedding night, waiting to submit to the demands of her spouse. But when I took her it was no virgin I took, but a woman, versed and capable, as accomplished a lover as any man could hope for. We were together as we had never been before, not even in the days of the Rue du Bac in Paris, a meeting of two people that was not only physical but spiritual as well, and if ever we knew one another, it was on that night when we had drunk from the Widow Fortune's little wooden cask and the flutes had played.

Afterward, while Beth slept, I rose again and went into the bathroom. From the window over the radiator, I could look down onto the terrace, the lawn, the meadow, and the cornfield, all moon-flooded, and it seemed that I could see one of the figures standing there again, where it had stood before. Not the woman; the man—a dark shape, forming the figure of straw and corn, waiting. For what? I told myself that now I was really imagining, but I have since thought differently. *Was* it he, truly, the Harvest Lord?

I looked a moment longer, trying to make out the figure, and then it was gone. If it had returned at all. Or if it had ever been there. Getting back into bed, settling myself under the sheet, my head on the pillow, my arm around Beth's shoulders, I pictured again the mysterious figure of the woman. Who was she? Or, rather, who was she *meant* to be? I recalled the Widow's words about the riddle of the sphinx; now I had been provided with my own riddle to solve. I remember that the last thing I thought of were the old lady's words: *A man must learn to discover what is possible.*

Then I fell into a dreamless sleep.

PART THREE

TITHING
DAY

16

One afternoon the following week I could hear the church clock striking five as I cleaned my brushes and palette and put my paints away. Then I rode my bike into the village to send off to my New York gallery some Polaroid prints of the bridge painting. I went into the post office, where Myrtil Clapp, the postmistress's assistant, sold me a stamp. Attaching it, I saw the postmistress herself, making tea from a singing kettle on a hot plate set on some file cabinets at the rear. Beyond, in the back room, I could see Constable Zalmon, feet propped up on his desk, smoking his corncob pipe and thumbing through a copy of *Field and Stream*.

Tamar Penrose glanced up from her tea things and gave me one of her smoky looks. I lifted a hand in a brief salute, dropped the envelope into the slot, and went out.

I checked my watch against the steeple clock, noting the spasmodic activity around the Common as I crossed it. Mrs. Green went into the library with an armload of books. Jim Minerva loaded groceries into the back seat of his Volkswagen and drove off, heading south along Main Street. A farm wagon creaked by, Will Jones seated in it with the reins drooping between his hands. He pulled up outside the Rocking Horse and went in. With tinkling bells, the sheep baaed and moved from my path as I headed for the church on the opposite side.

Some of the younger village girls were going up the steps, and through the open vestibule doors I could hear the soft lilt of organ music from inside. Coming up onto the sidewalk, I saw Mrs. Buxley hurrying from the beauty parlor; Margie Perkin had been at her hair. She dithered her fingers as she hastened to greet me.

"*Lovely* day," she said, as though she herself had fashioned it. And how was I, how were Beth and Kate, and how were my *lovely* paintings? Inside, choir practice began, and the bell-like sounds of the girls' sopranos and altos floated out through the doors.

"*Lovely* sound, isn't it? Our young girls are rehearsing for Tithing Day. You'll be coming, surely."

I said I hadn't heard about Tithing Day, and she explained that next Sunday would be a special service when the village offered their token corn tithes to the church. An impressive ceremony; we were certain to find it rewarding.

"See you in church." She dithered her fingers again and went into the vestibule. Amys Penrose came along, pushing his broom at the edge of the roadway, stopping when he got abreast of me to touch a finger to his hat brim. I waved to the Widow, whose buggy went creaking by on the far side of the Common. I had not seen her to talk to since the "experience," the weekend before, and I was anxious to hear what she would have to say about the epiphany of the Harvest Lord and the unknown lady. With rattling wheels and rusty springs, the mare clip-clopping along the dusty roadway, she, too, headed south. In a moment, Kate came riding her horse out of the north end of Main Street; she went flying onto the Common where the terrified sheep moved from her path in a huddled, woolly mass. I called to her not to disturb them; she waved and rode on.

"What's this Tithing Day Mrs. Buxley's been telling me of?" I asked Amys.

"More nonsense," came the succinct reply. He spat, his customary mark of disapproval. He wiped his mouth on his faded sleeve. "Could use a beer. I'm spittin' cotton."

I could take a hint. I offered to join him at the Rocking Horse for a drink, and, leaving the pile of leaves he had swept up in the roadway, he shouldered his broom and we went along to the tavern. The room was crowded, smoke layered the air, and there was the agreeable hum of voices as the locals gathered in groups and exchanged the end-of-the-day news; behind the bar, Bert was busy filling orders. We pushed our way through to find a place in the corner at the end of the bar. I let Amys order his beer, then asked for my usual Scotch-and-soda.

Will Jones leaned against the center of the bar, talking to Fred Minerva, Ferris Ott, and several others. They nodded at me when I lifted my glass to them. As Harvest Home drew nearer, there was a feeling of camaraderie among the farmers, and from all sides news was furnished, items for discussion. Item: Old Mrs. Mayberry had died. Item: Mrs. Oates, the undertaker's wife, had given birth to a boy. The village population was thus rebalanced. Item: What was Worthy Pettinger acting so all-fired cranky for these days: didn't he know when he was well-off? Fred Minerva just wished his Jim could've got a crack at being Harvest Lord. Item: Justin Hooke's rooster. Item: The weather. If it snowed before the second Wednesday in November, it would be a hard winter. Item: The hard winter of fourteen years ago. Item: The bad one. Item: The last Great Waste.

These topics variously reached our ears as I downed my drink and Amys his beer. When we had finished, I asked Bert for two more, then signaled him to pour a round for Fred, Will, Ferris, and the rest. They all thanked me, and when they had emptied their glasses they trooped out, Ferris Ott discussing with Fred Minerva the bad luck he'd had all year.

I turned back to Amys and contemplated him for a minute, then leaned toward him, adopting a careless tone but choosing my words carefully. "Tell me, Amys, how long have you been ringing the bell?"

"Eight ropes, maybe nine. That's the length of time it'll take to wear a rope out. Maybe six, seven years a rope, dependin' on how many's born, how many dies."

"When you ring, is there a difference—I mean for a man and a woman?"

"Sure. For a man you got to ring three times two, for a woman it's three times three." He took a long swig of beer, savoring it as it went down. "Hey, Bert, gimme some o' them nuts you got back there."

"Three times three?" I leaned closer. "Is that the way you rang for Gracie Everdeen?"

"Hell, no," he replied in a hoarse whisper. "No bell was never rung for her. I'd've done it if they'd let me, but they wouldn't. Not *them*. No bell tolled for Gracie. Not thrice times thrice, not thrice times nothin'. I rang her into the world, but there was none to ring her out." He rolled a cigarette and lighted it. "Oh, Gracie Everdeen." He blew out a raspy stream of smoke, then, dirge-like, returned to the topic of the lost Gracie.

"The Coombe never bred a finer beauty than Grace was. Nor a sweeter one. Sweet and delicate she was, a reg'lar pony. There wasn't a fellow in the village didn't hanker for her. She grew up tall, but slim, and pretty as a man could hope to see." He pressed my arm to convince me of the truth of his words. "I mean, she was *pretty*. It was nip and tuck who was gonter win her."

"Roger Penrose?"

"Ayuh. 'Twas the end of nip and tuck then. Roger'd been goin' with Tamar Penrose, who was one of them blamed Penrose cousins. Durin' that time, the ladies voted and the honor come to Roger—he was poor enough, but they balloted and chose him for Harvest Lord. Tamar was mighty proud, thinkin' Roger was bound to ask her for the Corn Lady. But he didn't. One year went by, then two, and still hadn't asked her. Hadn't asked any girl. Now Gracie's bloomin' like a flower, and—did I say was pretty? —I did and she was. Lemme think a minute. Roger's Harvest Lord, and there's pretty Gracie. He takes her for a ride in the Widow Fortune's buggy, and when they come back, Gracie's been asked. Everyone thought that was fine, 'ceptin' for Tamar, who's got her nose out of joint, bein' left out—Tamar's a sulky creature.

But there's Gracie, just—just radiatin'. Now—where was I? Yes. Roger's Harvest Lord, Gracie's Corn Maiden. Roger's got two years or so to go. The Widow's educatin' Gracie in her duties. Anyone who talks about her's got only the best things to say. Oh, wasn't she lovely, light and delicate as air—yes, she was. Well, sir, next thing you know, Roger's give her a ring."

"Engagement?"

"So to speak. He couldn't afford no fancy job. Then the banns was posted and read out. It's not often a Harvest Lord'll marry his Corn Lady—'ceptin' like Justin and Sophie, which come as somethin' of a shock. But Roger's decided on little Gracie. Then Mrs. Everdeen puts her foot down, and revokes the banns. Says Gracie's got to give Roger back his ring. Then, after a while, Gracie starts actin' funny. Long about the time she quit the fields and put on shoes, she just seemed to go haywire. Did all sorts of crazy things."

I motioned Bert for another beer. "Like what?"

Amys blew his nose and wiped his eyes. "Well, she stopped combin' her hair, for one thing. Took to wearin' the same dress day in day out. Sassed the Widow. Hitched her fanny at the pastor. At Midsummer's Eve, she slipped a whole pie under Mrs. Buxley's rear end just afore Mrs. Buxley sat down. Rolled her eyes at one of them Soakes boys. Roger was plenty mad. Everyone was. 'Cept me; I just felt sorry for her. None of this happened right off, mind you—'twas more gradual-like. One Spring Festival, she fought with the boys in the street. Right out there where you put down them Soakeses, she took on Ferris Ott and laid him in the dust. Then when Roger bought his horse—"

"The one he broke his neck on?"

"Ayuh. She challenged Roger to a race, and she won. Now, nobody could beat Roger's horse—but Grace did. Folks said she stole some of the Widow's herbs and put it in the horse's oats. Roger was so mad he says to Gracie to give his ring back. Then she disgraced the whole village—or so *they* think."

"How so?" I sipped my drink. Amys dragged on his cigarette, blew out the smoke, swigged his beer.

"Well, sir, you can see it, surely. She'd become a terror. Bare-footed, wild hair, screamin' and yellin', puttin' her nose up, swearin'. Folks were angry. She was the Corn Maiden. Roger'd given her the honor and she didn't seem to care. There wasn't nothin' she wouldn't do to shock folks or make them think ill of her. Then come Agnes Fair, and that was the end. Roger was bound to win the pole-shinny, but Grace denied him the pleas-ure. She loses him the wrestlin', too. Next, she has words with Ewan Demin', and then she's gone."

"She left."

"Ayuh."

"Where'd she go?"

He shook his head, drank, wiped his chin. "Nobody knows. Left on Agnes Fair day and didn't come back until almost two years later. But it was too late. Roger said if Grace was goin' to act that way, Tamar could be Corn Maiden, and come the play, Tamar was crowned in her place. But what most folks didn't know, Gracie'd returned the spring before. It was like she couldn't stay away. The winter after she left was a hard one. Snow on the Common five feet deep, people tunneling out to feed the livestock. I lost four of my sheep that year. There was a thaw, then a flood, then spring was behind the barn. And with it come Gracie Everdeen. And, wherever she'd been, she come back sad and sorrowful, and you can bet me, the heart in her poor bosom was cleave in two."

There was something in the simple country way he put his words together that painted a picture for me. I could see the fallow fields, the drab sky, the melting snow, and the tempestu-ous, strange creature that was Gracie Everdeen, victim of un-bridled passions, spurning the mother who broke her heart, the lover who betrayed her. "But she didn't come back to the village that spring, did she?" I was remembering Mrs. O'Byrne's part of the story.

"No, sir, she didn't. She was stayin' over t' Saxony, but she wouldn't cross the river. Wouldn't come over the Lost Whistle for hide nor hair."

"Why not?"

He ducked his head briefly, and faltered in his story. Then, regaining himself, "Who knows? Womenfolk do peculiar things sometimes. Roger Penrose heard she was over there, and he rode out and begged her to come home. Time after time, but she wouldn't."

"Why wouldn't Roger cross the bridge?"

"Wasn't supposed to. It's the rule. In the seventh year the Harvest Lord's not to go beyond the village boundaries. Same for the Corn Maiden. But Grace, on her side, she'd never set foot to the bridge. And Roger'd never go to her."

"But he did, finally." I told him what I had learned from Mrs. O'Byrne about the night Roger had galloped across the river and carried her to the Cornwall side, and that Mrs. O'Byrne had wanted to fire Gracie for immorality.

Amys stared at me, speechless, then spat again. "'Tain't true! Roger never touched her that night!"

"How do you know?"

"I—" He stopped uncertainly, glanced quickly at Bert, the bartender, then hollered for more nuts. When Bert had gone to the far end of the bar, Amys continued in a hoarse whisper, "Roger never laid a finger to her. The Harvest Lord can't have relations with no girl before Harvest Home. It's against the ways. Anyhow, Roger met her just before the Corn Play. That was poor Gracie's last chance. He rode back and Tamar was crowned in her place. Next day, the day before Kindlin' Night, when they burn the scarecrows, the Widow Fortune buggies over to talk to Gracie. She come back without her, too. So Tamar goes to Harvest Home."

"To do what?"

"Hell, son, don't ask me all these questions. I'm tryin' to tell you. Roger goes to Harvest Home as the Lord, and Tamar goes as his Maiden."

"Goes where?"

"To the woods. To Soakes's Lonesome."

"Harvest Home is celebrated in the woods?"

"The seventh one is, always. But then, Gracie comes too."

"And was a disruptive influence."

"Who says?"

"The ladies. Mrs. Green, Mrs. Zalmon—"

"Damn old biddies. If she was, the Lord God he knows."

"Then what happened?"

"Two days later, Irene Tatum finds her poor body in the river. Thrown herself off the Lost Whistle. I heard, and I went to toll thrice times thrice. But Mr. Deming comes and says I can't. He tells me to dig a hole."

"Outside the cemetery."

"Mr. Buxley—he says he can't read service for a suicide, and here come all the elders carryin' a pine box, with Gracie inside, and they set it in the hole; then Mr. Deming in his black suit tells me to fill it in, and they go away. Not a soul there for the funeral. Mrs. Everdeen packs up and leaves town for the shame, and there's the end of it."

"You buried her?"

He turned his head quickly and used the spittoon again. After a moment he said, "Buried her beyond the fence, where you see her stone. Where she lies without, in disgrace, and Roger lies within, in honor. And *herself* runs the post office and makes fast and loose with anything in pants." He clutched my sleeve and spoke fiercely. "Don't you listen to folks. Gracie was a fine girl. And a beauty, don't you forget. Pretty as spring, a reg'lar fairy, that was Grace."

Bert came and collected the glasses, obliterating with his rag the wet rings left on the bar.

Amys tottered off his stool, a sad, forlorn look on his wrinkled face. "Listen to me, sir. I loved Grace, and I never forgot her, even though *they*'d like to. Sometimes when I ring thrice times thrice, like when Mrs. Mayberry died, I tell Gracie that's for her."

He touched his hat brim, thanked me for letting him wet his whistle, and took up his broom and left.

I finished my drink, trying to piece together the threads of his story of the unfortunate Gracie Everdeen, and chalked it up to a case of unrequited love.

When I approached the church again, Amys was tolling six o'clock. Above the bronzy notes of the bell, the voices of the choir sounded, floating out through the vestibule door and hanging soft in the air. The sun was dropping behind the post office, and long shadows had crept across the Common, making the circles on the grass more pronounced.

I took a few moments to step into the church and sit in one of the pews, looking up at the choir loft over the doors, where the girls held their sheets of music in pairs and sang the lovely melody. Maggie was at the organ, watching in the little mirror over the keyboard as Mrs. Buxley conducted the voices, while, in the upper corner of the loft, the Widow Fortune sat leaning her head on her hand, lost in some private reverie.

The song ended, and the church was perfectly still for a moment. Then the girls moved from their places, gathering around the old lady as she spoke to them, praising them for their singing. When I went up the aisle, I glimpsed Mr. Buxley seated at a table in the vestry, writing in a ledger. I stopped for a word, and he explained he was entering the date of old Mrs. Mayberry's death. He brought down another, showing me the entry of her birth sixty-seven years before; then he returned both ledgers to the shelf. Each volume was dated by year, a whole history of village births and marriages and deaths, the three important events of a man's life, no matter where he may live.

I complimented him on the music I had heard; he said yes, it would pass very nicely for Tithing Day.

I walked along Main Street, looking at the houses with their neat gardens and fences, their windows, some with as many as eighteen panes of glass apiece, the handsome Colonial doorways. The kinds of houses I had never known in the city.

Passing Tamar Penrose's place, I saw the child Missy perched on the limb of an apple tree, playing with her doll while some chickens pecked in the dirt below. She lifted her head and stared at me as I walked by. Suddenly I thought of the other doll, the one from the cornfield, and was shocked to realize I didn't know what had become of it. As I tried to recollect the circumstances, I heard her give a little cry. She had caught her dress getting out of the tree, and when she tried to free it she lost her hold and tumbled to the ground. I ran back and opened the gate. She lay at the base of the tree looking stunned. I knelt and lifted her head and asked if she was all right. She stared at me; then her two hands came up and pressed her temples, as though to relieve the pain.

She was wearing a strange-looking cap of knitted wool, pulled down around her ears as though it were the dead of winter. Her dress had grass stains on it, her shoes were muddy.

"Hello," I said.

She regarded me emptily; then a look of recognition floated into her washed-out eyes.

"Missy, do you remember me?"

"Mnmm—mean, um—paint—"

"That's right. I'm a painter. Do you remember at Agnes Fair, what happened with the sheep?"

She shook her head.

"You pointed at me, remember?"

Another shake. She was staring at a chicken that was scratching in the dirt around the tree.

"Did someone tell you to point at me?"

A shrug.

"Did someone tell you to pick the Harvest Lord? Or did you pick him because you like Worthy Pettinger?"

Another shrug. She was watching the chicken's bright little eyes with her dim ones.

I tried again. "When people ask you questions and you tell them things, are they just things you make up?"

She giggled, then spoke. "Sometimes." Still she eyed the chicken. "Mnmm—um—sometimes not," she added thickly, sucking air through her mouth.

"When they're not, who makes them up? Where do they come from?"

"I don't know."

"You hear things? Things that someone says to you? Like a voice?"

"Sometimes. Sometimes I don't hear, I just see." Still staring at the chicken, she got up and started across the lawn to the porch. She stopped and gave me a quick look. I stepped toward her. She took another step. She seemed to be luring me to her. When I moved, she moved; when I stopped, she stopped, waiting until I moved again. She got to the steps and ran up, then spun around on the porch. When she saw I was coming up the steps, she threw herself in the porch swing and dug a loop of string from her pocket. She looked first at the place beside her, then at me. I sat on the faded canvas cushion and she set the swing in motion.

The rusty chains creaked. She looped the string over each hand, made a cat's cradle pattern, and held it up for me to take. I inserted my fingertips and lifted it, producing a new pattern. She gave me a sly look, took the string, and made another. Her look challenged me as she waited for me to make the next move. I dipped my fingers into the maze and lifted it. The pattern slid, altered, held.

"Mnm—" she murmured, staring at it.

Again I tried. "Is it a game you play? Like cat's cradle?"

"No game."

"What kind of things do you see?"

"Mnm—it's like looking through glasses," she said, suddenly speaking distinctly. "Sometimes red, sometimes blue, or maybe black, and then everything's colored black, and that's the way it looks. . . . When I see it like it's supposed to look, that's when they tell me what to say. Sometimes there's fire and lightning. Um—and music."

"Music?"

She thought a moment, a faint burrish humming issuing from her lips. "Like at the play. You know." She made a flute-like sound and played her fingers on invisible stops; then she made drum sounds and pantomimed rat-tat-tat. "That kind," she said. Without looking at me, she took my hands and laced the fingers, then began winding the loop of string through them. "Mnmm," she murmured, her brows drawn together in a scowl of concentration.

"There." She placed my hands in her lap and stared at me. I pulled at my fingers and discovered they were bound fast. As I tugged, she broke into a fit of laughter, hiking back against the cushion and waiting for me to free myself.

"Missy, untie the man." Tamar Penrose stood on the step. She took the girl by the hand and opened the door and sent her inside. I got up, trying to loosen the intricate webbing that bound my fingers. Tamar came and examined my hands. "That's a trick of hers."

"I can get it." I struggled to slide out of the knotted web.

"I'll have to cut it. Come on in." She stepped inside and waited for me. Out on the street dusk was falling; the occasional passing cars had turned their headlights on. I heard the familiar sound of a vehicle, then the more familiar clip-clop.

"Your little girl's a good rider," Tamar said, holding the door. "Missy, make a light." She closed the door and led me to the kitchen, where the child had turned on the light; then she looked for a knife in a drawer. A large cat blinked on the sill over the sink. "Missy, hon, run out and rustle us up a chicken for dinner." Missy went out through the screened-in porch. I heard her chasing around the yard, trying to catch a chicken.

"I didn't know it was little girls you liked," Tamar said in an insinuating tone, a smile playing at the corners of her red mouth as she sat me down and cut the string. "Isn't there a law about that sort of thing? Maybe I should just leave you trussed up and call the Constable. Child-molesting and all that?" She laughed and I caught the scent of her perfume. "There," she said when she had finally freed my fingers. "She's a dickens, that one. What's she been telling you?"

"Nothing. We were just playing cat's cradle and—" I stopped, realizing how silly it sounded. I got up. "Well, thanks for the girl-scout job."

"What's your hurry? Now that you're here, stay and have a drink."

"Thanks, I'd better be on my way."

"Come on." She was getting glasses from a shelf and setting them on the table, her dress stretching provocatively over her full figure. "Roy Soakes brought me a jug of his pa's corn whiskey. Ever tried moonshine? It's just behind the door there; bring it—I'll get the ice."

She stepped into the back area where the refrigerator was, then went out to peer through the broken porch screening. Missy had caught a chicken, which was making a terrible squawking while she tried to control it. The screen door clattered as Tamar took a hatchet from a nail and went down the steps. I watched her seize the chicken, lay its neck on a box, and decapitate it; then she released the body, which ran in crazed circles, dripping blood onto the dry earth. When it had keeled over and lay kicking on its side, she picked it up by the feet and carried it to a pan near the steps. She tied the legs together and hung the still-flapping body on a nail where the blood drained into the pan below.

She came back in and washed her hands, then got out ice, and presently we were seated opposite each other at the table. The cat on the sill wafted its tail as we clinked glasses for luck. The child must have gone off somewhere, for she did not come in, nor did I hear her out in the yard.

"So." Tamar hitched her chair closer to the edge of the table. "You're a painter, is that it? What kind of pictures do you paint?"

I explained about the sort of things I was trying to get down on canvas. "Are you interested in art?"

"I know what I like." She looked at me under lowered lashes, her eyes narrowing slightly. I had never been close enough to see that they were green. "That's what they say, isn't it?" she continued. " 'I don't know about art but I know what I like'?

I like pictures, all kinds, long as they're pretty." She stretched lazily. "It's a pretty village, I guess."

"Have you always lived here?"

She laughed. "Sure, what else? Where d'you go if you're born in the Coombe? That was our house, where you live."

"I know. We appreciated your selling."

She shrugged and held her fingers up and stared at her nails. "Wasn't my idea. We needed the cash, anyway." She went on, speaking of her father, who had lost his money through corn speculations during the last drought year. They'd had to move, then move again, always to a smaller place. This had all happened after the last Great Waste; the year Missy was born. Then Tamar's father had died, and her mother, and the elders awarded her the position as postmistress. "I haven't always worked at the P.O." Her eye had fallen on my hand resting on the table top. She was staring at it. I picked up the glass and drank.

"Pretty strong, this."

"Knock the eyes out of Justin's rooster. Folks say it's rare. Smoky flavor. They call it the old stuff." She lifted the bottle again; I declined and she splashed some in her own glass and rose to add water from the tap. I watched the lines of her body move, the easy sway of her hips and breasts, the arch of the neck while she turned the faucet. "I always figured I'd get married at least five times. Have a gang of kids. Shows you how things work out, don't it?" She looked up at the ceiling. "Well, I got one, anyhow. She's like her father, got the same nature when she's calm." She studied her reflection in the mirror between the windows. "Same nature when she takes fire, too. I guess she favors him in her coloring. Most girls would've tried to hide it— not having a husband, I mean—but what the heck. Nobody around here cares."

"She's an unusual child." I wondered who the father had been.

"Yeah. She is. She don't make much trouble for me. We get on fine. It's hard tryin' to talk to her sometimes. I mean it'd be nice to have someone who understands what you're saying."

She sat again. From the sink came the slow drip of water. "Darn that leak," she said.

"Needs a washer."

"Lots of things around here need lots of things."

"You knew Gracie Everdeen?"

Her brow shifted slightly. There was a pause. Then: "You're full of questions, aren't you? You interested in Gracie Everdeen?"

"Just trying to get the village history straight."

"I'll get it straight for you. Sure I knew Gracie. If it wasn't for her, we'd still be living where you're living. It was her who brought the Waste, her who ruined my father, ruined so many around here. She was a sly one, Gracie. Thought she had it all. And she did, for a time. Had Roger, got to be Corn Maiden; she was queen of the May, all right. But things didn't work out for poor Gracie. I got Roger, I got to be Corn Maiden, and there's Gracie pushing up daisies in the churchyard. If you want to know what I think about her, I hope she burns in everlasting hell. She *ought* to have killed herself, or if she hadn't, someone—" She broke off, controlling her anger. She leaned on her elbows; the scoop of her blouse slackened; I could see the deep firm line between her breasts.

"If you want to know the truth, Gracie was dippy. Pure dippy."

"You mean crazy?"

"I mean crazy. Crazy with love for Roger, and crazy she couldn't marry him. That's what sent her off the deep end."

"What happened?"

"She was supposed to marry Roger. Then Mrs. Everdeen revoked the banns. That's what drove Gracie crazy, because her mother wouldn't let her marry Roger."

"Why didn't she want her to marry him? Wasn't he good enough for her?"

"He was a Penrose! Lived just off the Common. Roger was poor, but the Everdeens never were any great account in the Coombe. People think the Penroses are—" She touched her temple. "But in this case it was the other way around. Gracie's brains went to pudding."

"How?"

"Lord, Roger'd picked her for Corn Maiden. That was an honor. What did she do? She tossed the honor back in all our faces, the little fool. Nothing she wouldn't do to shock people or make them think ill of her, she who had everything, Roger included. Know what she did on Agnes Fair? Roger was shinnying up the pole on the Common, and there goes Gracie up the flagpole in front of the post office in about the same time. They wasn't watching the Harvest Lord then, let me tell you; they were watching her. Then, when Roger was wrestling, out comes Gracie from the platform and throws a hammer lock on him and tosses him to the ground in front of the whole village. The Corn Maiden putting down the Harvest Lord? She was crazy, I tell you. Then she marches up to old man Deming and curses him out, swearing like a trooper. It wasn't any wonder she ran off, after that."

"And you were Corn Maiden in her place."

"Yes. I was. And I'd be again, if I could. Sophie Hooke, for heaven's sakes. Why, she and Justin are *married*. That's not right. I don't think that's right. Nobody does." She reached for my glass. I did not release it immediately and I could feel the light tracery of her nail against the back of my hand.

"What're we talking about Gracie for? People'd like to stop thinking about her, if they ever could. You've got good hands. Nice fingers. Long. I guess that means you're an artist." She was rubbing her fingertips over the dark hairs. "Nice," she said in a husky voice.

"Nice?" I let go the glass. She took it to the sink and put some ice cubes in.

"Nice. I mean, sitting around my kitchen. It's not often I have gentry sitting at my house." The cat stirred again as she poured two stiff fingers from the stone jug and brought the glass back, bending over my shoulder to place it on the table. I could smell her scent, not just the perfume but the whole womanly, feminine scent of her. I looked up, felt her hair brush across my eyes. I started to turn away; she leaned insistently and the red mouth came closer, the lips moist, parted. She kissed me. I slid an arm around her neck and held her mouth to mine. I released her in confusion, and she shuddered, burying her lips in my shirt collar, then stepping away. "I knew," she murmured, and her head nodded as though in private conversation. "I knew."

It had grown dark outside. I rose. "Sorry. I guess that was starting things that shouldn't have gotten started."

She leaned back against the sink, her breasts straining against her blouse. "Shouldn't have? I've been waiting these months for you to start something." She was running cold water in the sink; her red-nailed fingers sparkled under the gushing faucet. She turned the tap, shook her fingers, and came to me; her arms were around my neck, her face tilted to mine. "I've been waiting, and now it's happened. I knew it would." There was a light in her eyes that was not mere lust, but a gleam of triumph. I could feel the drops rolling from her fingertips onto the nape of my neck. I reached up and unclasped her hands. She took them away and placed them on my chest.

"I can feel your heart." A smile grew from the corners of her mouth. I felt unsteady on my feet, locked my knees so I wouldn't stagger. "The old stuff getting to you?" She laughed lightly. "You can have a high time on the old stuff." The invitation was now not only in her eyes but on her lips, in the caress of her fingers as they toyed with the fabric of my shirt under my jacket.

I returned her look with the same level gaze, trying to keep my balance. "Sorry, lady—you have the wrong guy."

"Don't want to play?"

"In my own back yard."

"Do you?" The curve of her brow rose, a mocking curve, questioning the truth of my statement. "Lots of play in your back yard? Sandbox and everything? Tin pail, shovel—playmate?"

"Why not? I'm married—remember?"

Her laugh became hoarse, unattractive. "Still waters don't run very deep in your case, do they?" she said, half choking, half laughing. "I thought at least you'd like to go wading." She looked at me another moment, then threw her arms about me, smothering me in her embrace. "I want you." I could feel the warm throb of her against my thighs. Her mouth was all over my face, then across my lips, my cheeks, kissing my eyes, my brow, the tip of her tongue drawing a wet path to my ear, down the side of my neck.

I grasped her forearms and forced her away from me. Her arms bent, her hands came up, wilted in my grasp. Then they took on a tension, resisting my force. Her eyes flashed, and she ran her tongue over her lips.

"You bastard!" she whispered. The fingers convulsed, became claws, as they sought my shirt and tore at the buttons. I stepped backward, struck by her fury, keeping myself steady only by grasping the back of a chair. "You son of a bitch! Get out of here! Go on, get out." As she came at me, I retreated to the doorway. She snatched up the glass from the table and dashed the liquor and ice at me. Her face had gone white, contorted in rage. She used words I had never heard a woman speak before. Now she flung the glass at me; I threw up an arm as it grazed my head, and it splintered against the doorjamb. The cat sat up. Tamar stood there looking at me, her fury ebbing. I held my hands up, palms outward, a gesture of futility.

"Sorry, lady," I said. Turning, I saw her hand come up to her mouth and cover it, the long red nails taking sheen from the light. "Sorry," I repeated dully. The cat meowed, and I turned to the back-porch doorway and stared in horror.

The child stood on the threshold, the front of her dress smeared with blood. In one hand she held the kitchen knife; in the other was the chicken, split down the middle, its insides hanging out in bloody riot. Bits of feathers were caught at the corners of her mouth, sticky with flecks of blood, and I could see her jaws working, trying to swallow something. Her eyes were glazed with some manic dream, while around whatever it was she had in her mouth, she spoke an unintelligible gibberish. I backed away from the disgusting sight as she advanced into the room. Her mother had not moved.

The knife fell from the child's hand, clattering noisily. Her neck stretched like a serpent's, the head angled forward, the eyes blank, unseeing. Cassandra, speaking with the tongue of the god.

"Mn—mm—mean, um—" She muttered on in a dead, hollow tone. I stiffened, waiting.

"Mean—um—mnm—" She seemed to be groping to see something that she alone could see, to hear what she alone could hear. There was still some unchewable matter in her mouth, and the parched syllables came with difficulty.

"Be—ware—" She was fumbling with the dead chicken, working her fingers inside the slit cavity.

"The—night—"

I looked down at the dripping entrails, and back as Tamar spoke anxiously. "When, Missy? Which night?"

"When—it comes—the night—beware—"

"When?"

A garbled response.

"*Which* night, Missy?"

Though she faced me, I was sure she did not see me. Yet, pillaging the insides from the chicken, yanking them onto the linoleum, she was speaking to me. "For you—the—"

"What, Missy?" Tamar strained forward anxiously to hear.

The cat dropped to the sinkboard and eyed the slimy guts on the floor. Missy bent, feeling with her hands but never removing her glazed eyes from my direction. She scrabbled at the feathers in the corner of her mouth and then, scooping up the loathsome mess from around her feet, she began hurling it at me, bit by bit, her arms windmilling, the gobbets flying in a spate of red before I could move.

"*Which night?*" Tamar demanded again.

Ugly blotches had appeared on the child's pale skin. Wet breathing sounds issued from her gaping mouth. "Mean—um—mnm—" Gently she fondled the last remaining pieces in her palms, then paused as though listening. She struggled to articulate, then gasped out the words.

"The—all—pre—vail—ing—night—"

Her hand flew up, she crammed the stuff into her mouth,

choked, and fainted. As I backed through the doorway, the cat sprang to the floor with a thud and began greedily devouring the chicken's heart.

17

At first when I turned in to Penrose Lane, I did not hear the horse. Then, absorbed in thinking of what had happened at Tamar's house, I thought that Kate was just giving the mare too much head. At last I realized Tremmy was running away with her. They were coming at a fast clip, and I could see the look of terror on Kate's face. I ran into the middle of the road and lunged for the rein. "Dig your knees in!" I shouted, grabbing hold and letting the horse drag my weight. At the same time, Kate pulled back on the reins and the horse reared and plunged, whinnying wildly and thrashing with its head. Still Kate kept her seat, grasping the mane with both hands as she tried to control the animal. Its head came up and knocked me sidewise, and again it reared, its hoofs just missing me as they came down. I rolled out of the way and shouted for Kate to kick free of her stirrups, then jumped and snatched the reins in one hand and an ear of the horse in the other. Twisting, I exerted all the force I could to quiet the animal, and as it moved past me, I let go, reached for Kate, and grabbed her from the saddle. The horse skipped away as I held her in my arms, then set her down.

"Gosh." She leaned against me for a moment, pressing her head to my chest with relief.

"Are you O.K.?"

"Sure. I'm fine." She looked up at me, rose on tiptoe, and kissed my cheek. I heard her laugh as I went back to the corner, where the horse had stopped to chew some grass. I came quietly up beside it, talking to it until I had got the reins, and gently led it around. Kate was still laughing.

The laugh stopped. She caught at her chest. Yanking the horse behind, I started to run. Her hands came up around her throat, she staggered slightly, and I let go of the horse and caught her just as her knees buckled. I laid her down in the roadway for a moment, watching as her eyes bulged, the veins appeared, and she fought for air. Frantically I felt in the pockets of her jeans for her Medihaler. It was not there. I picked her up in my arms and, running, carried her down the lane.

I brought her in through the door of the kitchen, where Beth and Maggie Dodd were sitting at the table having coffee. Beth jumped up, white-faced, and I told her to get the emergency Medihaler from the drawer, then took Kate into the bacchante room and laid her on the sofa. When Beth brought the breathing device, I forced it between Kate's lips and pumped the aluminum valve. In the other room I could hear Maggie on the telephone, calling Dr. Bonfils. Then she dialed another number, apparently failed to get a response, and a moment later hurried out the door.

The Medihaler seemed to be having no effect. As Kate lay gasping for breath, I could feel her pulse getting weaker. Hastily I forced her mouth open and began applying mouth-to-mouth resuscitation. I was still working over her when the doctor arrived.

He administered massive doses of adrenalin; I swabbed the arm for him when he injected the needle. Kate lay in a comatose state, her position unchanged. Behind me, Beth watched horror-stricken. The doctor rolled back the lids and looked at the turned-up eyes. I heard a truck in the driveway, and shortly Merle Penrose, Harry Gill, and another from the fire department rushed in with the respirator. The doctor supervised the application of the machine, taking his stethoscope from his bag and holding it to Kate's chest. I stepped back out of the way, groped blindly for Beth's hand, but failed to find it.

Kneeling, the doctor listened. I could see that the collar of his shirt was frayed; I remember thinking he probably got paid so little for his services in these parts that he couldn't afford a new one. Mrs. O'Byrne's Tiffany clock on the shelf chimed the

half-hour, and I became acutely aware of the ticking. Merle
and the fire department boys had moved to the corner, waiting.
I could hear the sound of raspy breathing, but I knew it was
Dr. Bonfils, who, with his shoulders sagging, crouched by the
sofa and listened for the heartbeat. He motioned to Merle; the
apparatus was detached. Merle and the others did not look at
me as they took it and went out. The truck backed out of the
driveway and went along the lane.

Dr. Bonfils stood looking down at the small figure on the sofa;
he did not turn immediately. Unable to wait longer, I stepped
to his side, put a hand on his shoulder, forced him to look at
me. It is still possible to hope when hope is gone; he read the
hope in my expression, and I could see it pained him to be able
to offer me none. I watched him lay the stethoscope in the bag,
heard the snap of the latches. Then he picked up his bag and,
without looking again at the figure on the sofa, left the room.
I heard the front door open and close.

In the space between the coffee table and the sofa, I knelt
and laid the side of my head along the cushion, my lips touching
the shoulder of my dead daughter. There was the odor of the
stable on her jacket. I took her hand and held it. What did one
do now? In the movies they always draw a sheet over the—

Body.

Again I heard the ratcheting sound of a motor; a car pulled
into the drive, doors slammed. I remained where I was, thinking
I must call Ed Oates and let him do what must be done. Amys
Penrose would be tolling thrice times thrice; wasn't that the way
you did it for a girl? Thrice times—

I heard them coming in, felt the floorboards give as someone
came up behind me. A hand touched my shoulder, and I looked
down and recognized it as the Widow Fortune's. Maggie Dodd
was standing behind her.

Without speaking, she motioned me aside, and I rose and gave
her my place beside the sofa. She lowered herself, the little black
valise beside her. I looked at Beth, who stood in the doorway,

shaken but dry-eyed, her hands at her breast, clutching a hand-kerchief.

"Open my bag," the Widow told Maggie.

It was useless, of course. For all her healing powers, for all her pharmacopoeia, for all her wisdom, there was nothing to be done. I had seen it in the doctor's eyes. I went to Beth and took the handkerchief from her clasped hands and used it myself, wiping my eyes and blowing my nose. She returned my look briefly—and angrily, I thought, as though Kate's death had been my fault. How mine? For the horse that I had bought her? For moving to the country where she could *have* a horse? For—what?

I put my arms around her and drew her against me. She held her body stiffly, and her hands at her breast kept us apart. Behind me I could hear noises, the rustle of the Widow's black dress, a few muttered words to Maggie. I turned to see the old woman bending, her ear to Kate's unmoving chest. She listened intently, then straightened; slowly she raised her hand, closing her fingers into a massive fist, which she held motionless for the space of three or four seconds, then brought it down with a firm blow. Quickly she moved her head to the listening position. She grunted; then, putting one palm over the back of the other hand and placing both on the chest, she began applying a steady pressure. When she had worked thus for perhaps a minute, she changed her position slightly, moving to the head, where she repeated the mouth-to-mouth resuscitation.

I could see it was no use. The girl had not stirred; there were no signs of breathing. As she applied her mouth, the Widow lifted her eyes and let her gaze wander the room. She pointed at the jar of bamboo pens on the piecrust table. Maggie handed them to her; she examined them, selected one, and flung the rest away. She sent Maggie for clean towels; then, pulling her bag nearer and beckoning me to her, she reached up to dig in my pocket. I knew immediately what she wanted: my pen-knife.

Maggie brought the towels, and relieved her of the mouth-to-mouth resuscitation. The Widow opened the knife and, without wasting a second, bent over Kate. She plunged the point in at the base of the throat, making a small, quick incision. Then she inserted the blunt end of the hollow bamboo pen into the aperture and began sucking. I held a towel for her as she spat out the fluids she was draining from the throat, a thick, yellowish-white substance, mixed with blood.

I glanced at Beth; she had not moved from where she stood. I looked down at the two women, both working stolidly, determinedly, Maggie with her mouth to Kate's, the Widow drawing out the deadly secretions that had caused the arrest. As she sucked at the hollow of bamboo, her broad, liver-spotted hand spread across Kate's chest, exerting the rhythmical pressure initiated earlier, pushing down as Maggie pulled the air out, releasing as it was replaced with fresh.

Still I knew it was impossible. I watched the collar of blood ooze from around the inserted pen, saw it flow down the collarbone onto the green velvet upholstery. I gave the Widow a fresh towel and took the soiled one, holding it in my hands. Kate's blood. Beth moved, came to stand beside me at the end of the sofa, and together we looked down at our daughter in this grotesque attitude of death. It seemed ignominious, and I wanted to tell them to stop, to leave her alone, let her be; don't do this dreadful thing to our child—the cut throat, the running blood, the streaming nostrils—

I must have made a sound, for Maggie stopped, then shook her head once, a firm shake, never taking her eyes from the Widow. I was struck by the horrible thought that the old woman had gone insane, was trying to suck the last bit of blood from the unmoving body, and again I thought, Christ, let them stop.

And then, before our eyes, the miracle took place. The chest heaved convulsively; the Widow quickly raised her head, and I heard the rush of air through the bronchial tubes. Never ceasing the rhythmical pressure on the chest, she shifted her position slightly, turning the head so that more liquid drained, while Beth reached for a towel and knelt to wipe up the excess.

"She's alive," I said aloud. The old woman shot me the quickest of looks, an unreadable one; then, cradling Kate's head with her free arm, she shifted her back to a supine position, still using the other hand as a bellows. The breathing continued for some seconds, then stopped. I felt my body sag. Again the Widow used her mouth. The breathing resumed. Erratically, but it resumed.

She would live, she would live, I kept telling myself. She would live because of this old woman who was bending over her, forcing her to live, pushing the breath back into her body, giving her air to breathe. Beth had laid aside the soaking towel and was leaning on the arm of the sofa, her hands before her face in an attitude of prayer. The rate of respiration quickened, slowed, and quickened. After several minutes, the Widow took her hands away. The chest seemed to rise and fall of its own accord. The uneven breaths wheezed in Kate's throat and chest, but they were breaths.

She would live.

Now the Widow was working at the hole in the throat, holding it closed with her fingers to stanch the blood flow. I came around her to a position between her and Beth, reaching for Kate's wrist that hung limply to the floor, feeling the vein for a pulse. It was there; faint, but it was there. Silently I kept thanking God. Thank you, God. Thank you, God.

Again I heard the Widow mutter something, and she motioned for Maggie to hand her Beth's work basket. She threaded up a needle, and as if she were quilting she calmly sutured the muscle and tissue together with a series of neat stitches.

I marveled at the way the ancient fingers worked, how deft and nimble they were, even in age, how carefully and gently they manipulated. When the stitches had been placed and the knot tied, she dug her fists into her back to ease the strain, but kept her kneeling position at Kate's side, her eyes taking in every slightest movement.

I continued holding the frail wrist, as if trying to draw from it a stronger pulse beat. Beth remained where she was; Maggie was poised at the other arm of the couch. I could hear the low sound of the Widow's voice; I thought she must be speaking to Maggie, perhaps to herself, perhaps making a prayer; I do not know what I thought. Crouched beside her, I began to feel the strength emanating from her body, a life force flowing out of her into the child. She bent close to Kate's ear, speaking into it, willing her, commanding her to live. The words made no sense to me, but the fervor with which she spoke them engendered in me the utmost feelings of trust. I glanced at Beth. Her eyes shone; there was a small, rigid smile of hope on her tightly compressed lips.

I felt the pulse flutter again. I jumped to my feet and ran into the kitchen. I had picked up the receiver and started to dial when I felt Beth's hand on mine.

"What are you doing?"

"Calling the firehouse. For the pulmotor—"

"*No.*" Her fingers pushed the button, breaking the connection. "I don't want them back here."

"Christ, Beth—"

"*No.* I don't *want* them." She looked toward the bacchante-room door. "She's doing it. Leave her alone. If she can't do it, no one can. Leave her alone. *Leave her alone.*" Her voice rose to an anguished pitch, the cry of agony of a mother for her daughter. I replaced the receiver and reached to take her in my arms. She pulled away.

"Beth—"

She spun on me, her eyes flashing fire. "I know where you've been."

Been? Where had I been?

I had forgotten. With Tamar Penrose. Even in my innocence, I felt a flood of guilt. Beth was clutching my shirt. I looked down at it: lipstick, two buttons gone, spatters of chicken blood. I opened my mouth to say something, but she went into the other room—past Maggie, who stood in the doorway.

Maggie took a glass from the cupboard, found the Scotch on the shelf, poured a stiff shot, got ice and soda, then set it on the table. She pulled out the chair and gestured for me to sit.

I did as she indicated, taking the glass she handed me. Absently I stirred the cubes with my index finger. Maggie pressed my shoulder, then took another chair, and sat across from me, offering me silent comfort. I could hear the faint, insistent effervescence of the soda in my drink. We waited. I could hear the low voice of the Widow Fortune.

Then, after a little while, I could hear Kate's voice, too.

18

I completed a painting of Fred Minerva's barn in less than four days, working at the site during the day, nights in the studio. When Beth's village activities required her elsewhere, I interrupted my work to stay by Kate's bedside, sitting in the club chair, which I had moved up from the bacchante room. We would talk, or play games, and sometimes I would sketch her, or objects in the room, or views from the window. Some noontimes the Widow would come in her buggy and fix lunch for me, thus relieving Beth of the extra duty. While I ate in the kitchen, I could hear the creaking of the club chair as she sat beside Kate's bed, and the low intense tones of her voice as she talked. Sometimes Kate would laugh, and that made me feel good. Sometimes the Widow would stay the entire afternoon, and then I could devote more time to my easel. She would often cook dinner for us, and through my open studio window I could hear her bustling among the pots and pans while tantalizing cooking smells drifted out to me. I decided she must be cooking for herself as well, for I would see her packing part of the meal in her wicker basket, first wrapping it in foil to keep it warm, and covering it with a linen napkin. Then, promptly at five, she would hurry off to where other important things demanded her attention.

Worthy Pettinger did not leave, as I had expected him to, and when he heard of Kate's illness, he came regularly after

school, scheduling his visits to coincide with the Widow's departure, when he would go up and visit with Kate until Beth came
home.

When the barn painting was done, I sent it off to the gallery
in New York. Some days later, I got a call saying it had been
sold and a suitable check would be forthcoming. Before beginning the portrait of Justin Hooke, I immediately set to work planning another for the gallery—Jack Stump's bait shack by the river.
The peddler's latest trip must have taken him up into Vermont
somewhere, for we had seen nothing of him for weeks, and I
had still had no opportunity to talk with him about my discovery
of the screaming skull in Soakes's Lonesome.

On the Friday following Kate's attack, I came into the kitchen
shortly after five to find the Widow Fortune still at the sink,
washing up the pans and bowls she had used to prepare dinner.
Through the glass window of the oven I saw a leg of lamb on
the rack, several slices cut away from the joint, which she had
doubtless wrapped and put into her basket. She was filling a
thermos with hot soup from a pot that simmered on the stove.

"Now, that's what I call soup," I said when she had let me
taste from the ladle. "What is it?"

She laughed. "I don't think you've yet come to trust my cooking. That's nothing but mushroom broth."

"Ah," I said.

"With a little borage thrown in. And some purslane. And a
bit of chervil."

"Ah," I said, tasting again. "That's it, is it?"

"Of course it's not. Think I'd tell a fellow—even a good-lookin'
one—everything I put in my soup?"

"Or in your mead?"

"Here, go wash your hands—you got smudges all over 'em."

I cleaned up the sink, while she sat down heavily in a chair.
She looked tired tonight, and I knew her care for us was taking
its toll of her strength. She smiled, a small smile of gratitude,
which seemed to say, *Well, haven't we come through it all nicely?*

Suddenly I was on my knees beside her, my arms around her waist, my head in her lap.

"Here, now—here, now," she said. "Come, don't do that."

"Thank you," I murmured into the folds of her long apron. She patted the top of my head, then down my cheek, then pushed at my shoulder, half pleased, half embarrassed by my display.

"Nothin' wrong with sentiment, if it's what you truly feel. That's the trouble with folks, they're too afraid to show what's inside 'em." As I rose, she gave my hand a solid squeeze, then looked toward the door behind me. "Evenin', Worthy. Late, en't you?"

Worthy Pettinger stood in the doorway, looking disconcerted at having come upon us at such an intimate moment. The Widow rose and went to him, brushed his hair from his eyes. He submitted to her careful scrutiny, squirming as she took his chin in her hand. "Thinner you are, and peaked. No, don't move." She opened the black valise. "Spoon," she said to me. I fished one from the drawer and handed it to her. She took a bottle, unscrewed the cap, and poured. Worthy's eyes rolled as she put the spoonful of liquid to his lips and made him swallow. "Another." She dosed him again, pushing the spoon at him while he bent back against the sinkboard. Then she capped the bottle, returned it to her valise, and rinsed the spoon.

"Don't take on so, boy," she told him shortly. "Go and bring the buggy for me—the mare's hitched to the garage doors."

When he had gone to do her bidding, she set the valise beside the splint basket and went up to tell Kate goodbye. In a moment I heard the station wagon pull up, and I opened the front door for Beth. Our greeting was constrained as she laid her things down on the hall table and took off her coat.

"How's Kate?" It was always her first question.

"O.K. Want a martini?"

"Afterward." She hurried up the stairs. Kate's bedroom door opened, then closed. I could hear the exchange of greetings and the drone of the women's voices. The kitchen door slammed and

in a minute I saw Worthy hunching in the shadows at the opposite end of the hallway.

"You all right?" I asked before stepping past him into the
kitchen.

Silently he followed me in, watched while I got ice from the
automatic dispenser, the glass martini pitcher, the gin, and the
vermouth. Soon I heard the Widow's footstep on the stair. I
mixed the drink, poured it into a stem glass the way Beth liked
it, and put it on the refrigerator shelf.

The Widow came in tying up the strings of her bonnet. As
she smoothed her skirts, I noted her shears were not in their
accustomed place at her side. She turned to Worthy, who stood
behind the table yanking his finger joints, which cracked loudly.
"Why such a long face, boy? You look like you was off to Arma-
geddon for the final battle." She picked up the black valise.

Again I felt compelled to express myself. "Thank you for your
prayers."

"Try some of your own. Sunday's Corn Tithing Day. Worthy,
don't shirk your duty to your Lord. You want things, come to
church and ask for 'em." He looked down, still cracking his
knuckles. "Leave off them anatomical detonations and hand me
my basket, I'm late."

He came around the table and gave her the splint basket. She
folded the linen napkin over its contents and went to the doorway, then turned.

"Sunday. Church. Tithing Day. Don't forget."

"*I won't forget!*"

I whirled, shocked at Worthy's tone. He stood with his shoulders hunched, the lock of hair falling down over his brow. He
made no move to push it aside; his hands hung limp at his sides,
and I could see the muscles in his jaw working as he glared
angrily at the Widow.

"Very well," she replied evenly, and went out. The buggy
springs creaked as she mounted; she clucked up the mare and
the wheels ground along the drive. Worthy went to the sink
tap, filled a glass, and drank.

"Bad taste," I remarked, meaning the two herbal doses he had swallowed. He nodded, wiped his mouth.

"Are you still planning to leave?"

"Yes."

"When?"

"I can't go till—" He broke off. "Soon. I'll go soon." His eyes narrowed as he stared into the sink. "I've got something to do. One last thing, then I'll get out and never come back."

He went upstairs, and when Beth came down a few moments later I carried her martini and my Scotch into the bacchante room. The sofa had been taken away to be recovered, and we sat on either side of the fireplace, she in the Salem rocker, I in a Windsor ladder-back.

"The Widow says Kate can come down for a little while tomorrow," she said, rubbing her finger around the edge of the glass.

"That's good."

"But only for an hour or so."

"Fine."

The Tiffany clock ticked, filling the silence between us.

"Beth."

"Mm?"

"Why are you acting this way?"

"I'm not acting any way. I just—"

"Just what?"

"I just didn't think it was possible."

"Possible for what?"

"Possible for you—" She took a sip of her drink. "Please, Ned, I don't want to fight—"

"I don't want to either. There's nothing to fight about."

"Then can't we leave it at that? Kate's going to be all right and—"

"Yes. Kate's going to be all right. But are we?"

"Yes. I guess so. I don't know."

"Look at me." She raised her head and returned my gaze. "I went to Tamar Penrose's, yes. But nothing happened. I promise you that nothing happened."

"Then it must have been a wasted visit." She drank again, and asked, "Why *did* you go?"

"I didn't go with her, I went with the kid—Missy. I—" I broke off. How could I explain to her why I had gone with Missy that afternoon? Or what it was I was trying to find out from her. Or my fears, which I considered foolish ones but which, nonetheless, I had failed to rid myself of. "It's true," I maintained stolidly. I felt hot and confused, hating the distance between us, wishing we could put down our glasses and hold each other. "It's true," I said again.

"You went home with a little girl at six o'clock in the evening? For what possible reason?"

"To find out something."

"From a thirteen-year-old child?" Her smile was the one she used when she wanted me to feel like a fool. And I did. How could I tell her about the red pointing finger, the mad child prophesying in her mother's kitchen, the bloody chicken, guts spilled all over the floor?

"She fell out of a tree—I went to see if she was all right— I followed her—we were sitting on the porch, in the swing. We were playing cat's cradle—"

"*Ned.*"

"It's true. She tied my hands. Tamar came home."

"Tamar . . ."

"What should I call her—Miss Penrose?"

"That's what you used to call her. Until things got on a different—footing."

I rose angrily. "Look, I'm trying to tell you the truth. I'm trying to tell you what happened."

"You said nothing did."

"It didn't."

"I didn't bother saving your shirt. I threw it out."

"Why?"

"Because I didn't feel required to sew back the buttons some other woman had ripped off my husband's clothing in her eagerness to avail herself of his body."

"I kissed her."

"Once."

"No—"

"More than once."

"Yes—"

"And you had a few drinks and got a little stinko, and she was there and she was so inviting you couldn't help yourself—isn't that the way it went?"

"I—"

"You couldn't help yourself. The male instinct. Loin lust. What did you do about the child?"

"She wasn't there. She went out."

"Nice. The mother sends the child out to play while she—"

I crashed my glass into the fireplace to silence her.

"You can believe me or not, however you choose, but I'll say it once more. Nothing happened beyond a couple of drinks and a kiss."

"I'd better get a broom," she said.

I watched her go into the kitchen, and above the ticking of the clock I heard Kate coughing upstairs. I took my car keys from the hook and left the house.

When I got home, it was after three o'clock in the morning. I tiptoed into the kitchen and put two quart cartons into the refrigerator, turned off the light Beth had left for me, and moved up the stairway. Outside Kate's door, I stopped and listened. I could hear the sound of her easy breathing. I went across the hall and opened the door to our bedroom. Beth was asleep in the four-poster bed. The light on the bureau was still burning. I undressed, and laid my things on the chair. For some reason I was thinking of Cassandra, the prophetess of Troy. Having spurned the love of Apollo, it had been given to her to speak with his tongue, but, speaking, it had been her fate that no one should believe her. But the hollow horse came, and the walls of Ilium were tumbled.

And the walls of Cornwall Coombe? It was Missy Penrose's fate that everyone should believe her, every last villager. I switched off the light. Outside, there was no moon. All was still and dark. A quiet night. I wondered what and who could make it "all-prevailing."

19

Even after I had had only four hours' sleep, the yellow bird managed to wake me the following morning at my accustomed hour. I could hear Beth in the shower, and when she emerged from the bathroom, pink and flushed, I wanted to pull her back into bed. She put on her robe, removed the towel she had wrapped around her, and sat at the dressing table brushing her hair.

"Morning," I said.

"Good morning." From her tone, I felt it was not. I yawned widely.

"You'd better roll over and have another six hours."

"Why?"

"You didn't get very much last night."

"No."

She brushed crisply for ten or so strokes. "I suppose the urge was irresistible."

"No."

"What, then?"

"I went for a drive."

"Oh?" She gave me a look in the mirror. "Till three in the morning?"

"Yes."

"That's a long drive, over to Main Street. They say the murderer always returns to the scene of the crime."

"I drove to New York."

She swiveled on the bench, brush poised at the downstroke. "You what?"

"I said I drove to New York."

"What on earth for?"

I threw the covers off and headed for the bathroom. "To buy Kate some proper chili."

When I got downstairs, my breakfast was cooked and in the warmer. There was a note saying Beth had gone to Mrs. Brucie's to pick up some quilts. When I opened the refrigerator door to get the cream for my coffee, I found another note pinned to one of the paper cartons from Pepe's Chili Palor. It read:

Not for breakfast ! ! !

(and watch for the man with the sofa)

The recovered sofa was returned about midmorning, and was ready for Kate when I carried her downstairs at noon. I laid her on it, with pillows and a blanket, then pulled the rocker up and sat beside her.

"Want the T.V. on?" I asked.

"In a bit. Not just now. Doesn't that bird know winter's coming?"

"He waited till you got better."

She nodded an absent affirmative to my remark, scrunching up her nose like a rabbit. Then she sniffed, and turned to me wide-eyed. "That smells like *chili!*"

I went into the kitchen, dished up a bowl, and brought it back on a tray with a glass of milk. "Pepe sends love."

"Oh, Daddy—" I settled the tray on the table and held the bowl and spoon.

"I can do it."

"You just lie there and let me spoon-feed you. You've been a sick girl."

"How many'd you get?"

"Two. We can freeze what you don't eat and you can have it another time. But not for—"

"Breakfast. I know." She swallowed the spoonful I held for her and waited for the next. "Did you and Mom make up?" she asked, blowing.

"You heard us, huh?"

"Mm. It sounded as if you were doing toasts, like in *War and Peace.*"

"I think it was more war than peace."

She let the subject drop then, and ate in silence, blowing on each spoonful as I held it for her. "Want some milk?"

"Mm."

I handed her the glass, she took a few sips, then lay back against the pillows while I used the napkin on her mouth.

"Anything else?"

"Could you open the window? It's sort of stuffy."

I raised the window behind the sofa. From the other side of the hedge came the Invisible Voice. We listened together, trying to determine what it was today. Neither of us recognized the work. I lowered the window slightly and turned on the television, handing Kate the remote control so she could choose her channel; then I carried the tray to the kitchen. When I came back, Kate was watching June Allyson struggle valiantly with a bull fiddle on the television screen.

I made sure she had what she needed, then went back to the studio to continue preparing a gesso board for my new painting. While it dried, I straightened up my paint taboret, sharpened my pencils, threw out a bunch of old sketches, and packed my drawing kit. From Robert's open window, the Invisible Voice continued reading, though I still had not yet caught enough of it to identify the work. When I came out the studio door, I found the buggy in the drive, the tethered mare contentedly chewing the grass along the hedge. The kitchen door popped open and the Widow appeared on the back stoop, fists on her hips, glowering.

"Chili!" The way she spat the word I decided it had a bad taste for her.

"Chili?" I replied mildly.

"Don't you go giving that child none o' that foreign muck. You want to upset her stomach? You feed her, you feed her what I leave to feed her, hear?"

"Yes, ma'am."

She gave me another look, then retired. Passing the hedge, I heard the Invisible Voice:

"'I am Charles Hexam's friend,' said Bradley; 'I am Charles Hexam's schoolmaster.'

"'My good sir, you should teach your pupils better manners,' replied Eugene."

I called over to Robert. "You've got me, Robert. What's the book?"

"Try *Our Mutual Friend.*"

"Never heard of it."

"Dickens."

By spring, I decided, Robert would have read his way through the entire works. I climbed on my bicycle, and pedaled out into the lane.

I stopped at the post office to mail the letter I had written to the gallery in New York. As I dropped it into the box outside, I could see the postmistress behind the counter, weighing a package. Her head was down, her face obscured by her hair. Suddenly she looked up, as if she knew I was watching. She stared back at me, her face a mask, then she picked up a rubber stamp and stamped the top of the package. I walked back to the bicycle.

Coming along the roadway in front of the church on the far side of the Common was the pink Oldsmobile. I got back on my bike and rode south along Main Street; I could hear the car behind gaining on me. When I got to the intersection of Main and the River Road, I made a sharp left, and the pink car went roaring past. Glancing back, I saw Old Man Soakes behind the wheel, while two other faces peered at me through the back window. I heard their hoots and jeers as the car disappeared beyond the end of a cornfield, and a plume of blue exhaust dissolved in the air.

Ten minutes later, I was seated on a box at the corner of the small plot where Jack Stump's bait shack stood. I spent an hour sketching the structure, then, dissatisfied with the results, concentrated on some of the details. There was a particular window I liked, with a piece of tattered shade, and a mud-dauber's nest in the corner by a broken pane of glass. I contented myself with this small particular for the better part of the afternoon, until the sun caught the broken pane, reflecting in my eye so that it became difficult to work. I made one or two brief erasures on my page, then reversed the sketch against the light to check for errors. Turning it again, I held it up and compared it with the original. Suddenly something odd about the sketch caught my eye. Or, rather, something odd about the window itself. In the drawing, as I had completed it, the window shade hung down only four or five inches, but now, in the shack, the shade was drawn to the sill.

Sliding the pad into the case, I zipped it up and approached the door and listened. From the other side I could hear a faint scraping sound. I knocked.

"Jack? You in there?"

There was no reply. I backed away, studying the housefront. Inside I heard a slight cough, and another shuffling noise. I tried the door. It was locked.

"Hey—Jack, it's me, Ned Constantine." I waited for a few moments, then walked around to the back where a small door was cut into the crude siding of the shack. I turned the broken porcelain handle and stepped in.

It was a small, dark room, with little more than a dripping faucet over a sink and a disreputable two-burner stove marking it as a kitchen. A kerosene lantern sat on a rickety table; beside it was a sack of groceries. On the window sill was a shaving mug and an ivory-handled razor which I thought I had seen before. I went around the table and pushed open a door, beyond which was a small hallway. I crossed the hall and opened the other door.

With the shade drawn I could discern only vague shapes—a table, some chairs, a bed with rumpled covers against the wall. Making my way to the window, I raised the shade; it flew up on the roller with a clatter. I heard a sort of whimpering sound behind me and turned to see the bedcovers moving. A hand emerged from under the blanket to pull it up. I stepped past a pile of magazines and looked down.

"Jack?"

Again there was movement, and I reached to turn down the blanket. The hand reappeared, fiercely gripping a corner.

"Hey, old-timer, it's me, Ned Constantine."

The whimpering sound continued, and I bent closer. "Hey, Jack—what's the matter?" As I pulled the blanket back, the peddler seemed literally to be shaking with fright. Cowering, he threw his head to one side and covered it with his arm. His skin felt hot and feverish, and the effort to restrain his tremors brought on greater ones, the shudders racking his frame.

I drew the blanket down farther, and knelt. He kept his head turned away, and it was only by my gentle insistence that he eventually turned it toward me, sliding the tattered sleeve of his shirt over the lower half of his face and gazing at me with red-rimmed eyes. The stubble on his face was shorter than usual, no more than a night's growth.

"Are you sick?" I asked. He closed his eyes and shook his head. "Did you just get back? You've been gone a long time." He nodded wearily. As I was used to doing with Kate, I reached for his wrist to feel his pulse. Instinctively he snatched his arm away, revealing his face.

"Oh, no. *Oh, no.*" I stared in horror. "Jesus, Jack, what's happened to you?" Even in the dim light, I saw the pitiful wound that passed for a mouth, the scabbed-over scars not fully healed. He huddled against the wall in fear, and I reassured him that I wasn't going to harm him. Little by little, his hand slid down to the blanket, his fingers plucking at the worn fabric. I patted the hand, bending forward trying to see in the dim light.

"Nobody's going to hurt you, Jack." Clearly, he was terrified of something. I carefully took the face between my hands and stared at the scars. They were set half an inch apart, top and bottom, with more random ones at the corners. As though in protest against my seeing such obscene work, he made a gurgling noise in his throat. He tried to stop it, couldn't, coughed, choked; the mouth opened and I stared into the dark maw. My stomach heaved at what I saw and I released the pained face.

I leaned across him and held him by both shoulders, shaking him slightly. "Jack? Jack, listen to me. I'm going to get a doctor. Can you hear me? I'm going to get help."

I heard a step behind me, then a voice. "Leave him be—he's been molested enough."

The Widow came in, set her valise on the table, and came to the cot. I looked from her to the huddled shape under the blanket, then back to her again. She took a flashlight from her valise and pulled a chair close to the cot.

"What's happened to him?" I asked.

Paying no attention to me, she switched on the light and held the lens against her skirt as she put her hand on his brow and felt it.

"Well, Jack, how is it this evening? Better?" The head turned slightly, nodded. As I had, she took his wrist and felt his pulse, then laid it back across his chest. "Yes, better, I'd say. Comin' along nicely." Then to me, "Wants a cup of tea, I expect. Maybe you'll put the kettle on?"

I started the gas burner, filled the kettle under the tap, and put it on the fire. When I came back, the Widow was holding the flashlight over his open mouth and gently urging him to open it. "Come now—you devil, you—don't be coy with an old lady. Open up and let me see how things are." At last he opened his mouth and permitted the examination. She looked for a moment or two, moving the beam around inside, then nodded for me to bring her valise.

I fetched it, and she gave me the light to hold while she took a bottle and dipped a cotton swab in it, then inserted the swab and ran it carefully around inside.

"There, now, that's good. Close now, Jack." She returned the bottle to the valise and took out a tin of ointment, which she applied to the scars around the lips. "Last time I used this was when they took to you with their fists. But they had worse than fists about them, didn't they?"

I stared at her. "The Soakeses?"

"Hush," she told me. "Now then, Jack, what you want is some tea, en't that it?"

He nodded; she gave his hand a pat and rose. I followed her back into the kitchen, where she took a box from the shelf and a teapot which she rinsed at the sink. I sagged against the doorway and must have made some sort of sound, for she spoke impatiently. "None o' that, now. There's trouble enough around here."

"They cut off his tongue?"

"Appears they did." She spooned some leaves into the pot, wet her finger, and touched the outside of the kettle. "Another moment." While the water continued to boil, she removed the linen napkin from the top of her splint basket and began laying out things on the table—several foil-wrapped packets, and the thermos jug. "Didn't know you was feedin' the unfortunate, did you?"

She had been taking the food from our house not for herself, as I had thought, but for Jack.

She filled the teapot from the kettle, then took up a rolled parcel from a chair and unwrapped it. It contained some shirts and a pair of pajamas, freshly washed and ironed.

"How?" I asked.

"Simple. They caught him. They hid in the woods—*their* woods, damn their eyes—and they caught him. They caught him and they savaged him. Old Man Soakes and his boys. A nice, well-mannered bunch. I always said Jack's nose would get him in trouble one day."

Unconsciously I touched the end of my tongue, thinking how close I had come to a similar fate. Old Man Soakes with his sharp knife, the boys with their—

"Canvas needles." I voiced my thought.

"Aye, canvas needles. They cut and stitched him up for fair."

"How did he keep from bleeding to death?"

"We stopped him." She took a cup and saucer from the shelf

and set it on the table. I recognized the box of One-B Weber's tea.

"It's steamin', Jack," she called to him, "so we'll let it cool a bit before you try it." In the other room, she resumed her chair and held the cup and saucer on her lap, testing the rising vapors with the palm of her hand.

"But almost bled to death he did, didn't you, Jack? Here, try a sip." She held the cup up, waiting for him to drink.

"Now, then, no recalcitrance today," she told him. "One-B Weber's is a restorative, if ever there was. And when you're done I've got soup and some good roast meat, courtesy of our friend here." Though he did not seem to want the tea, she waited, cup poised, until he sipped. She watched him carefully, her eye never wavering as she made him drink, and while he drank she related what she knew of the tragedy.

She and Asia Minerva, along with Mrs. Zalmon and Mrs. Green, and Tamar Penrose as well, had been quilting at Irene Tatum's house on the Sunday evening, when they heard a ruckus across the road in Soakes's Lonesome. There were gunshots and they had trooped out on the porch to investigate. Then out of the woods Jack had appeared, crazed with pain and hardly knowing who he was or where he was going. He saw the light and came to them, blood pouring through his sewn-up lips. They had cut the stitches and discovered the severed tongue. The Widow herself had put the poker in the stove and cauterized the wound; then they had laid him on the davenport in the living room and kept watch until he came out of shock.

"Ashes there were everywhere, en't that so, Jack?" she continued. The peddler nodded dazed agreement.

"Ashes?" I asked.

"Ashes. When they'd done with their fishing knife and canvas needles, they dunked him in water, then poured ashes from their still over him. En't that so, Jack?"

I saw him nod. *Ashes.* White *ashes.* Then it dawned on me. The phantom in the windstorm. Not the Ghost of Soakes's Lonesome, but the mutilated Jack Stump, his mouth stitched up into the grim red smile, the face ash-smeared. I remembered seeing the Soakeses as I was driving to Saxony to visit Mrs. O'Byrne, recalled the decoy-making implements, saw again the skiff on the water.

Patiently the Widow waited until the cup was empty, and when he wiped his mouth she gently took Jack's hand away. "Don't do that; you're wipin' off all the salve. Now you just content yourself until I get you shaved; then I'll fix your supper." Motioning me to lead the way with the lamp, she brought the cup and saucer into the kitchen and set it on the table.

"Only way to do is to joke with him, else he'll sink into a fit o' apathy and he won't recover. If we don't make too much of a thing of it, he'll be back on his tin-pan contraption come spring. Won't you, Jack?"—raising her voice again—"I say, Jack'll be back on his contraption, pedalin' up to my door fit as a fiddle come spring."

"What's being done about them?" I said.

"The Soakeses? Faugh, what's to be done? The Constable knows, but there en't a witness. Poor Jack can't speak for himself. Can't even write the tale."

I shook my head. "Jesus, to go through life like that."

"No need to take the name in vain. And no help for what can't be helped. Jack don't need syrup; he needs vinegar, or he'll never get up." All was being done that could be managed, she said. The village ladies were taking turns nursing him, and he was never alone for long. The mouth would heal; the main thing was to keep his spirits up. "There's a lot worse ways to go through life. Plenty of people who can't talk or hear, both. Some who can't talk, hear, or *see*. Look at Robert Dodd. A sorely afflicted man, but he's made a life, him and Maggie. Thing is to survive. You, now, you're a painter, you don't need to talk nor hear, but you got to see—ain't that so? But if you couldn't you'd survive, now, wouldn't you? You wouldn't let a pack o' Soakeses put you under."

She rinsed out the cup and set it in its place on the shelf. I marveled at her. She not only ministered to the sufferings of the body, but she dealt with the psychology of the matter, refusing to let the bodily ailment fall prey to the sickness of the mind. She had no time for feeling sorry, or for despair, or for weakness.

"Life at its worst is better than no life at all, en't that so?" Briskly she whipped up a lather in Clem Fortune's shaving mug, took the ivory-handled razor, and went in to shave Jack.

20

Beth went to New York overnight, driving the car filled with village handicrafts for Mary Abbott. That night, after Kate had gone to sleep, I brought the little wooden cask down from the cupboard shelf and, sitting in the bacchante room, drank from it again. I went out and stood staring at the empty cornfield. There was no music; no figures appeared. I put the cask away and went to bed.

Sleeping, this is the kind of darkness I saw: a visible, tangible thing; a fathoms deep ocean, with a thousand improbable shapes colliding, merging, separating; bright sea anemones folding and unfolding; and more intricate organisms, each geometrically perfect, blossoming scarlet, orange, turquoise, gold. It was as though I could reach out and dip my hand into the dark sea they swam. The dark had texture—soft, pliant, furry—like the pelt of an animal; it had dimension, seeming so high and so wide and so much across; immersed in it, my body displaced its own volume. Its flesh yielded, was weighted, ballasted. A breathing dark. A living thing, pulsing like a heart, throbbing with secret incomprehensible emanations, contracting, expanding.

And hidden in the dark, the eyes; the eyes of Missy Penrose. In dream blackness they stared at me. I leaned to the right, they followed; to the left, they followed still. The dark orb, oval, curved, unblinking. Upon its gelid surface I saw my own reflection, Bluebeard distorted. The eye became a solid sphere, an onyx globe, whose depths foretold events unborn, whose mysteries remained obscure. Saw in the eye great black birds hovering; saw cornfields in ruin; a scarecrow figure. The birds were crows, became harpies with human heads and women's breasts, and in hideous chorus they railed at me. And their eyes again became the child's eyes, and the eyes pursued me and I was running— and I was not running from, but to, for I had found the answer. In my dream I knew, the secret lay bared, and with the answer came realization, came—

Daylight, and I sat in our church pew, feeling the sweat running from my armpits down my sides, soaking my shirt. Surreptitiously I loosened my tie, felt in my pocket for a handkerchief, blotted my brow.

The windows of the church were open, bringing the outdoors in, and the breeze, and the beautiful fall. Outside I could see the knoll with its tombstones beneath the spreading branches of the red-gold trees. Gazing out, I was only half hearing Mr. Buxley's sermon, the text of which this morning was taken from the Book of Ruth: ". . . whither thou goest, I will go; and where thou lodgest, I will lodge: thy people shall be my people, and thy God my God."

Ruth, who had left her own land to follow Naomi into hers, where she had gleaned the fields of Boaz. Ruth in tears amid the alien corn.

Turning my head to the gallery where the girls sat, I saw the child, neither listening to the minister nor looking at him, her blank half-wit look instead directed toward me. I had the feeling that she had not taken her eyes off me since the beginning of the service.

As I had done each day, again I worked the riddle over in my mind. *Beware the night.* Which? *The all-prevailing night.* How would it come? When?

I flicked my eye up to her, once, twice, again. I tried to analyze my feelings about her, and I could not. Except the realization that I felt, in some mysterious way, akin to her. She confused me, and my dreams. I had told myself she was only a thirteen-year-old child. She was playing some sort of game with me, a child's game, nothing more; she was nothing but the village idiot.

Wasn't she?

Yet her staring eyes filled me with a feeling of dread, as though they foretold a terrible event yet to come.

Portent. Omen. Missy Penrose.

Tamar Penrose.

The mother sat below, listening attentively to Mr. Buxley, and I felt, or perhaps imagined, that she was aware I might be looking at her, might be giving thought to her. As the daughter confused me, the mother angered me. There was something about her that seemed not merely predatory but demanding. Hers were not just the requirements of the town doxy from the local turnip-heads behind a haystack. There was something else in her, a deeply ingrained sense of something primitive, of the Woman Eternal, who demanded to be served—not just between the legs but to make man utterly subservient. Tamar the castrator. Moth to flame, I had come close and had my wings singed if not burned. I would not hover near again. I would avoid her as I would contagion. There would be no more episodes in that lady's kitchen, no matter how the invitation was delivered.

And, torn shirt aside, how had Beth known I had been at Tamar's house rather than at the Rocking Horse, or at the covered bridge, or any other place I might have been? Though I told myself women know these things by instinct, still I did not entirely believe it.

From the pulpit, Mr. Buxley droned on interminably, as was his habit. I looked around once more and realized that Worthy Pettinger had changed his mind. He had not come to church, as he had promised the Widow. His seat in the boys' gallery was occupied by another, and there seemed no need for Amys Penrose's rod, though I thought the bell ringer looked unusually attentive as he lounged against the rear wall.

Mr. Buxley concluded his sermon with a stentorian list of begats, ending with Ruth's conceiving Obed, who became the father of Jesse, who became the father of David. He adjusted his glasses, coughed once, and left the pulpit to sit in a chair behind it. Now, from the pews, the village elders arose to station themselves behind a long harvest table below the pulpit. Mr. Deming nodded, and Justin Hooke stood up from his cushioned pew. He smiled as he put out his hand and drew Sophie to her feet; heads nodded and murmurs of approval were heard. Long after, I remembered the picture they made that day, Justin and Sophie, as they paused in their places. The sun streaming through the window caught their hair, turning it golden, surrounding it with a shining aureole. They looked at each other with tenderness and feeling, and I thought how blessed they were. Each bringing an ear of corn, they approached the harvest table below the pulpit, renewing the ancient and respected custom of the corn tithes.

When their symbolic gifts had been offered, the rest of the congregation rose to do likewise. I watched the faces of the farmers, their wives, and children as they filed past, tendering their corn ears to Mr. Deming, who then laid them on the harvest table. I saw the Widow's white cap and black dress as she joined the line, and when she came opposite Mr. Deming, she handed him not one but two ears. He took her hands and pressed them, then leaned to kiss her cheek as he thanked her.

She was the great lady of the town, and there was not a villager who didn't know it. She was equal to the respect and duty paid her, and I thought how much they owed her, and how much I owed her, including the life of my only child. As she paid over her corn tribute to the church, I silently paid her my own tribute.

Constable Zalmon and his wife, at the head of their pew, joined the line as it wound ceremoniously down to the pulpit. Apart from the antiquated badge of office pinned to his weekday vest, Mr. Zalmon had never looked to me much like a constable, and I supposed very little had occurred during his tenure to occasion his use of force or imprisonment. An ancient village law of durance vile, which could be at any time invoked to restrain drunks or disturbers of the peace, provided that—since the stocks had been dismantled from the Common—the alleged guilty party should be incarcerated in the back room at the post office until a town meeting determined innocence or guilt, and the penalty to accompany the latter. This was called being given a "ticket-of-leave," and the prisoner a "ticket-of-leaver."

Though the villagers had by a concerted effort kept the attack on Jack Stump private, it was generally concluded that it remained for Mr. Zalmon to press charges against the Soakes family, and he spent much of his time outside the post office, keeping a sharp lookout for the pink Oldsmobile.

Since I had for some days set up my easel near the bait shack, the window of which I was still painting, I had seen the continual passage of the village dames coming at all hours with their baskets of food, and almost without fail every day at five the Widow Fortune would arrive in her buggy to tend the results of the Soakeses' violence. The ladies washed Jack's clothes and linens, made him broths, kept him clean and shaven, and otherwise did whatever was required to revive him. It was the Widow's object to put him back on his cart by spring, a purpose she went about with diligence and dispatch. In the meantime, Mrs. Buxley had solicited funds from the parishioners to keep him in necessaries through the fall and winter.

I had taken the boat and rowed upriver to the Soakeses' jetty, but had seen no sign of any of them. Rumor had it they had gone off on a hunting expedition, and it appeared Mr. Zalmon's vigilance was in vain. Clearly, they had shut Jack Stump up as effectively as they had the revenuer whose skull screamed in the hollow tree.

The tithing line was dwindling. The Dodds went down the aisle, Maggie leading Robert slowly; he held his token ear of corn out from him as though feeling his way with it. Mr. Deming took the ear and laid it on the heap, which by this time had become considerable. The elder shook Robert's hand warmly, accepted Maggie's ear, and she brought Robert back to their pew.

In turn, I took my place in line, then handed Mr. Deming the three ears I had brought to church, one for myself, one for Beth, and the smallest for Kate. Mr. Deming took this last and held it up so all might see, and as I passed back up the aisle I knew I was receiving the good wishes of the villagers for Kate's recovery. I felt the warmth of their glances, saw Asia Minerva smile as I passed her pew, caught Will Jones's acknowledging nod as I passed his.

When the last of the children had come down from the gallery and passed before the table, the elders turned to Mr. Buxley, who rose out of his chair and, from the pulpit, held his hand above the piled ears of corn on the harvest table and offered a blessing, while the elders and the congregation bowed their heads. When the blessing had been given, Mr. Buxley readjusted his glasses and announced the closing hymn. I stood with the rest of the congregation and turned to face the choir loft over the closed doors. Mrs. Buxley lifted her gloved hand, nodded to Maggie at the organ, and we began singing.

The selection was a Thanksgiving hymn, and the strains, church truant though I was, rang familiarly in my ears. All around me, my fellow-parishioners sang with fervor, their faces uplifted to the streaming sun, mouths wide, hymnals held high, while with fierce determination Mrs. Buxley encouraged the choir:

"Come ye thankful people come,
Raise the song of Harvest Home;
All is safely gathered in, ere the winter storms begin;
God, our Maker, doth provide, for our wants to be supplied;
Come to God's own temple, come,
Raise the song of Harvest Home."

The voices joined, rose, the notes clear and loud, a fervent sound that surely could be heard in Tobacco City. Ardor lighted the singers' faces, and joy, and belief:

"First the blade and then the ear,
Then the full corn doth appear;
Grant, o harvest Lord that we
Wholesome grain and pure may be."

I was looking not at Mrs. Buxley, or at Maggie, or the choir, but at the clock under the choir loft. Suddenly the vestibule doors flew open with a thunderous crash, a metallic sound reverberating as one of them struck the radiator. The choir exchanged startled looks. One by one their voices dwindled away, and Maggie lifted her hands from the organ keys, turning with a surprised expression, while Mrs. Buxley leaned over the railing and craned her neck to discover the cause of the disturbance.

White-faced, and with a deep scowl, Worthy Pettinger stood on the threshold, his arms outstretched to hold the doors back. As his eyes swept the pews, I saw Mrs. Pettinger start, her hand flying to her mouth to stifle a little cry. Silent, staring, the congregation stood dumfounded, waiting to see what would happen.

Worthy lifted his right hand from the door panel and made a fist of it, and the fist trembled as he raised it and spoke in a loud, angry voice: "May God damn the corn!"

Immediately a babble of sounds arose, women covering their faces with their hands, some of the men turning to one another with angry mutters.

"May God damn the corn!"

He remained frozen in the open doorway, his clenched fist held aloft. *"And may God damn the Mother!"* Bringing his arm down in a swift gesture of denunciation, he wheeled and raced out the door. Behind him, the church was in pandemonium, the women crying out and sinking into their seats, the men struggling from their pews and up the aisle, while Amys Penrose appeared in the vestibule and, clutching the rope, began to yank it furiously. Listening to the wild peal of the bells, I thought the old man rang them with the sound of an "Amen."

PART FOUR

THE CORN
PLAY

21

The grain grew fruitful and the corn was ready in the husk, the fields seeming almost to groan under the weight they bore; then, when the Days of the Seasoning were over, and when the moon had attained its promised phase, it was time, and the harvest began. The villagers gathered at the Hooke farm, where custom decreed they were to commence the reaping; spreading out along the rows, they plundered the golden, opulent land, plucking the ears from the stalks and tossing them in baskets, which were then lifted and emptied into the horse-drawn wagons passing along the rows.

When Justin Hooke's south field had been picked clean and the corn taken to the Grange for the husking bee, the stalks were then cut with sickles and gathered into giant shocks, which were tied and set at intervals between the furrows, and soon the field was bare. As in the other harvested fields, all that remained were the shocks and the stubble and the scarecrow the Widow Fortune had made, and now the villagers moved to the next field, and the next, and the one after that, and so the days of reaping went by in Cornwall Coombe. Everyone knew that Harvest Home was soon at hand.

Since the incident of my assumed profligacy with Tamar Penrose the night of Kate's asthma attack, I had seen changes in

Beth which, naturally enough, I thought stemmed from her wounded pride. And yet they were puzzling. Much of the time she seemed merely preoccupied, as though trying to remember something. Seated in the bacchante room after dinner, I would catch her as her needle paused in midair while she stared off into space. I would hear a murmured word or phrase, as if she were trying by repetition to stamp it indelibly upon her memory. Or she would make a sign, absently; then, when I looked up, she'd smile as if she herself knew she was addled. Her smile, once so quick and bright, had become bland, almost irritating in its complacency.

And in my own complacency I understood, or thought I did, her secret. Thought I understood the precise urgings that were prompting this change, those stirrings that lie at the very core of womanhood.

She was waiting for something.

So I waited with her.

She developed a habit of crossing her arms over her chest and hugging her waist and making little rocking movements, as though in an effort to stave off the wound she imagined I had dealt her.

She gave up reading the paper, seemingly taking no interest in what was going on in the world. I would find the telephone off the hook, and when I asked why, she would say it must have gotten knocked off, or, more truthfully, that she just didn't feel like talking to anyone that day. She never watched her favorite television programs any more, preferring instead to be with Kate through her slow stages of recovery. She seemed indifferent to whatever suggestions I made for amusing her.

"How about dinner over on the turnpike tonight?" I might say.

She would look blankly at me and reply, "Turnpike?"

"At the Yankee Clipper."

"*Ohh.* All right. If you'd like to."

"I thought *you* might like to."

She would shrug as if dinner at the Yankee Clipper were the

furthest thing from her mind, then go and call the Widow Fortune to see if she minded coming to stay with Kate.

Though I was certain she had gone off into some impenetrable woman's haven to lick her wounds, I was equally sure that if I was patient and bided my time, she would return to me and all would be as before.

Sometimes I would reach for her hand and squeeze it and try to express what I was feeling. She would untangle her fingers, and give my cheek a pat.

"But I want you to believe me," I would say. "I want to know that you believe me."

"Of course I believe you, Ned."

But, I thought, extraordinary as she was, she did not.

Though she continued each day going about the village to gather up the newly produced handicrafts—the quilts and bedspreads, the carved figures, the woven things—the ruling passion of her existence, her obsession, had again become Kate. I saw the warning signals, but made no move to interfere. I told myself it was natural enough—a mother's response when her child has been taken from her, then through some miracle restored. I think if Kate at that time had asked for the moon Beth would have discovered some way to get it for her.

I had been thinking of how to repay the Widow Fortune for what she had done. Money was out of the question—she would never accept it—so I turned my mind to some token of our thanks that she could not refuse, some extravagance she would never indulge herself in. One day, an idea occurred to me.

To fill in some of Kate's time, the Widow had brought her a needlepoint canvas, which she had taught her how to work, and Beth moved her sewing things from the bacchante room to Kate's bedroom, where they would talk and stitch together, Kate on her needlepoint, Beth on her quilt. When the Widow came, I could hear the three of them up there, laughing and talking, and suddenly it came to me: the perfect gift for the Widow Fortune.

That night, after the old lady had gone and Kate was asleep,

I found Beth seated by our bedroom window staring out at the night sky, at the waxing moon and the bright frosty stars. I thought of the night I had found her sitting in the same chair, after the "experience."

I pulled up the dressing-table bench and sat beside her in silence. Her head rested comfortably against the chair back, and I saw how beautifully the moonlight caressed the most prominent features of her face, her cheekbones, the line of her upper lip, her brow.

I reached for her hand. "What is it?"

Her look was distant, and the complacent smile played at her mouth. "I was just remembering."

"That night?"

"Yes. That lovely music. So—different from what we're used to hearing."

"But you never *saw* anything?"

"No. I told you."

I described again the two people, the corn figure I was sure must have been Justin, and the veiled female figure.

"Sophie naked?" She laughed lightly. "I don't think so. More likely Tamar—if you saw anybody."

If I saw anybody . . . Perhaps she was right; perhaps, with the magic of the moment and the cask of honey mead, I had confused reality and fantasy. Maybe I had been hallucinating. I had read about fly agaric, the mushroom that the Widow Fortune had hunted in Soakes's Lonesome. Taken internally, its properties were capable of producing singular hallucinogenic effects; it was also capable of making one see and comprehend things with stunning clarity.

After a while, Beth, who had got up and was doing something with her hair, spoke again. "And if you *did* see her, but she wasn't supposed to be the Corn Maiden, who was she?"

Who, indeed . . .

And I felt then that it was not a hallucination, but real; I saw that she was the sphinx and that it had been given to me to attempt to comprehend her identity.

Then, with the harvest almost in, it seemed that summer was gone altogether. While in the fields the farmers hurried to bring in the last of the corn, the trees turned, as if they had been left outdoors too long and had rusted. The maples were the color of flame, the locusts the deep red shades of cordovan, the beeches spread their tops like golden umbrellas, and all of them were shedding their leaves rapidly. Pumpkins were brought in from the fields and set out by roadside stands where apple cider was sold, and the village began preparing for winter. Then, as quickly, the frost disappeared, the weather warmed again, and with Harvest Home approaching the valley enjoyed a magnificent Indian Summer.

On the morning before the husking bee, which would precede the Corn Play, I drove to an appliance store over on the turnpike. When I came out half an hour later, I had purchased a Singer sewing machine, a little pink beauty with about a hundred different attachments only a genius would know how to use. It would be a far cry from the Widow Fortune's old Fairy Belle with the footworn treadle; and it had an automatic bobbin.

On my way home, I passed Dr. Bonfils's car, and again my thoughts turned to Gracie Everdeen. I had for some time now been brooding on the fact that suicides often left notes, usually written in a fury of desperation, but sometimes shedding light on the motives behind their actions. I decided to pay a call on Mrs. O'Byrne in Saxony.

I found her hanging a wash on the line. "I thought they did that on Mondays in the country," I called, getting out. When she had pinned her pillowcase I told her the few additional obscure details I had gleaned about Grace's death, and that it had been suicide. The shock of the news set her down on the kitchen steps. I hastened to add I did not think it likely that her anger at the girl had in any way driven her to such extreme measures; it must have had something to do with Roger Penrose. Was there possibly—

"A letter!" She got up and hung her clothespin bag on the line, then led me up the steps. "She did write a letter. I found it on her bureau after she'd gone. It was all addressed, and I supposed she'd forgotten to mail it, being upset the way she was. I put a stamp on it and sent it."

A letter, but it had gone.

"Do you remember who it was addressed to?"

"To her beau, to Roger Penrose. But he never got it. Come along, I'll show you." She took me through the kitchen and down into the cellar, where she attacked a pile of cardboard cartons, each of which was crayoned with some identifying legend: "Christmas Ornaments," "Dick's Winter Things," "Grandma's Kitchenware." One bore the single name "Grace," and this she pulled around into the light. She undid the twine that bound it, and pulled back the flaps. I bent and looked. There were some dresses and sweaters, shoes, gloves, a small box with bits of costume jewelry, and a pocketbook. Mrs. O'Byrne took out the pocketbook and unclasped it. There was a letter inside.

I couldn't make out the cancellation mark, but the envelope was addressed to Roger Penrose, in Cornwall Coombe, and a faded rubber-stamp mark read, "Deceased—Return to Sender." The letter was sealed.

"May I open it?" Mrs. O'Byrne paused, then said that after fourteen years, and with Gracie gone, it wasn't like prying into a person's things. I took out my penknife, slit the envelope, and drew out the single sheet of paper. Holding it close to the light, I read the handwriting, wild, infirm, distraught:

My Darling,

Forgive me. I did not mean for it to happen that way. Which was why I did not want you to see me. But you know now why it is all impossible. What has happened isn't my fault. It doesn't matter, it will die when I die. What no man may know nor woman tell—how I hate the words! I wanted to be there to make the corn with you. I must be there! Oh, I am driven to madness! I will come! No one can stop me. Forgive me.

There was no signature. I read the lines again, then gave the page to Mrs. O'Byrne, and bent to examine the other contents of the carton. When Mrs. O'Byrne had done reading, she refolded the letter and slipped it in the envelope.

"Well, there's the answer—wouldn't you say? He'd gotten her pregnant. She was going to have a baby—wasn't that it? And after bein' engaged to her, he decided he wanted the other one. A ring he gave her, too."

I was examining the shoes. "She still wore his ring?"

"Not on her finger—around her neck, on a little chain, like a locket."

"Why not on her finger?"

"She couldn't. It wouldn't fit."

I returned the shoes to the box—large, heavy shoes. "Gracie must have been a big girl."

"Like a horse. But not strong like a horse is."

"Would you say she was delicate?"

She glanced at the shoes in the box. "Not with feet like them. But delicate in her constitution, yes. She was weak as all getout. She did the housework, but she'd get awful tired. I felt so sorry for her, the way she lagged. Just docile and quiet, and wanting to sleep all the time. Not an ounce of energy. I expect it was the morning sickness."

I remembered how tired Beth had been before Kate's birth. Still, Gracie had not long before been shinnying flagpoles and wrestling Roger Penrose to the ground. I picked up one of the gloves, looked at it, and asked her to put it on. She slipped her hand in and held it up; the glove fingers drooped over the ends of her own. I returned it to the box along with the pocketbook and letter, then put the carton back and went upstairs.

I thanked her and left, mulling over the contents of the letter. *I did not mean for it to happen that way. It will die when I die. What no man may know nor woman tell* . . . Very possibly, as Mrs. O'Byrne had pointed out, the frantic thoughts of an unwed mother. But when had he gotten her pregnant? Surely not the night he met her at the bridge.

Driving back over the Lost Whistle, I pulled up on the Cornwall side, got out, and walked back under the portal, peering through the open latticework. Twelve or so feet below, the placid river ran under the bridge in a slowly moving current, and I could see a school of brown-colored fish gliding in the depths. On both sides, the bank eased down to the water in a gently sloping, sandy stretch. I wondered from which point along the bridge Gracie Everdeen had thrown herself, and indeed how she had managed to kill herself at all, the drop being, to my eye, insignificant.

I thought over what I knew: Amys said Roger had ridden across the bridge the night before the husking bee. The husking bee took place on the night of the Corn Play, the beginning of Harvest Home. Gracie had died two nights after Harvest Home. If she was pregnant, Roger must have met her sometime earlier that summer, sometime when neither Mrs. Lake nor Mrs. O'Byrne had been watching. Then she went to Harvest Home and accused Roger. Leaving, she returned—where? Mrs. O'Byrne had stated that she went away without her things and never came back. But Irene Tatum hadn't found the body until two days later. Where had Gracie stayed before she jumped from the bridge? Had she been alone during her last hours alive?

I drove away, my mind both mystified and intrigued by the tragic girl, until my attention was diverted as I heard radio music blaring from the Tatum house: Sonny and Cher singing "I Got You, Babe"; rock and roll in Cornwall Coombe. Stirring her smoking soap kettle, Irene hollered over to the cornfield where some of the children were hauling down the old scarecrow and bringing it up to the house.

Making ready for Kindling Night. Now, all along the way, I noticed how the fields had been emptied of their straw-and-corn watchers, the scarecrows the Widow had done up for the various farmers. I pulled in at the Hooke farm, and talked with Sophie for a while. When Justin came from the barn I posed him by the flowering pear tree, as I had seen him when he planted it. When I began sketching him, Sophie came and asked if she might watch, and I said fine; since my student days, when

I used to draw on the subways, people looking over my shoulder had never bothered me.

When some task took her back to the house, I continued working, listening to Justin. He was his usual affable self until I brought up the subject of Worthy Pettinger and the scene in church several weeks earlier. Justin's sunny face had a way of clouding over when his thoughts were disturbed, and now it became thunderclouds on Mount Olympus.

Worthy, he said angrily, breaking his pose and turning his face away, was a young fool. His sin was double: not only had he refused the honor of the village by renouncing the role of the Young Lord, he had also damned the crops. Though this harvest would not be affected, who knew what the following year would bring? Again Justin spoke of drought and pestilence, and when he turned his face back, I could see the whole history of ancient superstition and fear written there.

Some of the responsibility he took upon his own shoulders. He had known Worthy was dissatisfied, had known he was unhappy and discontented. He, Justin, should have taken more pains; it was his responsibility as Harvest Lord to see to it that Worthy came 'round before the terrible and furious conclusion, one that was regarded to be as unfortunate as the Grace Everdeen episode.

I took up my bamboo pen again and Justin resumed his pose. "About Gracie—how was she a disruptive influence at Harvest Home?"

"She came—that was enough."

I tried another tack. "I don't think Grace Everdeen killed herself. Or if she did, she didn't do it by jumping off the Lost Whistle."

"Why?"

"Because a ten-year-old child couldn't drown in that water, if she could swim a stroke. It's not more than fifteen feet from the railing to the river, and if a person was determined to commit suicide that's not what you'd call a guaranteed result."

"River's high this year."

"Meaning?"

"Meaning that when Gracie killed herself the river was low. Not much water but lots of rocks along there. They're smooth, but they're hard. Hit one of them from fifteen feet and I guess you've got a guarantee."

I guessed I had, and that Gracie had, too. "How long ago was that? When Gracie—"

"Fourteen years," he replied quickly.

"How do you recall it so exactly?"

"If you'd lived here, you'd recall it too. Not a villager that doesn't, who was alive then. It was the year before the last Great Waste."

The last Great Waste. Which somehow in the minds of Cornwall Coombe lay at the hands of Gracie Everdeen. It became more tantalizing, a village mystery whose solution I more and more felt the urge to discover. What had Gracie's blighted love affair had to do with the blighting of the corn crop thirteen years ago?

I sketched awhile in silence, then said to Justin, "If Sophie wants a painting of you while you're Harvest Lord, you should have worn your costume."

Justin laughed. "I'd feel silly standing out here wearing that costume."

"The one with the corn leaves?"

His look was blank. "It doesn't have corn leaves. It's cloth."

"I meant the one you wore in the cornfield. Interesting show you people put on that night." I worked to put a touch of irony in the comment.

"What show?"

"You know. Behind my house? With the music?" Using my pen, I imitated a flute. "It was you, wasn't it? You and—someone else? Tamar, maybe? The night Mrs. Mayberry died?"

He regarded me stolidly, with no trace of a smile, and shook his head. "I don't know what you're talking about. Sophie and I went to the movies that night."

"I see." Clearly I was going to get no admission of complicity in the "experience" from Farmer Hooke.

When I finished my sketches of Justin, I left the farm for the village, where I found things busier than usual. Woven harvest symbols swayed in the breeze on the chimneys, and clusters of dried corncobs hung on the front doors of the houses, in preparation for Harvest Home. Cars were parked around the Common; people were hurrying to and fro with a general air of bustle. Men gathered along the street and in doorways, some peering down the street, others checking their timepieces against the church clock; women went in and out through the open doors of the Grange, bent on various errands. Two or three boys were up on the roof of the Grange porch, festooning the entrance with corn garlands, while Jim Minerva stood on a ladder, attaching to the corners bunches of unshelled Indian cobs.

Two girls came down the steps, their heads together as they spoke.

". . . want to run off for, just before the play?" Betsey Cox was saying.

"He's crazy." Sally Pounder's face was red with dismay as she looked up at the church steeple. "Amys," she called over, "is the clock fast?" Amys Penrose paused in his sweeping, leaning on his broom to reply. "Hell and tarnation, no," he snapped. Sally cast a worried look down toward the Penrose barn as she and Betsey hurried to join a gathering of women on the Common.

A wagon creaked down the roadway and pulled up in front of the Grange. Mr. Pettinger got down from it and began unloading some pumpkins, while his wife watched him from the seat. "Howdy," he said to Ferris Ott. "Brought these for the show."

"Don't think we need pumpkins, do we?" Ferris Ott asked Will Jones with elaborate indifference. Mr. Pettinger glanced uncertainly at his wife. Conversation in the vicinity had come to a standstill, and backs were presented as the farmer stood with his armload of pumpkins.

"No, we got plenty of pumpkins." Will Jones glanced at Mr. Pettinger. The pumpkins went back on the wagon, and as Mr.

Pettinger took up the reins and drove off, Mrs. Pettinger stole a look back from under her bonnet.

"What was that all about?" I asked Amys, in front of the church.

"Shunned. What you might expect around here," he replied loudly. Heads turned toward him; the bell ringer glared back defiantly. "The boy 'e run himself off, and I say bless the day he done it. Sometimes it takes the lesser fool to do the greater thing."

"Sweep with your broom and leave farmin' to them as farms," said Ferris Ott in Amys's direction.

Just then Mrs. Zalmon's head popped out the Grange door. "Where's those Tatums with the rest of the decorations?"

She called inside and was quickly joined by Mrs. Brucie and Mrs. Green, and they, too, hurried to meet the group on the Common.

"There's good luck," exclaimed Jim Minerva on the ladder, having hung one of the woven harvest symbols over the Grange doorway. Amys paused to spit in the dust, his bushy eyebrows contracting in a scowl.

"For them's fool enough to hope for luck around here, it should be luck aplenty. If I had my way, I'd see 'em burned, ever' last one." He wiped his sleeve across his mouth.

"Don't believe in luck, Amys?" I asked. The old man reflected a moment as though lost in some forgotten pocket of time. "Trouble is it don't seem wuth all the fuss." He drooped his head, and when he lifted it his face sagged more and the fierce gleam in his eye had been extinguished. "No, sir, it don't seem to me the candle's wuth the game."

"For shame, Amys Penrose, of course the candle's worth the game." Mrs. Buxley came dashing toward the hall, arms laden with costumes. She stopped in mid-flight. "'And God said, Let there be light,' remember?" She looked over at the harvest symbol. "Still, we mustn't put our faith in luck alone," she cried gaily, giving me a bright, expectant smile. "I mean, we're *not* medieval, are we? We *have* landed men on the moon, haven't we? Think of it, Ned, your first Corn Play. Our twenty-third. Hardly seems possible. I don't know how we're going to fit Sister Tatum into her costume this year unless we can get a brassiere on her." She resumed her flight, calling, "Jimmy, help me with these, can't you?" She loaded the costumes into Jim Minerva's arms and sent him up the steps.

He cast a worried look down the street. "Gosh, Mrs. Buxley, it's almost time—"

"Gracious, it's *not!*" She looked up at the steeple. "Amys, is that clock—"

"Yes, *ma'am*, it's right."

"Tempus *fu*git." Mrs. Buxley scrunched her brows mischievously at me, as if *we* knew one could do nothing about the fleetness of time. "Dear Amys, come with your broom, can you, and give our stage a sweep?" She shooed the laden Jim Minerva inside, then cajoled Amys up the steps. "See you in church," she called to me over her shoulder.

Skirting the Common and the waiting women, I glanced at the steeple clock, then entered the vestibule. Mr. Buxley's vestry room was locked, so I climbed the wooden steps leading up into the belfry. I could hear the gears of the clockworks stolidly moving as I passed the housing, and presently the great bronze dome of the bell itself hung above me. Through the arched portals of the tower, I could see out in all directions: up and down Main Street; behind me to the river, the cemetery plot—Gracie's gravestone, solitary beyond the iron fence; and directly in front, the Common.

Mrs. Buxley came hurrying from the Grange hall to join the ladies on the grass, the group growing larger each moment; several of them cast looks up to the clock below me. When the bell ringer came out with his broom, I descended the rickety steps again, passing the rope which hung down from the bell. I walked into the church and found Amys in the vestry.

"Nice view from up there."

"Ayuh."

"Got a minute?"

"Got two."

"I'd like to have a look in one of those." I pointed to the shelf with its line of dated ledgers, which Mr. Buxley took so much pride in.

He gave me a quizzical look, then nodded. "Help yourself." He left the room, and I brought down the volume marked 1958. Turning to the end, I worked backward from the last of November, checking every entry: births, weddings, funerals. At last, I found an entry, written in an authoritative hand, that read: "Grace Louise Everdeen, suicide, interred this day—outside church burial ground—no services."

I closed the book, returned it to its place, and went to find Amys, who was carrying a stack of hymnals from the big oak cupboard at the back of the church. I thanked him and left.

Whatever unformed suspicions I had harbored were resolved by the Reverend Mr. Buxley's register. The entry had proved it—the official church notice of Grace Everdeen's interment in unhallowed ground, the immemorial resting place of suicides. I resolved to let her bones remain in peace, and dismissed the subject from my mind. The church bell began to toll.

At the firehouse, Merle Penrose, a burly man, one of those who had come with the respirator during Kate's attack, was polishing the brass trim on the truck. As I passed, he and a helper left off work and hurried out; two others interrupted their checker game and followed, leaving the firehouse doors wide open.

In front of the drugstore was another group—some whittling, some smoking their pipes, some with hands in pockets—apparently waiting for Mr. Deming, for when he suddenly appeared they moved off in a body. Meantime the bell continued to sound, and more women were arriving from all directions to join the group waiting on the Common.

I entered the post office and found two ladies at the window, baskets on their arms. One was mailing a package. Through the grille I could see Tamar Penrose sorting letters into the initialed boxes. Her back was turned, and she had not seen me enter.

The teakettle steamed on the hot plate. The Constable hurried in, lifted the hinged panel, and went into the back room, and Tamar, carrying some letters, quickly followed. The door closed behind them.

"Hurry," one of the ladies at the window was urging the other, darting glances toward the Common and digging in her purse for change. When they finally made a hasty exit, I stepped up to the window and asked Myrtil Clapp for a book of stamps. While I paid for them, the door to the back room opened and the Constable and Tamar came out. She hurriedly finished distributing the mail, turned the hot plate off under the teakettle, and followed the Constable out the door.

Myrtil set her empty teacup aside and went to the letter rack. She looked in the A-B-C box, and returned with several envelopes, which she slid under the grille. "Lots today," she said, then turned a triangular block which read "Closed" on the inserted card. She lifted the counter panel and passed through. I looked around: the post office was deserted. I picked up my letters and began thumbing through them. A cry from outside froze my hand briefly; then, slipping the letters into my case, I hurried through the doorway.

The sunlight was blinding. When my eyes adjusted, I looked around. The street was empty. On the Common, standing in the yellow light and casting small pools of shadow on the green grass, the women waited.

"How's your late potatoes, Asia?" Will Jones's wife asked Asia Minerva.

"Poor, dear. They're awful poor by now."

"They want rain. Seems as though the corn took all the rain this year. Soaked it right up, it did. And after all that rain we had last spring."

Asia craned her neck around the shoulder of the woman in front of her, as if anxiously straining to catch a sound. It could not take much longer.

Then it was done. One of the women called out, another pointed; they broke from the Common, running across the grass and out into the street, milling in the thoroughfare to meet the men coming from behind the barn. Asia was hugging her son, and when she held him back from her I could see the bloody marks on his face. Asia pulled him to her again, clasping him to her bosom, while the rest crowded around, talking excitedly and reaching to touch him as the men stepped up and wrung his hand. Then the group began dispersing, casting looks over their shoulders to where Missy Penrose stood, a little apart, her incredible doll dangling from one red hand.

Going to the Widow Fortune's house, I noticed that her corn was yet unharvested. A trail of smoke was rising, not from the chimney but from somewhere behind the house.

"Did you think my skirts had caught fire?" she said, laughing, as I rounded a shed to find her bent over a bench with a row of beehives on it. Her face was protected by a net, and in one gloved hand she held a bee smoker, with a small bellows attachment. "Come along," she said as I stepped back, "no cause for alarm. Them that call this hive home is over in yonder tree. Some dratted raccoons have been playing havoc and eating up my honeybees. I'm giving their house a fall cleanin'."

She raised the hive at the end of the bench and scraped the insides free of wax and other material, then reset the dome in place and laid the apparatus aside. "Now all I got to do is catch that coon, then swarm the bees back, and come spring there'll start to be plenty of honey in the pot."

I helped her gather up her paraphernalia and carry it into the shed. While she put the things away, I noticed on a dusty shelf in the corner a row of small wooden casks, identical to the one she had presented to us. They were stoppered with pegs and lay under a caul of cobwebbing, seeming as if they had been undisturbed for many years.

She saw me looking at them, told me to come along, then hurried me from the shed. Outside, she dusted her hands and eased her back.

"Winter's comin'—my sciatica's kickin' up." She looked off at her corn, nodding in approval. "Pretty soon it'll be all in, and another year'll be over. Oh, yes," she continued as we walked along the edge of the patch, "your year ends come New Year's, but for a farmer the year's end comes with the harvest. Harvest, then the huskin' bee, then Kindlin' Night, then the Harvest Home, and that'll see us safe for another year. Bountiful harvest," she said, sighing gratefully as she took off her work apron and folded it with precise motions. "Come and have a cup of tea."

The kitchen was the usual potpourri of herbal fragrances. On the stove a large kettle was simmering, and she directed me to carry it to the back porch, where I set it on a table. As she covered it with a piece of cheesecloth, I saw pieces of what appeared to be the large caps of the mushrooms we had found in the woods, drained of their redness but nonetheless recognizable. On the shelf were half a dozen more little casks, newer-looking and un-stoppered. When I came back into the kitchen, she had cleared away the remains of herbs and spices and the water kettle was on the fire.

She got out her tea things and set them on a tray. The cups and saucers were a handsome grayish blue, with a Chinese design; looking at the bottom, I saw they were marked "Ironstone, Made in England." When I admired them, she said the pattern was called Canton, and that Clem Fortune had given them to her as a wedding present. While the kettle heated, she got down her box of tea and filled the little silver tea ball. The cardboard tea container being empty, she pulled out the lining, flattened it, and spiked it on a spindle on which she saved scraps of paper; the box was relegated to another cupboard. In the Widow Fortune's house everything was saved, everything was used.

While she carried the tea things into the parlor, I went out to the car and brought in my surprise. She was comfortably en-sconced beside her hearth, and I set the large carton on the hooked rug at her feet. Changing her spectacles for the occasion, she used her shears—a pair I hadn't seen before—to part the gummed tape and open the flaps.

"Oh, dear." She looked from it to me and back to it, bending forward with the eager expression of a child. "Is it what I think it is?"

"What do you think it is?"

"I think a sewing machine."

"I think you're right."

I lifted it out and set it on a table where she might examine it more closely. Then I showed her the array of attachments for zigzag and buttonholing and for all the other mechanical feats the machine was capable of performing. And the last—

"An automatic bobbin! I declare I thought I'd go to the grave without an automatic bobbin, surely."

"No one should go to their grave without an automatic bobbin, surely. That's—well, we just wanted to thank you for—"

"Here, now—here, now." She took and held my hand, gripping it firmly between hers, then releasing it. She removed her glasses and wiped her eyes. "You're a good man, Ned Constantine. You're a good family. Well." She folded her hands over her broad bosom and smiled. "Well, now, there's an end to Fairy Belle and I can't say as I'm sad to see her go." She peered again at the new machine. Without her spectacles, she had that curiously naked and unfamiliar look of people who habitually wear glasses. "How d'you s'pose I'll ever learn to run her, at my age?"

I said I believed it was not very difficult, and showed her the accompanying pamphlet of instructions and diagrams. She put her glasses back on to read, slipping her shears on their black ribbon into her lap. "Looks mighty complicated. Perhaps Beth can help me."

I stuffed the pieces of packing material back in the carton.

"New scissors?"

She shook her head. "Lord knows, I've left them others over to Asia Minerva's or somewhere when we were quilting." She sipped her cup, eying me over the tops of her glasses. "Leave that, your tea's gettin' cold." I took the chair opposite and stirred lemon and sugar in my cup.

"One-B Weber's?"

"Ayuh. You'd like the honey better'n sugar, though."

"Your bees make a good honey." I stirred with my spoon. "Interesting honey."

"How so?"

"Your mead, I mean."

"Oh. Did you like it, then—what was in the little cask?"

"Yes—I did."

Her face was deadpan. "I thought perhaps you might."

"We enjoyed the show, too."

"Show?"

"You know—the fellow in the corn."

"Was there a fellow in the corn?"

I smiled; she returned my look with one of watchful interest. "Yes, there was a fellow in the corn. A fellow you put there."

"Why would I do that?"

"I've no idea."

A flicker of disappointment in her expression. "None?"

"Perhaps I have. I'm not sure. The fellow had a—girl." Giving the single syllable a slight nuance.

"That's in the natural way, isn't it? A man and a maid—"

"In a corn patch—"

"You make it sound mighty pedestrian. Who was the—girl?" Duplicating my emphasis.

"I think she's a sphinx."

"Oh? Like we said, sometimes it takes awhile to riddle a sphinx. Sphinxes are notoriously puzzling, as we know. But if you saw something—mind I say *if*—if you thought you saw something, perhaps that something may have given rise to speculation."

"It has."

"Then maybe that's all it was meant to do."

" 'To discover what is possible?' "

"Certain. But maybe you only dreamed what you saw."

"That's possible. What do you spike your casks with?"

She laughed heartily. "A good drink don't need to be spiked. At least, not what's in one o' them casks. Spikin' generally dulls the senses, don't it? Take for example that homebrew of the Soakeses. That'll fog a man in plenty." She rummaged in her work basket, came up with a bit of crocheting, and proceeded to ply the hook as though her fingers could not bear to be idle. "Anyways, what you saw—or thought you saw—did you enjoy it?"

"Yes. I did. Very much."

"But—?"

"I didn't understand it. At least—" I wanted to query her about the identity of the female figure, yet though I was certain she had manipulated the proceedings in some manner, I could see that she didn't want to be questioned about it, but wished me to resolve what questions I had by myself. Her silver spectacle rims twinkled as she peered over them at the sewing machine on the table. "Amazing invention, a sewin' machine. Partic'larly since they electrified them. Interestin'—"

"What is?"

"The effects you can get with a little battery. Sparks, and all." Her look was sly behind her glasses. She returned to her sewing, and step by step led me away from the subject, but more than ever I wanted to solve the riddle of the sphinx, and to comprehend who the figure in the cornfield had been.

"Yes," she continued, "I believe you have an understandin' heart. How's things t' home?"

I shrugged noncommittally. "Um—"

"You been philandering?"

"No."

"As I told your wife. You're not the type. I can spot them ones a mile away." She moved her chair slightly to take the leg off a worn spot in the rug. "There's nothing worse than an unforgiving woman."

"Beth?"

"I s'pose if you'd been sowin' oats before now, she'd be used to it. Difference is she believes in you."

"If she believes in me, why doesn't she forget about it?"

"She's hurt. It's been part of her upbringing to believe in the institution of marriage as prescribed by the vows at the altar. Her faith in you was total. I expect the Tamar episode shook it up a bit."

"How do you know about it?"

"I hear things."

"You hear talk, ma'am."

"No need to get testy. Didn't I just say you were a good man? Beth was brought up a lady; she don't understand women like Tamar. But she'll come 'round."

"Will she?"

" 'Course she will. She wants a bit of talking to. She's bringin' her quilt over tonight. You let me have a few words with her; then you just go out of your way to be nice, and see if things don't work out. That Tamar's a devil. I brought her into the world, I've seen her grow up, and I know what goes on in that mind of hers. Don't flatter yourself she wants you. She don't. Or if she does it's only because she can't have you. Tamar's always wanted what she couldn't have."

"Like Roger Penrose?"

"Aye, like Roger. 'Ceptin' she got him in the end, just as she said she would. Or she got *of* him." I noted the slight emphasis, waited for her to elaborate; she did not. " 'A man's good as he ought to be but a woman's bad as she dares.' That's Tamar. Still, she got what she wanted."

"Which was?"

"Wanted to be Corn Maiden. And she was."

"In Grace Everdeen's place."

"A girl like Tamar can be the downfall of man and woman alike."

She was not altogether cryptic; her remark was not lost upon me. "It's not what you think it was."

"Me? Pshaw, I don't think anything. Haven't time. Besides, it's none o' my affair."

I smiled again. The Widow was much more interested in the caprice of the weather and the vagaries of nature and what the earth would yield than she was in the common pursuits of her

fellow-creatures. What was here yesterday would be here tomorrow, and if it wasn't it was no great matter. What mattered was
the earth and what it could provide.

The telephone rang. "Now, who can that be," she said, rising.
"Never get used to that contraption if I see the millennium."
She excused herself and went into the hall, where she picked up
the receiver. "Yes, Mr. Deming," I heard her say; then, not to be
eavesdropping, I carried the new sewing machine into the other
room and set it up on a card table.

"Everything all right?" I asked as she came in and I saw her
serious expression.

"Sakes, I don't expect anything's ever *all* right, do you? Mrs.
Deming's got a touch of somethin' or other. I must go and have a
look." She patted the machine, then thanked me again. At the
door, she offered me her cheek to kiss and said, "Happy you
came by. And"—almost an afterthought—"don't you worry none.
There's news t'home that'll take care of all."

"News?" I had turned, but the door was already closing. The
last thing I saw was the twinkle of her spectacles in the light.

I drove away feeling better. *News t'home that'll take care of all.*
Wondering what this mysterious disclosure might be, I scarcely
saw the other car as it swept by. It was coming from the direction
of the Common, traveling fast. I glimpsed Constable Zalmon at
the wheel, an unidentified man beside him in the front seat. I
waited until the car had reached the country end of Main Street
and turned onto the Old Sallow Road, then I continued on my
way home.

Kate was upstairs in bed; having eaten, she was resting for the
husking bee the following night. It would be her first time out
since the attack. Beth had decided that evening to have dinner
in the dining room, which lately we seldom used. The table had
a festive look to it: there were linen place mats on the dark,
polished table top, and linen napkins; a small bowl of chrysanthemums; candles. Usually when we ate there, we sat at

either end, with Kate between, but tonight Beth had placed herself at my left, and I wondered if this new proximity indicated a change in her attitude. Still, as we ate and talked of inconsequential things, I found her preoccupied and distant.

"I bought the Widow a sewing machine."

"Did you?"

"From us both. A little present."

"Did she like it?"

"She seemed pleased. She wants you to show her how to use the automatic bobbin."

"Of course." A silence.

I said, "Good soup."

"Black bean. I put some sherry in it."

"I can taste it."

I looked at her over the ironstone tureen between us. "It needs a little salt, I think," she said. I passed her the silver cellar and she added a shake to her cup.

"I was at the Hookes' today," I said.

"How are they?"

"Fine."

She was staring at the monogram on the napkin, an elegantly scrolled "E" in thick embroidery. "Elizabeth," she said.

"Hm?"

"It was my mother's name."

"I know."

She traced the figure of the letter with her nail. "I can remember her."

"Your mother?"

She nodded; a little smile. "I can remember the smell of her soap—Pears' it was—and I can remember her talking to me. She and Father had separate rooms, and in her bedroom there was a blue wicker chaise with a pocket in the arm for magazines or whatever. I can remember the chaise made a sound—the wicker, I suppose."

"But, Beth, you were only two—"

"I know. But I can remember. She had a tea gown—it was rose-colored pongee, I think, or some kind of silk, and it had lace cuffs."

I was astonished. I was certain it was impossible for people to have such early memories. "And she sang to me, naturally" —a little half-laugh. "It was a song about a bird. Something about Jenny Wren. Then Father would come in and I would be taken to the nursery."

"By the nurse?"

"No. Mother. She carried me. There was lace on her collar, too."

"And then?"

"Then she was dead. She just wasn't there any more. Only the nurse, and Father. Don't let your soup get cold."

"I'm not."

She was crying. I was aghast. Big tears shone in the candlelight and rolled down her cheeks. I reached for her hand; she put it in her lap with the napkin.

"Beth—I'm sorry." She bit her lip, ran her fingers through her hair, laughed, a small inconclusive laugh. She looked around the room, at the walls above the wainscoting.

"I love that paper."

It was a copy of an antique paper showing ships in a Chinese harbor, with men in coolie hats loading tea aboard. We called it the Shanghai Tea Party. "It's a handsome room, don't you think?"

"Yes." I waited until she got control of herself again. "You're not sorry?"

"About what?"

"That we came."

"No. I'm not sorry. I'm very glad we came." She gave this last an emphasis that had a touch of defiance about it, as though she were determined to make it work at all costs.

"More soup?" I picked up the ladle, heavy monogrammed silver. Another curly "E."

"Yes, please."

I filled her cup, then mine. She was quiet a moment, then

said, "Look how the leaves are falling. I hate to see them go. It seems so final, somehow."

"There's always the spring."

"The Eternal Return."

"What?"

"Just a phrase."

It was; still, I had the feeling she hadn't coined it, but had heard it somewhere. She started crying again. I put down my spoon. "Oh, Beth—"

"I'm going to have a baby."

"Huh?"

"A baby. I missed my period. It must have been that night we drank the mead. I'm going to have a baby."

"Are you sure?"

"Yes."

The Widow had said news, news to home. I couldn't speak, but reached for Beth's hand, which now she let me hold.

"How long have you known?"

"Since—since the day of Kate's accident."

I saw it then. She had been waiting for me to come home to tell me the news, and when I came it was from Tamar's house, with lipstick on my shirt and buttons off. No wonder she had got so angry. All these weeks she had been carrying the secret, had been frightened. I knew what she must have been feeling.

"Nobody knows yet. Except the Widow, of course. And Maggie."

I felt a pang of disappointment that Maggie had been told before me, but I guessed I'd had it coming, after the Tamar business. She let me kiss the clenched knuckles of her fingers, and I told her how glad I was.

"It'll be born in the spring. Just before Spring Festival." She fingered the monogram again. "Perhaps Elizabeth."

"If it's a girl."

"Yes. And if it's a boy—"

"Please, not Theodore Junior."

She smiled. "No, not Theodore Junior."

"What, then?"

She folded her fingers under her chin and stared thoughtfully out the window. "I have to ask Missy."

"What?"

"I have to ask Missy," she repeated.

I was shocked. "I'm not going to have that birdbrain naming any kid of mine—"

"We must. She wants us to."

"Who?"

"The Widow." She caught my look. "That's little enough, isn't it?" The terrible picture of the child's bloodied hands was spinning through my brain. "After what she's done for us. I want our baby to be special."

"Of course it'll be special. But—"

"We'll have to rake the lawn again." She laid aside her napkin, rose, and went to the window, where she stood, not saying anything, but just looking out. A long moment passed, and I suddenly had the feeling she had forgotten I was there. I went behind her and put my hands on her shoulders and drew her back to me.

"I don't know what we'll do," she said, "now that Worthy's gone. All the things that need looking after."

"We'll get someone else. When they've finished harvesting."

"Yes." She sounded faraway. "Harvest Home will soon be here. Worthy won't be in the play. I wonder where he went," she added musingly.

"Dunno," I said. I half heard a noise on the stairs as Beth turned to me. "He just said he wanted to go away and—" I broke off; she was staring at me.

"He told you he was going away?"

"Yes. That day we fixed the chimneys."

"And you didn't do anything to stop him?"

"How could I stop him?"

"You could have tried to talk him out of it. You could have told someone so they could have stopped him."

"Why should he be stopped? I think it's the best thing he could have done."

The color had drained from her cheeks. She pulled away angrily and turned her back to me. "A young boy like that, off on his own—"

"He's almost seventeen, almost old enough to vote, old enough to fight—" I stopped myself, remembering what Worthy said about trying to enlist.

"What's he going to live on?"

"He's saved some money. I gave him some more. And I'm going to buy his tractor—"

"You gave him money? That's just abetting him—"

"God, Bethany, he's not a criminal."

"It seems you're taking rather a lot on yourself, aren't you? Advising and all. I mean, it's really none of your business."

I couldn't believe my ears. We were having a fight about something that didn't concern us. I tried to sound calm and reasonable.

"Beth, what difference can it make, if that's what he wants to do? You're right, it *is* none of our business."

She wheeled on me. "Meddler. You're meddling in things that don't concern you. You had no right!" Her hands trembled as she picked up the tureen from the table and went swiftly through the bacchante room into the kitchen.

"Hi, sweetheart."

"Hello, Daddy."

"How's tricks?"

"Fine."

"Can I visit?"

"Sure."

Beth had gone out. I sat in my club chair beside Kate's bed, trying to make my voice sound more cheerful than I felt. "How's the needlepoint coming?"

She held up the piece she was working on, a bouquet of flowers tied with a ribbon. "For Mother's birthday."

"Mother?"

"Yes."

"You usually call her 'Mom.'"

"I know. Did you have another fight?"

"It wasn't a fight, Kate. It was just—a discussion." I watched her small fingers as they threaded the thick needle and carefully worked the yarn through the canvas and drew it out again. "You'll have that done in no time. Kate, what's the matter, sweetheart?" I raised her chin and looked at her; tears were welling. "Hey, don't cry. It wasn't a fight, honestly."

"Why did you let him go?"

"Nobody *let* him go. Worthy went because he *wanted* to." The stair tread: she had been listening. "He's a man, he has to do what he thinks is right for himself. We'd only be selfish if we tried to keep him simply because we wished it for ourselves." I bent closer and took her work from her hands. "Worthy's got a lot of growing up to do. Like all boys. There are lots of things he wants to find out about, and when he does, one day he'll come back, and by then you'll be grown up, too."

"Then what'll happen?"

"I guess that'll be up to you and Worthy."

She shook her head, the stubborn shake that was her mother's. "He'll be different and I'll be different, and we'll both have met someone else, and it won't matter any more."

"There are other boys. Corny Penrose is a nice fellow."

"He's a clod. And anyway he sent a cob to Elsie."

"Do you want to come downstairs and watch television?"

"No, thanks." She took back her needlepoint and began working again. "You go ahead. I'll be all right."

"O.K. I'll see you before you go to sleep."

I kissed her and went downstairs. I opened the door of the Victorian cupboard and switched on the T.V. I watched until Beth came home. She put her sewing basket on the floor, then came and kissed the top of my head. "I'm sorry, darling. Forgive me?"

I pulled her onto my lap. "Of course."

"I guess I'm jumpy—the throes of motherhood are looming.

I suppose we'll have to go bassinet shopping and all those things again. Can you still remember how to mix formula?"

"I can take a refresher course."

She went up to see to Kate and I started around the house turning off the lights and locking the doors, a habit I still could not get out of.

Coming back into the bacchante room, I saw my sketching case where I had left it on the piecrust table. I remembered the mail I had picked up at the post office, slipped the envelopes out, and glanced through them: a circular from a swimming pool company, a letter for Beth from Mary Abbott, a bill from Bonwit's, a letter for me from the insurance man, and another.

This was addressed to me in pencil. Turning it over, I read the return address: Mr. John Smith, 245 Franklin Street, Hartford, Connecticut. I slipped the single page out, put down the envelope, and read the lines from Worthy Pettinger. He was fine; he would be sending me another address shortly; next week he was going to New York. I could send him the money for the tractor there. I read the letter twice, then threw it on the fire. The white page burst into bright flame and immediately turned black, curling but preserving something of its original shape as it fluttered on the log. I took the poker and pulled the fire apart, and reset the screen. Then I picked up the envelope, and stood staring at its back, thinking that something was odd. Not that it had been written in pencil, or that Worthy had written it, but odd that the edges of the flap were puckered, and that it had parted so easily from the envelope as I lifted it.

Someone had steamed the letter open.

22

I had been right: Worthy Pettinger had left Cornwall Coombe because he was frightened. He had pledged me to secrecy concerning his whereabouts, inventing the mythical John Smith to protect himself. But someone had found out. Now Worthy was in danger. But what kind? I decided that I would go to Hartford and talk to him, tell him his letter had been intercepted, and try to learn the reason behind his danger. I would go tomorrow, after the husking bee.

For it had begun at last, what everyone had been looking forward to—the four-day celebration of Harvest Home. It was initiated by a grand and enormous feast at the Grange hall, and the husking bee, a prelude to the presentation of the Corn Play. I never got to Hartford, however, never met Worthy there, for it was this fateful night that saw my fall from favor among the villagers of Cornwall Coombe, and the beginning not only of my great disgrace but of the terrible things that followed.

The evening began well enough, certainly. Whatever words the Widow had had with Beth seemed to have brought about the desired effect: she was sweet and warm and loving, and with the news of the baby coming, I felt sure the Tamar issue was a closed book. We arrived at the Grange shortly after seven o'clock—Beth, Kate, and I, in company with the Dodds. The lights of the large building cast warm beams through the tall windows and streamed through the wide-flung doors onto the street, bidding all of Cornwall Coombe to enter and be welcome. On either side of the entrance, close to the kitchen, women were laying cloths on long tables while Mrs. Green and Mrs. Zalmon and others accepted the wealth of covered dishes prepared for the evening's festivities. At the far end of the hall, the stage was festooned with garlands, giant corn shocks and pyramided pumpkins flanking each side, the curtain painted with harvest symbols. In the middle of the floor was an immense pile of corn ears ready for husking, and in one corner a country orchestra was tuning up, five musicians whose notes competed with the tumult of voices while children ran everywhere, crying, "When do we start?"

In the opposite corner from the musicians sat the Widow Fortune, her look grave as she spoke with Sophie Hooke. When Sophie slipped away we went to bid the Widow good evening.

A place was found for Robert, and while Maggie went to speak to the orchestra he exchanged pleasantries with the old lady, who was wearing her best cap and her Sunday dress with the bone brooch pinned at her bosom.

"Well, Mary, this is one of my favorite nights in Cornwall."

The Widow laughed and winked at a passing crony. "Robert, you think the way to a woman's heart is through your own stomach." She laughed again, and began describing for him familiar faces and sights around the hall. There were the Tatum kids, jumping on the corn pile and making mischief as usual; there was Sally Pounder in a new dress; there was Sophie Hooke in another; and didn't Justin look handsome; and there came Asia Minerva—wasn't she lookin' proud; and there went Fred—she guessed she knew where *he* was goin', to join Will Jones and them others havin' a pull at the stone jug in the corner, and yes, the orchestra was tunin' and you could just see how Tamar was itchin' to get out and dance; and Missy had brought along her doll; and listen to "Turkey in the Straw"—didn't that bring back memories of Clem!

Mrs. Deming came to pay her respects and shake Robert's hand, but there was no sign of Mr. Deming. Other ladies, having finished their work at the tables, drew up their chairs and brought out their piecework. Robert said if it was going to turn into a hen party he and I had better join the men, and we went to the corner to have a pull at the stone jug, too.

While the men drank, the ladies sewed, the young children ran wild, and the older ones talked in the corners; there was activity galore backstage, where last-minute preparations for the Corn Play went forward. Mrs. Buxley's round face popped out between the curtains to scan the hall—looking, it appeared, for Robert, for now she came hurrying toward us.

"Here you are, Robert—no need to hide that jug, Fred, I haven't lived here twenty-three years not to know you can't have a husking bee without a spot of the old stuff. Robert, come along, I want to be sure you remember your way to the stage for the narration," and she went away propelling Robert behind the curtains.

The men passed the jug, tilting it to their mouths on the crook of their elbows and handing it to me to follow suit; I felt the mellow liquor slide down my throat, and accepted the tumbler of water Will Jones offered as a chaser.

A drum rattled, and baskets were brought in and distributed while the men rolled up their sleeves for work, the women fluffed out their aprons, and all began donning corn mitts. When the hands of the clock between the windows pointed to eight, the husking bee commenced, and all of us rushed to attack the giant heap of corn, forming a circle on the floor, stripping off the husks, and shelling the cobs.

In that token ceremonial, it seemed that the village had summoned up all its reserves of bonhomie and good spirits for this merriest of nights; the Grange walls resounded with the good-natured joshing of the farmers, the echoing chatter of the women-folk, the unquenchable spirits of the children. There was a joyousness in the labor, a high-jinks, devil-may-care attitude as though, the summer's labors done, now they could relax and share a comradeship that stemmed from the symbolic harvest that towered before them, a mountain of security for the coming year. Farmers I scarcely knew came and slapped me on the back and joked with me; their wives, whom I had seen only in church, stopped to exchange pleasantries and say how glad they were our family had come to Cornwall Coombe. Custom and reserve seemed abandoned, all was jollity itself, so jolly that one pull at the stone bottle surely called for another, and when one jug was empty there was another to take its place.

The time passed and we worked unstintingly; the dust from the husks rose in the air, the kernels falling in golden showers into certain of the baskets, the cobs thriftily reserved in others. When the baskets were filled, they were borne away, to be returned empty, ready to be filled again. Meantime the orchestra kept up any flagging spirits with one old tune after another.

I wiped the sweat from my brow, tilted the jug as it was passed again, and went back to work with renewed vigor. If there was laughter, it seemed I could laugh louder; if there was shouting, I could shout louder; singing, sing louder. The pile of corn dwindled, smaller and smaller, and it became a contest to see who would get the last ear to shuck. This piece of good fortune fell to Jimmy Minerva—an omen apparently of the utmost significance—he having engaged in a scuffle with the Tatum boys and several others for the prized trophy. A mighty cheer went up when Jim carried it aloft, crying, "I have't! I have't!" And the rest chorused, "What have'e?" "A neck! A neck!" he replied in the traditional Cornish formula, brandishing it as he brought it to the Widow Fortune herself to husk. Taking her cue, she rose and performed with ceremony, letting the kernels sift through her fingers into a basket, returning the cob to Jim, then dusting her hands on her apron and solemnly bowing all around.

By God, I thought, slapping my thigh, the old girl was regal. Reg'lar duchess. I took two short steps, listing slightly, then pulled myself upright. Was I tight? I felt tight. It was hot in the hall. Auditorium chairs were brought out, the dishes on the long tables uncovered, and there were "ooh"s and "ah"s along the lines that formed; nobody had ever seen such a feast as this one.

There were Mrs. Brucie's famous Boston baked beans and Mrs. Zalmon's famous German potato salad and Asia Minerva's famous buck stew and Mary Fortune's famous blood pudding, to say nothing of a host of other favorites. And when one was already full, there still remained to be eaten Irene Tatum's famous double-chocolate family-treat cake and Myrtil Clapp's famous apple cobbler and your choice of Mrs. Green's famous pumpkin pie or Mrs. Buxley's famous mincemeat.

I didn't feel hungry; I was much more interested in finding the stone jug again. Things were becoming a little bleary for me as I staggered out onto the porch. "Smell that air," I said, and turned to find another amicable farmers' gathering with another stone jug of the old stuff, and perfectly agreeable to sharing with me. I dribbled slightly as I tilted the jug to my lips, passed it on, then wiped my chin. I peered over the railing. What were those kids doing down there, peeking around the corner of the hall, all got up like cornstalks—the play? Oh, the *play*.

"Come spring, I'm goin' to plant corn," I informed the empty street, hanging on the corner post and swinging. Yessirree, come Planting Day I was going to be right out there with the rest of them, just a-hoein' and a-plantin' and a-dancin'—

They gave me the jug again and I raised it high. "Here's to crime." They laughed and thumped me again, saying I was a good fellow.

There was another drum roll and we trooped back inside where the eaters who had been corn huskers were now become an audience. The chairs had been rearranged in rows with a wide aisle between the two sections, and without display or haste the villagers moved between the rows to seat themselves—a little solemnly, I thought, a trifle grave. Moving along the back, I slid into the place Kate and Beth had saved for me, taking Beth's hand and waiting with the others while the last voice trailed off, the hall darkened, and the footlights came up on the curtain and music was heard.

The Corn Play was about to begin.

There was a brief murmur and stir as through the vestibule doors came the youngest Tatum girl, Debbie, looking like a bridal attendant while she ceremonially strewed her way down the aisle with flowers; her steps were slow and measured, the way she had been rehearsed, and she looked neither left nor right but stared straight ahead, pretending she did not know that the Harvest Lord and all his court followed in her train.

My fuzzed brain tried to recall the various figures in the corn quilt the Widow had showed us. These were the courtiers pouring through the doorway, a joyful procession of village boys and girls, singing in clear, melodious voices, and with music—strange music, I thought, but familiar—tambourines and pipes and drums; some shaking rattles, others ringing bells, healthy flesh agleam, expressions eager and delighted. I recognized Sister Tatum and Margie Perkin and Sally Pounder, smiling and not at all shy or modest with the laughing boys whose arms circled their waists, but singing and tossing looks to the audience, the procession becoming a dance as they made their way toward the stage. Great garlands of cornhusks woven with autumn flowers were carried on poles, swagged against the ceiling, while baskets like cornucopias spilled fruit and corn, and those who bore them looked back over their shoulders at who came after.

We all knew who this was: Fred Minerva playing the Harvest Fool—an outrageous country jester decked with bells and tattered ribbons, and for his head a tumble-down corn crown—doing a comical dance that made the people laugh to see someone more foolish than themselves.

Next appeared a lovely figure, all in white, a long shimmering dress trailing to the floor, her head covered by a white veil embroidered with flowers. She stood for a moment in the doorway like a bird poised for flight, then moved down the aisle, almost floating rather than walking, her features hidden, her hands clasped before her.

"The Corn Maiden," I heard people near me whispering, and I knew this was Sophie Hooke. When she got to the stage her maidens came and led her to her place.

Next came six young village bloods carrying aloft what looked like a giant ear of corn, its contents hidden by a wrapping of husks, and this ear was deposited on the stage.

There was a delay, a stage wait that seemed almost contrived, and the audience strained and fidgeted, as if the suspense were unbearable. "Bring him on!" shouted one man. "Show us him," called another. "Come and make the corn," a third urged. "Aye, make the corn—make the corn!" It became a clamor echoing to the rafters, with the women joining in, and I tried to recall where I had heard the phrase used before. A line in Gracie Everdeen's letter to Roger Penrose? Then, suddenly appearing, there stepped into the light the majestic figure of the Harvest Lord himself, a pleated mantle of bright scarlet swirling behind him. He went down the aisle with a long stride, and when he reached the stage he stood center in a spotlight, arms outstretched in generous acknowledgment, the women in the audience visibly charmed, the men now satisfied, all rejoicing at his presence.

Craning my neck as, with a quick flourish of red, he tossed the end of his cloak over his arm, I tried to discover if the costume beneath was the same the figure in the cornfield had worn. What I saw appeared to be sewn of handwoven fabric, embroidered, a duplicate of the figure in the quilt. Nor was he wearing the odd little corn cap I had seen on the night of the "experience."

The other players had taken up various positions around the stage: the Corn Maiden sat to one side surrounded by a ring of her ladies, the Harvest Lord beside her, all watching as Robert Dodd entered from the wings and began the story of the growing of the corn.

"*And the plow entered the earth,*" Robert said, "*to make the corn. The furrow was turned, and the seed was planted and the earth was fulfilled. Willingly the earth received the seed and the seed sprouted and put forth its leaf. Rain and sun in their changing but never to be broken cycles nourished the crop and it was good, this peaceful time of waiting till the harvest.*"

While the narration proceeded, the actors pantomimed the action. First the Harvest Lord and the Corn Maiden came center stage, facing each other. There was a general sigh of anticipation and an audible whisper of "making the corn" rippled through the audience as the Corn Maiden's ladies lifted away her veil, revealing the radiant Sophie Hooke. Her long blond hair was entwined with flowers and strings of corn kernels, and her blue eyes were huge and innocent as she looked up at Justin, who embraced her. Then they proceeded to "make the corn." They walked to opposite ends of the stage while two boys wearing great curving horns came drawing a plow. Justin seized the handles and guided the plowshare across the floor of the stage, and at the opposite end of the furrow Sophie held herself ready, ducking nimbly between the horns as they came at her, then skipping over the plowshare and running to the other end of the stage. The horns turned—the plow, and Justin, too—as he now recrossed the stage and the action was repeated. Sophie was waiting to meet him, and again she passed between the horns and over the plowshare.

"Plow the furrow!" someone called; the woman next to me clasped her hands before her, and her husband struck his thigh with enthusiasm. When the field had been plowed, the horned boys and the plow were taken away, while the women used hoes to till the soil all around Sophie and Justin, who again faced each other, in the middle of the stage, waiting for the rain to nourish the ground. The maidens dipped their hands in copper ewers brimming with water, letting the drops fall from their fingers to the earth. Next the seeds were planted, four kernels laid on the stage boards, the young men working with bags slung over their shoulders, just as we had seen them on the day we first came to the village.

All this took place on Planting Day, which was during the Moon of Sowing, and after more rain, the audience became very still, for now it was Spring Festival time and behind the players rose the waxing moon, a cardboard cutout pulled along on a string. Enthroned, the Harvest Lord was now invested: a magnificent crown of intricately woven corn ears and husks was planted atop Justin's corn-colored hair. Now Sophie, as his consort, was likewise crowned with ceremony and applause. Afterward, their outer robes were taken from them and the Harvest Lord and the Corn Maiden danced together, she demure and shy, a little frightened at his advances, yet encouraging them, too, he stomping heavily on the stage and moving around her in prescribed ritualistic steps.

The courting dance ended. Now—during the period called the Moon of the Good Gathering—the Harvest Lord strode to the footlights and addressed the audience.

"I am the Harvest Lord. The sower of the seed. The King of the Corn. You have made me all-powerful, and in return I offer you the bounty of the earth. I am he. I am he." As he spoke, he made gestures of giving, while the spectators half rose in their seats, their hands reaching as though to receive his largess.

"Give't! Give't!" the men shouted, fingers outstretched in a catching gesture.

"And do ye not," called another, "be ye curst."

"Aye, be ye curst."

"And damned."

"Aye, then do ye be damned."

Justin nodded to them, still holding out his hands in his great gesture of giving. "Shall I be cursed, then?"

"No!" they cried. "No!"

"Do I drought?"

"No!"

"Do I blight?"

"No!"

"Then tell me your bidding."

"Make thee the corn!"

"What, with the Mother?"

"Make thee the corn!"

"Yes—with another."

This response concluded, he smiled, showing his white teeth, then bowed and turned, striding about the stage and lingering briefly with each of the maidens as if he could have his way with any, and they eager to oblige him, but he had eye for no other than the Corn Maiden, the rapturous Sophie, who sat by watching.

Then Fred Minerva pranced about in his corn tatters and, as Harvest Fool, flipped up the skirt of Justin's tunic, making asides to the audience: "Hey, girls, now there's a plow to make the corn with! You'll be harrowed for sure." Nobody seemed to mind the ribald talk, everyone laughing good-naturedly; one man crowed to Justin, "Hey, old cock-a-doodle-doo!" and another cupped his hands and shouted, "There's a cock'll do!" When the fun was over Robert resumed the story:

"And in the way of the seasons and of time, the earth was quickened and proved fruitful and the ears swelled in the husk: the sun lent his glory, decreeing the Harvest Lord should be powerfully endowed; the moon gave him the magic that only

she may give; in her turn, she decreed that while the Harvest Lord sat upon his throne and was young and vital all the crops would grow, the people would prosper, that man would have to eat. And the earth burgeoned forth and readied her gift for the taking."

The Moon of Good Gathering waned and became the Moon of No Repentance, and during this time Justin danced with all the maidens. Though I watched carefully, thinking at some time to see the figure—or a similar one—from the cornfield, I watched in vain. Other than the Corn Maiden herself, no one appeared who might have given me a clue to my riddle.

Next, the children I had seen from the porch came onstage, dressed in corn costumes. They were the growing plants, and they formed the rows between which Justin and the girls danced. Then, as Justin appeared to grow tired and his movements became languorous, he knelt beside Sophie and put his head in her lap. Robert continued the narration:

"And there was wind and cold, but neither sun nor moon nor anything good, for the earth slept. But under her cold white pillow lay a secret, which only men who have tilled the soil may know, and while the earth received unto her the Old Lord, and held him in slumbering embrace, her womb at the same time prepared itself for new birth, and this was the secret that every husbandman knew. And when she threw aside her blanket once again, when Planting Day returned, the Lord who had been the Young Lord, but was now in his turn the Harvest Lord, would rise anew, strong and young and beautiful, and so it would continue, forever, the Eternal Return, for thus it was since the Olden Times."

Listening, the audience nodded, their faces eager and bright as the tale was told. The play was the duplication of the natural process, a pantomiming of life itself, and it seemed to me that at heart these people were primitives, a clan of ancient lineage, plain and clear in their wants and needs.

Onstage the corn children had clustered together, and when they parted again, a stir went through the audience. The giant cornhusk now lay in the center of the stage. The papery skins rattled, moved, then parted altogether, and with a bound Jim Minerva sprang to his feet.

"Ho!" someone called as he popped up.

"Have'ee't a new one!"

"New," they whispered, nodding and applauding as Jim stepped to the footlights and bowed. Then the corn crown was set on his head, the plow was brought again, and when he put his hand to it a great shout went up, and people rose to their feet while the curtains closed. When they opened again, the cast stood in a line, making the traditional stage bows; the curtains closed again, parted to reveal the principals. As Justin handed Sophie toward the footlights to curtsy, she stumbled slightly; a buzz went through the audience, but Justin set her safely, then raised her. Jim Minerva bowed again; then they all bowed to Robert, and Sophie brought him to center stage; Robert bowed, and the curtains closed for the last time, and the Corn Play was over.

Wasn't it a fine show this year, they all said. I heard murmurs about Sophie's having stumbled during her bow, but the rest had gone slick as a whistle.

When the chairs had once more been cleared to the sides of the hall, the dancing began. The orchestra played one or two standards to get people warmed up, and couples were moving out onto the floor a few at a time. Wondering if Beth wanted to dance, I looked around for her. The Widow was again speaking to Sophie, and nearby Mrs. Zalmon was showing Beth her latest quilt. I invited Kate instead, and led her onto the floor, but I could tell from her expression she wished I were Worthy instead, and I had trouble keeping from stepping on her feet.

The musicians swung into a plaintive waltz, and that went a little better. When Kate said she'd had enough, I took her to the sidelines and we watched the dancers. I saw Sophie Hooke go by in Justin's arms, holding her long skirt out as he turned her, her head back and a little to one side, her hand resting lightly on his arm that held her, their bodies dipping to the lilt of the music. He was looking over the top of her head with a sober, grave expression, and I wondered if he was enjoying himself. Or if Sophie was, for that matter. She was gazing up at him with that yearning, bittersweet expression she had for him alone. Then I saw there were tears in her eyes. Yet, watching them, it seemed impossible that anything should really spoil the happiness of those two, and when next Justin turned her, I saw the tears were gone and she was smiling again.

When the band began a reel, I went to get Beth to come and watch. The lines were formed, gentlemen opposite ladies, bowing, changing from parallel progression to circle, the couples breaking up into fours, crossing over, making small circles, then spinning in the do-si-do. Never having seen an American country square dance before, I marveled at the dexterity and grace with which these farmer folk, so awkward and shuffling in the field, now executed the intricate patterns. There was Fred Minerva beaming, his heavy farmer's shoes treading the lightest possible as he bowed to Edna Jones, linked arms, and spun her. There was the minister dancing with Mrs. Deming—where was Mr. Deming?—Will Jones with Maggie Dodd, Cyrus Perkin with Asia Minerva, the whole village mixed together in the community of dance.

When good ol' Justin passed, the Widow beckoned him with her thimbled finger and he leaned while she spoke in his ear; then he threaded his way through the dancers to Beth, and drew her into the dance, laughing as she got confused in the steps and straightening her out again, handing her along to Morgan Thomas, who passed her to Merle Penrose, as up and down the floor they went. When Will Jones left the dance to join the drinkers, Maggie came laughing and breathless and took my hand and pulled me onto the floor. It was hot and the music was loud and I was drunk and enjoying it immensely. Good ol' Maggie.

Then good ol' Maggie was somehow suddenly replaced by good ol' Tamar, who ended up the reel with me, and when the band began a slow number she was in my arms. Gliding around

the floor, I felt quite the stepper, and for the first time that evening I wasn't treading on someone's feet. Good ol' Tamar, she
danced like a dream, and who could say anything if we were
having one little dance together?

She danced closer than convention might have dictated, but
it was hard keeping our bodies separated, they seemed to fit so
naturally together. Good ol' Tamar, with her Medusa's curls and
her red mouth, and her red fingernails sliding under my collar,
and the smell of that perfume. Not saying anything, but just
dancing, and I recall asking her if she'd cut in on Maggie. Yes,
she said, she had. I asked if it was leap year and she said no,
just ladies' choice.

Then I saw good ol' Beth sitting between the Widow and
Mrs. Zee, and I decided we'd danced enough; I stopped and
let go of her, but she wasn't having any of that. She hung on
me, laughing. Which, as any fool could plainly see, didn't set
too well with either Mrs. Zee or good ol' Beth. I undid Tamar's
arms from around my neck and said she ought to cut in on Justin,
ha-ha, and good ol' Beth—there were two of her at this point—
had put on her you're-making-a-spectacle-of-yourself expression,
so I guessed I'd go outside for some fresh air.

On the porch another jug had been produced. I took a pull,
and they all whacked me, telling me what a good fellow I was
turning out to be. And wasn't that Tamar Penrose some hot stuff,
and wouldn't you know a sly chap like me would be getting
some of that, and was I ever going to catch it when I got home!
I thumped them back and told them what good fellows *they*
were turning out to be, and no, I wasn't getting any of that,
we were just dancing, and if my wife didn't like it she could
go frib a frabble. They laughed and thought that was funny,
and went back to talking corn. When the music started again
they all went back inside.

It was then the trouble began.

I was drunk, and knew it, but it didn't seem to matter—lots
of them were in similar condition—and with a last look at the
clouds scuttling over the moon, casting rolling shadows along

the deserted Common, I stumbled back inside, hearing the music
—not the band we had been listening to, but something with
a more exotic sound, the same kind we had heard on the night
of the "experience," and it was a pleasant sound, but I saw that
none of the men were dancing now, only the women, barefooted,
dancing in a circle, the floor strewn with fine grain laid in patterns with designs drawn in it, and Missy Penrose in the center
of the dancing circle and what was she wearing—some sort of
corn crown—and the women had joined hands as they moved
around her in the circle—heads now raised joyfully, now bowed
in contrition, now exultant again, backed by the syncopation of
drum and tambourine and flute—for the fiddle was silent—with
flex of knee and thrust of breast, graceful arms extending, lilting
left and right with a sowing motion, the feet tracing patterns
in the grain, brows glistening, and radiant Tamar, her Medusa's
locks winding, her woman's body arching and dipping—I couldn't
take my eyes off her—writhing almost, her face ecstatic, transported, seeking and calling forth with pride and longing, the
dance becoming a ritual, and I, uninitiate, trying to make sense
of it, bewildered by the mysterious weaving of hands, intertwin-
ing of figures back and forth, in and out, up and down, still
maintaining the form of the revolving circle, then a rush of awful
reality as though those circles marked by the women's slipping,
sliding feet and intertwined fingers manifested some impenetrable knowledge, imprisoned some mystical charm, and the men
hot and sweaty, all gape-mouthed and glassy-eyed, watching the
sinuous rotations, while I, feeling drunker than I had ever been
in my life, dipped the sweat from my forehead, somehow wanting
everything to stop now, but it would not, I could not make it—
my mouth gaping also as within the circles appeared other figures,
small, lewd, primal figures of fecundity, all breasts and buttocks
with great blank mouths and staring eyes, and NO, I shouted,
wanting to stop it, it was wrong, there was something terrible
about it, suddenly it was all serious and it seemed to have woven
some deeper, more sinister meaning into the circles round and
round, the straw figures bobbing on poles, the women crushing

them to their breasts with ecstatic moans, and where the children
had been dancing the boys were no longer there but only the
girls dancing in imitation of their elders, Missy Penrose dancing,
not merely dancing, but as she turned, dervish-like, pointing,
pointing around the hall, stopping, pointing at me—God damn
you! I thought; damn you and your pointing finger and your
chicken guts—and one or two of the girls were brought from their
circle into the other circle and— *What the hell!*—there was Kate,
dear Kate, sweet Kate, wearing a crown, a corn crown, and what
was this, some sort of payment for her life having been saved,
but no, I thought, God damn it, whatever was going on they
weren't to bring her into any God-damned circle and put a crown
on her, and I lurched across the hall, shouldering my way past
the men, dimly aware of Beth's protesting voice, then of her coming after me and trying to pull me back, and I was resisting
her, yanking free and breaking two girls' link in the circle and
stepping into it and roughly tearing Kate away, the crown from
her head, hearing hisses and sharp whispers, the children stopping, drawing back in shocked surprise, some crying out, attract-
ing the attention of the rest, an angry murmur arising among
the men, a rustling among the old women like wind through
dry grass, then my glimpsing an angrier face under a white cap,
risen from a chair, eyes flashing in flesh gone pale, closed fist
uplifted as though to strike, a sibyl become harpy, the dancing
women never pausing but whirling by, giving me deadly looks,
Tamar's face a mask of loathing; but, angry, confused, not knowing I should turn my head away in shame, still dragging Kate,
I propelled her to the entrance where I stopped, not letting go
her hand but then, astonished, releasing her as the music ceased
—not all at once, but by degrees, the dancing as well—all heads
turning to see who stood in the lighted doorway, and I blinked
in perplexity as I stared at Mr. Deming and the Constable, each
gripping an arm of the thin, dark figure between them, and I
shouted and lurched toward them, trying to break their hold on
the prisoner, staring at Worthy Pettinger's pale defeated face,
and reeling again or spinning or being pushed and the pale face

vanishing, the remaining faces no longer friendly as rough hands seized me, shoving me out the hallway and down the steps to sprawl in the roadway while on the porch moths spiraled in pale dementia around the light under the harvest symbol and unsmiling faces aligned themselves in drained fury and they flung cobs at me without passion but remorselessly, and even then I would not turn my head away but lay there, bloodied and astonished, wondering what it truly was I had seen that night.

23

Next morning, a deadly hangover. Vague recollections of disaster, of something—what? Couldn't remember. Downed Alka-Seltzer, aspirin, took one shower, then a second. Some better; not much. Still couldn't remember. What had I done? Kate: Skip it, Daddy; it's all right. Beth: Don't worry, darling, it was nothing. Giving me a smile, a pat, and I could smell Pears' soap when she kissed me lightly. About midmorning I remembered dancing with Tamar Penrose; bits and pieces of the evening impinged fractionally on my memory. Still dazed, I found the copy of the New English Bible and, confronting Beth in the bacchante room, swore on the Book never to have anything to do with Tamar again.

"Ned, I don't want your promise."

"But I want to promise," I said. "I want to swear I'll never have anything to do with her, never even talk to her again."

"Don't be so dramatic. It doesn't matter—really it doesn't."

But it did to me, and so I promised, and I felt better for having done so. My earnestness must have made some impression on her, for she laughed and acted sympathetic and was the indulgent wife.

She got up from the sofa and raised the window; she had noticed before I had: the yellow bird had flown. It was curious how silent the locust tree and the drive had become. "Robert says it will be back in the spring; it always comes back."

"The same bird?" I asked.

"Yes. The very same one. The Eternal Return." She turned and looked at me. "When it comes back—" Again the complacent smile; I knew what she was thinking.

"There'll be the baby."

She nodded, went into the kitchen. I followed.

"Are you sure? I mean—"

"Certainly."

There seemed no doubt of it. The morning sickness had begun; her breasts were swelling, and her belly. Still—

"Don't you think maybe you ought to see Dr. Bonfils?"

"Ned—don't *worry*. I don't want to see Dr. Bonfils. It's all right. I know. The Widow says so. And Missy. No—don't look shocked. It's true. She says there's to be a baby in the spring."

And if Missy, the village idiot, prophesied it, who was I to contradict? For whatever reasons, Beth seemed so certain, so safe and sure in her belief, so happy in it, that I would not have contradicted in any case. As she had made so many other things possible, the Widow Fortune had made this possible, too, for us to have another child.

But for me the prevailing wind that blew through the village of Cornwall Coombe remained one of mystery. I could not fathom the intensity of feeling against Worthy Pettinger's defection. It was as though they considered him somehow their property or the subject of their demands; as though regardless of his personal wishes, he must conform to theirs. I considered it a much-ado teapot, for they had their replacement, Jimmy Minerva, whom everyone seemed to regard favorably. But Worthy's anger had taken him beyond the bounds of reason, and his damning of the corn had shaken the village to its foundations. It was considered the worst of omens; Missy Penrose was being frequently and avidly consulted for prognostications, while in church Mr. Buxley offered prayers.

Even Mr. Buxley.

When my thoughts were not with the boy, I found myself, in spite of everything, returning yet again to what I was beginning to call—in my mind, at least—the Mystery of Gracie Everdeen. Some facts seemed clear enough. She had run away because her mother forbade the marriage. She had come back, and her sweetheart had got her pregnant. She had thrown herself from the Lost Whistle Bridge into the river, which was low, and dashed herself on the rocks. Irene Tatum had found the body, which had been buried without ceremony outside the church precincts.

It seemed simple and tragic, both. Still, I wondered. Phrases in the pathetic letter kept popping up in my mind: *What has happened isn't my fault. . . . It will die when I die. What no man may know nor woman tell.* In no way was I able to decipher the meaning of the words. And *I wanted to be there to make the corn with you.* I had seen the "making of the corn" in the play, the ritual tilling of the earth, Sophie jumping over the plowshare; but Gracie's reference remained lost on me. I recalled the shoes in the box—unusually large for a girl, and the gloves as well. Yet Amys had remembered her as pretty, girlish, delicate. And Mrs. Everdeen—why hadn't she wanted Gracie to marry Roger? Because he was poor? Because the strain was tainted? And why had she wanted Gracie to give Roger's ring back? And why had Gracie kept it? And, more important, why had she waited until two days after Harvest Home to do away with herself? Where had she spent the intervening time?

Putting these thoughts from my mind as best I could, I turned to the task at hand, the completion of Justin's portrait in the time promised. I drove out to the farm for a sitting; Justin's normally sanguine attitude was at first tinged with a slight coolness, and, though she was sympathetic, Sophie's demeanor also seemed altered. Her usually bright face was dull, shadowy, clouded by some kind of worry. I observed a growing sense of urgency in her; her actions were composed of quick, brittle movements, and she seemed impatient with the slow thoroughness of my work. I had set up my easel on the lawn between the drive and the harvested cornfield, and I could hear her in the kitchen, banging and rattling pots and pans.

I felt it necessary to make some remark about what had happened at the husking bee, though I was then still having difficulty putting the pieces of the evening back together. Justin laughed good-naturedly, and said I was not the first to have gotten a snootful and made a fool of himself. "I think Fred and the boys were out to get you, anyway."

"Out to get me?"

"To see how well you could stand up to the old stuff. I guess you didn't pass the test. They're annoyed with you, but it won't last. They're not down on outsiders as much as they seem to be."

"I'm a fair drinker, but—"

Justin agreed. "It's pretty strong."

"And it leaves you with a blank." I tried to explain the curious impression I had of something ominous growing out of the dance. He said I was imagining things.

"It's just one of the old ways, you know. If you transgressed, it was against them, not against the people."

"What are the 'old ways'?"

He was friendly and casual. "Well, let's say they're the things that are—handed down. Maybe they're not the most convenient ways, but they suit us. We leave people to live their lives the way they want and we want to live ours the same." He shrugged. "Hell, Ned, I'm supposed to be the Harvest Lord, and I'm not sure I understand it all myself. All I know is it's what I've been taught. And it's been fine for me. I'm a lucky fellow. I told them after you went home—you acted the way you did because you don't understand yet."

"Understand what?"

He regarded me quizzically for a moment, then glanced over at the cornfield, to the spot where I had discovered the doll. "Well—now don't get me wrong—but a fellow oughtn't to go around snaffling pieces out of a friend's cornfield. Some things are meant for a purpose, y'know."

I felt the flush of embarrassment at my theft of the corn doll being thus revealed. Who had known besides Worthy? Who had seen me? "I'm sorry, Justin, I didn't realize—"

"That's what I mean. I know you didn't. Don't worry, the crops are safe in. See—it's the way we're born. We can't help ourselves. It's all of our ancestors, all the way back."

"What was it—that little doll?"

"A man has to eat," he said in a penetrating tone. "His food comes from the earth. And the earth must be thanked."

"How?"

"It must be reverenced."

"With corn gods?"

His eyes held mine in a level gaze for a moment; then they took on a puckish gleam. "Did you figure out who it was—that night?"

"In the field? No—"

"We must learn to discover what is possible."

I heard him, yet I was miles away; not miles, but as far as Soakes's Lonesome, on the Widow's mushroom hunt. *A man must learn—*

"Did you like the little 'experience'?"

—to discover—

"The music? The little cask? Your friends?"

—what is possible. . . .

Justin's eyes now held a smile. "Is it such an enigma? Such a sphinx? Come on, Ned, a fellow as smart as you—"

I was trying to put it together. "It was you, then?"

He laughed again, a deep, rumbling laugh. "Not me. I'm no actor. I told you, we went to the movies. And I didn't mean him, I meant the lady."

I was mentally stumbling, trying to make the connection, to grasp on to the reality forming in my mind. The doll in Justin's field—the veiled figure below our meadow. "You mean they're the same?"

"There is only one."

"Who?"

His expression sobered. "She's been a riddle for a long time. We thought sure you'd get it."

"*Not* the Corn Maiden."

"No."

"Then—"

"She is very old."

. . . *older than Rome or Greece, older than Crete, than Babylon or Egypt; as old as the dawn of time* . . .

Suddenly I saw. Saw clearly. I knew now who she was: the sphinx unveiled. "I—" Fumbling for words.

"—didn't know. 'Course you didn't. Now you do." He nodded, his amusement gone. "Now you do," he repeated. "She's our Mother. The Mother Worthy Pettinger cursed."

A man must learn to discover what is possible.

A little "experience."

Not the Corn Maiden, but someone else.

The Mother.

"You worship something called the Mother? Mother—" He was waiting for the last word; I supplied it: "Earth."

He made an equivocal gesture with one hand. "She is—paid homage." If I had watched closely, he went on, I had seen it all in the Corn Play. This was not merely a play, but the enactment of a belief—namely, that the renewal of life is the natural counterpart of the sexual union of the Harvest Lord with a spirit of growth, a goddess of fertility. No, the Corn Maiden was not the Mother, but one acting in her place.

"Fertility is the important thing to us here. Death is a terrible thing. But for us barrenness is worse. If you're a farmer, that's about the worst thing that can happen to you. In the play, if the corn sprouts in due season, it's because the Earth Mother has been impregnated, and was caused to bear."

"Christ, Justin—fertility rites?"

"If you like." Again a gentle smile. "But what is to stop people from believing? There are stranger beliefs in this world. Ours is very simple. And it keeps us from—" He paused, gravely looked off at the annihilated cornfield.

"From what?"

"From being afraid. We fear only one thing, that something should interfere or change the cycle."

"Which cycle?"

"Of life. Of living things, of the seasons. Of the natural order of things. The Eternal Return." He spoke simply but earnestly, with a depth of conviction I found it difficult to fault.

"But they go to church on Sunday and sing hymns, like everyone else in the land."

"Is everyone like everyone else in the land? I don't think a Cornishman would agree with that. Being different's part of our heritage. Personally, I'm proud of it." It was not arrogance I read in his face, but a realization of himself, of what he stood for in the eyes of the villagers, and his responsibility to them. They had honored him; he would not fail them. "If you have questions, take them to the Widow Fortune," he said kindly. "And," he added, almost as an afterthought, "as you hope for tolerance from the villagers, so they must hope for tolerance from you."

"What about tolerance for Worthy?"

"What d'you mean?"

"Simply that it doesn't seem to me that anyone's taking into account what he wants for himself."

"I don't know if Mr. Deming will want to take that into account. Worthy understands."

"Understands what?"

"What he's supposed to do. Mr. Deming does not consider that the honor's to be taken lightly. Nor do the rest of the villagers."

I started to protest; he moved toward me, putting his hand on my shoulder. Even in his casualness, he gave me the feeling he was exercising all his influence, cautioning me not to behave rashly, trying to protect me from my own ignorance. That in some unspoken way he was to be trusted, that he of himself could control the situation.

"I understand. It's natural to doubt. Not to believe. But give it time."

Who was I to try to solve mysteries that had been insoluble for the ages. Napoleon, trying to solve the riddle of the sphinx. I would give it time—for now.

When Justin went back to work, I stowed my painting gear in the car, then drove over to the Pettinger farm. No one answered my knock at the back door; the barn was closed, the place deserted. As I left, I glimpsed Worthy's mother at an upstairs window; she made no sign.

Beth passed me going in the opposite direction, toward the bridge. She waved, then sped on without stopping, and I wondered where she was hurrying to. Returning to Penrose Lane, I stopped next door to speak with Maggie. I rang the bell; she answered, kissing me warmly and pressing my hand.

"Hi, Ned! I'm so happy about the baby!" I thanked her, and asked if she knew where Beth had gone.

"She said she had an appointment somewhere, then she wanted to look at wallpapers for the new nursery. Come on into the kitchen—I've got Robert's lunch on. Have some?"

I declined, accepting her offer of a drink instead. Carrying Robert's tray, she brought me into the sun porch. She set down the tray, waited for a pause in the narrative on the record player, then lifted the arm and shut it off.

"See who's here, dear," she said, "Ned."

"Well, m'boy, pull up a chair."

"Robert's reading *Anna Karenina*."

Robert readied himself while his wife unfolded a card table and set it up over his knees, put the tray on it, and opened a napkin and tucked it in his hand.

"Thank you, dear." He began feeling out the carefully cut meat with his fork, the tips of his fingers working like antennas over the implements; Maggie hovered to assist his hand in finding the glass of milk or the salt shaker. When he had finished, she took his napkin from his lap, removed the tray, and bent to kiss him before going out.

"Don't forget your drops, dear. Perhaps Ned will take down the card table—all right? Anything you need before I go?"

"Can I have a cigar?"

"Oh, Robert, you know what the Widow said." She gave me a wink, set the tray down again, and took a cigar from the humidor on the desk, did her ritual of preparing it for Robert, then held the match while he lighted it.

"That's quite a ceremony she performs," I observed when Maggie had gone.

"Yes, Margaret's father taught her." He blew three smoke rings, the last passing through the first. "Did I do it?"

"Bull's-eye. You should see them—" I stopped in embarrassment.

"It's all right, m'boy, no need for blushes. The worst thing is for people to be conscious of my—infirmity. I'm used to it. Always amazes me how much I can see."

"You have some vision still?"

"Blind as a bat. But I can see things in my head. The wonderful part is that for me they never change. Take Margaret, for example. I know she's older now, but I see her exactly as she was when I lost my sight. And I get along. I have her, and my talking books. After *Anna Karenina,* I'll undoubtedly get around to *David Copperfield,* finally. Is there a small bottle here somewhere?" His fingers were groping among the things at his elbow; I leaned over and put into his hand a rubber-stoppered bottle.

"That's it, thanks." As he removed his glasses and set them aside, I was astonished to see that he was not merely lacking vision, but that he lacked the very organs needed for vision. Drawing out the wads of cotton that filled the eyeless sockets, he put drops into each, set the bottle down, and replaced the cotton with fresh pieces. When he had screwed the top on the bottle, he felt for a paper tissue and used it on the lenses of his dark glasses.

"Haven't seen a thing for a long time, but I still wipe my glasses every time I put them on. Creatures of habit, that's what we are." He settled the lenses over the bridge of his nose and felt for his cigar in the chrome stand at his side, then smoked in silence for several moments. "I must admit," he said reflectively, "going blind came as quite a blow. Bound to, I suppose."

I thought for an instant he was going to reveal the nature of his accident, but he dismissed the subject with a spin of his cigar tip, as though life's horrors were unaccountable, and hence not worth discussion. "Some tragedies are unspeakable," he went on, "but we must endure however we may. I'll tell you something, m'boy, even though I enjoy my talking-books, I'd give up all the books in the world to see one star again. That's what I miss the most, seeing the stars. We go out on the lawn sometimes at night and Margaret describes them to me; quite a one with the stars she is."

"Quite a one with everything," I said admiringly.

He nodded. "She's a good right hand. Corrects my letters—I'm a rotten typist. Keeps me from bumping into things. Think of it, these many years of keeping a fellow from skinning his shins—that's a career in itself. Margaret's quite a woman." He felt for the cigar stand and tapped his ash. "Anything particular on your mind?"

"Why?"

"Something in your voice."

"Robert—what's going to happen to Worthy?"

He shook his head, and blew out a cloud of smoke. "Hard to tell about Worthy. Lot of feeling about that. You can't go around damning the corn crop in this village and not have people angry." Worthy, it seemed, had been given a ticket-of-leave, and was being held in the back room of the post office under the ancient statute of durance vile.

"But he hasn't broken any law," I protested.

"No—none that's in the books. But in Cornwall Coombe there's a code of ethics not to be tampered with. To go against one is to go against all. It's not really a village, you know. It's more a clan, a tribe."

"Penrose tribe?"

"Partly. But a man has to show respect for both the village and its ways. What time is it?"

I looked at the clock on the desk. "Ten minutes to two."

"They'll be starting soon." He ran his tongue around the inside of his lips, then ruminatively touched it to the tip of his cigar. "About Worthy. I suppose it's a matter of—choices." He paused, tapping his ash again. I had the feeling he was picking his words carefully.

"Some probably wouldn't agree with me, but I believe a man's fate is in his own hands. 'Not in the stars, dear Brutus,' as Shakespeare says. No matter what a fortune teller may say, or an astrologer or a seer, the events that come to a man are determined by him and how he adjusts to those events. We're all offered choices. Our very existences often depend on these choices. Making the wrong one can change our lives, but at least the decision has been made; the brake has been released, the machinery can go forward again. But in going forward, it may bring a man to meet the fate he himself has sought."

"Did Worthy make the wrong choice?"

"I couldn't say."

"But it's such a small thing."

"There are degrees of smallness. I can understand your being interested in the boy's welfare, but it's out of your hands. I wouldn't worry. Most likely the elders'll give him a lecture and let him off."

He made a gesture, dismissing the subject, but still I felt that there was more to be said and resolved. He seemed to sense this in the silence. Nodding, he repeated Justin's words.

"If you have questions, take them to the Widow."

The church bell was tolling as I drove up to the Widow Fortune's door and knocked. There was no reply. Nor was the buggy in the drive. I waited another moment, then continued on to the Common. Passing the church, I saw some women moving up the steps. Just inside the open vestibule doors, someone—Mrs. Green, I thought—was handing out slips of paper from a sheaf in her hands. I glimpsed the Widow's white cap as she took one and started in. Her head turned quickly—a flash of expression, no more, but before she looked away again I read in her face things I had never seen there until that moment. Was it scorn? Contempt? Or was it denunciation?

She entered with the others and presently the bell stopped. Amys Penrose came out, closed the doors behind him, and went down the street toward the Rocking Horse Tavern. I drove past the north end of the Common, where a large pile of debris was being assembled for the Kindling Night celebration; then I parked in front of the drugstore and went in. Except for the boy behind the soda fountain, the place was empty. "What's going on over at the church?" I inquired. The boy shrugged and gave me a peculiar look. I walked out and, continuing up the street toward the post office, I caught various looks, and had several backs offered to me, which made me think of the shunning of the Pettingers when they had come to the Grange with their pumpkins.

Approaching the entrance to the post office, I received dark and sullen stares from several men lounging in the doorway, and when I attempted to pass, Constable Zalmon came to the door and blocked my way.

"Sorry, son, closed today."

"Is this a holiday?"

"Nope. Just closed."

The coldness of his tone told me the frost was on the pumpkin; and not only in the fields. Taking a quick glance over to the church, I proceeded along the sidewalk toward Penance House. I could hear the men's voices behind me. I leaned against a telephone pole, waiting. They were watching me, I could tell. When I glanced up, they deliberately turned away, focusing their attention on the closed church doors. I slipped up the walk to Penance House, ducked around the corner, and moved quickly across the yard to the side of the barn.

I had not been there since the day of the Agnes Fair, when Missy had pointed her bloody finger at me. There were several outbuildings scattered around, and, a short distance away, what looked like an abandoned hatchway set into the earth. The double doors were secured with a heavy chain and rusted padlock. I wondered what the doors led to.

Across the way was the rear of the post office. There was only one window, with a heavy latticework of metal screening over it. I crossed the lawn separating the two properties and crouched under the window, listening for the sound of voices. There was none. I stood and peered through the grille.

The room was small and sparsely furnished: the Constable's desk with a wooden swivel chair, askew on a square of worn carpeting, and a folding cot along one wall; on it sat Worthy Pettinger. His hands lay listlessly in his lap, and he looked pale and harried. I ran my nail over the screening; the boy started, then came to the window and opened it.

"You all right?" I asked. He nodded. "What are they going to do with you?" He shrugged and jammed his fists in his pockets, returning my gaze evenly but saying nothing.

"Listen, son, I'm sorry. I guess I'm the one who got you in this jam." He shook his head again. "They saw your letter. Tamar steamed it open; that's how they knew where to find you."

"You told them."

"No—no, I didn't. Christ—"

"How did they know which letter to steam open? Why would they look for a letter from John Smith if someone hadn't told them? Nobody knew 'cept you and me."

I was perplexed. "I can't say, boy. But I swear I didn't tell them."

"It doesn't matter." He turned away, walked to the desk, and stared down at the tray of food on top. "Food's good, anyhow."

I examined the screening. It was riveted tight along a solid iron frame, the frame sunk into the stone surround of the window. But the screening could be cut. "Listen, Worthy, you sit tight. I'm going back to the studio and get some heavy cutters, and after dark I'll come back and get you out of here."

"Go away." He threw himself down on the cot, clasping his hands in front of his chest, drawing his knees up in a fetal position. "It wouldn't do any good. They'd find me again. It wouldn't do any good." He was shivering.

I thought a moment. "Christ, Worthy, make sense! What have you done? There's no law—"

He leaped from the cot and slammed his palms against the iron grille. "Yes, there is!" he exclaimed hotly. "There's a law for everything! You can't help me. Nobody can. Don't interfere or you'll only make trouble for yourself. It's what they want. They always get what they want!" His dark eyes blazed; then the light in them went out and he wrenched himself away and sat in the swivel chair. I waited another moment, then left.

The men were still in front of the post office, looking over at the church. I crossed the Common and went into the tavern. Amys was hunched over a beer on the corner stool. I asked Bert for a Scotch-and-soda, and pulled up a stool next to the bell ringer. "What's going on, Amys?"

"Little of this, little of that. Not much in a small town like this."

"That's not what I mean. What's happening at the church?"

"Meetin'."

"What about?"

"How can I tell—I ain't there." He tossed off the rest of his beer.

"Amys, over there in the back of Penance House—what're those hatchway doors in the ground?"

He choked, sputtered, then let go in the spittoon. "Root cellar." He spun a quarter on the bar, wiped his mouth on a soiled handkerchief, and went out blowing his nose. I saw him look over at Penance House, then back in my direction before he went off toward the church.

Some men came in, Will Jones and Fred Minerva among them, and as they gathered farther along the bar I could tell from their furtive looks that I was the object of their conversation. I finished my drink and went out. The Constable was still in the doorway of the post office talking with the other men. One or two glanced my way, then returned to their discussion.

The church doors remained shut. The clock said a quarter after three. I thought again of Worthy on his ticket-of-leave, secured in the back room of the post office, and I wondered what I could do to help him.

I had no idea how long the meeting in the church would take, but I still wanted to talk to the Widow Fortune. In the meantime, I drove south along Main Street, down the River Road to the bait shack. I found Jack Stump seated beside the cold fireplace. I thought it odd, his having no nurse; then I remembered that all the women were at the church meeting.

He turned his head to me as I entered, giving me a long look. Finally he lowered his lids wearily and rested his head against the back of the chair.

"It's cold in here, Jack. Why don't I poke up a fire?" He made no sign; I went about laying some kindling. When it began crackling, I brought a blanket from the bed and covered him. As I tucked it around his shoulders, his hand appeared from beneath the folds and grasped mine.

"It's O.K., old-timer. How about some tea?" He stared at the flames in the fire. "Some of the Widow's One-B Weber's?" A faint smile flicked in the corners of his mouth before I went to put the kettle on. When the water was hot, I got down the tea box and brewed tea in the pot and filled the cup. I held it for him while he sipped, but his look told me he found it unpalatable. "Sorry, Jack, I haven't got anything stronger on me." A sly look came into his eye. "You'd prefer some of the old stuff to the Widow's tea, huh?" He flashed another look, and I could see both fear and contempt in his eyes. He made a quick hissing sound through his teeth.

"Don't worry about the Soakeses, Jack." He shook his head, pushed the cup away. He leaned back against the chair and immediately fell asleep. I put the cup and saucer aside and carried him, blanket and all, to the cot. His body seemed to weigh scarcely anything, and when I laid him down I had the sudden premonition that spring would never see him back on his rig again.

As I slid my arm from under his neck, I felt something catch. The button of my jacket sleeve had become entangled in the little red cloth bag around his neck, and when I tried to free my arm the string broke. I slipped out the bag and held it between my fingers, looking down at the peddler's face, agonized even in repose.

The wood crackled in the fireplace, providing a dancing light against the wall. Jack stirred uneasily as a clock chimed the half-hour. Absently, I toyed with the cloth bag for a moment; then, feeling something inside, I opened it and spilled the contents into my hand. There were a few bits of dried, crushed herbs, the rolled scrap of paper the Soakeses had scribbled their warning on, and a ring—a small irregularly shaped circlet, carved in the village fashion from a piece of hollow bone. I smiled, thinking of the Widow Fortune's charms for toothache and for warts, and wondered what my own little red bag had contained. I blew away the bits of herbs, then unrolled the scrap of paper, the sinister note the Soakes had left in Jack's trap:

This is a WARNING!
At your peril
Keep OUT!

I stared at it for a moment, holding it up to the fire. My hand must have been shaking slightly for I saw a small bright shape rippling on the sooty wall next to the fireplace, the tiniest beam reflected back from my hand. I thought it was my wedding ring, but as I dropped that hand, holding the paper in the other, the small shape still remained, like the signal of a tiny heliograph flashing a message. I reversed the paper into the light and discovered what was causing the little ripple on the wall. When I had read the too clear words on this other side I felt a sudden chill, though the fire had warmed the room—the chill that comes not from any drop in body temperature but from those faint warning notes that are sounded in the dim recesses of the mind.

I tucked the scrap of paper in my pocket, and was returning the bone ring to the bag when Mrs. Green came with food for Jack. She stopped, and without greeting stared at me. Hurriedly I retied the string around his neck and slipped the bag inside his shirt. I left quickly. There was still time to get to Soakes's Lonesome before dark.

24

Two hours later, when I arrived at the Widow Fortune's, the small, gabled house looked gloomy and forlorn with the corn patches cut and shocked. The dying sun seemed to draw the fire from the maple leaves, giving the trees that framed the house a dark, foreboding air. Striding past the stubbled yard, I knocked on the door; again there was no reply. I went along the drive, where I found Fred Minerva's wagon parked near the beehives: two men had just finished loading the wagon with wooden casks of honey mead from the shed. I moved aside as Fred drove the team out, the men dour, silent, granite-eyed, surveying me from the tailgate. Out on the street, Fred pulled up as Mrs. Green came to meet them. She hurried away with one of the casks.

I went down the lane to the barn. Through the open doorway, I could hear the cow knocking her hoofs against the stall, and the rhythmical sound of milk squirting into a tin pail.

The old lady's long skirts covered the milking stool she sat on; the cow gave me a bland, uninquisitive look as I entered.

"Good evening."

"That it is." She glanced at me briefly, then returned her attention to the cow's teats, two of which she held loosely in her hands.

"Milking time," I observed.

"Comes 'round this hour reg'lar as sin. Cow that's got milk wants to give it," she replied indifferently, sitting stolid and taciturn.

"How's Caesar's Wife?"

"Not above reproach, as Caesar's Wife should be. But then, who is? Hold still, there, miss or ma'am, or whatever you are. Girl's edgy tonight."

"Why?"

"Hard to tell. Folks and beasts alike gets itchy long 'bout now, when the harvest's in and the work's done."

"And Harvest Home—?"

"Aye. Harvest Home." She looked up toward the rafters as though to peer beyond the rooftree to the heavens themselves. "Be a full moon, too. They call it the Moon of No Repentance around here."

I leaned against a joist. "Why's that?"

"Come harvest you take what there is—too late for repentance."

I gave her a thin smile. "Another tradition?"

"Certain."

"I keep hearing about tradition."

"'Pears some folks don't hear enough, the way they behave in public." The regular ping of the white stream hitting the side of the milk pail emphasized the deep undercurrent of her words. "Some folks, it appears, have a mind to meddle where it's none of their affair, and to scoff where they have no right to scoff. There are some hereabouts who don't take kindly to a man who makes fun at our ways.

"Your bein' an outsider, them old ways is a pretty hard thing for a man to seize on to. Outsiders always had that trouble; take Robert, for instance. He had trouble some years ago; he learned. But hereabouts in Cornwall Coombe we look on the old ways with partic'lar relish. You take a woman, now. A woman is different than a man. There's things in a woman a man may never understand. Hold still, there, girl." She rapped the cow's flank as its tail switched. "Bein' a man, you ought to think about the fact that there's things in women you can never understand."

I eyed her coldly. "What things?"

Her laugh was rough. "You think you know women? You think you know your wife? Think you understand her body, her mind? Her needs? They're all different than yours, every last one. But because you don't understand, you have no way but to accept it."

"Or perish?"

"Maybe. A woman is supposed by most men to be heavenly, but if the truth was known, she ain't heavenly a'tall. She's a creature of the earth, she works and loves and lives with her feet firmly planted on the ground, and them that don't is a sorry lot of dreamers. Look at your city ladies, in their beauty parlors and their lunch places and their shops and their love nests. Are they happy, them and their nail polish?" She released the two teats, wiped her hands on her apron, pressed the bony joints, then stripped the last drops of milk from the cow's teats. "There may have been a man before there ever was a woman in the Garden of Eden, but the man would have died long ere he did without her. If it weren't for the women, where would anyone be? Unborn. Just—not livin'. Just somewhere else in the universe. 'Ceptin' the women, you'd have men who'd never know the light or the air or whatever joys God may see fit to bring us."

"Or the horrors." I laid an edge to my voice.

"Horrors, too. That's what comes of bein' born of woman. But pity the poor creature for what she longs for and for what she never gets. But longin', they ought to be given their way. There's a good old girl," she told the cow, rising and walking to the doorway where she set down her stool and pail. Ignoring me, she crossed the lane and went into the field, looking off at the empty land. She remained there statue-like, and might have been carved from an immense quarried rock, a massive and columnar sculpture, dark, brooding, sphinx-like. But this riddle—I could read it now. I did not like her any more; the thought saddened me.

As I came up behind her, I heard her speaking, not to me but to the stubbled furrows.

"'I was born like the maize in the field, like the maize I was cherished in my youth, I came to maturity, I was spent. Now I am withered and I die.'" Becoming aware of my presence, without turning, she said, "There's an epitaph for you. It was an Indian's." Her voice sounded heavy, weary as she nodded and said, "Aye, she is a friend to man."

I took a step to her. "Mother Earth?"

Her head turned abruptly; she gave me a long look, searching, as though even now she would be friendly, still would command my respect and understanding. "Yes," she replied simply. Bending, she scooped up some soil, clenched it before my face, then opened her hand. The form of her palm and fingers remained pressed into the moist loam. "This is her. Look at her." She took my hand and laid the clod in it. "Feel her. Smell her. She is there, has been, will be, till the end. She is the beginning and the end. Who will deny her? Who *can* deny her? You have questions? Ask them. Listen to her, she will tell you."

"What will she tell me?"

"Do not be so scornful. She is all of woman, and more. She bears as a woman bears. She gives and sustains as a woman does, but a woman dies, being mortal. But she is not. She is ever fruitful. She is the Mother."

I stared at the mounded mass in my palm.

"Lay seed in her, she will bear. She will nourish and sustain, and in the sustaining will give forth and provide. And that seed you give her will make another seed, and that another, and another, again and again—forever the Eternal Return." Slowly her arms rose and straightened, her fists opened, spread broad, an impressive gesture of benevolence, a priestess acknowledging the deity. "Let us pay her tribute. Let us beg her for her strength and protection. Let us pray that she may bring forth her strong plants, her rich food, her very life. How selfish we are. We give her but a seed, a kernel, a dead thing. Yet see what she returns to us. Such bounty, such riches, such life! What mortal is there who cannot help but wonder at her, love her, fear her?

"The Bible says Eve was born of Adam's rib, but he was born of the earth, so there was woman before there ever was man.

She is not merely a mate, a life's companion, a helpmeet; she is the moving force, the power. And while Adam was abroad in the forest, she was in the fields planting and tilling. What man but a fool will reject the counsels of his spouse, who will give life to his sons? What man will spurn her, not venerate her, she who shares his bed and board, who tends his fire and his cookpot? The Lord preserve the women. The Lord preserve the fruitful Mother. And she will give, and give, and give, till there is no more to be given."

She took the clod from me, pressed it, and let it crumble and sift between her fingers, the particles falling into the furrow.

"And in the end she will take it all back. There's the irony. For as a man dies, so does a woman. It is the Mother who must succeed in the end, since everything must return to her. It is the tribute we must pay for her patronage." She stared down at the crumbled soil, spread it with her toe. "Come Planting Day, she will need even that moiety."

She turned and went back to the barn, and took up her pail and stool. "I bid you good night," she said.

"No." My voice rose sharply. She blinked at me, trying to understand my purpose in coming.

"You're angry," she said, a trifle wistfully. "Too bad. I hoped we might've been friends. You have something more, then?" I nodded. "Come along, say what you have to say." She motioned me to close the barn door; then, as I followed her, she made her way to the dooryard where she disposed of the stool and ushered me up the steps.

When she had poured the milk into a crock and put it in the refrigerator, she nodded for me to be seated as she put the kettle on to boil. The lamp she had turned on laid a warm pool of light on the scarred and ringed surface of the wooden table. She washed her hands, and when the kettle began to sing she took it from the stove plate. She brought down the box of Weber's tea; brewing it, she spoke over her shoulder. "Who shall say, 'Be like me'? 'Be like all the others'? If the bull cares to give milk, who shall say him nay? And if folks—folks like me—think about the old ways, who shall say them nay? Who shall say me nay? I have a cow, and if I believe the Mother fattens the plain for Caesar's Wife to provide me milk, no man's goin' to tell me no." She brought the cups on their saucers and laid them on the table. "If your wife tells you that it's because of women and their strength that men survive, who shall tell her no? Not you, if you're as smart as I think you are."

Her step as she laid out the tea things was scarcely as spry as I had seen it on other occasions. Her face looked tired, and without that inner spark that usually animated her every word and gesture, and I saw that she was a very old woman. There was pain in her searching look; in back of the hooded eyes lay a question—hers, not mine, a question in answer to my question. She sipped, then took a hank of wool from a basket and began winding the end around her fingers.

"Planting Day? Spring Festival? Midsummer's Eve? Harvest Home? Certain they're older than the hills and they're not like Santy Claus that you stop believin' in when you catch your ma hangin' up stockin's Christmas Eve. They're in people's blood and marrow and hearts and they been there for centuries. You don't take them things lightly, nor do you laugh nor interfere just because you've had too many pulls at the jug. And a man who dares is bound to come to grief."

Outside, it was dark. The light above the table was a single beacon in the shadowy room. She continued winding the yarn. "Adam delved and Eve span," she said wearily. Thinking of what I had discovered an hour ago in Soakes's Lonesome, after leaving Jack Stump's, what I had known I would find, I remained silent, aloof, watchful of her, one hand employing the spoon to stir my cup, the other deep in my jacket pocket.

I knew I would never come to this kitchen again, never sit at her table, never drink her tea. It was, in a way, like the end of an affair: bitter, hopeless, irreparable.

"Spinning is a woman's natural work," I said at last.

"Aye, traditionally."

"We were speaking of grief. Has Worthy come to grief?"

She bit her lip. Then: "We all come to grief, one time or another."

"What will happen to him?"

"That's no concern of yours."

"Because I'm an outsider? Worthy's like a son to me."

"He was a son before he ever met you."

"He's a kid! Sixteen! What did he do?"

"He damned the corn!" Her eyes widened. "He damned the crops. That's a serious business."

"All he did was run off from something he didn't want, to find something he did want. Is that so terrible? You never would have found Worthy if—"

"Yes?"

"—if Tamar Penrose hadn't seen my letter and steamed it open. She told the Constable, who told Mr. Deming. Mr. Deming called you, the night I brought you the sewing machine. You sent him after Worthy."

"Don't you go glarin' at me, you and them dark Greek looks. Worthy Pettinger knew what he was doin'; he had plenty of time to think it out—all them weeks I sent him 'round to you, hopin' he'd come to his senses. He was chosen. He was to be the Young Lord in the play."

"But you *had* the play. The Minerva kid was the Young Lord."

"How much better Worthy would've been. Made for it, he was. Proper age and all. Seven years younger than Justin, almost to the day." She shook her head sadly. "It's not so much for him, but for the other boys comin' along behind him. Can't have notions like Worthy's goin' abroad through the village. He's got to be taught—"

Now, I thought; now. Say it now. Say it and be done. I said, "Like the Soakeses taught Jack Stump."

"Aye."

"Rolling him in ashes—"

"Aye."

"Old Man Soakes cutting out his tongue with his knife—"

"Aye."

"The boys sewing his mouth with their canvas needles—"

"Aye. Poor Jack, all he did was talk, and for that they mutilated him beyond hope."

"No! For that *you* mutilated him beyond hope! You and the women. The Soakeses never touched Jack Stump!"

"Here, now—" She drew back from me as though to mantle herself in the shadows. I reached in my pocket and produced the scrap of paper with the writing over the skull and bones. "There's a warning the Soakeses supposedly left him in the woods—only it wasn't from the Soakeses, it was from you!" I turned it over and laid it before her. "Does that look familiar?" I reached to the shelf above the sink and grabbed a box from it. Tea sprayed around me as I tore out the liner and spread it beside the piece of foil paper, whose silvery reflection had caught my eye by Jack Stump's fire. "Read it."

"Can't see without my specs," she said truculently.

"You don't have to see. You can feel it." I seized her fingers and pressed them on the foil lining. "Weber's tea. Embossed. With 'One-B'—remember?" I turned Jack's message over and pressed her fingers there, on the identical foil, embossed the same way. "One-B Weber's."

"I don't expect I'm the only person to use Weber's tea."

"You have to send for it—remember? To London. You used one of those scraps from your kitchen spindle to write the note, and had it put in Jack's trap, the traps you moved yourself." She pulled her hand away; I seized her arm and gripped it. "Jack Stump was in the woods all right, and you didn't want him there any more than the Soakeses did. But you decided to do something about it. You caught him, you and the other women over at Irene Tatum's for a quilting party. He wasn't rolled in the ashes from Soakes's still, but in the ashes from Irene's soap kettle. Then you cut his tongue out. With these." I yanked my hand from my pocket, raised it, and brought it down. The teacup and saucer broke as the pair of rusty shears struck them.

"There's your missing scissors, Mary, and you didn't leave them at Asia Minerva's house. You lost them in the woods when you attacked Jack. You were looking for them the day we hunted mushrooms. After you cut off his tongue, you took your needle and thread and stitched his mouth up. You planned it all, the quilting party at Irene Tatum's house, all of it."

She looked at me across the broken pieces of the cup, something defiant in her eyes. "First time you ever called me 'Mary.' Seems strange. People don't call me that much. Clem used to, of course —Robert sometimes." One hand came from her lap and touched a fragment of china. "Aye, Jack was a talker. And a meddler, and that's a bad combination in any soul, man or woman. Tamar put the quietus to him."

"Tamar?"

"It was she who done the cuttin' and sewin' of poor Jack. Strong measures, I'll agree, stronger than was warranted, maybe, but sometimes Tamar's got to be restrained. Yet I couldn't say it wasn't necessary. Nobody would've been beholden to Jack for goin' off on one of his territory circuits and talkin' at every doorstep along the way."

"Talking about what?"

"Things we don't want talked about." She spoke angrily. "Some things are no one's business but our own. We got skeletons in our closets same as other folks. Jack was afflicted by tongue and nose, both. Went pokin' his nose around the Lonesome, where he oughtn't to have been. Went pokin' it around town and findin' out things outsiders oughtn't to be concerned with."

"I'm an outsider."

"But we didn't want you to be." She looked up at me with mute appeal. "*I* didn't want you to be." She waited for me to speak; I knew I must not, for my own safety. "Jack's a sly one," she continued. "Puts one and one together and comes up with two. What he saw, he knew, and what he knew, he was bound to tell. We got our privacies. Some more regrettable than others— even Jack would admit that."

I spoke coldly. "You don't have to worry; he won't talk any more. And you don't have to worry about getting him back on his rig by spring—he'll never see the winter out."

She stared at the shattered cup and saucer. "You think I'm evil. A bad old woman. Yes, I'm old, and I crave peace. I don't have much time to grow older. Soon someone's going to have to relieve me of my—duties. Someone will have to come after me."

"Missy?"

"You are too disdainful. Missy, perhaps. Or, before her, another. But while I live I'll be doin' my duties. I've lived as I was taught. I've lived in what I believed."

She looked down at the table, ran her fingertips along the blade of the rusty scissors. "I miss the old humbug, y'know. Hearin' him comin' 'round with his clatter and his bang and gabbin' a body's ear off."

I pulled my hands to me, thrusting them in my lap, wrenching my fingers that I should not strike an old woman. When I could govern myself again, I got up.

"What about Worthy?"

Her head lifted, her eyes blinked at the light, as if trying to see past it, past me, into some cloudy future. "Worthy Pettinger," she said softly. The light etched her features; she looked haggard, worn, as she began picking up the shattered pieces of the blue teacup. "Clem bought me them cups the year we was married. All these years, and not a one of 'em broke. Till now. I don't s'pose I can mend it, can I?" She thought a moment. Then: "No," she concluded, "some things is forever past mendin'." One by one she laid the broken pieces in the saucer.

25

It was the end of the great back-to-the-land movement. Henceforward it would be country mouse into city mouse again. What other answer was there? What else to do. But how could I bring myself to put it to Beth, to tell her how we had been fooled and connived against? To tell her what the women really were?

Tell her what the Widow Fortune was?

Perplexed, indecisive, but with a growing determination, after a sleepless night, the next morning I gravitated to the Common, my mind still working over the reason for the attack on the peddler. *We have our privacies,* the Widow had said. Something private, which Jack Stump had discovered. Still trying to conjure up an idea of what discovery, I watched Irene Tatum's pickup truck rattle down the north end of Main Street and pull up to the Common. Some of the Tatum kids leaped out and, under Irene's supervision, unloaded a stack of wooden planks and hauled them across the grass to the bonfire heap. The construction had grown considerably in the past two days, a crude frame of timbers and boards nailed crisscross to hold together the assemblage of boxes, crates, and debris that had been jumbled inside. Ladders were being used to hand material up to the top, where Jim Minerva was securing it with twine, while below groups of people viewed the work as it proceeded, pointing, laughing, chatting.

From the chimneys and eaves of the houses hung the woven corn symbols, swaying in the breeze: Harvest Home was coming.

Inside the post office, it was business as usual. I passed the open doorway, then slipped along the side of the building to the rear. I crept up to the window and looked in. The room was empty. The door was open and I could see Myrtil Clapp at the counter, stamping a package for Mrs. Buxley, sho stood on the other side of the window. Glancing at me, the minister's wife gave me a quick dither of fingers, and I hurried around to the street to intercept her as she came out, then walked beside her across the Common.

She gave me one of her best smiles. "Lovely day, Ned, isn't it the *love*liest? And tonight will be one of the most exciting—see the bonfire we're going to have."

"Mrs. Buxley, what's happened to Worthy?"

"Worthy? *Pett*inger? Why, nothing." She wrinkled her eyebrows. "Worthy's left."

"Left?"

She nodded, arranging the neckline of her dress. "Mrs. Zee drove him over to the turnpike to catch the bus. He's gone to New York. At least he *said* he was going to New York." She gave a little shrug. "Of course, one never knows what the young people are going to do these days, does one?"

"He simply left?"

She threw her gloved hands out palms up. "Simply. Ewan Deming had a little talk with him. I think he rather reprimanded Worthy. Set him straight, so to speak. Then he let Mrs. Zee drive him to the bus. Isn't it strange about the sheep?"

"The sheep?"

"Yes. See—they're gone. Amys has put them to fold. A sure sign winter's coming. Whenever the sheep are gone, I know it's time to get out my fur coat. Hope you've got plenty of warm clothes—our winters can be terrible. One year the snow was five foot high right here on the— Ned? Are you all right?"

"Yes. Of course."

"Suddenly you looked—well—" We crossed to the far sidewalk in front of the church, where she gave me her arm to help her onto the first step. "Thank you." She let out a little laugh, as if we were wicked. "See you in church." Waggled fingers, went on up the steps, patted the bell ringer's shoulder as he sat knitting. "*Pretty* colors, Amys." Went inside.

He gave her a look and plied his needles.

"Been here all morning, Amys?"

"All mornin'."

"Did you see Worthy Pettinger leave?"

"Ayuh. Old Deming gave him what-for; then Mrs. Zee drove him off in his car."

"Did he have a suitcase?"

"Ayuh." He began counting stitches. I went a little distance down the sidewalk and turned in to the cemetery, made my way up the slope through the maze of headstones, and stood on the knoll, thinking.

Then I quickly left and went down to the library, where I asked the librarian to find me a particular volume of the *Farmer's*

Almanac. When my theory had been corroborated, I thanked her and left. Margie Perkin's head hung out the window of the beauty parlor as she chatted with Betsey Cox, the bank teller, below. On the other side of the Common, the perpetual checker game at the firehouse was interrupted while Merle Penrose and Harry Gill stood in the doorway watching Mrs. Brucie come out of the grocer's and go into the drugstore. Jim Minerva tied a corncob on a stick and jammed it in the top of the bonfire pile. A cheer arose from among the onlookers, and Mrs. Buxley, who had brought Mr. Buxley out onto the church steps, waggled her fingers. Directly across the way, at the post office, Tamar Penrose came to see what the applause was about.

I stared moodily at the autumn sky, as blue as it had been in August, in June. I recalled the morning of the Agnes Fair, walking down Penrose Lane, pledging myself to the earth, thinking how right it all felt, how we would find our places in Cornwall Coombe. *You folks be happy here,* said the Widow Fortune; *That's all you've got, each other, and bein' happy together.*

My jaw clamped. I felt aloof, apart, a stranger. Who was I? Who were they? The villagers of Cornwall Coombe; and I an alien, an outsider, never to be an insider. But I no longer cared to be. They were altered, and so was I. All I wanted now was—suddenly I wanted terribly to see Beth, to talk to her.

Tamar went back into the post office. The back room was empty now. Worthy had gone. He hadn't cared much, after all; had left without saying goodbye. When you came down to it, he wasn't any different from the rest.

Myrtil Clapp came out of the post office, followed by Tamar, who locked the door and went toward her house. I stood on the knoll, thinking about Justin Hooke. Why had he lied? I kept wondering. Why would Justin Hooke tell me a deliberate lie?

I went down the back slope and stepped over the iron fence. The marshy ground squished under me, filling with water. I shoved a branch into the earth. It drove in easily and when I pulled it out the hole filled immediately. The place wasn't a grave; it was a bog.

Amys was watching me from above. I climbed up and stood beside him.

"Wet down there," he commented. "Good land if they'd drain 'er. 'Bout run out of room up here. Don't know where I'll put the next one that kicks the bucket."

"Why don't they drain that land?"

"Wouldn't pay. She'll wet up like that again."

"When it floods."

"Ayuh."

"Amys, what's Justin Hooke hiding?"

"How can I tell? I ain't Justin Hooke."

"Grace Everdeen didn't kill herself."

"She didn't?"

"No. At least not by jumping off the Lost Whistle. Justin says she dashed herself on the rocks, because the river was low that year. Only it wasn't. There'd been a flood that spring. You said yourself that the winter before Gracie came back was a bad one. Snow five feet deep, people had to tunnel, some of your sheep died. There was a thaw, and then the river flooded. The river was high all that summer, just like this year. The drought—the Great Waste—came *after* Gracie died, not *before*. So there weren't any rocks. Justin's lying." I paused, looked closely at Amys, then said, "And if it was flooded like this, you couldn't have dug a grave for her."

He turned away slightly, examining his horny palms.

"Amys? She's not there, is she?"

He did not reply immediately, and when he did it was with difficulty. "No, sir."

"You never buried her, did you?"

"Yes, sir. I did. Mr. Deming said to dig and I dug. But it was all mud, and water three inches deep in the bottom. Fast as I bailed 'er out, water seeped in again. Only a cold man like Ewan Deming'd consign the unhappy dead to such a place. I told him it was wrong. Deming said, 'Fill 'er in.' When the elders left, I pulled out the box and hid it, then filled in the hole. That night I put her on my barrow and took her where she'd be dry and safe."

He turned with a pleading look, his eyes watering. "In the name of God, don't tell. Please—they'll—"

"I won't, don't worry. What did you do with her?"

He looked once again down the slope to the grave marker, then motioned me with his head. I followed him across the Common to Penance House and out back to the barn. He took me behind it to where the sheds were, and, beyond them, the hatchway dug into the ground. Glancing over his shoulder, he crouched at the doors and undid the lock securing the chain.

Three beams set into the earth served as steps. In the musty dimness, I could make out the earthen sides of a small room lined with bare shelves where roots and vegetables had once been stored for winter use. Along the far wall, I saw a long, dark shape, shrouded by some kind of covering. Amys drew back a dusty tarpaulin and I looked down on the coffin of Gracie Everdeen.

"It's dry as the Sahara down here," he whispered hoarsely. "Never gets no water, never no rain nor snow. There she lies—the last of sweet Gracie."

The pine box rested on two sawhorses, and the boards were badly warped and shrunken, so that there were wide spaces between them.

"Weren't you afraid someone would find out she's here?"

"Nobody comes down here. I got the only key."

"It's not a very big box, is it?"

"No, sir."

"But Gracie was a tall girl, wasn't she?"

"But pretty," he said quickly. "Gracie was pretty as a picture."

"I remember you said so."

He shook out the tarpaulin, raising a cloud of dust, and I helped him redrape the box. He leaned to smooth a corner, and as he stepped back the toe of his shoe caught on a sawhorse leg, sliding it from under the coffin. The end tilted, then hit the floor with a dry, wooden impact. He bent quickly and lifted the end again, replacing it on top of the sawhorse. As he straightened the tarp again, I saw something underneath, a small pile of some substance on the floor. While I watched, it grew larger, a small cone filling out on the sides like sand in the bottom of an hour-glass. I knelt, looking closer. Overhead a faint trickle still continued through a crack where the coffin boards were shrunk apart. I caught them in my palm, brought them nearer.

Corn kernels.

Small, infinitesimally shriveled seeds of corn. I moved to the head of the box, motioned Amys to the foot, and together we lifted it. Another trickle of corn fell from the bottom. We shook the box, heard inside the dry rattle as more seeds sifted down, shook it until almost all the kernels had come out, until I was utterly certain there was nothing left inside, that for fourteen years this coffin had contained not the remains of Gracie Everdeen but only a sack of corn.

Requiescat in pace, Grace Everdeen.

But where was she resting? Why the carved inscription, the monument, the false grave?

With a sketch pad open on my knee, I sat on my folding stool, drawing the pear tree under the side window at the Hooke farm. As I laid out on the page the framework of the bare branches, I was reminded of the chestnut trees in the Tuileries in Paris, whose branches are cut back every autumn to grow again in the spring. I was trying very hard to think about Paris, and about anything that might keep me from thinking of what I did not want to think about.

I had not seen either Justin or Sophie when I came, nor were any of the men I had seen on former visits working on the premises. Justin's El Camino was parked near the barn, and there was bedding hung out to air.

I found it difficult to concentrate on my work, and presently it became even harder, for I heard voices coming from the open upstairs window.

"Don't, Sophie. Don't let anyone see you like this."

There was a pause, then again the low rumble of Justin's voice as he murmured something. Then, "You love me," he said.

"Yes."

"Then it's enough. For me, it's enough. If we can have a child, it will be raised as we have wished it, and that will be enough, too."

Her murmured response signified nothing to me.

"In the old ways," Justin said. "Trust them. Sophie?"

"Yes."

"*Trust them.*" Another pause. "And tomorrow, when we go to the Common—"

"I don't *want* to go to the Common—"

"We must. We must be there for them. When the bell strikes twelve, we must be there. You will behave as is fitting. Otherwise they'll hate you. You'll spend the rest of your life being hated, like—"

"Don't." I saw a flash at the half-open window as Sophie passed. She whispered something, and I dropped my head down over my sketchbook.

Justin called, "How's it going down there?"

"Fine." I nodded up to him; he lowered the sash and drew the shade. Soon I could hear them in the kitchen, talking in normal tones again, amid the rattle of silverware and the clink of china. Then something fell and broke, and Sophie was crying again; I heard her running upstairs. In a moment, Justin came out the kitchen door and down the steps. I returned to my work as he crossed the drive and stood beside me; from upstairs came the sounds of Sophie's sobbing.

Justin shoved his hands in his pockets. "Spilt milk." He drew a long breath. "She broke the cow pitcher." Making no comment about the drawing of the tree, he wandered a short distance away and stood at the edge of the field, looking off. He took his key ring from his pocket and jingled it, his hands clasped behind his back. He ran his fingers through his hair, then recrossed the drive.

"Well, I've got to get going."

I looked up. "See you tonight?"

"Kindling Night." He shook his head. "I don't think we'll be there. We've seen lots of Kindling Nights." He glanced at my page. "Nice tree. You're a good artist." He was holding out his hand. I rose and took it. "Goodbye, Ned," he said simply. I watched him walk to the truck, get in, and drive out around the other side of the house.

I moved my stool closer to the tree, making a few detail notes of the bark and tips. Then I heard something behind me and turned to find Sophie looking over my shoulder.

"Hi, Sophie."

"Hello, Ned. That's a beautiful drawing. How is the painting?"

I said the tree was the last thing to go in, and I would have it finished by tomorrow noontime. "If you and Justin are coming in, you can pick it up, if you like."

"Yes. Noon." She nodded absently, and I could see she was thinking of something else. She went to the tree and put out her hand, running her fingertips along one of the branches. "They never bear fruit, you know."

"Don't they?"

"No. Just leaves and flowers. I suppose that's why God gave them to us, just to be beautiful." She was silent for a moment, and when she spoke again it was with a forced control. "Ned, could you do something for me?"

"Sure, Sophie."

"Could you make it spring?"

"Spring?"

"Yes. Paint the tree in spring. Not with the bare branches, but with flowers. Make the tree all white and flowery. With little green leaves?"

"Well—" It had been part of the design of the picture that the branches be bare, the simple straight lines meant to play off the simple straight figure of Justin. I did not like the idea of putting in the flowers, particularly white ones; they would make the picture too pretty.

She saw my hesitation and smiled. "That's all right. It was just an idea." She turned away quickly and her hand came up and furtively brushed at one eye. I observed her as she stepped away to the tree and stood looking at the bare branches.

"Sophie, did you know Grace Everdeen?"

There was a quick, quivering motion about her shoulders as though a cold wind had touched her. "No."

"But you'd heard of her."

Still, head lowered, she looked at the lower trunk of the tree. "Yes." Her face was turned from me; I got up and approached her, saw her hand break off a dead twig from a branch. Her shoulders stiffened, her chin lifted. "She was bad. Grace Everdeen was bad. The baddest anyone could be. Bad—brought bad to the village—" Speaking by rote, as if hypnotized.

"How?"

Her eyes snapped, the color rose in her cheeks. "She came back for Harvest Home. She shouldn't have. She was *blighted*."

"What had blighted her?"

"She was *diseased!* That's why she ran away, so nobody would know. She never should have come back."

Diseased. Not pregnant, but diseased. Amys had said she was a fairy creature, Mrs. O'Byrne had said a horse.

"No one wants a Corn Maiden who's sick." Sophie's hands trembled at her breast. "Grace Everdeen was cursed by God. As I am cursed." She covered her face to hide the tears. "Jesus help me." She tore her hands away from her wet cheeks and looked at me, crying, "Help me!"

"How, Sophie? Tell me. I'll help you."

She stared a moment longer, as if she thought I might truly help. Then, "No—you can't. No one can." With a wild, despairing look, she spun and ran across the strip of lawn into the field, stumbling along between the gathered corn shocks, her pale hair streaming behind.

When I had gathered my things together, I went into the kitchen and telephoned Dr. Bonfils in Saxony.

Strangely, he seemed to be expecting my call.

When I came out again, Sophie was a small figure in the distance, crossing the field toward the road as the Widow Fortune's mare appeared around the bend. The buggy slowed, then stopped, and the old lady got down from the seat, and when Sophie came to her she put her arms around her, the blond head resting against the black dress, and I saw the Widow's large hand as it made comforting gestures about Sophie's shoulders.

I started up the drive to my car, then turned back, looking again at the pear tree. I decided that when I painted it I would make it bloom for Sophie Hooke. As it would in the springtime.

The Eternal Return . . .

Dr. Bonfils had agreed to see me if I could come to his office during his lunch hour; I had said it was important. When the nurse showed me in, he was having a "takeout" hamburger and chocolate milkshake at his desk. "Well, Ned," he began quickly, "I'm sorry. As I told your wife, as right as the old lady is most of the time, unfortunately even she makes mistakes. I'm sure it's a disappointment but surely one you can bear up under, eh?" He opened a little foil packet and squirted ketchup on top of the hamburger. I stared at him.

"I'm sorry, Doctor, I'm confused—what are you talking about?"

"Your wife. She came to see me yesterday. I'm afraid there's been a mistake. She's not going to have a baby."

"Not?"

"No. I'm sorry, but the examination was negative." He took a bite of his hamburger, allowing me time to absorb the shock of his news. "She didn't tell you?"

Beth passing me yesterday on the Old Sallow Road. Maggie telling me she had an appointment. Worried that I had been right; which I was.

"She was disappointed, naturally," the doctor went on. "All the signs were there. She's not the first case, of course. A woman wanting a baby, showing all the symptoms of conception. It's a form of physical hysteria."

"Doctor, can you do a test on me? To find out if I'm sterile?"

"Of course. Do you think you might be?"

I told him of Beth's obstetrical problems, but that I had always thought it might be the mumps I had caught from 'Cita Gonzalez when I baby-sat for her.

While we waited for the results of the test, I told the doctor my real reasons for having come to see him. "I wanted to ask if you remember a girl named Grace Everdeen."

"I remember her well. What do you want to know about her?"

"During the summer of 1958, while she was living over at Mrs. O'Byrne's, you were treating her, isn't that so?"

"I was treating her a good while before that."

I looked at him, surprised. "You were? Was she pregnant?"

It was his turn to show surprise. "Pregnant? No, nothing of the sort. As a matter of fact, as far as I know, Grace was still a virgin when she—ah, died."

"You knew she killed herself."

"Certainly."

"Do you know why?"

"I believe I do."

"Was it because of Roger Penrose?"

"Indirectly, I suppose—" He broke off. "Mr. Constantine, what exactly is your interest in the case?"

I said I was a friend of Mrs. O'Byrne's, and that through her I had taken an interest in the tragic story, and was trying to substantiate for her and for myself the facts of Grace's death. The doctor listened, and then, wiping his mouth and fingers, he said, "Grace Everdeen killed herself because she had contracted an incurable disease."

I leaned forward. "Which was—?"

"Acromegaly. It's a not uncommon condition. Did you know Grace was Swedish?"

"No."

"On her mother's side. For some reason, acromegaly seems to have a high incidence among Swedes. It is a condition arising from a hypersecretion of the growth hormone. A pituitary disorder."

"Is it fatal?"

"Often. In its early stages, it can induce in the patient the ability to perform extraordinary feats of strength. Then, as the disease takes hold, the patient suffers a gradual enfeeblement. He becomes emotional, distraught—manic, even. As it was in Grace's case—she was subject for some time to acute depression and delusions. Those are some of the mental stresses. In regard to the physical aspects, in extreme cases acromegaly can produce a giant."

"A giant."

"Indeed. When the adult body has attained its full growth, it stops. But with the incidence of acromegaly, the extremities continue to become enlarged, the hands and feet, the bones and cutaneous tissues of the face. Where skeletal overgrowth happens, the fingers may become excessively long or thickened. The frontal ridge of the head becomes enlarged, the jaw prognathous, the cheekbones knobby. It may, as in Grace's case, set the teeth wider apart. The tongue often becomes gross, causing difficulty in talking, and the lips thicken. Generally, the condition produces a monstrous physical change in the patient."

"How long does it take?" The irony of the situation struck me: all this medical information—I had come to find out one thing, and was on the point of discovering several.

"Sometimes the manifestations are slow to reveal themselves; in other cases—like Grace's—it can come fast after the initial onset."

"Not a *fairy*, but a *horse*," I repeated softly.

He glanced at me, crumpled his napkin, and tossed it in the basket. "In a short while, Grace Everdeen would have been an extremely unfortunate-looking young woman. If she had not run away, I might have been able to arrest the symptoms, but during her absence the disease had taken a fierce hold on her. I reinstituted the course of X-ray treatment, and I administered large doses of estrogens to slow down the pituitary action. The radiation, however, had to be repeated at two-month intervals, and by the time Grace returned, it was already too late. If you could wait a moment—"

"Of course." He finished his milkshake, then went out, dropping the carton in the wastebasket as he passed. When he came in again, he was carrying a large manila folder.

"I kept the X-rays. It was such an unusual case." He flipped a switch on a light panel and ranged half a dozen negatives on the rack. Several showed the entire figure, several the head and torso. One was of the hands, another of the feet. In some of them the light form of the ring chained around the neck appeared.

"Is something wrong?" he said. I was staring at the remarkable shape of the ring.

"No— Please go on."

Before he had completed his comments, his nurse came in with a printed form which she placed in front of him. When she went out, the doctor studied the report for a moment, then looked at me.

"It's as you thought."

"Sterile?"

"I'm afraid so. There weren't any little fellows swimming around. Undoubtedly the mumps."

Well, there it was. Me, mumps: sterile. Such a stupid disease. Much more stupid than Grace's. And less far-reaching. I couldn't have a child. Grace had died.

But, leaving the doctor, I knew now that he was wrong about one thing. Grace Everdeen had not chosen to do away with herself. She had been murdered. On the night of Harvest Home.

In the outer office, I paused to ask him one final question. "Tell me, Doctor, how is the Widow's health?"

"Mary Fortune? Why, it's the best. She's old, but she's got a sound heart. At the rate she's going, she's good for a lot of years yet. Providing she doesn't overdo."

I intended to make it my business that the Widow Fortune should not overdo.

I crossed the Lost Whistle Bridge again, and drove back along the Old Sallow Road. Fred Minerva's wagon was pulled up along the roadside where some men were clearing a path through the brush. Others were unloading the kegs of mead and carrying them into the woods. Though several glanced at me, none offered any sign of acknowledgment. When I got to Irene Tatum's orchard, I drove my car behind a shed, ducked across the road, and entered the woods. Hurrying, I found the blazed trail and quickly picked up the stream. I had little time; I knew where the kegs were being taken. When I got to the gap, I went through, scrambled onto the bank, and from there walked into the clearing.

The crow sat in the dark shadows of the pine branches. No wind poured through the gap; there were no moans today. *We have skeletons in our closets same as other folks,* the Widow Fortune had said. But her skeleton was in no closet; it was hidden in the hollow tree—not the supposed bones of the missing revenuer, but those of the murdered Gracie Everdeen. Then, approaching, I saw the skeleton was no longer hidden; it was gone. The tree tomb was empty.

I might have expected as much. They had come and taken the evidence away. They had killed Gracie and hidden the corpse from chance prying eyes but putting her in the hollow tree, under the vines. But why? Why hadn't they buried her body, or sunk it? Why in the tree, here in the grove? Prying eyes *had* found it—Jack Stump's. And for that he had been silenced. As I would be, if they learned I knew of it. But the *corpus delicti* had been removed elsewhere. Yet I knew there was a piece of evidence they had forgotten existed. One that Jack Stump knew of, and still had in his possession.

I fled the grove, the scene of Gracie's murder, and headed toward the river instead of the road. I did not want to go back to the village and to Beth—with the truth I knew I now had to tell her. Following the path of the stream, I tried to work it out. There had been the brutal cranial fracture, where I had supposed the Soakeses had struck down the revenuer with a heavy object. Someone had hit Gracie, causing her death. She had come to Harvest Home, and had been a "disruptive influence." She had been killed then, not two nights later. They had waited two days and then had Irene Tatum say she found the body under the bridge. Then they brought the corn-filled coffin to the cemetery to be buried, while Grace's body had been hidden in the tree.

The stream widened; ahead I could see the river through the trees. I came out on a grassy bank and looked down into the cove where Beth and I had swum that day. I saw the log I had leaned against. Across the river were the bare tobacco fields, the sheds low against the line of trees rising behind. I lay down on the grass and leaned my head against the log, thinking.

Beware.

The all-prevailing night.

The filthy bird hanging from her hand. Chicken blood and madness. It was I who was mad. Or if not, I had to do something.

Do something.

We all make our own fate, Robert had said. *We all have choices; the thing to do is make the choice.*

Right or wrong, make the choice.

I felt a tickling in my ear, then along my neck. I looked down to see small insect shapes swarming from the log, pouring out of the pulpy fibers onto my shoulders and down my back. Jumping up, I began stripping off my clothes, then ran down the bank and plunged into the water, rubbing at my skin to dislodge the insects. When I was free of them, I did not come out immediately. I swam, trying to tire myself, and when I came out I lay on the sand in the shallow water, feeling the sun on my body, the water sluicing along my shoulders and legs. I took deep breaths, trying to relax. I placed my hands on my stomach muscles, felt them constrict. I splayed out my fingers, bent them back against the wet sand to relax them, felt the smooth knuckle joint where the wart had been.

What had happened on that night of Harvest Home fourteen years ago? Fourteen years ago tomorrow night? How had Gracie

Everdeen been a "disruptive influence," for which she had been killed? Killed? Or executed? Where were her bones now? My speculations, like circles, went round and round, always coming back to the women. *What do you talk about at the Widow's?* Oh, just girl talk. Superstitions? Country notions? Perhaps. And in Justin's cornfield, the face with the staring eyes. The little corn god. Goddess. Mother Earth. Bountiful harvest. Moon.

Circles.

Choices.

"Circles," I repeated aloud.

"You're talking to yourself." The voice, followed by a laugh I recognized. I turned my head, looking up at the bank behind me. Tamar Penrose stood in the grass. She had been wading, her skirt was tucked up; I could see her legs white and glistening, her thighs, her melony breasts. Her red nails flashed as she tossed her hair back.

Not in shame but in contempt, I rolled onto my stomach, resting my head along my arm, the water sliding around my mouth.

"I talk to myself sometimes," she said. I glanced up at her as she sat in the grass and dangled her legs over the edge of the bank. She plucked an autumn daisy and twirled it between her fingers. I ventured my question.

She was pulling the petals from the daisy. "Loves me, loves me not. Gracie? How should I remember? I'm too busy with parcel post to keep track of people's comings and goings from this world to another. Loves me, loves me not . . ."

"What happens on Harvest Home?"

" 'What no man may know nor woman tell.' I guess that's the oldest saw in the village. You want to know about Harvest Home? I'll tell you."

She had put flowers in her hair, and the blossoms trailed down among the dark tendrils to her shoulders. She lifted the corn necklace at her breast. "This. This is Harvest Home. And these" —touching the flowers in her hair—"and this"—scooping some earth from the bank and lumping it in her hand. "It's to celebrate this." She opened her hand and looked at it, her voice curiously pitched.

She tossed the lump of clay and it fell near my shoulder. She rose and came slowly down the bank. I put my head down again. I could hear the light splash of her feet and felt a coolness on my back where her form eclipsed the sun. She bent, gently running the tips of her nails between my shoulder blades. I felt her hair brush against me as she came closer. I could feel her knowing fingers toying at the base of my neck.

"You don't say what happens."

"I'm not going to." There was an allure in her voice, as though she wanted me to urge her. "It's just what people do."

I shrugged her fingers away. They immediately returned, kneading the cords of my neck. Despite the coldness of the water, against the sandy grit, I could feel a stirring: loin lust. I pulled away. "And Jack Stump. Is that what people do? Savage their fellow-man?"

"It was necessary." She spoke lightly, as if the matter were of no consequence.

"Why not have killed him?"

"I could have. I'm very strong. Feel how strong."

"You bitch."

"Yes." An affirmation, a caress, both.

With my head turned away, I called her other names.

"Yes. But feel me. Feel my skin." She took my hand and invited my touch. "Feel how soft." I snatched my hand away, swore at her. She accepted my abuse willingly, her fingers gliding over my flesh as I accused; and as I accused, beneath me I could feel myself growing harder.

I spoke angrily. She had silenced the peddler, had cut his tongue and stitched him. Still she caressed me. Yes, she answered in a small voice, she had done these things. "With these hands." Ran them over my shoulders, down my spine to my buttocks, my legs. I pulled away. "Grace Everdeen died on Harvest Home."

"Yes."

I could feel my hardness in the sand, and as though knowing

it, she murmured things that sent the blood coursing to where she commanded it.

"She didn't kill herself," I said.

"No."

"She was murdered." I looked at her quickly, saw the answer in her eyes. "You killed her."

"Yes."

"Jesus."

"Jesus saves. But not Grace. She came. To Harvest Home. Where she had no right. She was diseased. Unclean. She couldn't be Corn Maiden, and she didn't want me to be. She came to blight the crops. To blight Roger, if she could. But she couldn't have him. I did. She came, and I hit her with my hoe. Here." She had straddled me, her hair brushing my shoulders as she bent and laid her fingers on my temple, showing me the place. "I killed her like she should have been killed. She was put in the tree so she would be there for all the Harvest Homes that came after. So she could watch. You want to know what happens at Harvest Home? I'll tell you. They make the corn."

"They—"

"Make the corn! Not like in the play. But really—truly make—the—corn. Roger and I, we made the corn together. Missy is Roger Penrose's child. We made her that night. At Harvest Home. Justin will make the corn. With Sophie. If Sophie can have a baby from it, it will be good. Then there'll be a surer chance of good crops."

"*You* had a baby and there was a drought."

Her eyes flashed. "The drought was Gracie's! And Missy's the best thing ever happened to this village!"

I loathed her. Her fleshy weight made my stomach heave.

I spread my palms against the pebbles and thrust upward, toppling her sidewise into the water. A light danced in her eyes, a triumphant gleam. I rose to my knees and she uttered a tiny mewling whimper as she saw what her touch had erected. She put out her hand; before she could reach me I leaped up; she lay back with a moan. I stood over her, the sun at my back, my shadow slicing her in half.

With panicky little moaning sounds, she scrabbled to me, sliding her hands up along my thighs, seizing and laying her cheek against me; I could feel the bite of her red nails where she had forced me to power. I lifted my foot, placed it against her shoulder, shoved violently. She fell back in the water, her mouth wet and red, then came to a crouching position and raised her arms as if she knelt upon an altar. The goddess pleading to be fulfilled. I would not. I would not pleasure the goddess; I would destroy her.

Even as I moved toward her, I knew I wanted to kill her. I flung myself on her, my hands murderous as they sought her throat, fingers closing on her windpipe. I seized her chin, wrenched it from side to side in the shallow water. I half rose and, bending, dragged her into the deeper part, thrusting her head up and down, her tantalizing smile appearing amid a froth of bubbles. I drove her under, holding her submerged, watching her hair rippling outward, undulant as seaweed, snakes—Medusa's head. I would obliterate it.

Again I drove her downward, held her there, watched the bubbles rise, saw the mocking smile, as though she defied me to do it. Her head drifted upwards, the cool, ripe breasts surfacing, the water draining between them. Then, scarcely realizing my intent, as she floated limp but smiling, I dragged her to the clay bank and propped her against it. She lay there, her breasts still rising and falling. She was not dead; but would be. There was another way, a better way. My body imprisoning hers, my hands began tearing at her dress, stripping it from her, shucking her bare. She had revived, but she did not understand what I meant to do. Her hands came up, caressing the back of my neck. She pulled my head close, her lips on mine, her tongue forcing its way into my mouth, her hand fumbling its way between us, stroking, manipulating me. I grabbed her wrists and flung her arms from her sides, using my knees to force her legs farther apart. She drew her thighs around the outsides of my thighs and pulled me in toward her. Her nails dug into my neck, my shoulders, and in return I flailed her breasts with my muzzle, using the beard stubble to abrade the tender skin. And then, fully aroused, I began ramming at her.

The light had not died in her eyes; their whiteness blazed at each thrust, her thighs sliding against me not in protest, but widening, opening herself to let me find her, to make me take her. Digging my feet into the ground for purchase, I felt my buttock muscles knot as I arched my back and drove myself into her. She shuddered and cried out then, but when I freed her hands her arms welcomed me in embrace. I wound my fingers in her wet hair and gripped, still wanting to kill her, not with my hands but with that other part of me that she had aroused. I worked at her and worked, then halted, watching her eyes roll, wild like an animal's, holding her impaled on me, for I would not finish yet, and when I had mastered myself I worked again, rearing and plunging, and mixed with my curses and her passion were the sounds of our clashing bodies, muscles and tissue, the bulging noises I could force from her, the thud of my chest against hers, the slap of our wet bellies.

It became a duel. Willingly she would take from me, but I would not give to her. There would be no ecstasy for her, only pain. But her pain became her ecstasy. "Oh, yes," she moaned, "my Greek, my Lord. Plow me, plow me." A full-throated plea and the water ran from her body in rivulets down the bank, mixing with the dark clay, and I dug handfuls of it and, riding her, ramming her against the ground, I smeared it in her face, the substance of Mother Earth, rubbing it in her eyes and ears, stopping her mouth with it, forcing her cheeks to wallow in it, her shoulders and breasts, ever driving, thrusting, pulling back, and ramming her again, sucking the saliva up from my throat and spitting it in her face, the face of the Mother goddess, driving against her, twisting, to batter her pliant flesh, to drive the goddess back into Mother Earth and bury her there.

She did not stop her words and though I battled her and thought the battle mine, she worked upon me to have her way, inviting my violence, glorying in it, using all her parts, and I, losing, thought that no machine had ever been so cleverly invented, so beautifully crafted to provide pleasure. I fought her with the strength of my body, but hers was stronger. As I surged into her, I heard my curses soften, heard them become endearments. I put my mouth to her breasts and sucked. Murmuring, she held me gently in her arms and I knew I had lost then. The duel was hers. Fulfilling me, she had vanquished me. I had not taken her and violated her, for the earth was not to be taken or violated, and she was of the earth. She was earth itself, the Mother goddess, and even as my semen flowed I could feel my eyes sting as the tears came; the man unmanned, defeated by the woman.

I grasped her wrists again and shudderingly withdrew, our bodies parting with a hollow sucking noise. As she lay panting against the wet clay, I could see her bruised, triumphant smile and I saw she knew it, too; she was the victor.

I tasted earth in my mouth. Turning, I spat, then filled my lungs and, wheeling, flung myself in the water, submerging, rubbing my hands over my flesh, cleansing it, watching the dark clay loosen from my body, break up, and float away in the current. When my breath was spent, I limply pushed myself to the surface. I slicked my hair from my eyes and looked at the bank. She was not there, but imprinted in the wet clay was the hollow of her form, and it seemed as if she had entered there, the goddess returned to the earth.

26

The goddess. I comprehended it, or thought I did. The doll in Justin's cornfield represented the Mother. The Mother was the goddess. The goddess provided fertility. Fertility was needed. Without it, there would be no corn. Without corn, no money or food. Without them, people died. Doll; Mother; fertility. Hope; belief.

They all believed. All the village. They wanted me to believe, too. It was shocking, yet terribly simple.

And Harvest Home was coming.

Harvest Home! A time o' joy and celebration. Eat, drink, and be merry. It means success and thanks and all good things.

But this, the seventh year, was special. Not all good things, perhaps. "What no man may know nor woman tell." This was the heart of it. A secret revealed; but what?

I slowed my car as the Tatum farm rose at the crest of the hill on my right, the silhouetted buildings bleakly huddled together. There was no sign of the pickup truck, nor indeed of any activity, other than the youngest girl, Debbie, standing in the dirt track, twisting the hem of her dress and wailing, evidently frightened by the fierce clamor of hogs in the pen near the barn.

I stopped to investigate. I could hear the pigs' grunting bodies heaving against the sty, their wet eyes inquisitively surveying me. A board had become loosened, and I pounded it in place with a rock, then drove off. Begrimed, with a runny nose, Debbie watched me go.

Beyond the house the landscape lay in somber peace. A smoky haze drifted over the cornfield, the cornstalks lying helter-skelter among the bearded stubble, the shocks diminishing in size as they stretched away from the road to the ridge. Behind them slid the sun.

Pulling to the roadside, I gazed off at the desolate vista; then, listening carefully, I got out, crossed the road, and stepped into the field. Dead stalks cracked underfoot. From somewhere ahead in the field was coming a strange sound: an uncanny, hollow clank or rattle, faint at first, then more distinct. In the amber light, the hulking sheaves seemed forbidding, sinister. Then I recognized the sound: tin cans swaying on the ends of their strings, the pebbles inside making a dull clanking noise, but doing little to repel the two crows which, shiny and black, sat huddled like felons, one on each shoulder of a solitary scarecrow.

It was impossible to account for the tumult of the pigs; squeals and cries pierced the air as their fury drove them to fresh efforts to break from the sty. I got back in the car and began driving down the road; then behind me I heard Debbie's cry. I looked back to see her dashing for the porch as the boards of the pen gave way and the pigs raced past her, charging across the lawn, heads lowered, a tide of frenzied shapes spilling down the slope and into the field, their short legs trampling the earth, overturning the piled shocks as they swept across the furrows.

Debbie sat down on the steps and wailed louder than ever.

Lights had come on in the windows of the houses along the way, and I could see people sitting down to early supper before Kindling Night. I was tired, and awash with guilt. I cursed myself for a fool, scarcely remembering the scene with Tamar on the mudbank—not what had happened, but how it had come about. Arriving at the country end of Main Street, I drove past the dark figure of a man leaning on a rake handle, watching piles of leaves smolder and burn. As the smoke drifted, blue and pungent, I heard the sound of a horse's hoofs, and the familiar creaking of wheels; ahead, the Widow Fortune's buggy emerged from Penrose Lane. The mare looked docile as she moved along; not so the old lady, who sat upright on the seat, her shoulders thrown back, her hands gripping the reins. I couldn't see her face, only the white cap tied under her chin, nor did she notice me coming along; or if she did she made no sign. She wheeled onto Main Street and headed the horse in the direction of her house. I watched the white cap disappear into the gloom; then I drove into the lane.

"Hello, Ned." Maggie Dodd was out in front of her house, laying plastic covers over the flower beds along the side of the hedge. I called good evening.

"I've just been putting my bulbs to bed. Have a good day?"

I made some reply and turned into my drive. The Invisible Voice came from Robert's sun porch. Beth's station wagon was in the garage. Leaving my car in the drive, I went in through the kitchen door. There was no light on, except for the fluorescent stove panel, which glowed eerily. Kate was standing by the table—not doing anything, just standing there.

"Hi, sweetheart." I lay down my sketching case and kissed her, dredging up a semblance of cheerfulness.

"Hi."

"Nice day?"

"Yes."

"What's wrong?"

"Nothing." She picked up my case from the table and laid it on the counter, then stood with her back to me. I went to her and turned her, holding her face between my hands. She looked pale, a little tired.

"Nothing?"

"Honest—nothing."

"Where's Mom?"

She nodded toward the closed door of the bacchante room, beyond which I could now catch the low sound of the T.V. set.

Kate placed something in my hand: my pencil flashlight. "I borrowed it from your studio."

"O.K."

She started out, stopped in the doorway with a look I couldn't read. Then she went out through the hall.

I dropped the flashlight into my jacket pocket and opened the bacchante room door. Beth did not look up as I came in, but sat on the green velvet sofa, hands folded in her lap.

"Hello," I said.

"Hello." An imprecise emphasis, betraying nothing of her present mood.

"No martini?"

"No. I didn't think so. Tonight."

"Guess I'll have a Scotch."

"All right."

"Anything wrong with Kate?"

"No."

I made a drink, then sat down in the club chair. A small fire crackled in the grate, and a large bowl of fresh chrysanthemums bloomed on the Victorian sideboard. I moved a copy of *House and Garden* and put my feet up on the coffee table. "Have a nice day?" I asked over Walter Cronkite's voice.

"Umm." She placed her palms together and rubbed them with a slow rotary motion. "Did you?"

I tried to force my voice to sound casual and light. "Yeah. I was out at the Hookes'."

"How are they?"

"O.K. I guess. Sophie seems upset for some reason. I wanted to make a couple of sketches of the pear tree for the painting."

In the light from the screen, I could see a little furrow of impatience appear between her brows. She picked up the remote control and switched off the set. I sipped my drink, watching the firelight play on her face.

"Cozy," I said.

She turned on the floor lamp and pulled her work basket to her.

"You all right?" I asked.

"Yes. Of course." She gave me a quick glance, then drew the quilt onto her lap and pulled the needle out. I listened to the ticking of the Tiffany clock.

"Coming right along," I offered, referring to the quilt.

"Yes. I should have it done by Christmas."

I held my glass up, watching the play of firelight in the swirl of amber Scotch and ice cubes. I caught her staring at me. Her eyebrows lifted the faintest fraction, then she resumed her work. Something was terribly wrong, I could tell. Her face was pale; she needed lipstick.

"And—?" she said.

"Hm?"

"And then what did you do?"

"After the Hookes'?"

"Yes."

"I—uh, I went to see Dr. Bonfils."

She gave me a quick, tight glance, then looked down again at her work. I put my glass on the table and sat beside her on the sofa, trying to take her hands.

"I'm sorry, Bethany."

"Sorry?"

"About the baby."

"He told you."

"Yes."

"He shouldn't have. He should have let me." She made a futile gesture with her shoulders, then laughed. "It appears I'm a wishful mother, nothing more."

"Beth—"

"Please. I don't want to talk about it."

"It's not you, it's me."

She shook her head uncomprehendingly. "There's no fetus. Nothing growing in me—"

"I know. I'm sterile. It was the mumps. The doctor did a test. You can have children, but I can't. It's my fault."

"It's—not—me?"

"No. Me."

She paused, holding herself rigid, motionless. Then she visibly relaxed. She dropped her head to hide the tears in her eyes. "It's all right. It doesn't matter. Any more." She spoke calmly, matter-of-factly, dismissing the topic as if we'd been discussing an unfortunate change of weather.

I stood up and looked around the room. It suddenly seemed different—not a room we had made, part of our house, but—simply a room. I glanced at Beth; she seemed different too, somehow. A stranger-wife. I knew she was upset about the baby, but there was something else as well, something she had not said yet.

She raised her head. "What is it, Ned?"

"I was wondering . . ."

"What?"

"If maybe we ought to move."

She looked at me, then around the room, then shrugged her shoulders. "I don't understand."

"I mean, I'm thinking maybe we ought to leave Cornwall Coombe. Sell. Get out."

"What on earth for?" She laid aside her work and gave me all her attention.

"I don't know. I just have this feeling."

"Where would we go?"

"Mm—back to New York, maybe. Europe, maybe."

"But we've been so happy here."

"Have we?"

"I thought we were. And if we haven't—really, Ned—I don't think you've given this much thought, have you? I mean, it isn't exactly fair to Kate. Taking her out of school again. And there's all the work we've done on the house. The money that's been spent."

"We can get it back."

"On a resale? I don't think so."

"Why not?"

"Because they won't— Because somebody isn't just going to buy us out and move in."

"Why?"

"Because." She looked at me. "Because they won't let anybody. Not just anybody."

"Weren't we 'just anybody'?"

"No. We weren't. You know that. They wanted us."

"The hell they did."

"Yes, they did. It took some time, but they did. The Widow wanted us."

"Did she?" I set my glass down rather sharply.

"You knew that."

"No, I didn't."

"Well, she did. That was the reason Maggie called us. It was all because of—"

"The Widow. You mean, she arranged it."

"Yes."

"She can arrange for somebody else, then."

"I don't think so."

"Bethany, listen. I don't know what's happening around here, but I don't like it. I don't know what's happened to you, or to us, or to anything. I want to get out. Now! Get the hell out while we still have the chance. Can't we? Beth, remember Paris? And the lilacs?"

"I remember."

"We could go back to them again."

"You've got lilacs outside that window, if you can wait until spring. Besides, who can ever go back again? Can we?"

"Sometimes it's not a bad idea, going back."

"I want to go ahead."

"To where?"

"I'm not sure."

"Bethany?"

"Yes."

"Do you remember that night?"

"Which?"

"*That* night. The 'experience.'"

"Yes."

"That was arranged too."

"Who—?"

"Who do you think? When I came into our bedroom, you had been watching, hadn't you? I mean, you'd seen?"

"Seen what?"

"Whoever it was that came out of the cornfield."

"No. I didn't see anyone. I was waiting for you. I was—"

"What?"

"Dreaming, I imagine. Ned, listen. Some things are better left not talked about. Some things are better left—"

"Unsaid."

"I like it here. You've liked it here. Kate does, too. It's the first time I've felt—"

Safe. I saw it then. In Cornwall Coombe she had found a place. She was secure. And not only secure, but changed. It had become more and more apparent. Not only city mouse into country mouse; she seemed in some way on the brink of something, as though poised for some indefinable leap. I saw her as she had been, blazing with unfulfilled yearnings, something she had been searching for. Baby—loss—

There are things women long for, and longin', ought to be given their way.

The Widow, Edna Jones, Asia Minerva, Ruth Zalmon . . .

Mothers. All of them, all mothers. For her. Mothers. And the Mother.

"You don't like me very much, do you?" I said the words before I realized it.

"I love you," she replied simply.

"It's not the same, is it? It's not the same at all."

"You make all the decisions," she said. "You always decide what's to be done. Even about coming here. You decided. I'd like to do my share."

"Is that what you want, to run things? Go ahead." I finished my drink. "Or do you want to run me? Some women do."

"I'm not that kind."

"Make sure you're not, or go find another fellow."

She gave me a long look, then drew out her needle again. "How was the rest of your afternoon?"

"All right. I—went for a swim. Can you beat that? This time of year."

"What happened to your lip?"

"Huh? Oh, I must have hit it on something. A rock, maybe." Remembering how I must look, I started quickly for the kitchen. "Guess I'd better change. What's for dinner?"

"Crab casserole. Ned."

"Yes."

"I don't want to sound like *True Confessions,* but tell me it isn't true."

"What?"

"That you raped Tamar Penrose."

"Ohh—listen—Beth . . ." The Widow in her buggy. And I

had thought the old lady wasn't interested in gossip. Beth was returning my look, waiting. I tried to fumble an explanation. I had no defenses. How could I explain what had happened? What excuse could I make? "Beth, listen to me, it's not the way you think. It's not that way at all. It happened—but it didn't happen that way."

"She says you raped her."

"It's not *true!* Beth, *listen.*"

"I am." Her tone was weary, as if she weren't really interested. I pushed the table aside and crouched, took her hands in mine. They felt unresponsive, lifeless. I had so quickly run out of anything to say. She faced my imploring look quietly with no sign of emotion.

"Why did you promise?"

"I meant it. I *meant* that promise. Honest to God I did."

"Then. But not now."

"Beth. Don't listen to them. Don't listen to what they told you. Let me tell you what they're like. I didn't want you to know. I didn't want to tell you. Because I know how you feel about her."

"About whom?"

"The Widow. Mary Fortune. But she's not like that at all." Now the words came spilling out, and I told her about Jack Stump, about the attack, about the paper from the One-B Weber's tea box, about finding the shears. She tried to pull away and I held her by the wrist, forcing her to listen. "And that's not the worst. They killed Grace Everdeen. Murdered her."

She pulled away again and jumped up. "Don't talk such rubbish!" I had never seen her look so angry. "After what she has done for us, after saving our child's life, after the days and weeks she's spent in our house looking after us, cooking for us, helping us, you try to make me believe such things! You must take me for a complete fool. You made me a promise. Which obviously was impossible to keep. You *had* to have her. Not just have her, but against her will—"

"It wasn't against her will—"

"And then to get out of it you tell terrible things about the Widow. Everyone knows who attacked Jack. Everyone knows Grace Everdeen committed suicide—"

"She didn't. I can prove it. The Widow—"

"Stop. I don't want to hear any more about the Widow. Not another single word." Her face was drained of color, her mouth was pulled down in an angry curve, her body trembled. "Just because you've had a lark in the woods with the town slut and you're sorry—oh, yes, you're sorry, not sorry you did it, but sorry you were found out. Did you think she'd never tell? Never say anything? And just because you were found out, you try to turn the facts all around, you try to besmirch the name of the finest woman who ever walked God's green earth."

"She murdered Gracie Everdeen. She and Tamar and the rest of the women. On Harvest Home."

"Don't speak about Harvest Home. You don't know anything about—"

" 'What no man may know nor woman tell?' " I could not resist the taunt. She started forward, then managed to restrain herself. I could not believe what was happening. I fought down a feeling of panic. She was going to tell me again—as she had that other time—that she was going away, that she wanted to leave me, to take Kate, get a divorce. Just as it had happened then.

Still I could not resist. "They're murderers." The word hung there, sounding ridiculous. Murderers were people you read about in the paper, in New York or somewhere—not in Cornwall Coombe. I looked at her, then away, through the dining-room doors; my eyes absently traveled the Shanghai Tea Party—ships in the harbor, coolies with pagoda-shaped hats—familiar and curiously real. I looked back. I went on. "I can bring you proof."

She was making visible efforts to keep herself calm. She pressed her palms together again, rotating one against the other. "Bring it. It won't prove anything." Her eyes were wet; her chin took on the stubborn tilt that had been her father's. "I will have the child. . . . I will . . . I will . . ." In the blind and futile assertion, I sensed a kind of withdrawal. At that moment she looked quite strange, not only in her features but in her whole manner, her being. A sudden flash went through my mind that she wasn't Beth at all, but someone else entirely.

She stared back, saw, failed to recognize me. The stranger-husband. Each of us now was imprisoned behind the bars of mistrust, of doubt, of disappointment. What could heal the breach? For no apparent reason, I thought of the rainbow we had seen on that first day, bridging us between the life we had known and the life that was to be. *This* was the life that was to be. This room would be peopled with ghosts, not of others who had inhabited it, but our own, future ghosts, relic-specters of a might-have-been. At that moment I knew we were doomed. She had already retreated from me spiritually; now it would be physically as well. She would leave me.

"*I will . . . I will . . .*"

With her free hand she struck the flat of her stomach. "If there is no child here, it's because you couldn't put one there. I'm not the barren one—you are."

I looked at her again, backed away to the door. "Murderers," I said; said again I would bring proof.

Upstairs, Kate's door opened; her footsteps sounded along the hall. I opened the front door and stepped out. Kate was coming down the stairs. Closing the door, I heard from the other side the whispered word.

"Mother . . ."

But it was not Kate who whispered it.

I drove to the bait shack. Mrs. Brucie was doing things in the kitchen; Jack was in the chair by the fire. He seemed not to know me at all; I suspected they must be keeping him drugged on something the Widow had concocted. He looked at me as I fumbled inside his shirt, but showed no sign of recognition. Mrs. Brucie came and stood in the doorway, watching. I pulled out the red cloth bag and tugged it open, then inserted my finger and felt. It was empty. The ring was not there. The oddly shaped bone ring that had been not the Widow's charm but Gracie Everdeen's engagement ring, which I had seen hanging at her throat in the doctor's X-rays. I dropped the bag back inside Jack's shirt. Mrs. Brucie was smiling at me, saying nothing.

The evidence gone. Jack Stump cut and stitched . . . by the women . . . because—because why? What were they trying to hide? The peddler had been silenced because he had found Gracie. Gracie had been murdered because, blighted, she had come to Harvest Home. . . .

Harvest Home . . .

What happened on Harvest Home?

Suddenly I became terribly afraid. And as suddenly I felt certain that Worthy Pettinger had never left town at all.

At the Common, the street lights had been turned off, and in the dark the villagers waited expectantly for the bonfire to be lighted. I pulled my car up near the post office and went looking for Amys Penrose, stopping to stare up at the gigantic wood structure, towering thirty feet and more into the air. The doors of the firehouse were thrown wide and the beams of the engine headlights illuminated the applauding crowd as the apparatus was brought onto the turf and hoses were run to the hydrants. The ladders that had been used to build the pyramid and to set the scarecrows on it were taken to the curb and stacked, while the firemen, donning their helmets, walked around the base, moving the spectators back to a safe distance.

I found myself caught up among them, and as I backed away with the others, the firemen ran to fling burning torches onto the pile. The bonfire began in clear limpid pockets of bright flame, glowing here and there. Then, as the wood and debris gradually caught, it became an awesome sight. I stopped where I stood, watching it grow, the flames slicing their way up the outside shell, orange, yellow, red, eating away at clapboards, boxes, beams, whatever they discovered, while from the wooden heart of the pile came the roar of the conflagration.

Of its own volition, the crowd retreated from the intense heat, and into this widened breach leaped a troop of living scarecrows, an array of ragged, wildly prankish straw-clad figures, bobbing and turning, doing a crazy dance while the onlookers joined hands and began circling the blaze in a clockwise direction, forming a great urgent chain.

Scornfully I watched. It was like a grotesque sports rally, and as they passed, link after link in their human chain, I hated them, these hayseeds with their stupid dance, their stupid singing, their stupid beliefs. "The old ways"—how I despised the phrase. I moved aside as more came to break their way into the circle, which grew larger, spreading out toward the edges of the Common, moving counterclockwise now.

Then, without apparent signal, the moving circle bulged outward toward me. Hands parted, arms lifted over my head, and I was swept up into the line by two incredible straw-and-rag men, who seized my hands in an iron clasp, drawing me along with them. Their effigy heads nodded at me as I, too, was forced to participate, moving faster and faster, the great blaze spinning past my vision. Another circle appeared before me, countering my own circle, and dark heads passed before the flickering light like figures in a silent movie. I was pulled along; the circles broke and re-formed into a serpentine braid, human ropes weaving themselves together, while the fire mounted.

Within the labyrinth of movement, distinguishable faces appeared: Robert's, Kate's, Beth's; and faceless details: Mr. Buxley's clerical collar, his wife's hat, the Widow's bonnet, whirling, kaleidoscopic; another face, rubicund, choleric. "That's him," cried Irene Tatum, "that's the one let the hogs out! Debbie seen him! He let the hogs out deliberate!" I could feel her hands snatching at me from behind, tugging at my clothes, trying to yank me from the circle, but still the straw hands held me fast and willy-nilly I was dragged away.

The line swept out again and, like a giant amoeba, divided itself from the larger circle to form a smaller one. Someone shoved me and I was propelled into the center; wheeling, I saw fire-washed faces, peripheral and with the sheen of exertion on their brows, now bright, now dim in the leaping light, all somehow sinister. They closed in on me with menace; I could feel the press of bodies, feel their hot breath, the air being pushed from my lungs by the sheer force of their weight.

Quickly they moved toward me and as quickly withdrew, as if I were the butt of some enormous joke, and all was merriment once more as they rejoined the larger circle, bringing me with them, a swirl of leaping forms, my scarecrow cronies gripping my hands as they circled the flaming heap. The rancorous hag-cry sounded again— ". . . let my hogs out!" —as I passed, the voice fading, becoming lost; and pull as I might I could not free myself. I gave up all resistance. They took me where they might, and the scarecrow men were laughing and nodding at me as though I were not in thrall to them, their jester faces wild, looking upward at the whirlwind of fire and smoke—See! See!—their eyes glittering with ardor as they reflected the blaze.

I looked up, too. Saw a picture. A picture no man could paint, or scarcely dream. Saw a hell of burning scarecrows: straw and sacking and button eyes, cross-poles and uprights, hats and coats all lost in flame, a holocaust of straw men, saw in the picture one higher than the rest, arms outstretched in cruciform supplication, leaning backward into the fire that licked at the tattered war tunic, the tarnished epaulettes, the cocked hat, saw the wind enfold the flames around the face as though in a caress.

"Worthy!"

The scarecrow in the field. The pigs gone mad with the scent . . . !

I shouted and struggled, but they held me and pulled me back as in the picture the giant structure seemed visibly to swell, to belch and heave in its last convulsive throes. Shouting with all my might, I saw it lean away from the wind, totter, tremble, and with a thunderous crash of flame and charred timber the hideous pile tumbled to earth. Still I shouted, saw people fleeing past me to safety, saw hot sparks spiraling upward in a fiery shower, saw the ashes borne like feathers on the breeze, sifting in a gray

spectral snow among the tombstones in the churchyard, saw a
hand raised over me, brought down on my head in a savage blow,
saw the picture crack, break into fragments, saw . . .

Nothing.

PART FIVE

HARVEST HOME

27

I awoke from nightmare to see the fragments pieced together, then realized they were the cracks and seams of a ceiling. I was in a strange bed, in a room unfamiliar to me. My jacket was on the back of a chair, my shoes beside it. A blanket had been drawn over me. The window shades were down. My head throbbed, and when I put my hand to the back of my skull I felt pain. I looked at my watch: it had stopped at ten minutes past five—a.m. or p.m.? I leaned from the bed and pulled the shade up: the sun was high.

I had come to in a bedroom at Penance House. I was looking out at an oblique angle toward the church. The hands of the church clock read twenty minutes to twelve. Men were working on the Common, some using rakes while others shoveled burned debris onto a giant chicken-wire frame. The sifted ashes were being scooped into burlap sacks and loaded onto the back of a truck. Soon all that was left to mark the night's events was a giant scorched circle on the grass.

I fell weakly back against the pillow, my stomach churning as the picture of the previous night reformed itself in my memory, the carnage of the fire, the scarecrow that had not been a scarecrow. I squeezed my eyes shut, grimaced. It wasn't possible; I had imagined it. There had been no face, only a straw head. I could make myself believe it if I tried. I tried. Could not. The face remained a face—Worthy Pettinger's face. A conspiracy of cremation.

I looked through the window again. Men were taking down the harvest symbols from the chimneys and eaves. Others had appeared at points around the Common, casually loitering. I saw no women, no children, no animals. No cars went by. The men appeared to be waiting, smoking their pipes and looking at the burned circle.

I heard the sound of a motor, and Justin Hooke's El Camino passed below the window, went around the Common, and pulled up at the curb in front of the church. Justin helped Sophie out, and she threw a furtive glance up at the clock on the steeple. When they came close to the circle, they halted. Justin released her arm and he looked up at the clock. It was five minutes to twelve.

More men had appeared, solitary, silent, stationing themselves beside the trees or the lampposts. Mr. Buxley came out on the church steps. He looked around, went back inside. Justin was talking to Sophie. Listening, she lowered her brow and leaned it against his chest. He shook his head, made an angry gesture, and raised her chin to him. She tried to leave, and he seized her hand, forcing her to listen. She drew away and flung herself down on the ground.

Justin glanced at a group of men, then quickly knelt and brought her to her feet. He lifted her face again, gently, and spoke some more words. She seemed acquiescent as he reached for her hand and began to lead her toward the circle. She halted once more, staring at the blackened earth, glancing indecisively at the clock and back again. Finally, she snatched her hand away and began to run. Justin took three or four steps after her, then stopped. The lounging men became more attentive, watching the departing figure as it disappeared up Main Street.

The steeple bell began striking the hour. When the final stroke rang, Justin stepped into the circle, under trees whose autumn leaves seemed to have hemorrhaged, seeping blood. The men watched him, never speaking but closely observant as he moved toward the center. Amys Penrose came through the vestibule doors and down the steps. He did not look at the figure in the ring, but rounded the Common, crossed the roadway, and disappeared beneath my window.

I pulled the blanket off, swung my feet to the floor, and went into the adjoining bathroom to wash my face. I looked dirty and disheveled, and in need of a shave. My head hurt worse than before as I bent over the basin. I soaked the washcloth and laid it against the swelling. The bedroom door opened and Amys's face appeared behind me in the mirror.

"Some bump."

Holding the cloth to the back of my head, I went and sat on the edge of the bed.

"How did I get here?"

"They brought you. Merle Penrose and Morgan Thomas."

They had slugged me, then carried me to bed. "Just goes to show you, nobody's all bad."

Amys eyed me. "Nice bed?"

"Comfortable enough. Were you there last night?"

"Hell, no. For that damn foolishness? Was over t'the picture show. When I came back, they was just lugging you up on the church steps. I told 'em to bring you here."

"Do you know what happened?"

"They had their Kindlin' Night."

"And tonight they'll have their Harvest Home. Amys, listen to me—" He turned away; he knew what I was going to say. I told him about Jack's discovery in the hollow tree, about his finding and taking Roger's ring. Irene Tatum had never found a body in the river; the coffin had been weighted with a sack of corn and a fake marker put up over her grave.

"She wasn't pretty, Amys. Not when she came back."

He nodded dumbly. "I know. I seen her."

"You—?"

"I seen her. The night Roger rode her back across the bridge on his horse. I'd been hidin' in Irene's orchard every night, waitin'.

I knew one of 'em was bound to cross the river. He rode her into the orchard. Her face was done up in some sort of scarf—he took it off. When he saw what had happened to her, he left her there. She swore she'd come to Harvest Home. Roger told the Widow, and she rode out and ordered Gracie not to come. But I knew she would. She was bound to. Bound to—even though she knew they'd kill her."

"You knew."

He shrugged simply. "Everybody knew. Gracie's tragedy was that she fell in love with Roger. No girl ought to do that when she's Corn Maiden—not with the Harvest Lord."

"Then that must be Sophie Hooke's tragedy, too. Why did you lie to me and say that Mrs. Zalmon had driven Worthy Pettinger away?"

"They told me to. Old Deming and the elders, they—" Tears came to his eyes. "They knew we was friends—"

"Are we friends?"

"Yes, sir." He turned to me, squinting against the light, his eyes streaming. "I know what you're thinkin', but listen to me. I've prett' near lived my life out now, and I done just about what I wanted to, but when you've lived as long as I have, you learn one thing—to keep your nose out of what don't concern you. I don't meddle with folks' doin's, and they don't meddle with mine. I don't know what happened last night. And if you do—or if you think you do—I wouldn't go around spoutin' off about it. Folks can get mighty cranky hereabouts."

I glanced out the window at the watchers: the farmers watching Justin standing immobile in the circle. Not a woman in sight, except for Missy Penrose.

"What will she do?" I asked, indicating Missy, "now that the sheep are put to fold?"

"She'll wait. Everyone will wait."

"For what?"

"Hoping Jim Minerva will choose a—"

"Corn Maiden."

"Ayuh."

"Who will it be?"

"Someone—young."

He was sounding a warning; my wits, dulled from the night before, were slow to take it in. I stared at him.

Then: "Kate?"

"The Widow wants new blood. That's why she got you the house. Villagers didn't want outsiders here. They had a meetin'. The Widow says yes, they should let you come. She saw you the first day you came here."

I remembered the Polaroid photograph of Kate that I had written our number on, the Widow's immediate interest. More conspiracy. I seized Amys's wrist, held him. "Amys, what's going to happen at Harvest Home?"

"What no man may know nor woman tell."

"*You* tell me." He tried to pull away; I tightened my grip. Amys looked down at Justin, the focus of all eyes.

"He won't tell, neither. Not before he goes, not when he comes back." With his free hand, he released my fingers from his wrist and stepped away. I remained at the window, staring down at the figure on the Common, waiting at the center of the ring.

The enigma. The baffling mystery that still eluded me. Amys was lying; he knew. They all knew; all but me. And though the Harvest Lord stood at the exact center of the circle, he did not stand alone; there was another with him, and though I did not know Her, I knew now who She was.

I vowed war on Her. I vowed death and destruction. New blood —for Her? If it came to that, I would set a torch to every barn in the village, to every field that grew a single stalk of corn. I would pollute the earth with some poisonous substance that would kill Her. I would rust the blade of the plowshare, I would break the handles. I would make a wilderness of briars and weeds. No matter how fair it flowered, no furrow or hill or meadow would not feel my hand, to lay low the spirit of the holy Mother—Earth. I cursed and damned Her, and I swore that She would not win against me.

Amys was looking at me. Had he read my thoughts? "Son,

there's only two ringin's today. I just done the first. The second's at moonrise. That's a special ringin'—curfew, you might call it. When you hear that bell, you make sure you're to home." He touched his fingers to my arm. "And son," he added, almost an afterthought, "make sure you stay there."

I intended nothing of the kind. "Well," I said, "pray for rain."

"Why's that?"

"The farmers need it."

I paced the rug in Robert Dodd's sun porch, my hand trembling as I drank a Scotch-and-soda. Though he had asked me several times to sit, I could not. The talking-book machine remained silent, the arm lifted from the record. Immobile in his chair, head slumped, the Professor listened to me, his dark glasses shielding his sightlessness.

I had come home to find my house empty. The station wagon was gone, so were Beth and Kate. There was no note, no communication of any kind. None of Beth's clothes were missing, or Kate's either. I was out of my mind with worry. Robert had told me that Maggie had driven down to the city, and that perhaps Beth and Kate had gone with her. Still, this didn't explain the station wagon's not being in the garage.

In my agitated state, I found it difficult to collect my thoughts. As coherently as I was able, I repeated the story of last night's events, going back to the afternoon, to the Hookes' farm, then to the river, meeting Tamar—I had got to that part of the story before I realized it, tried to explain my way out again: "It's not what you think. I didn't— She wanted it—she—" I stopped, then went on. The field had been empty, the scarecrow was taken down; then there was another scarecrow. The Widow had long before showed us the things in her parlor, the Spanish-American War tunic Jack Stump had sold her, the cocked hat, the boots. A scarecrow where there had been none. The pigs going berserk at the smell of blood. They had taken Worthy from the post office, and killed him. Then the scarecrow was put on the bonfire.

"They murdered him. And they cut off Jack Stump's tongue."

Robert shook his head. "It's not possible."

"No? I'm telling you! And they killed Gracie Everdeen!"

"Calm down, my boy. You're in an overwrought state. Grace Everdeen killed herself. It's why she was not permitted burial in our churchyard."

"She was murdered, and they wouldn't bury her because of whatever it was she did. At Harvest Home. Out there—in Soakes's Lonesome. Fourteen years ago tonight!"

"Yes. Tonight. I've been sitting here this morning thinking, Tonight is Harvest Home."

"I'm going."

"Going where?"

"There. To the woods. For Harvest Home." Angrily I put my glass down and started from the room.

"Ned—wait!" Robert's voice rose sharply. "If you won't sit down, stand there and let me tell you one or two things that might interest you. Are you familiar with what are commonly referred to as the Greek Mysteries? The Eleusinian Mysteries, for example?"

"I've heard the name."

"Back in the old days there was a cult of women who worshiped a goddess called Demeter. She was the earth goddess."

"The Mother—?"

"In one of her varying forms. But these so-called mysteries were celebrated annually, and the secret of what occurred when those Greek women got together to worship in their grove was so well guarded that to this day scholars don't really know what went on. But the important thing is that in each case where the secret was breached, it resulted in death.

"Those women didn't want anyone watching them while they were doing what they deemed necessary, or what they believed in. This is a very serious thing, as it is with any sort of fanaticism. And their fanaticism stemmed from their belief in a deity of grain. And the god—or, in this instance, goddess—who provided it was revered."

"Worshiped."

He nodded. "Agricultural societies in certain periods of history have been known to be especially primitive and savage, and also particularly secretive. And our agricultural ladies here in Cornwall who happen to believe as they do don't want any men knowing what their particular 'mysteries' are all about. So no one's ever seen 'em. That's about all I can tell you."

"I'm going to find out." The conviction in my voice produced a long silence in Robert.

"If you go," he said finally, "you'll live to regret it—if you live."

"But I'll *go!*"

"You'll never get there. They'll have guards posted. Along the road—the bridge, by the river. No one goes to the woods tonight, except the women. No Soakeses, no one."

"*I* go!"

He sighed wearily. "Let me tell you one more thing. Fourteen years ago, there was another man. He was curious, too. He tried to find out."

"Did he?"

"Before the mystery had even begun, he was discovered—and he suffered grievously. I beg you don't go!"

"If this 'he' you're talking about got caught, he was a fool."

"*You* are the fool."

"Everybody seems to think so. Why do you?"

I waited for him to continue, sensed that he had more to say. Sensed, also that in some way he, too, was afraid, was constrained not to go further. The room had fallen silent, and I suddenly knew I was waiting for something. Something that had nothing to do with what we were talking about; something from outside, beyond us. Something had happened—or was about to, I couldn't tell which. In a second more, I knew what it was.

Distantly, the church bell began a slow, solemn peal. Two tollings, Amys had said. This one was unscheduled; yet I had known it was to come. I counted, trying to remember what Amys had told me about the sequence of bells.

"Someone has died," Robert said. We listened. The bell rang three times, three again, three again.

"Thrice times thrice. A woman." Robert rose. "Have you got your car? Drive me to the church."

The bell continued tolling as we drove to the Common, and when we arrived at the north end of Main Street people were hurrying from all directions, crowding around the steps. On the top one stood the Widow Fortune, her white cap hidden by a dark shawl as she angrily gesticulated at Amys Penrose, who was pulling on the bell rope. A man ran up the steps and listened as the old woman spoke, then shouted to the crowd: "Amys oughtn't to be ringin'."

I drove to the curb and helped Robert onto the sidewalk, looking up at the Widow, who was shading her eyes against the sun, peering up the street we had just driven down. Soon I saw a vehicle making slow progress under the trees, and the crowd shifted as it approached, forming two lines outward from the church steps to the roadway where Justin's El Camino halted. He got out, lowered the tailgate, and came bearing his burden between the silent lines, moving up the steps, then bending before the Widow and placing at her feet the dead body of Sophie Hooke.

The Widow had not moved, but remained where she was, looking down at the still form, an enigmatic expression on her face. "What did she do?" I heard a voice asking. The Widow made a slight movement, acknowledging the question but offering no answer. Mr. Buxley stepped forward.

"She hanged herself." He clamped his mouth in a grim line, then continued. There would be no reading from his Book for the repose of Sophie's soul, nor would she be buried in the churchyard. She would rest outside the iron fence, and I pictured the real grave beside Gracie Everdeen's false one.

I watched the faces around me as they heard the pronouncement. Sally Pounder's mouth opened and closed in blank perplexity; Betsey Cox scowled and bit her thumb; Tamar Penrose, standing behind Missy, held herself in a breathless attitude of waiting, a kind of exultation on her face, expectant, transfixed.

Nowhere did I hear anyone say "Poor Sophie," nor indeed did anyone appear to be struck by the tragedy, or even by the fact of her death—only that she was dead *now, today.*

"Of all days," said one.

"Not a thought for anyone else," said another.

"Amys shouldn't have rung," said a third. "Dead by her own hand."

Justin Hooke stood stolidly, looking at the Widow as if for guidance, but saying nothing.

"Should have known better—" a third put in.

"A sinner's heart!" It was the Widow, who had lifted her head and begun speaking. Though she did not shout, her voice reached all quarters of the assembled crowd. "She has done away with herself. She has done it in spite and in malice. She has lived a foolish child and she has died one. I brought her into this world with these hands, and would that I had sent her from it with the same. Mr. Buxley is right—she will find no resting place in our churchyard. *She is bane.*"

"What will happen?" Sally Pounder called out.

"Yes, what will happen now?" It was Margie, the beauty parlor operator. "Will there be a Harvest Home?"

The Widow's features drew together. "Don't talk nonsense, girl, of course there'll be a Harvest Home. It's the seventh year—got to be!"

"But who'll be the Corn Maiden?"

"Never doubt the Corn Maiden will wear her crown tonight." Her voice was strong and angry. "But it's late. There's little enough time. Missy, come up. Tamar, send her to me."

As the child went up, I pushed through the throng, mounting step by step until I was eye to eye with the Widow. The child retreated toward the doors, her pale eyes fixed on me as I addressed the old woman.

"You speak of bane. If there is bane in this place, it comes from you. Not from your herb basket, but from yourself, from your stories and tales and talk. Sheep's blood and corn crowns and holy God knows what else." I turned on the crowd, "How can you listen to her? How can you let her do it? Can't you see what she is?"

The Widow was not angry. She turned her smile on me, a profoundly sad smile, as though she had lost a dear one; the ironic, knowing smile of fanatics whose beliefs are so ingrained it is impossible to communicate with them. She folded her large hands below her bosom, two fingers toying with the ribbon from which her shears were suspended.

"It appears your sarcasm is lost on these people here," she began, "bein' simple folk. But simple though they may be, this is their village, their home. Their ancestors founded it for them and it's been kept as they wanted it, and it don't seem to me they'll take kindly to such criticisms from an outsider. We let you come and let you stay, if that was what you wanted. We gave you the old Penrose house and let you fix it up and make a place to paint your pictures, if it was what you wanted. We don't believe in meddlin' with other folks, long as they don't meddle with us." She turned her vindictive look to the crowd below. "We were his friends; aye, and Justin was, too. Our Harvest Lord. But there are things beyond friendship. This man is a fool. He don't care for our ways. The old ways." She turned back to me. "You didn't come only to fix up a house; you come to make trouble. You come to nose around in places folks should know better than to go. You come to make your wife unhappy—aye, and your daughter, too—and you come to get drunk at public affairs where only the kindness of the village admitted you through the portals. And when you was done with that, what did you do? You tried to suborn Worthy Pettinger, him that was chosen. And now you have the temerity to come here in front of these folk and laugh at the things they believe."

She raised her closed fist in a swift denunciating gesture. "Let it be understood," she called out in a thunderous voice, "this man is pariah. Henceforth, in this village he is an outcast and will remain so. Let us turn our backs on him, and our hearts. Let us lock our doors to him, and hide our childern from him. Let none of us, neither the youngest nor the oldest, show our face to him again. Let us shun him as we would the rabid dog, the venemous serpent, the leper. He is forbidden. He is anathema."

With outspread arms, she invoked what powers lay beyond the bright blue span of sky to sweep me from her sight, drawing her shawl from her shoulders and muffling her features so only the implacable, remorseless eyes—the Cornwall eyes—showed as she turned her back and faced the vestibule doors. One by one, those below followed suit, turning where they stood, and, looking down, I saw only backs, no faces other than Robert's, his chin drawn down, his glasses black circles in his face.

Then the bell began again. A clang; another, louder, more resounding; another and another, increasing in rhythm and clangor. They turned back, looking past me to the vestibule where the child was tugging wildly on the bell rope. Her feet touched, she sprang up again, and again it rang; she performed a demonic sort of dance as she struggled against the weight of the bronze. Again her feet touched, again her body leaped; again the bell.

Her mouth was frothing, her eyes bulged. Tamar rushed up the steps; the Widow's arm blocked her passage. "Let her be." The child continued. Ring! Ring! Ring! Then she let go the rope, dropped to the brick floor, and while the bell echoed, she came from the vestibule; coming, she pointed; pointing, she screamed.

"He is there! He is among you! Guard him or you will be sorry!" Her head lolled back, then snapped forward, and she turned the full vent of her insane fury on me. *"And you will be sorrier!"* She seized my hand and sank her teeth into it, drawing blood as she had from the sheep, from the chicken, to feed vampire-like upon it, to feed her prophecy.

I tore my hand away, lifted it, and brought it down. She reeled and fell beside the outstretched form of Sophie Hooke.

Justin's eyes flashed fire as he grabbed me and pinioned my arms. I struggled, but no strength of mine could match his. With overt menace, the crowd pressed closed around the steps.

"Kill him. Kill him."

Merle Penrose and Morgan Thomas, my scarecrow masters of the night before, took me in custody and dragged me roughly down the steps, Mr. Zalmon following. Below, Sally Pounder pushed her way through the throng.

"But who will it be?" she cried. "Who will be the Maiden tonight? Who will make the corn?"

The Widow turned to Justin. "You must choose another." He shook his head. Looking down at the fallen child, she gestured for the men to carry her away. "The Harvest Lord will not choose. Then we must vote!"

Tamar stepped forward, her hands clasped over her breast, a turbulent, ecstatic look on her face. Sally Pounder stared at her sullenly, her mouth falling open. "But Tamar's been. For Gracie Everdeen. It ought to be someone else. Me—"

"Or me," Margie Perkin's face appeared before me. Others clamored.

"Tamar makes the corn better," someone shouted. Tamar—Tamar—Tamar.

The name swept through the crowd, and looking back as I was led across the Common, I saw Tamar Penrose lift her head proudly and enter the church to be voted upon, while the Widow, who had been speaking with the minister, spun swiftly, her skirts flying out in a black swirl, her hands again raised in a hieratic gesture, of both benediction and blasphemy.

Then she, too, went into the church and Amys Penrose closed the doors behind her.

28

The clock, an oaken one, clacked monotonously over the wall calendar above the Constable's desk, steadily marking off the minutes. I knew I had little time. The Constable sat across from me in the swivel chair. Tamar Penrose came in with two cups of tea, set them on the desk, and went out. I remembered the teakettle on the hot plate—the teakettle she had used to steam open Worthy's letter.

I unwrapped two cubes of sugar and dropped them in the cup, squeezed the lemon and tossed it in the wastebasket. There was no spoon.

"Must be in a hurry, Tamar," the Constable said. He slurped at his tea. Outside it was growing dark; I could see through the iron grille on the window. The Constable switched on the light and got up and went out, carrying his cup.

I could hear them talking in the post office room—the Constable, Morgan Thomas, some others. The outer door opened and I heard a woman's voice: Maggie Dodd. The Constable opened the office door and she came in carrying a tray.

"I got Bert to fix you something at the Rocking Horse." She set the tray down on the desk and looked at me. Then she came around the desk and touched my shoulder sympathetically. "I'm so sorry, Ned. Robert told me what happened. I've been in the city all afternoon, picking out some music." She drew off her gloves and took the Constable's chair.

"Hello, Maggie." Suddenly I felt sheepish. "Seems I've been given a ticket-of-leave."

"What happened, Ned?"

"I guess you'd have to ask Missy Penrose—"

She made an impatient gesture as though to do away with the thought of the malign Missy Penrose.

I asked, "What time did you go to the city?"

"This morning."

"Did you see Beth?"

"Yes. Didn't you?"

"No. She wasn't there when I got home. Where'd she go, Maggie?"

"I'm not sure. I know she had some quilts to go to New York. Perhaps she took them down herself, after she dropped Kate off."

"Kate?"

"She was driving her over to Ledyardtown to stay the night

with a school chum. Then—" She made a gesture of futility. "I don't know—she said she wanted to think things out."

"She didn't go to the Widow's?"

"Not that I know of. She might have. I can stop on my way home and see, if you want."

"I've got to get out of here."

She gave her rueful half-laugh. "Certainly you do. I've never heard of anything so ridiculous. I'm sure tomorrow—"

"I've got to get out of here tonight. Help me, Maggie."

She watched me with a bland expression. "How, Ned?"

"Get the wire cutters from my studio and bring them to the window. You can cut the screen."

"Stay here tonight, Ned. It's all a tempest in a teapot, anyhow. I'm sure by tomorrow things will have cooled down."

"I've got to get out of here tonight."

"Why tonight?"

"It's Harvest Home. The women are going to Soakes's Lonesome—"

"Which women, Ned?" Smiling, she had adopted a patient tone, as if speaking to a child or a madman.

"All of them—"

"All?" Still she smiled, but the amusement had turned visibly, and horribly, to scorn. When she spoke again, her voice was hard, dispassionate. " 'All' would include me, wouldn't it?"

I stared at her. "You?"

"Of course, Ned, dear. Have you forgotten? I was born here." She laughed, flicking the empty fingers of her glove against the edge of the desk. "You want to go to Harvest Home, is that it? Curiosity killed the cat, remember."

I stared; was it possible?

"You are a fool." Low, contemptuous; the kind Maggie-eyes were gone; in their place a small burning defiance, a triumph, as I had seen in Tamar's face when she went into the church for the voting. I could not believe it; Maggie, our friend. I felt something like an electrical jolt, as if I had sustained a physical blow. I drew a dry shuddery breath and shoved my hands in my pockets. The swivel chair squealed as she rose and began putting on her gloves. I took a step toward her.

"It was you, wasn't it? On the other side of the hedge. That day you were planting bulbs—"

"Go on," she said.

"You heard Worthy telling me he was going to run away. You told Tamar to watch for a letter from John Smith. You got him killed."

"Killed?" She worked the gloves on, finger by finger. "I don't know what you're talking about, Ned. Nor would anyone else. Mrs. Zee drove Worthy to the turnpike to get the bus to New York. If he didn't arrive there—well . . ." She shrugged.

"And you took the doll—"

"No—*you* took the doll. I merely returned it to the place it was supposed to be—in Justin's field. It was put there for a purpose." Her eyes narrowed appraisingly. "You may not have noticed, Ned, dear, but you have about you a certain air of—futility. You look tired. What you must do is eat and get some rest and not try to do anything. About *anything*. Then things may look different."

"After tonight."

"Yes. After tonight. After Harvest Home. If you are careful, and do not interfere, if you try to understand and be a good husband, things may look different. They may look different to Beth as well." She rose, picked up the napkin from the tray, and offered it to me. "Dinner?"

"The condemned man ate a hearty meal? Thanks, no." I stared at her, thinking of how she led me on all along the way; Robert, too. He had known, had been in on it all. Pretending, like the rest of them.

I turned back to the window. I heard her picking up the tray; she kicked her toe at the door and the Constable unlocked it. She handed someone the tray, looked back, then went through the door. The Constable came in.

"Not gonna eat?"

I shook my head. Chewing on his lip, he regarded me, then nodded at the cot against the wall. "You can sleep there."

"When do I get out?"

"We'll know tomorrow. But tonight the ladies want you in safekeepin'." He chuckled, made a circuit of the room, started out. Then he returned, asking me to empty my pockets. I laid my wallet, money, car keys, and penknife on the desk. He picked up the knife, opened the center desk drawer, and tossed it inside.

"Don't want no more suicides."

"Why should I commit suicide?"

"There's worse things." I heard the men in the other room laugh. He swept the other objects into the drawer, then felt in my jacket pockets, found the flashlight, and dropped that in too, and locked the drawer. He went out, and the door was swung shut and bolted. Feet scraped on the floor, the outer door was closed and locked, and I was left alone, immured in the post office for the night. Was it just for the night? What would happen tomorrow? I looked at the clock again; the moon would be rising soon.

I stared at the door. The lock was old but looked strong—strong and solid like the room itself. I sprang up and rubbed my hand along the stone surface of the walls; small chance of getting out.

But I must get out. I had a plan. I went to the window and opened it, pressing my forehead against the wire latticework. I examined again the surround where the screening was riveted fast.

The clock ticked. I could hear voices out on the street, could just catch sight of the Rocking Horse Tavern; men were coming out and getting into the cars parked in front. They drove off. Bert came out, locked the door, hurried away.

I stared over at the Penrose barn.

Gwydeon Penrose. What had he been like? One of the hardy Cornish forebears, like the rest of the village settlers. Had he believed in the old ways? Certainly, I decided; they all had. Their fathers and their fathers before them. Crafty farmers, clever. I recalled Amys's story of how Gwydeon had outsmarted the Indians, hiding his family here in the forge, and when they finally broke in they found—

Nothing.

I straightened, feeling the stubble on my chin. They had found nothing. Gwydeon hadn't been there. Nor his family. They'd escaped—isn't that what Amys had said? I made a rapid circuit of the room, pounding at the unyielding stone walls. If they'd got out, they'd had to do it from inside. How would I do it? Go up the chimney? I bent, feeling around the metal flanges of the flue. Though the fireplace opening was large, the flue was much too small and there was an ancient metal plate over it.

It wasn't the fireplace. Where, then? A trap door in the floor. I slid the desk aside and pulled up the scrap of carpet. The floorboards ran from wall to wall, pegged and in varying widths. I pounded with my fist, testing; felt the resistance of solid timberwork beneath. I went around the room jouncing my weight. The boards did not give.

I stopped, listening to the clock, my eye taking in the room again. Four walls, ceiling, floor, fireplace, the closet next to it—

The closet!

I turned a small wooden catch and opened the door. It was less than eighteen inches wide and ran from floor to ceiling. It appeared to have been a woodbox, nothing more. Dried mortar had oozed between the stonework. I knelt, examining the floor. The light was bad; the floor appeared to be covered by a square of linoleum that stopped at the threshold. I felt its surface, then tapped. It returned a hollow sound. I could see a bulge under the linoleum that could be the spine of a hinge. I felt with my fingers; there was another: two hinges. I tried to get my fingernails under the linoleum. One or two small pieces broke off; something was required to pry it up. The penknife.

I went to the desk and rattled the drawer. It gave slightly, but the lock held. I sat on the floor, braced my feet against the front, inserted my fingers along the underside, and pulled. The drawer resisted, then loosened, then came away altogether. I found my knife and began laboriously peeling off the linoleum.

At last—almost an hour later—I had exposed the metal that hinged the trap. Dirt had caked in the crevices and bound it fast. I used the knife point to scrape the dirt out, then tried again. With a screech of hinges the door moved. I lifted it an inch at a time, and when it was open I looked down into a narrow black hole. A crude arrangement of rungs descended along one side of the shaft and, taking the flashlight from the drawer, I climbed down into Gwydeon Penrose's tunnel.

There was hardly room to move, and I was sure I would suffocate in the fetid, airless chamber. I crawled, wriggling and pulling myself forward. Dirt had fallen from the ceiling, and I had to scoop it past my shoulders and under to get through. Overhead I could hear a faint thrum. A car, perhaps. Maybe I was under the street. And what lay at the other end? Another piece of linoleum, blocking my way out?

The tunnel narrowed to a point where I could barely get my shoulders through. Holding the flashlight, I slid my arms out in front and drew myself along, pushing with my feet. The passage widened again, and movement became easier. I came to a kneeling position, then crawled on all fours. There was planking under my hands and along the sides of the tunnel. In a moment I was standing, and I swung the flashlight beam in an arc, determining what lay ahead. I looked down, saw some stone steps. I mounted, and at the top I found a small door. I opened it to discover a closet of some kind. I could feel clothing hanging on hooks, and my hand struck a stack of books. Books and more books. There was a latch; I lifted it and the door partly opened. A gleam of light showed through the crack; I heard the drone of a voice. Quickly catching the door before it could swing farther, I peeked through the crack; I realized where Gwydeon Penrose's tunnel had led me.

The church. I was in the cupboard where the hymnals were stacked, under the choir loft. The voice belonged to Mr. Buxley, who stood in the pulpit saying a prayer; the pews were filled with the village women. Heads bowed, they sat with their backs to me, row after row of white-clad figures. I listened as Mr. Buxley completed his prayer, then left the pulpit and sat in his chair. Nervously he ran his finger around the front of his collar several times, watching the women, who remained with their heads bent. Mr. Deming appeared from a point past my line of vision, and stood under the pulpit behind the long harvest table which, I now saw, bore a large number of long-handled hoes. The rest of the elders ranged themselves on either side of Mr. Deming, and when the women lifted their heads, he nodded gravely, I heard a stirring, and presently the Widow entered in her black dress and white cap. He took a hoe and placed it in her hands. She turned and started up the aisle. Now certain others of the women rose and went to the table to be given a hoe, and they, too, proceeded up the aisle. When the hoes had been distributed, the men inclined their heads to the congregation in a gesture of acknowledgment, then one by one filed out through the small door behind the pulpit, to be followed by Mr. Buxley.

At the same time, women were coming up the aisle and leaving through the vestibule doors. The last person to go out was Maggie Dodd, who locked the door behind the pulpit; then she, too, came up the aisle. I heard her go out through the vestibule, heard the key being turned in the lock on the front door.

The church was silent. I waited another moment, then opened the cupboard door and stepped out. I tried the door behind the pulpit, next the side doors; all were locked. I went into the vestibule and tried the front door. It also was locked. The windows were too high, and in any case only the top ones opened. I was sealed in the church.

I shined my flashlight upward, along the steps leading to the belfry. Then I began climbing step by step into the steeple, passing the door to the choir loft, then into the small square room that had been the old watchtower, and was now the clock turret. Still climbing, I came into the belfry. Directly below on the Common, the women had congregated after leaving the church. I ducked as I saw several faces lifted, looking at the clock. When

I raised my head again, I saw Amys Penrose coming along the roadway under the street lamps. He reached into his pocket as he came up the steps and in a moment I heard, far below, the door opening. Then the bell rope tautened and the bronze dome over my head began to swing.

I crouched under the arch, holding my ears as the iron tongue struck the first curfew note. The entire chamber reverberated with an enormous peal like bronze thunder that slowly diminished in a chain of echoes in my ears, then sounded again. The bell rang twelve times. At last it came to rest, the clapper hung vertically, and the rope went slack; then the door closed and locked again, while below all along the roadway one after another the street lights dimmed and went out.

29

Hunched on my perch in the belfry, I watched the moon rise— the Moon of No Repentance. Over black treetops whose branches seemed to reach upward for it, it rose, imponderable and potent, hanging low on the horizon like some titanic disk vast and orange and glowing, and on this night of Harvest Home it seemed its path was not around the globe in its accustomed orbit, but a trajectory propelling it cataclysmically at the earth, so huge and bright did it seem.

Generously it lent its light to this most ceremonious of occasions as the women of Cornwall Coombe gathered below me on the Common. They seemed to meet in a community of spirit and endeavor, but with little of festival or celebration in their demeanor: a solemn convocation, rather, their apparel suitable to the event, full-skirted with drooping hems and long sleeves, a druidic look, the moonlight causing the white folds to shimmer and gleam.

One pointed, then another, and I turned my head to look up

Main Street where, under a porch light, beside the rusty glider, the child Missy Penrose appeared and came down the steps. The light went out, and now out of the darkness came another figure, their last-appearing sister, she whom they awaited: the Corn Maiden herself.

Veiled and ceremonially dressed, she came eagerly along the walk, her head proud and erect, surrogate for the dead Sophie Hooke. Tonight, Justin would make the corn with Tamar Penrose; Sally Pounder and Margie Perkin had lost.

They brought her onto the Common, where a festooned cart awaited her; her face was discreetly hidden by the embroidered covering. She mounted into the cart, and I saw the Widow's white cap moving through the white-clad figures as she draped the great quilt that told the story of the growing of the corn across the front of the cart.

They held themselves in readiness, but they did not start out, for still there was one missing: Justin Hooke, Tamar's partner in the night's events. Below me I could hear the internal workings of the clock, its iron gears ratcheting and settling into place again, the metallic clicks as the hands moved. I looked up at the bronze hull of the bell and the great iron clapper suspended above me, then down at the rope that trailed from the rocker to the vestibule below.

I saw Justin before the women did. I did not know where he came from, but he was there, at the end of Main Street, his blond head shining in the moonglow, his body shrouded in the same red mantle he had worn in the Corn Play. He was standing there, then he came on, walking slowly—operatically, even. The women saw him, and they fell silent at his advance, a dark, majestic figure, looking neither right nor left, but coming straight toward them, his red mixing and mingling with their white as they offered token aid for his ascent into the cart, where he stood beside the Corn Maiden.

They were a pair.

Even with Sophie dead, and with whatever the night might hold, they were a pair, Justin and Tamar. I watched them as they linked hands, standing proud and erect when the wooden tongue of the cart was raised, the vehicle with its two passengers drawn in a wide arc, torches—two, four, six, or more—flanking the sides of the cart, one figure running ahead to light the way, while musicians joined the moving troupe, flute and tambourine and drum, and the flower-braided cart was pulled not by any beast but by the women themselves, along the roadway where dogs hugged the shoulders, trailing in inquisitive pairs, but silent, as if they, too, comprehended the meaning of Harvest Home in Cornwall Coombe.

I watched it out of sight, then began drawing up the bell rope, arm over arm, pulling it up to me. When it lay coiled at my feet, I took off my coat and wrapped it around the bell clapper, tying the sleeves to secure it. Then I dropped the rope outside the arch, put my weight on it so the bell tilted, and stepped out, clutching the rope and sliding down. The bell gave off one dull reverberation, which muted itself and floated away into silence as I let go of the rope and dropped to the ground.

Against the perfect circle of the moon, paler than an hour ago, I watched the crow wing to its perch on the far side of the clearing. Somewhere in the cavernous fastnesses of Soakes's Lonesome the fox barked, the fox I had heard on my first visit, he who watched the watchers, who hunted the hunters. The hollow curve felt uncomfortable against my back and sides as I huddled under the network of vines that sutured the gaping cavity of the blasted tree.

Girdled there, a thick leafy screen securely hiding my head where once the screaming skull—the skull of Grace Everdeen—had rested, I waited, watched, listened. At my feet the dead roots convulsed themselves outward from the base of the tree to the spring which bubbled and fretted its way along the rocky stream bed. The thick grass of the clearing was a silvery-olive color in the mooonlight; more silvery were the trunks of the birch grove ringing the open space, and beyond that the trees were dark, receding in black corridors into the woods.

Then, from afar, I heard the sound of voices being funneled toward me through the gap. Soon there were other voices—I had no idea whose—speaking in low tones. Above the flow of water I could hear them approaching behind the tree, then pass in a group, and I could see the backs of four women carrying between them an object which proved to be a large chair—not an ordinary one, but a sort of throne, woven with straw and corn, which they placed toward the edge of the clearing directly opposite my hiding place. Then, like me, they waited.

Beyond the gap, the singing grew louder. It had taken them half an hour longer than it took me to get to the grove; I had followed the shorter route across the fields, avoiding the men posted along the Old Sallow Road and entering the woods through the meadow. They were coming through the gap now, processionally, their way lighted by the torches. I listened for the sound of the cart, but the Corn Maiden appeared on foot and was at once encircled and greeted by those who had come first, several clasping her to their bosom, then leading her to one side of the clearing where a large piece of cloth was spread; she sat, veiled, the white mantle she wore drawn around so no bodily part showed. Eight or ten of the girls grouped themselves about her.

I had not yet seen the arrival of the two other important characters in the drama: the Widow Fortune and the Harvest Lord himself. The women had arrayed themselves in a large circular group about the clearing, waiting. I saw some of them whisper to each other, then look in my direction, and as they joined hands and came toward the tree I felt the fear of discovery. Suddenly Robert's warning came back to me: the Eleusinian Mysteries, that no man had seen and lived to tell of. They came close, their faces turned directly toward me, but they had not discovered my hiding place.

Meanwhile other women were arriving in the clearing, many carrying hoes, some bringing wooden kegs, the ones I had seen unloaded from Fred Minerva's wagon. Several large baskets were brought out, from which came chalice-like cups. These were filled from the kegs and passed around, the recipients tasting as though examining for flavor, then drinking.

Cups were carried to the Corn Maiden's group, sitting on the ground, and they, too, drank. Presently I heard the sound of the instruments, and the celebrants arranged themselves again in a large circle around the clearing, cups poised in midair. I could hear someone moving behind me, and in a few moments I saw the Widow's broad black back and her white cap as she walked into the clearing, leading Justin Hooke, whose eyes were blindfolded by a white band, tied behind. The Widow brought him to the throne, where she aided him in sitting, arranging his red mantle so it covered him to the ground. A cup was quickly brought and offered to her. She signaled impatiently, and it was placed in Justin's hands, while another cup was given to the Widow, and they both drank.

The cups were passed, and passed again; the women drank long and eagerly, as if anxious to absorb the contents. They had broken up into groups, which in the most casual fashion began a loose form of dance, not the dance they had executed at the husking bee, but of a more impromptu nature, with no prescribed form. Someone started a song, its melody totally unfamiliar to me, with an odd cadence and odder pattern, a still odder tongue.

Suddenly I heard a sound behind me. Someone had come through the gap and was crossing toward the clearing, with slow, measured, almost furtive steps. A twig cracked, then another. I waited for a figure to appear within my range of vision, but no one came. Whoever it was had stopped at some point just in back of the tree and I froze, thinking she must be investigating the trunk. But no; I knew the person standing there was only watching the proceedings in the clearing.

Several women came toward the spring carrying a large metal ewer. They submerged it in the water, and while it filled they looked past me, one of them making a beckoning gesture, an acknowledgment to whoever it was waiting behind my hiding place. She beckoned again, gave a slight shrug, then the filled ewer was borne away, to be placed close to Justin's throne. Now, one by one, numbers of the women separated from the others and gathered around the Harvest Lord. His blindfold was removed, the cup given into his hands again. The women dipped napkins into the ewer and began washing his feet, a ritual of cleansing and purification.

Ivied garlands and chains of flowers were produced and hung around his neck and shoulders. Then the same corn crown that had been used in the play was brought to the Widow and she placed it on his head.

These women now withdrew, leaving the Harvest Lord to watch the dancing.

The dancers were accompanied by the instruments, a primitive strain similar to the music I had heard from the cornfield on the night of the "experience." From time to time, the circles broke while the women refreshed themselves from the cups continually being filled from the kegs and passed among them. Unfailingly, one was always carried past my line of vision to the unknown presence standing behind my tree, and I would hear low urgings, then a muffled response; then, the cup drained, the bearer would return to the group, where their somewhat stilted, ceremonial aspect was now wearing off. Their movements had become erratic, their singing often off key, their gestures more abandoned.

All the time, I kept careful watch for a clue in the proceedings that would tell me what it was Gracie Everdeen had done that had caused her death. Or what it was about the ceremony that had caused Worthy's. Or why Sophie had taken her life. The upright lord, seated on the throne, muffled in his red mantle, seemed gradually to relax; his shoulders slumped slightly, and as his head moved from side to side with the rhythm of the music, I saw in the flickering light that his features had taken on a glazed, drunken look. The mead was having its hallucinogenic effect. I remembered the cask Mrs. Green had been given from Fred Minerva's wagon: they had drugged Worthy before executing him.

The moon rose higher, and from time to time the Widow looked up at it; I judged she was using it as a clock. The torches were hardly needed now, for the clearing was illuminated by a light etching every detail. Again the cup was passed to the Corn Maiden, who took it under her veil and drank, turning to one or another of the girls around her, and from the pitch of their babble I could tell that the mead was having its effect on them as well.

Then, as the music built, the Widow walked to the center of the clearing and lifted her hoe to the sky. The moon was directly overhead. The dancers withdrew in groups around the periphery of the clearing while the old woman turned slowly, pointing around the ring with the tip of her hoe. I saw it swing toward me, pass, then stop. An angry look came over her face and she marched in my direction. Yet she also was not looking at my hiding place, but behind it. I could hear her decisive whisperings to whoever was waiting behind the tree. Then she reappeared, her step lethargic as she came to stand before the throne. With difficulty she assumed a kneeling position at Justin's feet, where she bowed her head in prayer; the others were silent and watchful until she lifted her head again, then rose unsteadily to her feet. Her face looked flushed, and she blinked her eyes behind the spectacles. She made motions with her tongue as if she found her mouth excessively dry: she was not drunk but narcotized. Laying a hand on Justin's shoulder, she spoke in a hoarse, uneven voice.

"Behold. This is our anointed. Give eye unto the chosen among us, give tongue to his praises. He was chosen for us, and for seven years we have loved and honored him. Trophy and tribute have been his, and the worship of all. He has been our Lord of the growing corn. He is our god, whose godhead is the crops."

The voices of the women punctuated each sentence with responses of approval, which sounded to me like the "Amen"s of a church service.

"As it was in the olden times, so it has been and ever shall be. It is the way. The spirit has been in our Lord for these seven years, and he has brought us good harvests. It was the flesh of his body, his strength and sinew, his limbs and brain, his blood that did this for us. The corn is his, each kernel, and for it we thank him."

"We thank him," they chorused.

"This is something to have done in a life. It is something to have been made for. To have been set upon the earth to cause the earth to bear."

"Oh, yes. *Oh, yes.*"

"Then let him be gloried!"

"Gloried. *Gloried.*" I heard the feverish response, saw the bright glistening eyes of the women as they lavished adoring looks upon him, some in their dazed state unable to withhold sudden emotional outbursts, pushing their way toward him and prostrating themselves before him.

The old woman's body had begun moving slightly; I could see her shoulders lifting and lowering as though to engender more deeply the force of the drug in her system. Her torso made small circular motions while her hand lay upon Justin's head.

"Hear me, for I speak with the tongue of the Goddess who dwells in the earth. I remind you again of Her promise. She will provide for us, She will give us the—" Here she broke off, as though to remind herself what would be provided. Having recollected, she went on in a thick, harsh voice: "The bountiful harvest, if—if we Her servants tend well to Her business. If we will *believe.*"

"*Believe.*" The word was repeated through the throng which forced its way nearer, the closest throwing themselves to the ground, reaching to touch the hem of Justin's cloak. "Let no man gainsay us. Let no outsider comprehend Her. In a time when faces have been turned on the other God, let us acknowledge the Mother of us all. She will sustain us."

"Yes. *Yesss.*"

"As She has sustained this, Her son."

Cries arose, a piteous lament, and some had come behind the

throne, leaning forward to touch Justin's head and caress his neck and shoulders.

"From his hand has come the gift, and in return we have shown him our secret. The soil has quickened and proved fertile and the rains have been plenteous and the sun of the world has shone on us."

"Has shone. Has *shone.*"

"The corn grew. We have prospered."

"*Prospered.*"

"And—" She faltered again, making a tight movement with her lips to master herself, as if the next moment were of the greatest import.

"And in the gratitude of our hearts we now offer him the pledge and token of our esteem, as is customary upon the seventh year of Harvest Home, that he may know of us the secret heart of that which he himself has given us. He alone of all men may know the secret which has been given to us, the secret of the Sacred Mother."

For an instant, I reeled back in time to Tithing Day, when Worthy had appeared in the church doorway and had damned the Mother. The answer was at hand. The secret was to be revealed, and with it the heart of the mystery I had so long probed. The secret heart of Mother Earth. The Widow's last words filled my head: "He alone of all men may know . . ." I realized my peril: if I was discovered, they would kill me.

The women had formed a melting, slow-moving configuration across the clearing and, before I realized it was happening, from the midst of the throng was produced the core of the night's mysteries, which no man but the Harvest Lord was permitted to look upon. Covered with a woven cloth, resting upon a silver salver, the mysterious and awaited object was given into the Widow's hands, who now turned and held it before Justin. From her seclusion, the Corn Maiden arose with her court, she, too, to gaze upon what lay hidden under the cloth. It was not large— this I could easily see—and I felt a tremor, wondering at this rare and precious treasure, this strange, forbidden object none but the initiated might look upon.

Yet when the Widow lifted the cloth and revealed it, I saw it was the commonest of things, something I had seen constantly since coming to the village of Cornwall Coombe. Was it for this these ceremonies took place? Was this the heart of the mysteries of the great Mother, which had been handed down from generation to generation, century after century? Was this what Worthy had feared, what Grace had refused to acknowledge, what Sophie had ended her life in dread of? What no man may know nor woman tell?

An ear of corn. A single, simple ear of corn. It lay upon the salver in its husk, the salver held before Justin's eyes as he gazed on it. What, I wondered, did the fact of it reveal to him? What had it been given him on this night of Harvest Home to read in a single ear of corn? Then I saw, as he must have, that what had been given to him was the exact and precise nature of the world he lived in, where the fact of the corn was the fact of his life. Like most simple facts, it was the truest, and the most easily overlooked. On the tray, hidden in the husk, was the whole vision, the life of the corn and the life of the man, inextricably bound together in oneness, bound in the tilling and the planting and the growing, in the harvesting and in—

I knew it then. *I knew it!* And was terribly afraid. The corn was the revelation; the revelation was in the corn: the ear in its husk held before the Harvest Lord by the hands of the Widow Fortune. Its deepest significance had been obscured by the tangle of mysteries, yet in a single chilling moment all the mysteries now became clear. I felt a shiver, like a strange paralysis, creeping up my body. I swallowed and, in the silence, thought someone surely must hear. But I did not fear for myself; I feared for Justin. I knew then the terrible secret of Harvest Home.

They were going to kill him.

Here, in the grove, in this temple of the Mother Earth, the Harvest Lord was to be offered in ritual sacrifice. Here, in the moonlight, with the dancing and singing women, Justin Hooke was being drugged, was then to be murdered, murdered for the corn.

This was why they had revealed to him their mystery, because he would never live to tell what he had seen. Bound together in oneness, the Harvest Lord and the corn, and as the corn died and was reborn, so would he die and be born again, not in himself but in the young Lord. The Eternal Return.

I felt shock, disgust, rage, felt again the hatred I had felt at the burning—hatred for their stupid, primitive beliefs. I wanted to shout out to Justin: Do not drink, run away; never hear, never listen.

I looked at him. He did not seem afraid. In his drugged state, he showed no loss of dignity; he sat regal and aloof, watching as the corn ear was covered again and taken from sight, as if he comprehended what he had been shown, and what he must now do.

The Widow was speaking again: "And as our Lord has accepted honor and tribute at our hand so he must likewise find his passing at our hand."

The Harvest Lord made immortal. The pride of Justin Hooke.

The old woman continued, recalling for them the last Great Waste, when Loren McCutcheon had been Harvest Lord—Justin nodding agreement—and the cause of this visitation had come at the hands of Gracie Everdeen, blighted in soul and body, she whose Lord had been Roger Penrose, and who had defied the traditions of Harvest Home, had brought to the reign of Loren McCutcheon waste and dearth.

Perfidious Grace Everdeen.

Dead, all of them. Loren McCutcheon, but not from drink. Roger Penrose, but not from a horse fall. Clemmon Fortune, but not from an axe blow.

Murdered for the corn.

The Widow Fortune.

Widowhood in exchange for good crops. And everyone, all the villagers, had known it, man, woman, child alike. And he, the victim, had also known. And I, the fool everyone said I was, had not known.

I saw it now. Loren McCutcheon had been the Harvest Lord and had reigned for seven years; on the seventh year Justin had been chosen the Young Lord at the Agnes Fair. At Harvest Home, Loren had been dispatched by some unknown means and Justin had taken his place. For seven years there had been no Great Waste, the crops were bountiful; and now, tonight, the seven years were done. Worthy Pettinger had been chosen the Young Lord, with Missy Penrose's bloody hands on his cheeks, signifying he would reign for the next seven years. But Worthy had not wanted to die. He had run away, been brought back, and killed. Insult to the Mother.

And Justin would die, in the prime of his manhood, to give place to the new Harvest Lord, Jim Minerva, who in another seven years would also die.

The King is dead, long live the King.

Now the women could not stifle their ready tears, and they began an orgy of cries, voices calling out in farewell. I strained to hear the Widow. She had become somewhat incoherent, and I caught only fragments.

"Land has offered up its gifts—bounty—his hand given freely—be grateful—in gratitude mourn him—" The hoarse, uneven voice rose and fell in a fanatical paean of praise and sorrow. "Land will sleep—so must he—lay him to rest—recall with love—the farmer Justin Hooke."

Generously the moon lent its light to the scene, which little by little became more agitated. Never while the Widow spoke had the cup ceased being passed among the celebrants; never had Justin not been offered it. His eyes glittered, his tongue betrayed the dryness of his mouth, while his glazed features seemed illuminated by some dread inner light as he listened to the doleful lamentation, prefacing what was to follow.

They would poison him, undoubtedly. Some baneful mixture the Widow had prepared would be administered, put into his cup, and given to him to drink. But this was not yet, this was later, for now there was something to come before.

I should have realized what it was to be, yet until it actually began, I did not. Had I known, nothing could have kept me where I had hidden myself.

But even this part was for a time delayed, while the dancing began anew—another kind of dance, a brutal, fierce expression of emotion. Justin was brought to a standing position, and the red mantle taken from his shoulders, to be folded by numerous hands and passed from sight. Now he stood before them in god-like glory, his body covered only by a short tunic extending from neck to thigh and made of strips of corn leaves, and I could see his glistening flesh through the spaces between the strips. Again he took the proffered cup into his hands, fingers spread around the curve of metal; I watched his Adam's apple rise and fall as the liquid slid down his throat. He returned the cup, staggering slightly, pulled himself erect, and stood, spread-legged, waiting.

Everyone was waiting. And then I saw what was to come. There was one figure in the ceremony I had momentarily forgotten: the Corn Maiden. Until now she had sat by, accepting the cup as it was handed her, bending forward in rapt attention as the Widow spoke. Now her outer robe was taken from her and she was brought forward, moving across the trampled grass with a slow, undulating walk, an aggressive sexuality revealed in her movement, the embroidered veil hanging to her waist, the rest of her body covered to the thighs in the same sort of corn-leaf tunic that Justin wore. While she gazed at him through her veil, the women took hoes and dug at the turf, turning the soft ground. Little by little, the green of the grass disappeared and the sod was dug up, revealing the dark earth beneath. As they worked they sang, their faces flushed from the drink, their gestures feverish, as though anxious to accomplish their labor.

Among them walked the Widow, putting her hand to their hoes, each in turn, encouraging their endeavors, her white cap catching the light as she lifted her head and offered reverence to the Mother; and as she spoke, each word was taken up in turn by the women, so the singing became a liturgical incantation, picked up one by one, the next repeating it, and the next, and so it spread all across the tilled clearing, the Widow making gestures of transference from her mouth to theirs, offering them the words, they antiphonally returning them.

"We offer Thee, O Mother, Thy husband, as Thou hast given him to us, so we return him to Thee, into Thy keeping."

"Thy keeping . . ."

"As Thou has provided him strength, take him in strength."

"In strength . . ."

"For tonight he shall be gloried. They shall stand by his tomb and remember him. He shall not have been Justin Hooke, the corn farmer, but the Harvest Lord. He shall be immortal."

"Immortal."

"Take him to Your breast, great holiest of Mothers, this Your son, and succor him, receive him, forgive him. *Blessed is he . . .*"

"Blessed is he . . ."

"Body of Your body . . ."

"Body of Your body . . ."

"Soul of Your soul . . ."

"Soul of Your soul . . ."

"Soul of the corn that grows, the receptacle, harborer of the seed . . ."

"Harborer of the seed . . ."

"Receive him . . ."

"Receive him . . ."

"O Mother . . ."

"O Mother . . ."

"O Mother . . ."

"O Mother . . ."

"O Mother-r-r . . . Ma Mère . . . Mía Ma-a-adre . . . Mawtharr . . . Mo-der . . . Ma-ter-r-r-r . . . Me-e-ee-eter-r-r . . ."

"Me-e-ee-eter-r-r . . ."

"De—meter-r-r-r . . ."

"Demeter . . ."

Thus continued the chant, a canticle in a gradual declension of words that saw its passage from the tongue of every day through tongues that had been spoken for century upon century and that at last became another tongue entirely:

"O *Mag–thyr* . . . *Da–mag–thyr* . . . *Da–myyg——ar* . . . *Ah, ldhu, Mag-thyr* . . ."

A tongue spoken before any of those preceding, and the women, hand-locked in circle within the grove, had the tongue, for the old woman gave it to them, but though they did not know the meaning of the words they comprehended their import, for this was part of the mystery they shared in; and as they chanted, the flutes fell silent and only the drums and tambourines continued, their repeated monotony bringing the celebrants closer and closer to the magic that lay behind this night of nights.

"*Mag–thyr* . . . *Da–mag–thyr* . . ."

A steady tempo measuring out the cadence and rhythm. And the tongue became tongueless, became sounds only, iterated again and again as the old woman turned the circle, her fisted hand giving the meter to the drums and tambourines, giving the women the chant, and the words she knew, the syllables, the sounds of the tongue that was no tongue at all:

"*Ah, ldhu* . . . *ldhu* . . . *yah* . . . *halg* . . . *ogrl* . . . *na* . . ."

Neither English nor German nor Latin nor Celtic nor Sumerian nor any other language, for it was the tongue men had spoken at the dawn of time, when they first learned to communicate.

And at length, as the old woman circled, giving to them the sounds, some of the women's heads began to sway and their bodies followed where their heads led them and their joined hands parted while, their throats giving utterance to the sounds, they fell to the ground and tore up the grass and dug at the earth like animals, swine rooting, groveling, rolling upon one another, writhing in hysteria, with heaving breast and flailing limb, and the old woman stood above them, driving them, her fist metronomic against the moon, rising, lowering, giving them the tempo and the words. Nothing could stay them now, nothing still them. Wildly they flung themselves where they might, heedless of injury, unaware of reality, swept into hypnotic oblivion, their stomachs expanding, contracting, drinking air that they should rise and chant again, and again fall in frenzy.

And there were some who fell at the feet of the watching Harvest Lord, who had laid his cup aside and sat unmoving and upright, observing the secret rites as they swooned before him, permitting them to extend their quivering hands to touch him: piteous, tender hands, despairing hands; surely they must touch their last. Beloved Lord, O lively, warm male flesh, O magnificent Lord, we thank thee, the Mother thanks thee—

"O Mother . . . Magthyr . . . ldhu, ah, ldhu . . ."

Louder grew the cry, louder the chant, more serpentine their writhings as they yearned toward him, rushing from him to tear their hair, heads flung back, open-mouthed to shout unintelligible obscenities at the heaven that was to deprive them of their beloved.

Now it would be his death, the end of Justin Hooke. But no; still it was not yet. There was more for the living Justin, one thing more for him to do. They swooped upon him and brought him from where he stood beside the Corn Maiden to a spot near the center of the clearing where the earth had been hoed, and from my hiding place I could see the blank glitter of his eyes, the half-lidded look of pleasure as they strewed themselves about his feet, rubbing their cheeks along his legs, upward to his thighs, their eager hands reaching under his tunic to fondle and caress him. His head dropped back and a deep-throated moan of pleasure issued from his mouth as he became aroused, and through the parted strips of corn leaves appeared the living malehood of the Harvest Lord.

"Ya—ldhu!" they screamed, rushing to touch it, feel the erect object of their adoration, the great rooster that had occasioned the ribald comments at their kitchen doors. "Ya—ldhu! Ahm—lot! AHM—lot!" Cries of torment, their frenzy now insupportable. The sight and touch of the Priapean object induced a wild pantomime of devotion, an obscene reverence to the maleness of the Harvest Lord.

They were working at his back, binding his hands behind with braided thongs, rendering them useless. Then the Corn Maiden was brought to him and I realized what must follow. Together, in front of the others, they were to make the corn!

The veiled figure stood before him, leaf strips from neck to thigh, white legs gleaming, and arms, as she brought them up in a worshipful gesture, violently trembling.

Hands reached to draw away the veil, and as it fluttered, then slid away entirely, I stared, only half hearing the twig crack behind the tree as the waiting presence took a step forward. I paid scant attention to my danger as in that single terrible moment I realized the mistake I had made, and to what extent I had underrated the Widow Fortune's powers of persuasion. If Tamar Penrose had been a candidate, and Sally and Margie, they had all lost. The Widow had wanted new blood for the Corn Maiden; she had got it.

It was Beth.

Like one entranced, she stood as if she had stepped from a sleeping dream into a waking one. Hands reached to support her as she faced Justin; the Harvest Lord and the Corn Maiden: the man and the woman: my friend and my wife. She had eyes for nothing but him. In a blinding flash, I thought back to the night of the "experience": Beth in the chair, her hand raised. She had not been pulling down the shade; she had seen him, was acknowledging him. Already the Widow had begun her corruption.

Her body swayed as if drawn to him by a magnet. She tried to lift her arms, they dropped to her sides; she went slack, crumpled under the power of the keg liquor. Hands bore her down, where her fingers dug at the tilled earth. Dirtied, they became claws and began rending the thin fabric of the leaves that covered her, exposing her breasts and belly; then, looking up at the figure towering over her, she moaned and her hand reached upward.

She wanted him. She wanted to take him, to take him inside
her, to couple with him.

I cried out, and began tearing at the covering of vines across
the tree hollow, hearing the step at my side, twigs cracking, then
being confronted in my struggle by the red-lipped face of Tamar
Penrose, her red-nailed fingers ripping at the screen of leaves
to expose me, calling loudly, *"He has seen!"* heads turning while
I sought to free myself, enraged that the vines which had sequestered me now became my fetters and held me fast, while with
angry cries they came at me, a wave of vengeful harpies. I cursed
them, trying to free my hands and feet, feeling the sharpness of
their nails as they tore at the vines, and "Defiler!" they shouted,
astonished and furious, "he has defiled us," while I yanked and
pulled, saw Tamar's glittering eyes, in my mind saw Missy's
deader ones, heard her say "You will be sorrier!" the blank yet
knowing look; "Kill him!" they cried. Justin and Beth turned with
uncomprehending stares, not knowing what had happened. "Kill
him!" the women cried again.

"No!" someone commanded—the Widow's voice, but not the
Widow at all: some bedeviled creature, unearthly in her fury, her
cap fallen off, hair wildly hanging about her shoulders, her black
dress smutted. The Widow in the madness of her own dream,
into which I rashly had intruded.

"No! He shall not be killed yet. He has come to see. He has
come to witness. Let him see. Let him witness. Let him see the
Harvest Lord at work. Let him see the furrow plowed! Let him
see the making of the corn." While many hands imprisoned me
in the hollow of the tree, she turned back and at her signal the
drugged Justin was brought again to stand spread-legged over the
supine body of Beth, his arms pinned behind, while they spread
her legs apart and he stepped between them and knelt, and eagerly
they guided him into the darkness between her legs.

I went mad. Waves of nausea and horror swept me. A stop-
page in my ears as if all sound were suddenly cut off, a switch
thrown, a plug pulled, leaving only dull interior explosions, painful sparks behind my straining eyeballs, the blood surging through

the taut veins in my neck, my teeth clamping onto my lower lip to stop the soundless words I screamed, trying to turn away, to shut my eyes, feeling the sting of Tamar's nails as they bit into my arm until I was made to watch again.

"See! See him plow the furrow. Watch!"

I watched. She was not his lover, nor he hers, but both were instruments of the women, his arms bound, hers held outstretched on the earth as he probed her, and my cries broke from my lips again, mingling with the ecstatic chant that moment by moment mounted in tempo and pitch, *"Ldhu, ldhu,"* thrusting their shoulders as he thrust, grunting as she grunted, *"Ldhu,"* and *"Ldhu,"* some moving behind him, their fingers tracing the curve of his back as it arched and bent again, rose and sank, their passion spurring his passion, she beneath him crying out in lust and pain. In the madness and the moonlight, his face contorted in spasm as he pushed his way farther. And then, in the moment of complete knowledge, they worked each other, met shudderingly, and capitulated. The corn was made.

I screamed out, but all eyes were on the locked pair. As they lay on the ground, he covering her, the handle of a hoe was thrust through his bent arms and across his back, and he was torn from her. They brought him to his knees with his spine arched like a bow. A tremendous roaring sounded in his throat. Some of them had lifted her away, and she lay panting as she was covered over with the mantel and the veil was drawn over her head. His bull-like roars continued; he knelt, dripping onto the ground. I shouted again, trying still to pull away from the hands holding me.

What followed took only seconds. There was a quick flash of movement as Tamar sprang forward. A woman whose fingers were tangled in Justin's hair forced his head back and moved aside when with a wild look Tamar thrust herself at him. A silver crescent gleamed in her hand; she raised the sharpened sickle and, holding the tip with the other hand, in one swift movement she slashed it across the exposed throat.

His roar became a wild bellow, then turned to a gurgle; a torrent of red appeared, a brightly flowing curtain melting down the neck and onto the chest. They bent him back farther and came with cup and bowl to catch the precious liquid, stumbling as they bore it to all quarters of the clearing, spilling his blood among the upturned clods.

It was an ugly death. They struggled to hold him through the series of convulsive heaves that wracked his body, the giant muscles bulging, arms flailing, a slow agony as the red life drained from him and was poured into the ground. Then the great shoulders heaved, slanted sidewise, and he buckled like a gored bull and toppled over, the blood still gushing from the crescent wound.

They had dragged me from the hollow and pushed me forward the better to see this horror, the death of the Harvest Lord. I watched as I had watched the eye in dreams, unable to do anything else. It was not happening, it could not be happening; yet I knew it was. I shut my eyes, trying not to look; yet I looked. The massive chest rose in a thickly glutted cough, there was a final eruption of blood through the mouth, the lids flickered, the eyes rolled upward, then the great heart ceased pumping and he lay still.

They changed his position, straightening him out on the earth, laying him on his side, resting his head along one bent arm. Then, the final horror: Tamar flung herself down on the ground beside him, pulling herself to him, entwining her arms about him in bloody embrace, her red lips kissing his redder ones.

The hands relaxed their hold on me as the women watched the hideous sight. I pulled free. The moon had gone behind a cloud and the clearing had become dark. Beyond the clearing were the trees, beyond the trees lay safety. I began running. But what tree was there to shelter this fugitive, to harbor the defiler of the temple, the heretic? Like nemeses, they appeared from all sides of the clearing, blocking my every way. I wheeled, my foot caught on a bared root, and I went down, feeling the taste of earth upon my tongue. It was not bitter. As I waited for them to attack, it seemed the ground was strangely warm, and I strangely comforted. In those few brief moments, I pressed my cheek against the tilled soil, the very bosom of Mother Earth, feeling it assuage the burning flesh, felt the firm yet yielding body of it under my flattened palms. It was as though, beneath my beating heart, I could sense the heart of the land itself, the heart that lay within, the heart of Mother Earth. Through all my being I could feel Her massiveness, Her power, and Her strength. She did not spurn me; She seemed to draw me to her, to embrace me. Though She, who had given me life, would give no more, She would receive me back to her, and as I had never prayed to God for my soul's repose, now I prayed to Her, not for succor or protection, but for absolution.

She was clement. She would forgive.

Then, as I lay there on the steaming earth, out of the shambles of the night the women fell upon me.

30

"It's too lovely a day"—raising the window—"to keep it outside the house. Feel that glorious spring breeze."

"Mother—your dress!"

"Like it?"

"It's beautiful."

"I thought perhaps—"

"No, it's just perfect."

"I'm glad." She went from the bacchante room to the kitchen, leaving behind the scent of the lilacs she had arranged on the sideboard.

"What about dessert?"

"In the refrigerator, darling."

The refrigerator door opened. "Chocolate mousse. How many?"

"Six. Two for Maggie and Robert, two for you and Jim, one

for me, one for the Widow. Open the window over the sink, Kate, would you?"

The window slid in its frame and, as though in response, beyond the hedge Robert's sun-porch window was raised.

"Morning, Robert."

"It's Maggie, Beth. Marvelous day for a picnic. How's it coming?"

"In a jiffy."

"I think you're crazy, always doing the whole thing yourself."

"I want to. Got the martinis?"

"Iced and ready. Here's Robert—"

"Morning, Beth. Spring at last, hey?"

"Oh, yes. I thought it would never come."

It was true. After the long winter, the balmy caressing air already had a hint of summer in it. And where it slipped under the window of the bacchante room it mixed with and circulated the perfume of the lilacs. From window to window, they discussed the yellow bird in the locust tree.

"I told you," Robert said. "It comes back every year."

The Invisible Voice began:

" 'Though certainly I don't know why you should,' said Dora— 'And I am sure no one'—'Jip, you naughty boy, come—' I don't know how I did it. I did it in a moment. I intercepted Jip. I had Dora in my arms. I was full of eloquence. I never stopped for a word. I told her how I loved her. I told her I should die without her. I told her that I idolized and worshiped her. Jip barked madly all the time.

"When Dora hung her head and cried, and trembled. . . ."

"We're having chocolate mousse," Kate called over to Robert's window; Robert replied briefly over the sound of the Invisible Voice.

"Well, well! Dora and I were sitting on the sofa by and by, quiet enough, and Jip was lying in her lap, winking peacefully at me. It was off my mind. I was in a state of perfect rapture. Dora and I were engaged. . . ."

Presently, down the drive came the clop of a horse's hoofs, and the creak of wooden wheels sounded under the bacchante room window. Beth's light step carried her to the sink. "Good morning."

"Springish, ain't it? Where's Kate, now? Kate, come out and see what I have for you."

Scrambling noises in the kitchen, the back door opening, feet clattering down the steps.

"Mother—come see what the Widow's brought!"

Beth hurried out to join the others. "Oh, just look at them," she crooned.

"For me?" Kate asked.

"Aye. If your mother says," came the reply amid myriad cheepings. "If you're goin' to have eggs, you got to raise hens. These here now are real Easter chicks."

A car honked out on the street, a door slammed.

"Here's Jim Minerva."

"Congratulations, Harvest Lord."

"Morning, everybody. Morning, Kate."

"You're lookin' spruce for Spring Festival. How'll it feel to be crowned? Here, take these creatures out to the hen house and put 'em in the brooder."

Kate's and Jim's voices trailed away as they went off to the studio. Beth said, "What are you giving Jimmy today?"

"I sewed him a new shirt."

"I picked out cuff links."

"Just the thing."

"That you, Widow?" came a voice from the house beyond the hedge.

"Mornin', Robert. Fine day for Maypoling."

"The Eternal Return."

"*Chapter Twenty-four. My Aunt Astonishes Me. I wrote to Agnes as soon as Dora and I were engaged. I wrote her a long letter, in which I tried to make her comprehend how blest I was, and what a darling Dora was. I entreated Agnes . . .*"

"Dickens," said Robert.

"Ayuh, Dickens."

Presently Kate and Jimmy came back up the drive, laughing and talking in low, significant tones. "You're lucky you've got that skylight," Jim said. "But if you expect those hens to lay at night, we're going to have to put in electric lights."

"Listen to Jim, Kate," the Widow said. "He's one o' the best hen-raisers in the village. Eggs galore, eh, Jim?"

"Eggs galore, Widow." His voice, though bright and cheery, seemed to have taken on an air of depth and solidity.

"Mother, Jimmy says it's all right with him if I drive his car."

"If it's all right with *you*, Mrs. Constantine."

"Kate, darling, you're bound to have your driver's license, aren't you? Determined girl."

"It's the Greek in her," the Widow observed.

"*Half* Greek, don't forget," Kate laughed.

They made their goodbyes, and when the car had driven away the Widow said, "A handsome pair, aren't they? Makes me think of when Clem would take me to Spring Festival durin' our courtin' days." A pause, then: "Wouldn't it be wonderful if—"

"I know what you're thinking." Beth drew a tremulous sigh.

"She'd make a lovely Corn Maiden, no doubt of it."

"I never thought I'd see the day when my daughter would be going into the poultry business. The way those two have worked cleaning out that studio."

"Good for each other," the Widow replied succinctly. "Like I say, a handsome pair if ever there was. Pretty dress you're wearin'."

"If anyone ever told me I'd be wearing maternity clothes again—"

"Are you takin' your elixir?"

"Yes, and I can feel him kicking stronger every day. Missy thinks a 'J.'"

" 'J'? John?"

"She says it's got to be six letters. I thought 'Joshua.'"

"Capital! The battle of Jericho and all." Pause; then: "Sophie's pear tree's all a-bloom."

"I saw."

"Just like in the portrait. Pity it never got finished. Good painter, he was."

"Yes."

When the Widow's buggy had gone, Beth came back in the kitchen and busied herself with the remaining details of the lunch. The wicker of the Hammacher Schlemmer hamper creaked as she packed it. The refrigerator door opened and closed several times, and her brisk footsteps took her from one area in the room to another while she went about her work. In another moment the sink tap was turned on.

" 'My dear Copperfield,' cried Traddles, punctually appearing at my door, in spite of all these obstacles, 'how do you do?'

" 'My dear Traddles', said I, 'I am delighted to see you at last, and very sorry I have not been at home before. But I have been so much engaged . . .' "

The gush of water from the tap stopped; then there was a quick zip as Beth tore a paper towel from the roll. She dried her hands, humming lightly, then opened the door under the sink and raised the lid of the trash container.

" 'Dear me!' said Traddles, considering about it, 'do I strike you in that way, Copperfield? Really I didn't know that I had . . .' "

She lifted the hamper and set it on the chair by the kitchen door. "I'm forgetting my quilting," she told herself in a surprised tone. She came walking briskly from the kitchen, softening her step as she came into the bacchante room.

" 'Now you mention it, Copperfield, I shouldn't wonder at all. I assure you she is always forgetting herself, and taking care of the other nine.'

" 'Is she the eldest?' I inquired.

" 'Oh dear, no,' said Traddles. 'The eldest is a Beauty!' "

The passage ceased abruptly. "I'm going, dear." She lifted the pickup arm and set it aside and switched off the talking-book machine as she went on speaking. "It's such beautiful weather. Nothing like a New England spring. Kate's gone on ahead with Jimmy Minerva. I wish you'd change your mind and come with us. Ned?"

I could hear her leaning to take up her work basket from the end of the hunter-green sofa.

"The sun would do you good—being cooped up in here all winter. No? Well, you know best what you want to do—I won't urge."

I knew what was coming next.

"Oh, Ned," she said in the nurse's tone she had made her own, "you didn't eat your lunch again. Won't you try a little? It's calf's liver—your favorite."

I could hear her lifting the fork, the tines striking the plate as she speared a piece of the carefully cut liver. I raised my hand to forestall her. Though I find it difficult learning to feed myself, I do not care to have her do it for me.

"All right, darling," she said in her bright, indulgent way. "There's crackers in the cupboard and cheese in the refrigerator, if you get hungry. And tonight we'll have dinner at the Yankee Clipper, if you'd like that. Ned?"

I made no reply for I could not. It was as Robert had suggested: some tragedies were unspeakable. I would never speak again. I heard her murmur, and knew she was making an inventory of the things on my table. I recognized the familiar sound of the rubber-stoppered bottle as she moved it closer. "Don't forget to put in your drops," she said. "They're right here"—taking my hand to feel where the bottle was—"and the cotton's just beside them. I have my sewing, and Jimmy's present, and the picnic," she said, and I knew she was standing in the middle of the room, checking for anything she might have forgotten to do for me. She bent to kiss me, her cheek grazing the frames of my dark glasses, which she took pains to straighten again. "Bye, darling," she said, pressing my clenched hand, then starting out. Her footsteps halted briefly and I heard the rustle of leaves; I knew she was making a last-minute rearrangement of the flowers she had brought in. Lilacs for Heart's Desire . . . Then she laughed softly, the light, rueful laugh that was a copy of Maggie Dodd's. "I'm forgetting your talking-book," she said, switching on the phonograph and resetting the needle on the record.

" 'Very pretty!' said I."

When she had gone, I sat in my club chair, finding it extraordinary that she could unfailingly locate the precise place where the narrative had been interrupted. But then, she had always been extraordinary.

Somewhere in the distance a child called, another answered; a dog barked; and still the warm May breeze slipped over the sill, rustling the chintz curtains and softly stirring the leaves of the lilacs on the sideboard. Their heavy odor hung in the room. For no apparent reason, I was thinking of Joshua: it would be a boy, as Missy had predicted; I was sure it would have Justin Hooke's blond hair and blue eyes. Outside, in the bitter spring, the yellow bird sang as it built its new nest. I folded my hands in my lap. The clock ticked. The Invisible Voice continued.